SARAH MORGAN

The Summer Swap

HQ
An imprint of HarperCollins*Publishers* Ltd
1 London Bridge Street
London SE1 9GF

www.harpercollins.co.uk

HarperCollins*Publishers*
Macken House, 39/40 Mayor Street Upper,
Dublin 1, D01 C9W8, Ireland
This edition 2024

1
First published in Great Britain by
HQ, an imprint of HarperCollins*Publishers* Ltd 2024

Copyright © Sarah Morgan 2024

Sarah Morgan asserts the moral right to be
identified as the author of this work.
A catalogue record for this book is
available from the British Library.

ISBN: 978-1-84845-921-2

MIX
Paper | Supporting
responsible forestry
FSC
www.fsc.org
FSC™ C007454

This book contains FSC™ certified paper and other controlled
sources to ensure responsible forest management.

For more information visit: www.harpercollins.co.uk/green

Printed and Bound in the UK using 100% Renewable Electricity
at CPI Group (UK) Ltd

To Margaret O'Neill Marbury, with love and thanks.

1

Lily

Running away from her life wasn't something she was proud of, but with a view this good it was hard to regret the decision.

Lily tightened her grip on the handlebars and pedaled harder. Here on the northern tip of Cape Cod while the rest of humankind were still sleepy and had barely reached for the coffeepot, the place was hers alone.

All around her were sand dunes and the ocean stretching as far as she could see. She cycled the same route every day, and every day was different. Today the sky was a deep kingfisher blue, but she'd seen burnt orange, flame red and smoky silver.

It was a place favored by migratory birds and tourists, and generally she preferred the first to the second. The day before, she'd seen a blue heron and two snowy egrets. As far as she was concerned the fewer humans the better, but she owed her current job to the influx of summer people, so she wasn't complaining.

She breathed deeply, letting the salt air fill her lungs and her mind. She felt free here on this windblown, sunbaked strip of seashore. For the first time in months, she felt better. Stronger. As if she might survive after all. The pressure had eased. She no longer woke at two in the morning drenched in sweat and panic, trapped in her life and hating every moment.

She felt something close to happiness, and then her phone buzzed and the feeling left her in a rush.

She pedaled faster, trying to outrun its insistent demand. She didn't have to look to identify the caller. It was ten in the morning exactly. Only one person called her routinely at that time.

Dammit.

Guilt and an unshakable sense of duty made her squeeze the brakes and she pulled over, breathless, and dug out her phone. If she didn't take the call now, she'd be taking it later and the thought of it looming in her future would darken the skies of an otherwise cloudless day. This was the price she had to pay for running away. You could run, but with today's technology you couldn't really hide.

"Lily, honey? It's Mom."

She closed her eyes briefly.

She'd been expecting this call, ever since she'd declined their invitation to come home and "talk things over." As if talking it over yet again would change the outcome.

Every time she saw her mother's name pop up on her phone screen her stomach churned. Guilt sank its fangs into all the soft, vulnerable parts of her. Her parents had made huge sacrifices for her, and she'd as good as slapped them in the face. And she hadn't even given them a reason. At least, not one they could understand.

They deserved better.

"I'm on my way to work, Mom. I can't be late." Never had dirty pots and pans and other people's laundry seemed more appealing. She'd rather deal with that any day than talk to her mother. Every conversation dragged her backward and left her so twisted with guilt she lost all confidence in her chosen path. "Is everything all right?"

"No. We're worried about you, Lily." Her mother's tone was shaky. "We don't understand what's going on. Why won't you tell us?"

Lily tightened her grip on the phone. "Nothing is going on. And you don't need to worry." She repeated the same words she'd said hundreds of times, even though they never seemed to settle.

"Can you blame us for worrying? We have a bright, brilliant daughter who has chosen to throw away the life she worked hard for. And with no reason."

No reason? As if it had been a whim. As if she'd woken up one morning and decided to waste all those years of hard work just for a laugh.

"I'm fine. This is what I want."

It wasn't that her parents weren't wonderful people, but communicating with them was impossible.

"Are you eating? Have you put on some weight? You were skin and bone when you left here."

"I'm eating. I'm sleeping. I'm good. How are you and Dad?"

"We miss you, obviously. Come home, Lily. We can cook for you, and spoil you and look after you."

Anxiety settled on her like a cloak, blocking out sunshine and her hopes for the day.

She knew what going home would mean. She loved her parents, but they'd hover over her with frowning concerned faces until she'd end up worrying more about them than herself. And then she'd do things she didn't want to do, just to please them.

And it wasn't as if she hadn't tried staying at home. She'd done that in the beginning (mostly because her options were limited) and the pressure of pretending to be okay had been exhausting.

"I'm happy, Mom. I just need some space. It's beautiful here. You know I always loved the ocean."

"I know. I remember when you were six years old, and we couldn't drag you away from the sandcastle you'd built." There was a pause. "Honey, Dad made some calls. He thinks it's not too late for you to go back to medical school if you want to."

Lily's heart started to pound. The sweat of anxiety threatened to become a full-blown panic attack. Her chest tightened. Her hands shook so badly the phone almost slipped from her fingers.

Interference, even well-meaning interference, should be designated a crime.

"I don't want to. I know you and Dad are disappointed—"

"It's not about us, it's about you. We tried so hard to give you all the opportunities we didn't have."

Lily stared at the ocean and tried to find her inner calm, but it had fled the moment the phone had rung.

They'd made huge sacrifices for her, and she'd thrown it in their faces. She felt terrible. But staying would have made her feel worse.

"This is difficult for me, too, Mom." The lump in her throat made it difficult to speak. "I know I'm hurting you and I hate it, but this is where I want to be. I can't be a doctor. I want to be an artist."

"You say that, but you're cleaning houses."

"To earn money while I try to find a way to do something I love." While she tried to loosen the knots of stress in her body and untangle the mess in her head. "There's nothing wrong with cleaning houses. I like it. And it's a respectable way to make a living. You did it."

"Because I didn't have the opportunities you had."

Lily felt guilt overwhelm her.

Her mother sighed. "Do you need money? We still have some savings."

And she knew just how hard it would have been for her parents to pull that together after everything they'd already spent on her. She'd vowed never to take another cent from them.

"I don't need money but thank you." She didn't want to think about the dire state of her bank account. She was determined to manage on her own now, no matter what.

"Lily—" her mother's voice was gentle "—your father would kill me for asking because I know I'm not supposed to ask, but did something happen, honey? Did someone hurt you? Your dad and I always thought you'd make a wonderful doctor. You're such a kind, caring person."

"Nothing like that." Lily's throat burned. She badly wanted this conversation to end. "Could we talk about something else?"

"Of course. Let me think…not much has happened here. Your father has been busy in the garden." Her mother spoke in a cheery *I'm changing the subject to a safe topic* voice.

"The hydrangeas are beginning to bloom. They're going to be stunning. I made the most delicious orange cake last week. No wheat. You know your father. Ground almonds instead of flour."

"Sounds yummy." She imagined them at home together and felt a pang. Despite everything, she missed them. Part of her just wanted to run home and be looked after but she knew that feeling would dissipate the moment she walked through the door. Within minutes the bands of pressure would tighten, and she'd be gasping for breath.

"I'm sure there was something I wanted to tell you." Her mother paused. "What was it? Oh, I remember—I bumped into Kristen Buckingham last week. She's always so charming and friendly. So normal."

The last person Lily wanted to think about now was anyone with the name Buckingham.

"Why wouldn't she be friendly and normal, Mom?" Lily knew how self-conscious her mother was around her friends and she hated it. It reminded her of being back at school and feeling like an imposter.

Her parents had scrimped and saved and worked multiple jobs in order to send her to the best school. They'd believed she'd have a great education and make influential friends. She would absorb their greater advantages by osmosis. It would be her ticket to a better life. They imagined her living her life in a bubble of success, mixing with people whose parents owned mansions and yachts and jets. People whose fridges were loaded with food and never had to worry about making it stretch to the end of the week. People who had drivers, and housekeepers, and staff who cleared the snow from their yard.

And she had met people like that, but most of the time

Lily had felt like a stray dog that had somehow wriggled its way into a litter of pedigrees. She'd been afraid to reveal anything about her background, because she knew it was different from theirs. She'd masked her true self because she'd known that she didn't fit. Despite her attempts to blend, she'd been badly bullied. To make things worse she'd also felt crushed by the pressure of work and parental expectation. To fail would have been to let them down, these people she loved so much and who loved her back. They'd half killed themselves to give her the opportunity. She couldn't let herself fail.

Panic had hovered close to the surface the whole time, threatening to suffocate her. The only thing that had driven her from her bed in the mornings was the knowledge of her parents' sacrifice and their pride in her. She hadn't felt able to tell them how unhappy she was, or that locking herself in a cubicle while having a panic attack didn't feel like success to her.

She'd been thoroughly miserable until the day Hannah Buckingham had rescued her from a bully who was trying to remove her ponytail with a pair of scissors. After that, everything changed.

Hannah was the granddaughter of the famous artist Cameron Lapthorne. She was a champion of the underdog. She had a fierce urge to protect anything threatened. She wanted to save the whales, and Sumatran tigers, and Antarctica. Lily was added to the list, and they'd become best friends from that moment. Hannah had said Lily was the sister she'd never had. Hannah hadn't cared about the differences between their household incomes. Hannah hadn't cared that Lily didn't have her own bathroom, or a housekeeper to keep her room tidy, or tutors to make sure her grades were the best they could possibly be. Hannah had found Lily interesting. Hannah had wanted to know everything about Lily. She'd wanted to access her every thought. For the first time in her life, Lily had been able to be herself.

They'd been inseparable. Protected by Hannah, the bullying had stopped and Lily had flourished. With Hannah as her friend, her confidence had grown. She'd no longer felt like a misfit.

They'd gone to the same college where they'd both studied biological sciences and then they'd applied to the same medical school. When her acceptance letter arrived, Lily's parents had cried. They'd been so proud and thrilled. It was the happiest day of their lives.

Lily had been happy and relieved that she'd achieved their goals. That she was everything her parents wanted her to be. That she hadn't let them down. For a brief moment she'd believed that maybe she could do this.

But medical school had turned out to be a thousand times worse than school. She was surrounded by people who were brilliant, ambitious and competitive.

When the pressure started to crush her brain again, she tried to ignore it. She was going to be fine. She'd survived this far. There were many different branches of medicine. She'd find one that suited her.

It didn't help that Hannah had no doubts at all. She'd known from the start that she wanted to be a surgeon like her father, Theo. Hannah wanted to save lives. She wanted to make a difference.

On the few occasions she'd met him, Lily had found Theo to be terrifying or maybe it was more accurate to say that she found his reputation terrifying.

Hannah's mother, Kristen, was equally intimidating. She

was an art expert, a whirlwind of brisk efficiency with a life so busy it was a wonder she fitted in time to breathe.

And then there was Hannah's older brother, Todd, who was smart, handsome and kind, and the object of lust among all of Hannah's friends. Lily was no exception. Teenage Lily had fantasized about Todd. Twenty-three-year-old Lily had kissed Todd in a dark corner during a school reunion.

Lily was in love with Todd, but now Todd was dating Amelie.

Lily had trained herself not to think about Todd.

"I just mean that Kristen is very important, Lily, that's all," her mother said. "But she always takes the time to talk to me when I see her."

"She's just a person, Mom. A person like the rest of us."

"Well, not really like the rest of us," her mother said. "Her father was Cameron Lapthorne. I don't pretend to know anything about art, but even I know his name."

Hannah had taken her to the Lapthorne Estate once. It had been the best day of Lily's life. She'd gazed at the paintings hungrily, studying every brushstroke, in awe of the skill and envious of anyone who could build a life as an artist. Hannah had given her a book of her grandfather's work, and it had become Lily's most treasured possession. She'd thumbed the pages, studied the pictures and slept with it under her pillow.

Ever since she was old enough to hold a paintbrush, Lily had loved art. She'd painted everything in sight. When she'd run out of paper, she'd painted on the walls. She'd painted her school bag and her running shoes. She'd said to her parents *I want to be an artist*, and for a while they'd looked worried. They'd told her no one made money that way and that she was smart enough to be a doctor or a lawyer. Lily knew how much they wanted that for her, and she knew how much they'd sacrificed. She couldn't bring herself to disappoint them. And so she had dutifully gone to medical school, underestimating the toll it would take on her.

"Lily? Are you still there?"

Lily tugged herself back into the present. "Yes. So how was Kristen?"

"Busy as ever. She was in the middle of organizing a big event at the Lapthorne Estate. Celebrating her mother's birthday and her grandfather, the artist. It's happening today, I think. Todd will be there with his fiancée—I forget her name. Amelie, that's right. And Hannah will be there of course. Kristen invited us, and you, which was generous of her."

Fiancée?

Lily started to shake. "Todd is engaged?"

"Yes. A bit of a whirlwind according to Kristen. They'd only been dating for a few months, and she thought it was casual. Had no idea it was serious and then suddenly they announce that they're getting married. I'm sure that wedding will be quite an event. Kristen said it was yet another thing for her to organize, although I don't understand why the responsibility would fall on her. She's such an impressive woman."

Lily wasn't thinking about Kristen. Lily was thinking about Todd.

She imagined Todd in the gardens of Lapthorne Manor with a glass of champagne in his hand, and Amelie gazing up at him with that flirtatious look that fused men's brains and made them do stupid things, a large diamond glinting on her finger.

Amelie had been the most popular girl in the school. She'd had the highest marks, the fastest time on the running track and the biggest smile. Amelie was the girl most likely to succeed. She was also the girl who had tried to cut off Lily's ponytail with a pair of scissors. And now she was marrying Todd. Kind, funny, clever Todd.

Todd had broken Lily's heart, and he didn't even know it.

Her palms felt sweaty as she tried to focus on the call. "Are you going to the party?"

"No, of course not. Your father wouldn't know what to say and I wouldn't know what to wear. They're your friends really, not ours. Kristen mentioned that Hannah is enjoying her clinical rotation, but you probably know that as she's your best friend."

Lily didn't know that. Lily and Hannah hadn't spoken since that terrible fight on the night Lily had packed her bags and left medical school for good.

Every time Lily thought of Hannah she wanted to cry. They'd sworn that nothing and no one would ever come between them, and they'd truly believed that.

They'd been wrong.

"I must go, Mom. I'll be late for work, and I don't want to let people down." She winced as she said it, because she was all too aware that she'd let her parents down. "Don't worry. I'm happy. I like my life."

"We don't want you to waste your talents, honey, that's all. You're capable of so much. You could be curing cancer—"

Curing cancer? *No pressure, then.*

"I hated medical school." The words spilled out of her. "It wasn't for me." And the pressure of trying to keep up had almost broken her. She didn't expect them to understand. They believed that if you were smart enough to be a doctor, why wouldn't you be one? And she couldn't figure out how to make her parents proud, but still live the life she wanted to live. "I want to be an artist, Mom. That's all I've ever wanted. You know that."

"I know, but where's the future in that? Your dad and I just don't want you to struggle financially as we did. Life can be hard, Lily."

Lily closed her eyes. She knew that. She knew how hard life could be.

"I'm managing fine. And I'm going to pay you and Dad back."

"That's not necessary, honey. We love you and remember there's a home and a welcome here whenever you need it."

Lily's throat felt full. It would be easier to disappoint them if they weren't so decent. If she didn't love them so much. "Thanks. Give my love to Dad."

She ended the call, wondering why big life decisions had to feel so difficult and wondering why, when there were so many people her mother could have bumped into, she'd had to bump into Kristen Buckingham.

Her little bubble of happiness had been punctured.

Todd was engaged. He was going to marry Amelie, and no doubt they'd have two perfect children and a dog and live a long and happy life with not a single bump in the road.

But she wasn't going to think about that now. And she wasn't going to think about Hannah. Twice in the last few months she'd almost texted her. Once she'd even typed out a message, but then she'd deleted it. Hannah had been furiously angry with her, and Lily had been angry with Hannah. They'd both been hurt, and Lily had no idea how to move past that hurt. Given that she hadn't heard from Hannah, presumably she didn't know, either.

The friendship that they'd believed could never be damaged, had been damaged. Broken. Amelie might as well have taken her scissors to it.

But that was in the past now.

Hannah was living in the city, and Lily was here on the Cape, and even though she'd brought all her emotions with her it was still preferable to being in the smothering atmosphere of her parents' home. And at least it had been her decision to come here. For the first time ever, she was living the life that was her choice.

She just wished it felt easier.

Eyes stinging, she dropped the phone back into her bag and pedaled hard. The call had cost her ten minutes, but if she moved fast she'd still get the work done.

The breeze blew into her face and dried the dampness of tears. One day she'd make it up to her parents. She'd find a way to make them proud, even though she wouldn't be curing cancer.

She turned into the driveway of a large mansion and cycled up to the house, her sudden stop creating a small shower of gravel. Grabbing her backpack, she sprinted to the front door and waved to Mike, the gardener, who was hauling trays of plants from the back of his truck.

This particular house was a prime beachfront property and was booked solid throughout the summer months. It slept fourteen, and the last fourteen to occupy it had clearly had a good time if the state of the kitchen was anything to go by.

The company she worked for catered to the luxury end of the market and it always surprised Lily that those people seemed never to have mastered the basic art of clearing up after themselves.

She scooped up empty pizza boxes, removed a discarded

lobster shell from one of the kitchen chairs (she could be curing cancer, but instead she was clearing up lobster shells) and cleared half a dozen empty champagne bottles into the recycling. She wiped, she spritzed, she mopped, she polished, and once she'd restored the kitchen to its usual pristine state and reassured herself that there was no lasting damage, she headed toward the bedrooms.

By the time she'd finished it was midafternoon.

She took a large drink of water from the bottle she kept in her backpack and retrieved her bike.

"I'm all done." She pushed her bike across to Mike, who was hunkered down over a flower bed.

Mike had worked for an investment bank until he'd suffered a serious case of burnout. Now he worked as a gardener, and said it was the best decision he'd made. It helped, of course, that he'd made himself a tidy sum of money before changing direction.

He straightened, stepped over a clump of petunias and walked over to her. "Where are you off to next?"

"Dune Cottage."

"That place is a mystery." He pulled his hat down to keep the sun from his face. "Have you ever seen anyone staying there?"

"Never. Easiest cleaning job I do all week. A bit of light dusting. Clean the windows, sweep the deck. Freshen the bed linen occasionally. Report anything that needs repairing."

"Who do you think owns it?"

Lily shrugged. "I'm guessing some billionaire from Manhattan who can afford to keep it empty."

"Isn't it a bit small for a billionaire?"

"Maybe he's a small, single billionaire."

Mike grinned. "A single billionaire. Does such a thing exist? Money is a powerful aphrodisiac."

"Not to everyone." In her experience, money didn't always bring out the best in people. "I have to go. See you tomorrow, Mike." She climbed onto her bike and pedaled down the drive and onto the cycle track that led to a remote part of the Outer Cape. The trail took her over sandy dunes and past salt marshes, and then finally the cottage appeared, nestled among the dunes, separated from the ocean by soft sand and whispering seagrass. Its white clapboard walls and shingle roof had been weathered by the elements, but still the building stood firm. It had become as much a part of the landscape as the shifting sands that surrounded it.

Whoever owned it was the luckiest person in the world, Lily thought. And the most foolish, because who would own a place like this and not use it? It was a criminal waste.

She and the people she worked with occasionally played guessing games. It was owned by a rock star who had ten mansions and never quite got around to using this one. It was an FBI safe house. The owner was dead and buried under the deck (as she spent a lot of time alone there, that wasn't Lily's preferred theory).

Whoever it was had made sure that they couldn't be identified. The management fees were paid by an obscure, faceless company. No one could remember when the cottage had last been inhabited. It was as if it had been forgotten, abandoned, except not entirely abandoned because it was maintained as if the owner might be coming home any day. And Lily was responsible for keeping it that way.

It was, in her opinion, the perfect job and if she was ahead of her workload she occasionally sneaked an hour or more to paint because the light and the views in this particular stretch of the Cape were spectacular.

She leaned her bike against the wall where it would be protected from the elements, hoisted her backpack onto her shoulders and headed up the wooden steps to the deck that wrapped itself snugly around the cottage.

If Lily had been asked to name her dream house, this would have been the one. Not for her, the mansions that were dotted along the coast from Provincetown to Hyannis. She didn't want marble, or hot tubs, a games room, gym or a cinema room.

She wanted this. The ever-changing light. The views. The feeling that you were living on the edge of the world. When she was here, her misery lifted. Her energy returned and she wanted to grab her sketchbook and record the view so that the memories would stay with her forever.

She delved into her pocket for the keys and opened the front door. Every time she stepped over the threshold, she fell in love all over again. She didn't care that the place was weathered and worn. To her, that was part of its character. This place had been lived in and loved. It had history.

She tugged off her shoes and left the door open to allow the air and sunshine to fill the place.

The interior was simple, every item carefully chosen to complement the ocean setting. The sofa was shabby, up-holstered in a blue fabric that had faded over time and had once matched the armchairs facing it. There were hints of nautical everywhere. The coffee table was made from timber salvaged from a shipwreck, no doubt a casualty of the dangerous waters and shifting sandbars. It was stacked with books and sometimes Lily curled up in the evening and read while listening to the sounds of the sea floating through the open windows.

The living room opened onto a wide veranda, which Lily was continually sweeping. At the back of the cottage there was a studio, north facing, with large windows that flooded the room with light.

Upstairs was a master bedroom with glorious views across the dunes, a large second bedroom and a third bedroom built into the eaves.

Lily headed upstairs, ducked her head to avoid banging it on the sloping roof and dropped her backpack in the smallest bedroom. She felt a stab of guilt and had to stop herself from glancing over her shoulder to check no one was watching her.

Just one night, she'd told herself the first time she'd stayed here. And then one night had become two, and two had turned into a week and she was still here two months later. At first she'd felt so guilty she hadn't even slept on the bed. She'd unrolled her sleeping bag and slept on the sofa in the living room and woken when the morning light had shimmered across the room. She'd used the shower in the smaller of the two bathrooms and told herself that occasionally running the shower and flushing the toilets were an important part of her caretaking responsibility.

She hadn't always lived here. Over the winter she'd shared a room with two other girls in a house in the town, but then the tourist season had taken off and every bed was needed for visitors. Lily's funds didn't stretch far enough to cover the cost of a new rental.

That was what she told herself, but the truth was she couldn't bear to leave this beautiful place. Sometimes she felt as if the cottage needed her as much as she needed the cottage. And who was ever going to know? No one came out this far once the sun had set, and she'd already decided that if someone found her here during the day she would simply say that she was cleaning the place. That was her job after all.

Gradually the cottage had embraced her and made her feel at home. She'd graduated from the slightly lumpy sofa to the smallest bedroom in the eaves (the master bedroom was taking it too far) and now her sleeping bag was stretched on top of the bed and she even kept a few toiletries in the shower room.

Over time she'd started to think of the cottage as hers. She cared for it as lovingly as a family member. She couldn't do anything about the peeling paint or the slightly tired furnishings, but she could make sure it was clean and always looked its best. Sometimes she even talked to the cottage as she was shaking out cushions and dusting down surfaces.

Why does no one come and stay in you? What sort of people are they that they'd leave you alone like this?

Whenever she was asked where she was living she gave a vague response, leading people to believe that she was couch surfing until she found somewhere permanent. The truth was, she'd stopped looking. Partly because her days were full, but mostly because she couldn't bring herself to leave and saw no reason to do so as the place was empty.

She loved being alone here. It meant that she could be herself, and not have to pretend to be something she wasn't. She loved the fact that in the evenings she could sit on the deck and watch the setting sun throw streaks of red over the sky and water. If she couldn't sleep, she could switch on the light and read without anyone asking her if she was okay. She could eat, or not eat, knowing that no one was policing her food intake. She could feel what she wanted to feel without the added pressure of knowing she was worrying someone.

She didn't have to pretend to be fine.

Because she wasn't fine. She hurt, inside and out, and until she stopped hurting she didn't want to be anywhere but here. She couldn't think of a better place to be wounded.

The cottage nurtured her, tempting her to sit on its sunny deck, or venture into the cozy kitchen to make herself a sandwich or a mug of creamy hot chocolate. With its old wooden cabinets and butcher-block countertops, the kitchen had a warm, welcoming feel that was a contrast to the sleek, modern kitchens that graced most of the homes she cleaned.

But the biggest comfort for Lily was the paintings. The walls were crowded with them. Sketches, oils and pastels— she'd studied them all closely, examining every brushstroke and every line because they were all extraordinary. And she couldn't believe that paintings of this quality were hanging on the wall of an almost abandoned beach cottage, because they weren't prints of the sort that were sold by the thousands in various shops along the Cape, or the work of an amateur. She was sure—or as sure as she could be—that at least some of them were the work of Cameron Lapthorne. His initials were in the corner. CL. And she recognized his style.

The best, in her opinion, was the large watercolor hanging in the living room. She'd stared at that painting for hours, seduced by the subtle blend of colors, intrigued by the figure of the woman standing on the sand, staring out to sea. Who was she and what was she thinking? Was she simply admiring the view, or was she planning on plunging into the freezing waters and ending her misery?

Every time she looked at the painting it seemed different. The shadows. The soft flush of light across the ocean. It was as changeable as the scenery that had been its inspiration. Looking at it made her chest ache and her throat close. It wasn't just a painting; it was a story. It made her *feel*. Whoever that woman was, Lily felt an affinity with her.

And if she was right that it was an original then this painting alone was worth *millions*. But she didn't care about its monetary worth. For her its value was in its beauty. Being able to gaze for hours at that painting was a privilege. It was like having a private view of the *Mona Lisa*, or Monet's *Water Lilies*.

She suspected Mike was wrong when he assumed the cottage wasn't owned by someone with pots of money. Maybe not a billionaire, but whoever it was had enough money not to care that they were leaving valuable art unattended.

Or perhaps it wasn't an original.

She'd studied Cameron Lapthorne's work in depth but had never seen any mention of this painting, and it differed from his usual style.

She tore her gaze away from it now and headed for the studio where she kept her paints and canvases carefully hidden in one of the cupboards.

She'd skipped lunch, but she didn't want to waste a moment of the light by preparing a meal for herself and, anyway, the conversation with her mother had chased away her appetite. Instead of eating, she reached for her pad and her oil pastels and headed toward the deck.

She wanted to paint. And even if nothing she produced ever came close to capturing the magical light of the Cape in the way Cameron Lapthorne had when he was alive, she would keep trying.

Food could wait. And so could finding alternative accommodation.

There was no urgency. After all, it wasn't as if anyone was using the place.

2

Cecilia

She was far too old to run away from something difficult, but she wasn't going to let that stop her.

Cecilia Lapthorne gazed out of her bedroom window at the top of the old sprawling mansion and wondered how best to make her escape. She could climb through a window, but that seemed a little dramatic when there was a perfectly good staircase within easy reach of her bedroom. Or she could walk boldly through the front door (it was, after all, her own front door) and if challenged by her children simply tell them that she would return when this ridiculous party they'd insisted on throwing was over.

She watched with mounting frustration as the lawns and the terrace were prepared for an invasion of people she had no wish to meet. Was there anything less satisfying than small talk? She'd rather have one decent conversation about something, than a hundred conversations about nothing.

She knew that Kristen and Winston were doing what they felt was right for her, but what they felt was right and what she felt was right were two different things. When they'd first told her about the party they had planned, she'd tried to talk them out of it, but they'd insisted it was exactly what she needed to lift her out of her grief. She wondered if it was revenge for all the times she'd insisted they eat broccoli when they were toddlers.

Either way, they'd ignored her entreaties, which shouldn't have surprised her. She was seventy-five years old and for a little over fifty of those years she'd lived in Cameron's shadow, dominated by his large and loud personality, the mouse to his lion (less generous folk used to say that Cameron's voice arrived in a room at least five minutes before he did). At public events she was "Cameron Lapthorne's wife," or sometimes "the artist's wife." She was an accessory, although not, she liked to think, as useless as that ridiculous pocket watch he'd taken to wearing in the mistaken belief that it made him seem endearingly eccentric.

They don't notice me, she'd once said to Cameron who had replied without a trace of irony, *Of course they notice you—you're with me.*

And that was how she'd spent most of their married life. She was a plus-one. An also. A satellite. Images in the press were captioned *Cameron Lapthorne and his wife, Cecilia.* Never *Cecilia Lapthorne and her husband, Cameron.* There had never been any doubt as to where she ranked in order of importance. Most of the time she hadn't minded. She was a quieter, altogether more private person than her loud, ebullient husband. She was happy for him to live in the limelight, while she hovered on the fringes away from unwanted attention.

Cameron had been dead for a year, but his passing hadn't released her from his shadow. Now, instead of being his wife, she was his widow, her existence still defined by her relationship with the man.

She was the keeper of his legacy, the custodian of his bright and brilliant talent.

She needed to move on. But how?

It was hard to step into a new life when you were surrounded by the old one. Cameron's presence was everywhere, wrapping around her like tentacles, holding her in place.

A month after his death she had moved all Cameron's personal items into one room and locked the door. She'd removed his paintings from the walls of her bedroom. She would have done the same to the rest of the house but it would have raised eyebrows as well as leaving a large number of blank spaces on the walls.

She'd briefly contemplated moving, but she couldn't bear to leave the beautiful gardens she'd spent three decades nurturing. When she was younger, her passion for art had been as great as Cameron's. She'd painted, sketched, lost herself in a visual world. These days the gardens were her canvas where she experimented with shape, color and texture. Her gardens had received national acclaim, but she didn't do it for the attention or the affirmation. She did it for her own enjoyment. Garden design satisfied her own need to be creative without in any way competing with her husband.

And now there was this party. A celebration of the artistic greatness that was Cameron Lapthorne. A retrospective of his work, displaying some pieces never before seen in public, offering fresh insights into the man.

Cecilia could have offered plenty of insights into the man,

including the fact that much of what the public knew was false. They saw only the genius. They didn't see the insecurities or the flaws.

The party had been Kristen's idea of course. Kristen, their eldest child. Daddy's girl. Kristen, who was so much more forceful than her younger brother, Winston.

Did Cecilia love her? Yes, of course she did. But did she *like* her daughter? Not always. Not right now.

It was Kristen who handled the day-to-day management of the Lapthorne legacy. While Cameron was alive she had helped him with the archive, carefully cataloging each piece that he produced. She collaborated with museums, galleries and private collectors, arranged storage, shipping and installation of artwork. Along with a small, carefully selected team, she handled the press and all research requests.

And she'd organized this party to jointly celebrate Cameron's life and Cecilia's seventy-fifth birthday.

Kristen was the reason Cecilia hadn't divorced Cameron.

When Kristen was nine years old, Cecilia had broken the news that she and Cameron were getting a divorce. She hadn't shared her reasons with Kristen because she hadn't wanted to drive a wedge between father and daughter. She'd been proud of her restrained, adult behavior given the circumstances. Sadly, her restraint had backfired and the result was that Kristen placed all the blame on Cecilia. Cecilia was the one still in the house. Her father had been forced out against his will. Kristen had made up her mind that her mother was a horrible person. (Winston had been five years old and almost all of it had gone over his head.)

Kristen had been so upset she'd refused to stay in the same space as her mother. She'd sprinted from the house crying and been hit by a car which just happened to be driving down Commonwealth Avenue as she was running across it with tears blurring her vision. For days her life had hung in the balance. Cecilia and Cameron had put their differences aside and reunited by her bedside. Cecilia had blamed herself and she'd known from Cameron's ostentatious silence that he had blamed her, too. When Kristen had finally woken up, she'd wanted them both by her bedside and they'd been so relieved she was alive, and so determined to make up for the trauma, that there had been no more talk of separating.

Cameron had been smugly relieved that the accident had achieved something that all his apologies and entreaties had failed to do.

The day before Kristen was due to be discharged from the hospital, Cameron had quietly moved back into the family home.

Cecilia had put her children's needs ahead of her own. She'd been consumed by guilt that her actions had inadvertently led to their daughter's accident.

Somehow, she and Cameron had stumbled through those early years after their separation and Kristen's accident, and gradually they'd settled into a rhythm.

Kristen had slowly recovered, but her relationship with her mother was forever changed. She became fiercely protective of her father, taking his side in everything. The two of them grew close and stayed that way.

Gazing down into the gardens now, Cecilia could see her waving her hands and delivering instructions to the flustered staff who normally led quiet, untroubled lives. They ran her household with little interference from Cecilia, who believed in employing someone to do a job and then letting them do it. Her daughter, on the other hand, believed in giving someone a job and then overseeing every moment of the task for the sole purpose, or so it seemed, of telling everyone where they were going wrong.

She'd been dictating everyone's actions since the day she'd arrived home from the hospital.

When she'd decided it was time to marry, she'd married a surgeon who was so dedicated to his work he was more than happy to allow his wife to run every other aspect of his life. Cecilia's feelings toward her son-in-law, Theo, were complicated. He was without doubt a brilliant man and a skilled surgeon by all accounts, but on the rare occasion he made it to a family event his mind was elsewhere and more often than not, thanks to endless urgent calls from the hospital, the rest of him soon followed. His professional importance wasn't in question although occasionally Cecilia wondered who would save all the trauma victims of Massachusetts if Theo died of a heart attack brought on by overwork. There were times when she'd been in mid-conversation with him only to suddenly find herself talking to an empty space because he'd felt the vibration of his phone and absented himself to answer it. Despite that, she had developed a deep fondness for him. It was hard not to care for someone who was so committed to his job and the preservation of human life, although having spent most of her life with a man who prioritized his work above everything else, Cecilia also sympathized with her daughter. But Kristen didn't seem to mind. She didn't seem to suffer any of the frustrations that Cecilia had experienced. Kristen was busy working for her father and keeping the house and, until they'd left home, raising the kids.

Since Cameron's death she'd taken to visiting Cecilia once a week to "check on her," an experience they both found stressful. Kristen wanted to talk endlessly about Cameron. Cecilia wanted to think about anything other than Cameron.

"Mom?" Kristen's voice came from behind her. "What are you doing hiding away up here?"

Cecilia gave a start and turned from her contemplation of the seven catering vans that had just arrived. (Seven? Were they feeding the whole of Boston?) She'd been absorbed in her own thoughts and hadn't noticed her daughter leave the gardens, but now here she was in the doorway of Cecilia's bedroom in full control mode. The concern on her face barely masked her exasperation.

Cecilia was exasperated, too. She'd intended to somehow do a vanishing act before Kristen appeared.

"I'm not hiding. I'm taking my time."

Kristen stepped into the room. "The guests will be arriving soon, and you're not even dressed. Is something wrong? Does the suit fit? You've lost weight since Dad died. I wish you'd see a doctor."

Fix, fix, fix. That was Kristen's approach to everything. She didn't seem to understand that some things couldn't be fixed and had to be endured and accepted.

She didn't understand that Cecilia's grief was complicated.

Her solution to Cecilia's negative response to the party had been to buy her a new outfit. It was currently laid out on the bed ready for her.

Cecilia had no idea if it fitted because she hadn't tried it on. It wasn't her clothes that she needed to change; it was her life.

"I don't need a doctor. I have no wish to attend this party, that's all. Something I've made clear to you from the beginning." Did that sound petulant?

Kristen obviously thought so because she took a calming breath and closed the bedroom door.

Cecilia sighed. The closed door meant they were going to have "a talk."

She often wondered if she was the focus of her daughter's regular sessions with her therapist. *My mother is difficult. We don't have the easiest relationship.*

Kristen had collapsed when her father died. When she'd been given the news she'd literally fallen to the floor and screamed. (She'd done the same when Simon Overbrook had dumped her in her second year of college because she absolutely had not wanted it to happen but it had happened anyway and the realization that she couldn't control everything and everyone around her by willpower and the sheer force of her personality had come as a searing shock.)

She'd shouted *Why? Why?* And Cecilia had assumed she was asking why her father and not her mother.

No one had been able to comfort her because apparently no one would ever be able to understand, and no one could ever replace her father. At the funeral Theo had stood frozen, immobilized by the sheer scale of his wife's grief. Physical hemorrhage in no way daunted him, but dealing with emotional hemorrhage was beyond him.

Kristen had seemed to gradually pull herself out of her debilitating grief and had thrown herself into work. She was busy, busy, busy, as if determined not to allow herself even a moment of space in which to think about her father.

It occurred to Cecilia that perhaps this exhibition was Kristen's way of keeping her father alive.

She crossed the room now with a brisk stride and dropped

35

into a crouch by Cecilia's chair (flexibility courtesy of two yoga sessions a week and a private Pilates instructor) and took her mother's hand.

"You're sad, I know. Grief is a terrible thing. Relentless. Exhausting. You must feel devastated." She squeezed, presumably to offer reassurance that everything Cecilia was feeling was normal.

Cecilia knew that nothing she was feeling was normal. She was supposed to feel devastated, but she didn't. It wasn't that she wasn't grieving. She was. She'd spent a lifetime with Cameron. But the one thing she couldn't admit was that she also felt free.

And she had yet to decide what to do with that freedom. For the first time ever, she had only herself to think about. It was both exciting and terrifying.

She breathed in a waft of her daughter's perfume.

From this angle she could see that Kristen's hair was freshly highlighted, her style a little softer than her usual blunt bob. Her dress was a figure-skimming swirl of blues and greens that could have been inspired by one of her father's earlier watercolors. She looked younger somehow. Different.

For the first few weeks after Cameron had died Kristen hadn't moved from the bed, but lately she seemed to have recovered her energy and today she was positively glowing.

"This must be very hard for you." Kristen was looking at her with sympathy. "It's emotional seeing so much of Dad's art displayed together, isn't it? I understand. It's like seeing the story of his life."

Cecilia blinked. Story of his life?

Knowing that a response was needed, she latched onto the one part of Kristen's observation that was true. "It is hard."

"I miss him, too. Every day." Kristen's eyes filled, tears never far from the surface when she thought about her father. "But this event is a celebration. It's our chance to show the art world and his devoted fans who he really was. The whole of his career, beginning to end. And we're lucky it's such a beautiful day. We thought you could give your speech in the garden."

She'd forgotten about the damned speech. Kristen had written it for her, and Cecilia had seen it only a few hours ago. She'd known immediately that she wouldn't be able to deliver it. She didn't want to talk about Cameron. She didn't want to talk about their life together.

"I can't do that."

Kristen patted her hand. "That's fine. We can cram everyone into the garden room if that makes you more comfortable."

Cecilia stirred. "I mean the speech itself. I can't give it, Kristen."

Now would be a good time to confess she had no intention of going to the party. But she couldn't stand the confrontation.

She was a coward.

Alarm flickered across Kristen's face. "All you have to do is say a few nice words about Dad. It's that easy."

Cameron, Cameron. It was always about Cameron.

What had happened to her life? Where, in all this, was the real Cecilia?

"Mama?" Kristen sounded anxious and Cecilia sat upright.

"I won't do it, Kristen. You speak if you want to, but I won't."

"But why?"

Because she wasn't confident that the words that left her lips would be the right ones.

It was time to leave the past in the past. Time to move on.

"I'm too old to give speeches," she said finally and Kristen stood up abruptly.

"Fine. I'll do it."

Cecilia could see her mentally reordering her never-ending to-do list. She watched as Kristen checked her phone quickly, as if she was waiting for something.

"Is Theo here?"

"No. He couldn't get away from the hospital, but he sends his apologies and his love." Kristen slipped her phone back into the pocket of her jacket. "You should get dressed. You know things take you a little longer these days."

"Things don't take me longer." She resented the implication that she was a crumbling shadow of her former self. "I choose to take more time over things because I can."

Secrets made you lonely, she realized. There could be no deep human connection without honesty, and she'd hidden too much from her children to expect them to understand her. It created a distance because there were so many things she knew that they didn't.

Kristen swept across the room and picked up Cecilia's suit. "I can't wait to see you wearing this. It's going to look stunning on you and you'll look great in the photographs."

Cecilia imagined the caption. *Cameron Lapthorne's widow, Cecilia.*

"When you were six you often refused to get dressed and go to school."

Kristen held the suit against her body. "Is this revenge for something I did when I was six?"

"No. The reason you didn't want to get dressed and go

38

to school was because you didn't see the point. It wasn't something you wanted to do."

"And you're saying that today is like that? You don't see the point? That's hurtful, Mom." Her eyes shone. "Planning this celebration has been a ton of work. Do you have any idea how much stress it has caused?"

"I'm sorry if you're stressed," Cecilia said, "but you were the one who insisted on it."

But she was partly to blame. She should have expressed her views more strongly before now. Instead, she'd let it happen.

So much of her life had been spent letting things happen. It was time she took control, but she wasn't sure she even knew how. Could you really change the habit of a lifetime?

Hurt crossed Kristen's face. "This party is for you, too. I've put hours and hours of work into making it perfect."

Perfect for whom?

Cecilia studied her daughter. There was definitely something different about her, but she couldn't put her finger on it and there was no point in asking because they didn't have that sort of relationship. They'd never had mother-and-daughter shopping trips, or mother-and-daughter spa days. She felt a stab of guilt because she knew that was partly her fault. She should have tried harder to bridge the gulf that had appeared between them.

But even so she wished that Kristen would ask, just once, what *she* wanted and then pay attention to the answer.

"We both know this party is not for me, Kristen."

Kristen was still holding the suit. "We are celebrating your birthday. Of course it's for you. I don't understand why you don't want to do this. Is it the paintings? Is it because we chose to use this opportunity to present a retrospective of Dad's work? Is it upsetting you?"

"Leave it, Kristen."

"No, I won't leave it. All we do in this family is ignore things that are uncomfortable and frankly it's exhausting. Let's be honest for once. Is it grief? Does seeing his art on the walls upset you?" Kristen glanced around her. "Obviously we've noticed that you don't have a single painting of his in this room."

She imagined her children speculating. *What is going on with Mother?*

Cecilia could feel her heart thudding hard. It pounded against her ribs, as if giving her a warning. Was she having a heart attack? If she collapsed, then she wouldn't have to attend the party. She could leave in an ambulance, which was a method of escape that had only just occurred to her. She wondered briefly if she could fake it. She could throw herself to the floor and clutch her chest, but there was a danger that Kristen might feel compelled to move in to look after her and that would be alarming for them both.

"His paintings are all around the house. I don't want them in my bedroom."

"Because it hurts too badly?" Kristen was looking at her with mounting concern. "You need to talk to someone. I've thought it for a while." She paused, trying to find answers from Cecilia's brief responses. "Or is it something else completely? Is it the fact that his work has gained even more attention since he died? It's a constant reminder, isn't it? It's both wonderful and difficult."

It was more difficult than wonderful. There was no moving on. In many ways her life hadn't changed at all, except that Cameron himself was no longer part of it. Her life continued, only this time her companion was the ghost not the man.

"Kristen—"

"I understand," Kristen said, "but it wouldn't be right for us to keep his talent to ourselves. Other people have a right to enjoy his work. This is an unprecedented exhibition, of international importance. Many of the paintings have never been on display before. Fifty years of Cameron Lapthorne."

Fifty years? Two-thirds of her life. No wonder she felt lost. She was adrift on the ocean, with no idea where land might be.

So much of life was chance.

If she hadn't been on the beach that day of her twenty-second birthday, and if she hadn't happened to turn and smile at the deliciously handsome young man sprawled on the sand with a sketchbook in his hand, she might be in a very different place right now. She would have led a different life. A life where she had played the lead part, and not the supporting role. If Seth hadn't just broken up with her...

Seth.

She hadn't thought about him in years, and then a month after Cameron's funeral the card had arrived.

She'd thought about him then, and she thought about him now and wondered about his life. Had he made good choices? Did he have regrets?

Cecilia felt suddenly tired, weighed down by past decisions. It was impossible not to look back and think, *What if?*

And yet part of her felt sympathy for the woman she'd been. That woman on the beach with the sun on her face and the wind in her hair hadn't intentionally stepped into the life she'd ended up living. It had happened by accident, step by step, moment by moment, one choice followed by another choice, and surely it wasn't a crime to have trusted fully and loved deeply? Even though many years had passed she could still remember the intensity of her feelings and the heady excitement of those early days.

"I know you're sad," Kristen said. "And I know it's hard. I'm sure you're lonely—" She paused, as if her mind was on something else. "Life is no fairy tale, is it?"

Cecilia looked closely at her daughter. Was she talking about Cecilia's life or her own?

Was something wrong with Kristen? Had something happened with Theo?

She opened her mouth to ask, but then closed it again. Even if she asked, Kristen was unlikely to tell her the truth. They never talked about things like that.

And they weren't going to do so now because the door opened, interrupting their conversation.

Winston stood there. He was four years younger than his sister and bore a strong resemblance to Cameron at the same age. A little on the stocky side, but handsome enough to compensate for any deficiencies in height. He'd arrived alone because his wife, Nina, had sprained her ankle playing tennis and was lying on the sofa with her leg buried in ice packs.

"Is there a problem? The guests are arriving, Kris, and I have no idea who anyone is. I'm worried I'll ignore someone important. Why aren't you downstairs?"

Kristen swung round. "Mom doesn't want to speak at the party. I'm handling it."

She was something to be handled. A problem, like not enough glasses or a catering issue.

As always, Winston was quick to side with his sister. "Kristen has worked hard, Mom."

Cecilia roused herself. Enough. She stood up. "I can hardly dress with you two standing in my bedroom. I need privacy."

They glanced at each other, not sure if they'd won the battle.

Cecilia wanted badly to be rid of them both. She glanced out of the window at the chairs that were currently being carefully set in rows. Presumably that was where Kristen had planned for her to address the guests.

Thank goodness Kristen had agreed to deliver the speech herself because Cecilia would have choked on the paragraph of sickly prose. It painted a fairy tale, not reality. Did people think Cameron had made it big by himself? Did they really think he would have become as famous as he had if she hadn't been there?

They had no idea of the part she'd played.

But Cameron had known.

"I came to tell you that a couple of journalists have arrived," Winston said. "One of them is asking questions about a painting called *The Girl on the Shore*. I asked Rita and she has no record of such a painting."

"That's strange, because someone else asked me about that painting recently. I checked with Rita, too. She worked for Dad for forty years. If she can't remember it, then I doubt it exists." Kristen tapped her fingers against her jaw as she trawled through her memory. "Maybe it was one of his early works. Dad frequently destroyed paintings that didn't come up to his standard. All part of his creative temperament. Mom? Do you remember it?"

The Girl on the Shore.

Cecilia felt suddenly dizzy. Her chest felt tight, and now she wasn't faking it.

It had all started with that painting. Everything could be traced back to that work. It had changed their lives in ways neither of them could have imagined.

Cameron had been unknown then. Just another struggling artist living a pared down, self-indulgent existence where the only focus was art. Eight of them had crammed into a small, clapboard cottage tucked in the dunes of the Outer Cape, close to the seashore. They'd cared more about the light and the landscape than sleep and food. Rest was something they did to pass the time until they could paint again.

For a moment Cecilia was back there with the sun on her face and the wind blowing her hair and Cameron smiling at her in the way only he could smile.

"Mom?" Kristen's voice cut through her thoughts. "*The Girl on the Shore*?"

It had been decades since anyone had mentioned that painting. She'd assumed—hoped—it had been forgotten.

But clearly not. Someone was asking questions.

Cecilia couldn't breathe properly.

"Mom?" Kristen's voice held a note of alarm. "Are you okay?"

"She's not okay," Winston said. "This party is too much. A huge public event when she's still grieving—maybe it wasn't such a great idea, Kris."

Cecilia barely heard them. What was she going to do? How had a journalist ever found out about it? Neither she nor Cameron had spoken of it for years. They'd agreed that destroying it was the best course of action. He'd promised her he would get rid of it. So many years had passed that they'd been confident that the painting was forgotten.

Except it clearly hadn't been forgotten.

A chill came over her and she rubbed her arms, trying to warm herself.

Why would someone be asking about that particular work now, after all this time?

If Cameron had done what he'd promised to do, then the painting shouldn't still exist.

But what if he hadn't? He'd made other promises he hadn't kept.

"Mom? Are you all right? Do you remember a painting by that name?"

Feeling distinctly unwell, she assembled her features into an expression she hoped was suitably vague. "My memory isn't what it was. I forget things." *If only.* There were some things she would have been relieved to forget, and *The Girl on the Shore* was one of them. "If it once existed then your father must have destroyed it."

It wasn't entirely a lie. He was supposed to have done just that.

But she couldn't squash the anxiety that the painting might still exist.

Winston frowned. "Could it be in a private collection?"

"Definitely not." Kristen shook her head. "If that were the case then we would have a record of it. What does this journalist look like? I'll go and talk to him."

"Slightly shorter than me. Fifties? Glasses. Academic looking. He asked to talk to you, but I didn't know where you were."

Kristen's cheeks turned pink, and she dropped her phone. "Sorry." She stooped to retrieve it. "Right. I'll talk to him."

For the first time since his death, Cecilia wished Cameron were here. He would have dispatched the journalist with a few sharp words.

Her feeling of anxiety increased. "Why do we have journalists here?"

"Because we are celebrating Dad's life and work. He's probably an art editor, rather than a journalist."

That explanation did nothing to soothe Cecilia's anxiety. If the person asking the question was knowledgeable about art, then that was even more concerning.

"Uncle Winston!" Another voice came from outside her room, this time it was Todd, Kristen and Theo's son.

Cecilia was relieved to see a friendly face. She was close to her grandchildren and considered that she'd been a better grandmother than she ever had been a mother.

Grandchildren were a second chance.

At twenty-eight years old, Todd was handsome, good-natured and very much his own man. Cameron and Theo had wanted him to study law, but Todd had chosen to major in environmental studies and sustainability, and nothing they said had changed his mind. There had been several uncomfortable family dinners during with Cameron had bellowed at him, and Theo had lectured him on secure careers and giving back to society (and also having a guaranteed income for life). Everyone had been tense except Todd, who had carried on calmly eating his dinner and asked for second helpings. Fortunately, his younger sister, Hannah, had stepped up and announced her wish to study medicine and be a surgeon just like her father, which had taken the heat off Todd.

After Todd had graduated, he'd worked for a year for a Fortune 100 company trying to polish their green credentials before leaving to work for an artisan carpentry company that used reclaimed and sustainable materials. He'd trained as a carpenter and now he worked for himself, accepting commissions, and sometimes working freelance for the company who had originally employed him.

Cecilia admired his quiet strength. He listened respectfully to his parents' views and then went ahead and did what he felt was right for him, undeterred by their strongly expressed opinions.

Todd was living the life he wanted to live. He was something of a hero to her.

In her eyes he could do no wrong, at least until last week when he'd unexpectedly become engaged. Amelie Watkins wasn't at all the woman that Cecilia would have chosen for Todd, and she'd been astonished when he had given them the news. They seemed entirely wrong for each other, but what did she know? She wasn't exactly an expert on love.

Flourishing a balloon and a wrapped gift, he crossed the room and hugged her. "Happy Birthday, Nanna." He kissed her on the cheek and presented her with the gift and the balloon. "Open it later when the crowds have left. That shade of blue suits you. You look glamorous and not a day over forty."

Kristen sighed. "She is wearing her nightgown, Todd."

"So what? It looks great. Nanna looks fantastic whatever she wears. Not that it matters what anyone else thinks, and, anyway, I'm sure they'll simply excuse her as a famous and eccentric artist."

"Except that she's not the famous artist," Kristen said, "so unless the gene for eccentricity passes through marriage, she can't really use that excuse, can she? And I'm sure she doesn't want to see photographs of herself in her nightwear all over social media. I bought her the perfect outfit so there is no reason for her not to look her best."

Todd kept his arm round his grandmother.

"A person should be allowed to wear what they like to their own party."

Cecilia was about to point out that it wasn't her party at all, but she didn't want to draw Todd into this web of family tension.

She changed the subject. "Thank you for setting up my new phone, Todd."

"You're welcome. Everything working fine?"

"I'm sure it is." She patted his hand. "You know me and smartphones. In my case the least smart thing about it is the user, but I'm managing thanks to you. I'm sure I'll get used to it."

"You have my number keyed in there," Todd said, "so if you need help call me."

"I'll do that. Where's Amelie? Is she downstairs?" She tried to sound enthusiastic. If her grandson loved Amelie, then she was determined to love her, too. Maybe the woman was cold and distant because she was shy. Maybe she'd warm up in time.

"She's not downstairs," Todd said. "She's not coming."

"What?" Kristen frowned. "Where is she?"

"She's not feeling too good." Todd looked at his mother. "I need to talk to you about the wedding at some point."

"Can it wait? I need to focus on this event, and—" Kristen broke off as her phone buzzed. She checked the screen, then flushed deeply. "I need to answer this. Excuse me. And, Winston, tell anyone who asks that they've been misinformed. There is no painting called *The Girl on the Shore.*"

Flustered, she headed to the door leaving Winston staring after her, flummoxed.

Cecilia decided this was the perfect time to clear them all out. She needed to think. She needed to plan.

"If you'd all give me privacy, I'll change into something that won't embarrass Kristen. Thank you for the present, Todd. You're the dearest boy."

Still holding tightly to Todd's gift, she managed to usher them out of the room and closed the door behind them. Her hands were clammy, her pulse racing.

The Girl on the Shore.

She leaned against the closed door, trying to think clearly. There was no way she could go to the party now. What if the journalist asked her about the painting directly? She was a hopeless liar. She'd give herself away.

She needed to stay calm and figure this out.

The guests had already started arriving. Soon there would be hundreds of people milling around, mostly people who wouldn't want to miss an opportunity to nose around the Lapthorne mansion. It was all so impersonal. She'd be expected to mingle, make small talk and accept condolences. Yes, there would be art lovers, but there would also be people who were there for the free champagne, the free food, the chance to see and be seen. Then there were the people who wanted to be able to drop into conversation that they'd been at the Lapthorne mansion for the party. They might casually mention some of the paintings they'd seen and pretend a level of knowledge they didn't possess. There would be few guests who would be there because they loved Cecilia. When she was younger, she might have mistaken the attention for friendship. One of the advantages of reaching the age of seventy-five was that you saw the world as it was, and not how you wanted it to be. There would be no one there who had known her in those lean years before fame had shone its light on them. There would be no one who really knew *her.*

She walked to the window again, staring out across the estate.

The extensive gardens were bordered by woodland and beyond that was the road. Driving north would take her to Boston, with its harbor and history. Heading south would take her toward the wind-battered shores of the Cape where their story had started.

Finally she allowed her mind to go there, to think about things she tried never to think about.

She'd avoided the place for so long. She'd had no reason to go and every reason to stay away. Until now.

She walked across the bedroom and opened the small drawer in her nightstand. The envelope had been given to her by the lawyer, six months after Cameron's death. After she'd read it, she'd tucked it inside her worn first edition of Henry Thoreau's *Cape Cod* and spent a long time digesting the fact that Cameron's last act had been to confess to another lie.

She'd been so angry and upset she'd simply left the letter inside the book where no one was likely to find it. At the time she hadn't been in the right emotional state to contemplate doing anything with the information that the letter contained. But now?

She still wasn't in the right emotional state, but now she had no choice. It was no good telling herself that everything was fine. She had to see for herself. She had to find out what else Cameron had lied about. She had to see for herself whether the painting still existed.

She had to go back.

3

Kristen

Kristen tightened her grip on her phone, glanced over her shoulder to check that Winston and Todd weren't following her, and slid silently into her old bedroom. It looked the same as it always did, mostly because no one ever slept in it. Kristen herself had only slept in it a handful of times since her marriage, and that had been early in their relationship at Thanksgiving when Theo had a rare night off and had been able to celebrate away from the city. They'd had sex in this very bed, although Kristen hadn't been able to relax because she was always waiting for Theo to be called back to the hospital. Coitus interruptus. It was a characteristic of their relationship. Drinks with friends, walks along the Charles River, dinner at their special restaurant on Beacon Hill, sex—thanks to the demand of Theo's job, everything inevitably ended before it was supposed to. Her entire life was a cliff-hanger. It was a wonder they'd managed to have one child, let alone two.

She sometimes joked with her friends that the reason she and Theo were still married when so many of their acquaintances were getting divorced was because they hadn't spent enough time together to grow tired of each other. *Marriage interruptus.* They'd built a life that worked for them. Or so everyone thought.

But no one really knew what was going on inside someone else's marriage, and that was true of hers. No one knew how lonely she was, and she was careful to give no hints. She smiled, she laughed, she played the part of a happily married woman even though most of the time she felt so alone and isolated she might as well have been living on a desert island with only a few palm trees and the odd seashell for company. There were days when she'd wondered if she was clinically depressed, but she knew deep down that she wasn't.

She was grieving for her father and had no one to share that grief with. Her mother didn't want to talk. Her children were busy with their lives. Her husband prioritized his patients and didn't seem aware that underneath her carefully groomed exterior his own wife was seriously injured, too. At her lowest point she'd fleetingly wondered whether stepping in front of a car might be a good way of getting his attention. Maybe then he'd notice that she wasn't herself. Maybe he'd feel guilty. *All this time you've had a broken heart, and I didn't even notice. What sort of a doctor am I?*

She felt so alone that a month after her father had died she'd called a grief helpline that she'd found on the internet (she'd withheld her number and given a false name), but the stranger on the other end of the phone had been so overwhelmed by the scale of Kristen's grief that her only suggestion had been that Kristen should nurture herself and maybe take a soothing bath or treat herself to a new hand cream.

She might as well have suggested using an umbrella in a hurricane.

That was the point where Kristen had realized she was on her own with this. She didn't blame her children for not noticing how bad she felt because like most mothers she hid her own anguish from them (it wasn't their job to support their grieving mother), and she didn't really blame her own mother because they'd never been close. But she did blame Theo. She felt resentful toward Theo and that resentment layered itself on top of other layers of resentment that had built up during their marriage.

Theo had missed the birth of his first child. Theo had been absent when Hannah had been admitted to the hospital with severe croup. Theo had missed parent-teacher conferences, sports days, Kristen's birthday (twice) and their wedding anniversary (four times).

Kristen had managed to forgive all that. (The man was a surgical genius, after all, with big responsibilities. Also, she'd known who he was when she married him and she refused to be a hypocrite.) She hadn't been able to forgive his absence when her father had died.

She'd called him from the hospital where her father had been taken. She'd left six messages, each of them more desperate. *Theo, I need you.*

It had taken him four hours to get back to her. Four hours during which she'd needed his support. His love. Four hours when she'd needed his medical expertise (why couldn't they save her father?) and a shoulder to cry on. Instead, she'd cried on the doctor who had broken the news of her father's death to her and her mother. She'd cried on the kind nurse who had arrived with tissues and she'd cried on her mother, although not for long because her mother had been unnervingly composed. By the time Theo arrived, her intense grief had morphed into anger. Her resentment had grown into a huge barrier that separated them. In the days that followed she couldn't find a way past that barrier.

Losing her dad was the worst thing that had ever happened to her. Nothing had prepared her for the depth of her grief. She was an independent woman with her own family, but when her father died, part of her had died, too. The knowledge that he was never coming back, that she would never see him again, sent her into a pit of despair.

Her father had loved her unconditionally. When she'd been with her dad she'd felt important and interesting and truly loved, and she was never going to get that feeling back. She'd gone from feeling alone to feeling crushingly, miserably alone.

And then, at her lowest point, she'd met Jeff. Jeff had listened to her when Theo hadn't. Jeff had allowed her to pour her heart out. Jeff wasn't scared of her emotions. Jeff switched off his phone when they were together.

And now Jeff was downstairs.

Heart thudding, she walked into the bathroom and locked the door. She had a list of jobs to do, every one of them urgent, but all she wanted to do was reread the message waiting for her on her phone.

Can't wait to see you x

Kristen read it twice and then pressed the phone to her chest as if that message were a living thing that she could absorb through her skin straight into her heart. Those words filled the big empty space inside her. They made her feel warm and cared for and connected. It was ridiculous that a simple message could make her happy, and yet it did. It was the kind of happiness that anesthetized you against all the trials of life, and there was no shortage of those, particularly right now when she felt raw and bruised by her mother.

Kristen had spent days planning the party to make it perfect, and yet her mother was behaving as if she was doing Kristen a favor by being there. They'd never had the easiest of relationships, and normally this latest episode would have upset Kristen so much she would have reached the point of screaming at herself in the mirror (an escape outlet with fewer consequences than actually screaming at her mother), but right now she didn't even care. She'd done what she could to celebrate the birthday and her father. She'd done everything she could to support her mother after Cameron Lapthorne's death. She'd tried to be thoughtful and caring and now she was *done*.

You couldn't help someone who didn't want to be helped. Her mother could turn up to the event in her nightdress if she wanted to. She could give a speech or not give a speech. She could read from the Kama Sutra. It didn't matter to Kristen. Everything that had seemed important to her, no longer seemed important because her priorities had changed over the past few weeks.

The only thing that mattered was the message and how it made her feel.

It turned out that the woman on the end of the grief helpline had been right about her needing self-care. But she hadn't needed a hot bath or hand cream. She'd needed Jeff.

Of all the problems Kristen had encountered in her life,

she was completely unprepared for the one she was currently dealing with. She was obsessed with a man who was not her husband.

Even thinking it shocked her. Occasionally she wondered what had happened to her. Had she had a personality change overnight? Fallen asleep and woken up in someone else's body? Knocked her head in her sleep? Taken something without knowing it?

For twenty-eight years Kristen had been a loyal and devoted wife. She'd raised two children, juggled the demands of the home with the demands of her very busy job (she adored her father but working for him hadn't been easy), supported her husband even though there were days when they saw so little of each other she could barely remember what he looked like. Even when she was spending yet another night alone in their house, she'd still been proud of him.

But losing her father had changed everything. She'd lost a piece of herself, too.

Did she still love Theo? Under the layers of hurt and resentment, was the feeling she'd had for him alive? Maybe. But right now Theo couldn't, or wouldn't, give her what she needed.

She should be feeling guilty, she knew that. But she wasn't.

Her feelings for Jeff weren't about satisfying a whim. This was about survival. This was about *her*.

Thanks to Jeff she felt better than she had in a long time. Thanks to Jeff she no longer felt like killing Theo. Jeff had saved two lives.

She put the phone down and gazed at herself in the mirror. She tucked a strand of her softly styled hair behind her ear and wondered why no one had said anything about her new look. Instead of her usual chic, sharp bob she'd gone for something choppy and textured. Feminine. Her stylist had added streaks of light gold and champagne and the overall look had been so different and dazzling that for a moment she'd had to check it actually was her in the mirror and not someone else.

You look like a different person, her stylist had said, and Kristen had started to panic because although she loved her new look, she was worried she would draw attention to herself and she didn't want that. She'd walked out of the salon feeling nervous, but still she'd been unable to resist the temptation to move her head from side to side every few minutes just so that she could feel the silken swish of her newly styled hair.

She'd felt jumpy all day, braced for someone to notice but no one had said anything. Theo hadn't noticed because he rarely noticed details about anyone unless they were bleeding or had a limb hanging off. Hannah had been home from medical school for the evening looking exhausted and far too pale, but she'd been distracted by something and had barely seemed to notice her mother.

Thinking of Hannah dimmed her happiness slightly.

Kristen had been determined that her relationship with her children was going to be different (and by that she meant better!) than the one she had with her own mother. She'd always made sure they knew they could come to her with anything, and that she would listen and never judge (and if she did judge, she would do so silently). She'd wanted them to know that they never needed to feel alone with their problems. That she would always be there for them.

She never wanted them to feel the way she'd been feeling for the past year.

She'd waited for Hannah to tell her what was wrong, and when she hadn't Kristen had probed gently. She'd asked about work, she'd asked about sleep and eating, she'd asked about boyfriends (she'd trodden very carefully there because there was a fine line between being a caring parent and overstepping), and finally she'd asked about Lily. Lily Thomas was Hannah's closest friend. At that point Hannah had roused herself from her state of gloom and misery sufficiently to snap that she hadn't heard from her since she'd dropped out of medical school. *We haven't spoken.* Given the reaction, Kristen surmised that this was a friendship issue, which was surprising because Hannah and Lily had been inseparable since they were young.

She'd felt the usual anxiety that came from witnessing your child in distress, but she knew there was nothing she could do to help with this. It was between Lily and Hannah.

And at least Hannah's preoccupation with her own issues meant that she wasn't paying attention to the changes in her mother.

Todd had dropped by briefly to talk to her about something but had left the moment he'd discovered his sister was there, which had upset Kristen because her children had always been close. Unfortunately Hannah didn't like Amelie, which was going to make for fun family gatherings in the future.

But right now, her children's problems weren't her priority.

She was her priority. At this precise moment she was the most important person in her life (it felt sacrilegious to think that because usually being a parent was all about coming last).

She'd arrived at the Lapthorne mansion earlier in the day and no one had so far seemed to notice that she'd changed her hair and bought a new dress that skimmed her new, slimmer frame (she'd never be a size zero but she wasn't sure her personality would fit into size zero, so she was fine with that).

She might have been depressed at this apparent confirmation that women over forty were invisible had it not been for the fact that to one person at least, she definitely wasn't invisible.

She'd read somewhere that to be truly happy a person had to be living a life aligned with their values, but that clearly wasn't true because she was happier than she'd ever been, and her values were currently being overridden by her impulses. She, Kristen Jennifer Buckingham, who disapproved deeply of people who had affairs, was about to embark on an affair. It hadn't actually happened yet, although she'd been emotionally unfaithful on multiple occasions in recent weeks.

The night before she'd eaten her dinner alone at home but instead of feeling upset and lonely, she'd thought about Jeff. She thought about Jeff when she was doing the laundry, when she was driving to the office, when she was staring at her computer. She thought about him so frequently she was terrified she was going to start talking in her sleep. *Jeff, Jeff, I love you, Jeff.* As a precaution, she'd taken to sleeping in one of the spare rooms using the excuse of Theo's unpredictable hours.

Theo's job meant that he was often called in to operate on complicated cases, usually at the most inconvenient moments. When they'd met, she'd been drawn to the sheer heroism of what he did. He was a trauma surgeon. He worked eighty hours a week and slept six hours a night. But he saved lives.

As someone whose life had been saved by doctors, Kristen couldn't think of a more important profession. Without doctors she wouldn't be here (without doctors she wouldn't now be in a position to contemplate having an affair with Jeff). But being married to a surgeon had its downsides, and one of those was the unpredictability of her life.

It was the unpredictability of life that had caused a woman to fall down three flights of stairs in her apartment building two months previously. If it hadn't been for her injuries Theo wouldn't have been called away from the dinner party they'd been attending, and Kristen wouldn't have shared a cab home with Jeff Singer, the art editor of a major newspaper, whom she knew vaguely from her work with her father. He had flirted shamelessly with her from the moment Theo had left the room. If Theo hadn't been called to the hospital that night, Kristen might never have felt the way she was feeling now.

And the way she was feeling was extraordinary, not just because of her age—she was forty-eight and had always assumed she was well past the age to be considered affair material—but because she just wasn't that type of person.

There had been a moment in her childhood when her parents had separated, and she still remembered the trauma of that. She had no idea of the reason behind her parents' near split, because that period in their lives had never been spoken of again, but she knew her mother had instigated it and the knowledge had made her protective of her father.

They'd got back together, but Kristen had never felt secure again. She'd vowed that her children would never have reason to doubt her and Theo's relationship.

They would stick with each other through thick and thin. And even now she wasn't contemplating divorce.

She would not disrupt her children's lives or scar them in any way. (Every time she thought about what divorce had done to her friend Trisha's kids she shuddered—the amount spent on therapy alone would have bought a house on Beacon Hill.)

She was simply making her own life a little happier, and surely no one would blame her for trying to find some joy in her life.

Despite her loneliness and her confused feelings toward Theo, she knew she probably wouldn't have let the relationship with Jeff develop into anything had he not pursued her so relentlessly. It had been flattering, at her age, to be irresistible to someone. And it wasn't just that he was interested in her physically, he was interested in all of her. He encouraged her to talk about everything and anything. He wanted to know every detail of her childhood, particularly her memories of her father. No one else wanted to hear her memories of her father, but Jeff did. He listened attentively and asked endless questions until she'd ended up telling him things she'd never told anyone before, even Theo. And if occasionally she felt a brief shimmer of worry that he knew so much about her, she dismissed it. Trust was all part of intimacy, and true intimacy was a gift.

She read the message again.

I've arrived. Can't wait to see you.

Their messages were usually neutral and safe, in case someone else caught a glimpse.

And what was he doing asking Winston about *The Girl*

on the Shore? He'd already asked her about that painting, and she'd told him it didn't exist. Presumably he'd been establishing his credentials to avert any suspicion.

Was she in love with Jeff? Maybe. Or maybe not, it was too soon to know. But she did know that he was exactly what she needed right now.

He'd started pushing to spend more time with her, which was flattering. But even if she could conjure up a plausible excuse for an overnight absence, where would they go? The idea of checking into a motel as Mr. and Mrs. Smith and paying cash didn't appeal. It felt sordid, and Kristen was determined never to be sordid.

But that problem was for later. For now, she had an event to host.

She refreshed her lipstick, took another look at herself in the mirror and then almost jumped out of her skin when her phone rang.

Maybe she wasn't cut out for this. She hadn't actually embarked on an affair yet and already she felt alternately giddy and guilty. It was like the impulse you had to eat fast food, even though you knew it was bad for you.

She grabbed her phone and saw Theo's name on the screen.

Theo never called when he was working and it was unsettling that he was calling now, when she'd been thinking of another man.

"Theo? I wasn't expecting to hear from you. Have you been operating?"

"We lost the patient."

"Oh." Kristen had a momentary image of a patient running undetected around hospital corridors, even though she knew that wasn't what he meant. "I'm sorry. I hope you're not blaming yourself. If you couldn't save the patient, no one could." She believed that. The fact that Theo had turned out to be a semi-absent husband was in part due to the fact he was fully present in his job.

"His car was hit side on by another car. The driver was looking at his phone."

She knew how difficult he found this part of his job. When someone died, no matter how severe the injuries, Theo felt a sense of personal failure. He'd told her once that he had to believe he'd succeed, or he wouldn't have the confidence to try. But she also knew that he had a perfectionist trait that made him single-minded. Hannah shared that trait. It was both admirable and aggravating to those around them.

"Do you want to talk about it?" The question was a formality. She knew he wouldn't want to talk about it. Theo never talked about it, just as he didn't want to talk about how lost she felt without her father. Theo didn't like talking about emotions, his or other people's. His cure for a bad day was a large gin and tonic and half an hour on the sofa with his headphones and Brahms. "Theo?"

"Maybe."

Maybe? Kristen couldn't have been more surprised if he'd announced that he was giving up surgery and joining the church. "All right." She trod cautiously on unfamiliar territory. "I'm listening."

She tried not to think about Jeff waiting for her downstairs, or the other guests, or all the things she still had to do.

"Not over the phone. I'm on my way to you. I should be with you in an hour. We'll talk then."

On his way? "You're coming here?" It was hard enough to get Theo to show up somewhere when he'd made a commitment, but in all their years together he'd never surprised her by showing up when he wasn't expected. *He hadn't shown up when her father died.*

"That's why I'm calling. I know it's not the perfect time, but I just want to be near you and the kids. If that has to be with a crowd around us, then that's fine."

Kristen's shock (when had Theo ever said *I just want to be near you and the kids?*) was followed by a rush of panic as another message arrived on her phone.

Drinking champagne in the rose garden.

Jeff was drinking champagne in the rose garden. Jeff was waiting for her.

And her husband was about to leave the hospital and join them.

"I thought you couldn't make it?" Kristen thought frantically. This was not a situation she'd anticipated. "You don't have to come. I've already told my mother you won't be here. We understand, Theo. Your work is important. More important than us."

"That's not true. And if ever I needed a reminder of that, I've had one." His voice sounded strange. Thickened and distant and difficult to understand.

She kept thinking of Jeff in the rose garden. Her new shiny hair. Her plans.

"Theo, the signal is terrible. Your voice sounds weird. I can't understand what you're saying."

"The guy who just died—it wasn't some stranger, Kristen. It was Michael."

"Michael?" Her mind went blank, possibly because the only name in her head right now was Jeff. She rummaged in her memory for a Michael. "Michael who?"

"*Our* Michael. Michael Dent."

And she realized that the reason Theo sounded strange was because he was crying. Theo, who never cried about anything, was crying so hard she couldn't make out his words. Her strong, emotionless husband was so overwhelmed with emotion that it was virtually pouring down the phone.

"Oh, Theo—" The room reeled, and she leaned her shoulders against the wall. "Not Michael."

Michael Dent had trained at the same time as Theo. They'd done their surgical residency together. He'd been best man at their wedding and Theo had been best man at his. They'd been close to his wife, Trisha, and had taken several vacations together. Michael and Trisha had two kids a little younger than Todd and Hannah. In the early days, Trisha and Kristen had met for lunch once a month and commiserated on the challenges of being married to a surgeon who was married to his job. Trisha had joked that at least they didn't have to worry about their husbands having affairs, because they didn't have time. And then Michael had apparently found the time, because three years ago he'd left Trisha for a woman called Candy who he'd met online, which Trisha felt made things worse because it meant he'd been actively looking. She'd vented her feelings in a long phone call to Kristen. *He didn't have time to take the trash out, but he had time to find himself a new woman.*

Michael had lost weight, bought a sports car and married Candy. Kristen and Theo had stopped socializing with them. (Even if Kristen could have made it through a whole backyard barbecue without impaling Candy with a chicken skewer, she would have felt too disloyal to Trisha who had been a mess for the first year.)

It was all very awkward because Theo was still loyal to Michael and the two men worked together, but Kristen had seen how close to the edge Trisha was and was adamant that she wasn't going to make it worse by enveloping Candy into their social circle. In the end they compromised, and Michael and Theo played golf once a month and grabbed a few drinks together occasionally after work.

Kristen hadn't seen Michael for ages, and now she would never see him again because Michael had been hit by a car. Michael was dead.

What would Trisha think? Trisha had dropped off the radar lately and Kristen suspected she might be seeing someone. She hoped she was. She deserved happiness.

And so did Kristen, but right now her husband was crying, and her lover-to-be was waiting for her in the rose garden with a glass of champagne in his hand, and life was a complicated, unpredictable mess.

"Theo—"

"I try and detach from cases." Theo was still crying, great thumping sobs that turned his words into something close to unintelligible. "It's the way I operate—literally—but this was Michael, and he wasn't just a surgical challenge he was my friend. And the family member waiting for news wasn't a stranger, it was his wife."

Kristen thought, *Which wife?*

"Candy was there?"

"Trisha. She had Lulu and Richard with her. They were dressed in shorts and T-shirts because they'd been waiting for him to come home so they could have a backyard barbecue. They do it once a month to try and keep things civil."

Kristen remembered Trisha talking about it. *I do it for the kids and it almost kills me.*

And the reason it almost killed Trisha was because despite everything that had happened, she still loved Michael and playing happy families had been torture.

"How was Trisha?" If this had happened a few years earlier when Michael had just met Candy, Kristen might have suspected Trisha of being the one who had T-boned the car.

"Distraught. She threw herself at me and said *Tell me you saved him, Theo*, and I almost told her I had because I so badly wanted it to be true. Instead I had to tell them that there would be no more backyard barbecues, and the whole time I was talking I was wondering how many barbecues Michael had missed over the years because he was working and if he would have got himself to more had he known he had a limited number, and I tried to remember the last time I was present for a whole family meal."

"Don't think about that now. It's not the time."

"It's the perfect time." He was still crying, and Kristen realized that she was crying, too.

She was crying for Michael, who had been a sweet and kind man before he'd decided to leave his wife, and she was crying for Trisha, who had now lost Michael twice, and for their kids, who would go through the rest of their lives without a father present for their key moments. She was crying for Theo, who hadn't been able to save his friend and maybe she was crying for herself because she was poised on the edge of a new and better life, and she could feel herself being dragged back inside the confines of the old one.

She tried to calm him down.

"It doesn't matter that you missed a few family meals. You and Michael are both dedicated surgeons. This is who you are, Theo. And your families accept that because we're proud of what you do." She realized she'd used the present tense, which was correct for Theo but not for Michael, who was now in the past tense.

One unpredictable event and suddenly you were moved into the past tense. Life was brutal.

"What if I don't want to be this person anymore, Kristen? What if I don't want to prioritize strangers over my own family? Michael was on his way to work. If he'd stayed home with his family, he'd be alive now. What if I don't want to be the guy who misses the barbecue. What if I want to be the guy who is there for his kids?"

What about being the man who is there for his wife?

"They're not kids anymore. Todd is twenty-eight. He's about to get married." She didn't want to think about that right now. "Hannah is twenty-four. And they're proud of you."

She tried to be tactful. It might be a bit harsh to point out that the time to be there for his kids had passed. That this sudden revelation might have had more relevance had it happened a couple of decades ago.

"Maybe what I'm saying is that I just want to spend more time with my family. When I was looking at Michael's body, do you know what I was wondering?" His voice was still thickened, but steadier. "I was wondering when he last kissed Trisha. When he last made love to Trisha."

This was surreal. "Er—a while ago, I should imagine. He's been married to Candy for two years."

"Yes, Candy. I—I meant Candy. Except—"

"Except what?"

"Nothing. It's nothing. Just something that—no, never mind."

Was it nothing or was it something? And if it was something then what was that something? And did she want to know?

Theo was all over the place, and it was so unlike him Kristen was alarmed. "You should sit down for a moment, Theo. Do you want me to come and get you?" She hoped he didn't want her to, but if he said yes she would go because this was Theo, and they had two children together, and he was a good man, and she probably still loved him even though he hadn't been there for her when her father died. (Why couldn't she get that out of her head? It was buried there like a splinter.)

"I don't need you to come and get me. I don't know what I need. That's why I'm coming home. The strange thing is we know better than most that life is fleeting and can change in an instant, but still we sometimes forget that. I'm not going to forget it again, Kristen, I promise."

"Okay." What did that mean? She didn't recognize the guy on the phone. This just wasn't Theo.

"I don't know when I last told you I love you, but it was probably too long ago. I love you, Kristen. When did I last tell you you're beautiful?"

"I—" She was about to say *yesterday*, and then remembered it had been Jeff who had told her that when they'd sneaked a quick meeting in a gallery coffee shop.

"You are beautiful. I thought so this morning when you were standing in the kitchen with the sun shining on your hair. I should have said so, but I was in a hurry to get to work."

The conversation was becoming more unsettling by the minute.

It had been years since anyone told her she was beautiful, and now she'd been told it two days running by two different men.

"Theo, you need to breathe and calm down."

"You probably think I don't notice, but I do. I love your new hair. I love your new dress with the blue swirls that looks like a Monet."

Theo never noticed what she was wearing. He didn't notice when she'd done her hair, or when she had a new outfit. She'd accepted that as part of who he was. His mind was usually on higher things.

But now he'd noticed. And his attention could not have come at a worse time.

The irony wasn't lost on her.

She'd smartened herself up for Jeff, and in doing so had caught Theo's attention.

Michael was dead and now Theo was coming to the party because the death of his friend had affected him in the way the death of hundreds of strangers hadn't. The loss of that particular life had made him question how he was living his.

And she understood because wasn't that exactly what had happened to her? It had taken her father's death to make her realize that she needed to do something about her unhappiness.

She'd waited all these years for her husband to be more present and now, when she'd finally found a way to fill the void, he decided to show up.

She wanted to scream at the unfairness of it. Images of her and Jeff sneaking a quick kiss in the rose garden were tarnished by another image that included Theo bursting through the blooms to look for her in this new spirit of closeness.

It was much easier to contemplate an affair when your husband wasn't present in your life. She'd almost convinced herself that Theo wouldn't even care. He was big on outsourcing—*get a nanny, get a gardener, get a cleaner.* In her head she was simply outsourcing her loneliness and her sex life. *Get a friend and a lover.*

All that would have to go on hold for now until Theo reverted to his normal self, which she was sure would happen quickly. Theo was addicted to work.

"You've had a horrible shock, Theo." Her phone buzzed and she checked it quickly, but this time it wasn't Jeff. It was Amelie's mother.

Call me! Urgent.

Kristen felt a ripple of irritation. The woman was so rude. And why would Amelie's mother be calling, and today of all days when Kristen was in the middle of masterminding the most important event she'd ever run?

As well as the party, Kristen already had Jeff to think about, and her mother, and now Theo. There was no way she had time for Amelie's mother. Whatever it was that was "urgent" was going to have to wait. But the call stirred up another anxiety that she'd been trying to ignore, which was that her son was making a horrible mistake by marrying Amelie, and not only because his mother-in-law would make his life a misery. Todd and Amelie were utterly wrong for each other. She had no idea why Todd had proposed, but as a parent there was only so much you could say or do to steer your child away from disaster. Sometimes you just had to watch the crash happening and prepare yourself to clear up the mess afterward.

Thinking about messes made her realize Theo was still talking.

"I'll be there soon," he said. "Bill is going to cover for me.

This is an important day for you. It's a celebration of your parents. I want to be there with you, Todd and Hannah."

"I haven't seen Hannah. I don't think she's here yet." She thought of Hannah's pale face and hollow eyes. She thought about Lily. *We haven't spoken.* And she remembered that Todd had said he'd wanted to speak to her. Was that related to the fact that Amelie's mother was calling? Maybe she was calling about the party. Was she upset that she and her husband hadn't been invited today? Kristen had finalized the guest list weeks ago, before Todd's out-of-the-blue proposal. She'd been determined not to make any more last-minute changes.

"I'll message Hannah," Theo said. "If she's still at the hospital I can give her a ride out. Will you call Trisha?"

Kristen's head started to throb. Maybe Trisha would hate hearing from her because Theo was the one who hadn't managed to save Michael. Did Trisha blame Theo? Did Trisha even care? Had she looked at Michael's body and thought, *No! I can't believe you've gone*, or had she thought, *You got what you deserved.*

But Theo was right. Whatever her reaction, Kristen needed to call her, and she needed to find Jeff, just in case Theo did show up.

And amidst all the chaos, she had to mastermind the event she'd organized, keep an eye on her mother, find time to talk to Todd, call Amelie's mother back and give a speech.

It was enough to make you want to run away.

4

Cecilia

Cecilia took the outfit that Kristen had laid out for her and hung it in the closet between her long black coat and a silver evening dress she'd never worn. Instead of dressing for a party and a public appearance, she pulled on a floaty summer dress that was cool and comfortable and covered all the parts of her she had no wish to display. It didn't really matter what she wore because providing her plan worked, no one she knew was going to see her.

Through the open window she could hear the string quartet playing Mozart and she wished they'd play something else because Mozart made her think of Cameron and right now she didn't want to be reminded of Cameron.

She checked that her bedroom door was locked, and then pulled out one of her larger suitcases and placed it on a chair.

Part of her couldn't believe she was doing this.

She'd promised herself that she wouldn't ever go back to Dune Cottage and here she was packing a case.

Any guilt she might have felt for not attending her own party was neutralized by the knowledge that she'd made it clear that she hadn't wanted this event to happen. Kristen would just have to handle it, and no doubt she'd do so with her usual competence.

She filled the case without wasting time. Underwear, nightwear, dresses, capri pants and several warm sweaters. Anything she saw, she stuffed into the case. When it was full, she threw the novel she was reading on top of her clothes, along with the birthday gift Todd had given her, and then zipped the case shut.

Now all she had to do was find a way to leave the house without being seen. Fortunately, her car was parked next to the stable block, which was separate from the rest of the house and gardens and out of view of the guests.

What would Kristen say when Cecilia didn't make an appearance? She'd be frustrated, and then concerned.

Cecilia didn't want her daughter to worry, so she reached for a piece of paper and scribbled a note.

I've gone away for a few days. I think your generation calls it "me time." Don't worry about me. I'll be in touch.

No doubt Kristen would take this as further evidence that her mother had finally lost her grip on reality and needed urgent medical help, but the only other option was not to leave a note and she wouldn't put it past Kristen to report her as a missing person. The last thing she needed was a search party looking for her.

She placed the note on the bed where Kristen was sure to see it, then walked to the window and looked down into the garden. Crowds of people had already arrived and were enjoying the gardens. She could see Winston making polite conversation with two elderly women who she recognized as being members of a local art society, and there was Todd talking to a young woman who wasn't Amelie.

Cecilia wondered why Amelie wasn't coming. She barely knew her, but she'd seemed the type that would have to be half-dead before missing an event like this. And just as she had that thought she saw a car pull up at the front of the house. Amelie stepped out, balancing on heels that surely should have given her altitude sickness.

She stalked across the lawn to where Todd was in conversation, swiping a glass of champagne on the way.

Did Todd know she'd changed her mind about coming?

Cecilia opened her mouth and closed it again. What was she going to do? Shout from the window? She was too far away for him to hear her. And it wasn't as if Todd was doing anything he shouldn't be doing. He was talking, that was all. Socializing.

Still, she watched with a sense of foreboding as Amelie finally reached him and then winced as the contents of the glass hit Todd full in the face.

She couldn't hear what Amelie was saying but judging from her body language and the way her face turned puce as she shouted, it wasn't anything polite. Heads turned as people tried to locate the source of the commotion.

Cecilia stood still, transfixed by the drama unfolding below.

Two security staff stepped forward and Cecilia saw Todd give a quick shake of his head and gesture to them to stand back. He wiped his face with his other hand and tried to take Amelie's arm, but she shook him off and said something in reply that made his shoulders tense.

Cecilia's heart ached for him. She had no idea what had happened between them, but she refused to believe that Todd was to blame. Even if he was, she would still be on his side. She adored him. Whatever he'd done or hadn't done, she was in his corner.

She scanned the crowd again, wondering if Kristen was aware of what was happening. Cecilia knew how important this event was to her daughter. The last thing she needed was more family drama.

At first there was no sign of Kristen, and then she spotted a swirl of blue and saw her daughter in the rose garden talking to a man who had his back to Cecilia. From Cecilia's vantage point it didn't look like a casual conversation. Like most artists she was observant, and there was something not quite right about what she was observing now.

Cecilia squinted to get a better look. Who was it? Not Theo, obviously. He wasn't coming, and, anyway, Theo was taller than this man, who seemed to be eye level with Kristen. Theo had wide shoulders and slightly messy hair because he could rarely find the time to get it cut. This man had close-cropped hair and was standing really close to Kristen.

As she watched, she saw Kristen reach out and touch the man's arm in a gesture that could only be described as intimate. He was clearly someone she felt comfortable touching.

Celia found herself repositioning the pieces of the puzzle that had been forming in her head. Kristen's newly highlighted hair. Kristen's slim figure and new dress.

And she felt a ripple of alarm because she knew what this was.

She recognized the signs. If Kristen and the unknown man currently standing in her garden weren't sleeping together yet, they would be soon. And then what? What did it mean?

Cecilia felt shaky.

Kristen, having an affair? Why? Was she unhappy in her marriage? Had Cecilia missed something? Had Theo cheated on her, and this was about revenge? Or was this a delayed reaction to Cameron's death?

She had a thousand questions and no answers.

Sickness swirled in her stomach because this was a trigger for her. Even after all these years, it was a trigger.

Cecilia took another look out of the window and from her vantage point high up in the house she saw something else. She saw Theo's car pulling into the long, tree-lined driveway and heading toward the house. No. That wasn't possible, was it? Theo was at the hospital saving lives. Theo wasn't coming to the party.

But as he parked and stepped out of the car there was no mistaking him.

And unless Kristen ended her assignation in the next two minutes, Theo was about to find his wife in the rose garden with another man.

First drama with Todd, and now drama with Kristen. Should she stay? She hadn't thought her absence would make much difference, but now she was wondering.

Should she message her daughter?

She was about to reach for her phone when she saw Kristen appear alone from the rose garden and head toward the area where champagne was being served in long-stemmed glasses.

There was no sign of either Todd or Amelie, who must have disappeared while Cecilia was watching Kristen.

And now that Kristen had moved, Cecilia could finally see the identity of the man she'd been talking to.

She gasped and stepped back so suddenly she knocked her calves against a chair.

No. It couldn't be.

But it was. She recognized him instantly. And she had no need to ask herself what he was doing here.

Jeff Singer.

And now she knew exactly who had been asking those questions about *The Girl on the Shore*.

Oh, he was clever. So clever. Cameron had known that and hadn't trusted him. And he'd been right not to do so. If Cameron were still alive, this man wouldn't have been allowed to set foot in the place. She hated him, and Cameron had hated him, too.

But Cameron was no longer alive, and the presence of this man wouldn't raise a single question. He was an art editor, known for his often brutal opinions and blunt commentary. He was famous in the art world, having worked at an auction house and then as an art dealer before following in his father's footsteps and finding his way into journalism. It was logical that he would be on the invitation list. His presence here wouldn't be a surprise to any of the other guests, but it was a surprise to Cecilia (the fact that he *dared* set foot on her property made her blood boil), although it shouldn't have been because she was acquainted with his ruthless ways and underhand tactics.

The bigger surprise though was the fact that he'd been

almost holding hands with Kristen in the rose garden. Cecilia didn't know what was going on, but she was confident that Jeff Singer's interest in Kristen had nothing to do with her freshly highlighted hair or newly minted body. Unless she was mistaken, he had a very different agenda.

Did Kristen know that? How well did she know him?

She felt concern for her daughter. What did this relationship mean to her? Was this a fun flirtation or something more? Did she care for the man? Because if she did, then she was in trouble and a world of pain lay ahead.

If she had a closer relationship with her daughter, she might have found a way to steer Kristen away from him.

For the first time since his death, Cecilia wished Cameron were here so that she had someone to discuss this with. *Someone to deal with Jeff.*

She stood, frozen by indecision. Should she warn Kristen? No, she couldn't do that without revealing that she'd been watching them. And she couldn't warn her without revealing secrets that she and Cameron had kept safe for a long time.

And seeing Jeff had put an end to her indecision. She had to leave. She had no choice.

She didn't want to see him. It said a lot that she preferred the idea of going back to the cottage on the Cape, even though the thought of it made her feel nauseous.

And as for Kristen—she was a grown woman. Cecilia knew that any interference from her would not be welcome and might even push her daughter closer to Jeff.

Right now, Cecilia had more important things to worry about than the state of her daughter's marriage.

She lifted her case, took a final look at the envelope waiting for Kristen on the bed and left her bedroom. She took the back stairs, just to be safe, and met no one as she walked through the door that led directly to the stables.

Her car was parked where she'd left it, and no one was around to witness her hasty departure.

She drove toward the roughly made track that led through the woodland to the road. Few people knew about this entrance, and it was the perfect way to avoid being seen. Still her hands felt sweaty on the wheel, and she kept expecting someone to stop her.

It was a relief to reach the road. She tried not to think about what was going to happen when they discovered she'd gone. It was possible that Kristen would be so tied up handling the surprise appearance of her husband, or the drama unfolding in Todd's life, that she might not notice for a while. And when Cecilia's absence was eventually noticed, no one would know where she was.

She'd stop on the way and pick up some provisions to keep her going for a few days. Cameron had said in his letter that he'd arranged for the place to be maintained and kept ready for guests, so hopefully the place should be habitable.

One of the advantages of Dune Cottage was that they had no immediate neighbors. Early in their marriage it had provided an idyllic escape. She and Cameron would spend their days painting, absorbed by the landscape, their work and each other. They'd walk on the beach, eat lobster rolls dripping with butter and sleep with the windows open, the sound of the ocean filling their heads.

But then everything had changed. And *The Girl on the Shore* was the reason for that.

He was supposed to have destroyed it.

Did you destroy it, Cameron?

Trying not to think about that, she focused on the road. Even though it had been years since she'd last done this drive, it was so familiar it felt as if she'd driven it yesterday.

She took the historic "Old King's Highway" which followed the northern coast of the Cape, because she wasn't in a hurry and was willing to tolerate some congestion in exchange for the scenery and a dose of nostalgia.

She tried not to think about the times she and Cameron had driven this route in those early days, driving with the top down, wind blowing her hair into a tangle.

The road wound its way through Sandwich and Barnstable, past the beaches of Cape Cod Bay and along tree-shaded roads dotted with wildflowers, historic houses and quaint local stores. She stopped in Yarmouth and bought herself an ice cream, and then drove onward to Orleans where she bought a lobster roll and ate it while gazing at the sea.

For a moment she was transported back in time. She was young again and madly in love with Cameron, full of optimism and hope for the future.

The world had seemed like a wonderful place.

From Orleans she headed toward the tip of Cape Cod, past miles of sandy beaches.

She stopped outside a small store to stock up on provisions. She bought fresh bread, milk, berries, thick sliced ham, a mixture of French cheeses and an expensive bottle of white wine. That would do her for now, and she'd figure the rest out later.

She paid and then loaded her bags into the car.

On impulse, she checked her phone, but there was nothing. No missed calls and no messages, which presumably meant that Kristen either hadn't yet discovered her absence or hadn't had time to do anything about it.

Knowing that this was the last time she'd have a reliable signal, she dropped the phone back into her bag and prepared to make the last stage of the journey.

She stared straight ahead for a moment, bracing herself for what was to come.

This was the part she'd been dreading. Up until now she'd managed to fool herself that this journey was nothing more than a scenic road trip. An escape.

What was coming next was reality. Cameron was gone, but the farther she drove north the more he seemed alive again. The memories were everywhere and once she reached the cottage, she'd be surrounded by them.

She had a sudden urge to delay her arrival for as long as possible.

Switching off the engine she retrieved Todd's gift from her suitcase and unwrapped it.

At first she thought he'd given her a notebook, but then she realized it was a planner, the cover inlaid with silver foil, the pattern subtle and beautiful.

A planner, for the year ahead.

She didn't know whether to laugh or cry. What was she supposed to do with this? She didn't need a planner for the life she was living.

She opened it and a note fell out. She recognized Todd's writing.

Take it a day at a time, Nanna.

Her vision swam and for a moment she clutched the planner and then put it carefully back in her bag.

She had no use for it, but she appreciated the sentiment.

Right now, the only day she needed to get through was this one.

Grabbing her sweater, she locked the car and headed toward the beach.

Perhaps what lay ahead would seem easier if she arrived after dark.

5

Lily

Lily worked on her painting, lost in her own creation, until the sun set and the light faded.

It calmed her mind and she wished, for a moment, that this could be a job. That her parents might understand and say *our daughter is an artist* with the same pride they would have said *our daughter is a doctor*.

But she wasn't an artist, was she? She was just someone who enjoyed painting.

And her parents didn't understand.

It was up to her to find a way to make this life work. So far she hadn't managed that.

She took a shower, changed into shorts and an old T-shirt, and poured herself a glass of homemade lemonade from the jug she'd filled the day before.

She didn't feel like eating so she sat for an hour on the deck, nursing her lemonade and appreciating the warmth of the evening. Slivers of light danced across the surface of the water and the air smelled of salt and summer. She shifted her gaze from the ocean to the vast inky sky patterned with shimmering stars and felt her problems shrink.

Here, perched on the edge of a continent, her past life felt a long way away.

It felt like a place for forgetting. For forgiving. For planning a fresh start.

Somewhere out there medical students were hunched over laptops studying. They were studying anatomy, physiology, pathology and pharmacology.

She was relieved not to be one of them. She might not know what she wanted to do exactly, but she knew what she didn't want to do.

She finished her drink, and headed to bed.

It wasn't late, but she was tired. Since the night she'd packed her bags and walked out of medical school she often felt tired, mostly because she didn't sleep well. The moment she closed her eyes her past swirled round and round in her brain. During the day optimism won. She felt hopeful and saw possibilities. *Everything was going to work out.* At night her brain punched optimism in the face, and she saw only obstacles and looming catastrophe. Instead of thinking *I've done the right thing*, she thought, *What have I done?*

She could have been a doctor. She could have made her parents proud.

They'd believed she could have had a good life. Been a success.

One day she was going to figure out exactly what really defined success. She wasn't sure, but she knew it wasn't hating every minute of what you were doing. She knew it wasn't waking in the morning dreading the day.

Tired of overthinking, she lay on top of the bed in her sleeping bag, listening to the sound of the waves. She left the blinds open so she could still see the stars through the skylights.

She pushed aside guilt about her parents and instead thought of Hannah. Did Hannah think about her? Presumably not, because she hadn't sent a message and it had been months now. Too many months.

She missed Hannah so much.

And now Hannah was going to have Amelie as a sister-in-law.

Amelie would be a member of the family. She'd be there for Thanksgiving and Christmas. For the rest of his life Todd would be smiling at Amelie. Kissing Amelie. Amelie, who had made her life a misery. Amelie, who hid the less wholesome side of her nature behind a dazzling smile that blinded most people to her more narcissistic tendencies. Maybe it was wrong of her to think it, but Amelie didn't deserve anything as good as Todd to happen in her life.

Which just went to prove that you didn't get what you deserved.

With a groan of frustration, Lily pushed her face into the pillow. She had to stop thinking about Amelie. She had to stop thinking about Todd. But how?

She loved him with every aching bone in her body. She needed to find a way to stop loving him, but she was still working on that. And in the meantime she had more immediate problems to deal with—like the fact that she was now a college dropout with no future.

She needed a new life, a different life, but it wasn't as if you could order that online.

Her parents knew about her career crisis, but they didn't

know about Todd, and she had no intention of telling them. They'd tell her that she was still young, that there were plenty of fish in the sea (hadn't they heard of overfishing?) and that she'd meet someone else eventually. She'd tried that. She'd dated a couple of guys in college, and one when she was in med school. They'd all fizzled to nothing. One was a good guy and maybe, just maybe, if she hadn't known Todd existed, it might have turned into something. But she did know Todd existed. And that was the problem.

Lily didn't want to meet anyone else. She didn't want to fall in love with anyone else. She didn't want to fall in love ever again. It was too painful. As far as she was concerned, love was like malaria or yellow fever. It was to be avoided. There had to be a vaccine. There had to be *something*, because surely someone must have invented something to make sure human beings never had to feel this bad. And she couldn't even blame Todd, because he'd done nothing. There had been that one kiss (the single best moment of her life by a long way) but he'd never mentioned it, so she assumed that he either wished it hadn't happened or didn't remember it. The one good thing was that he had no idea she felt the way she did, which was a relief, because if he *had* known she would have had to move to another country.

Hating herself for not having more willpower, she checked Amelie's social media and saw a photograph of her and Todd, followed by a stream of hashtags: #soulmate #manofmydreams #truelove.

Lily wanted to add a few hashtags of her own, but she used all her willpower and put her phone down instead.

She closed her eyes, not anticipating that she'd sleep but she must have done because she was woken by a loud noise coming from somewhere beneath her.

She lay without moving, and then flinched as she heard breaking glass and a voice.

Heart pounding, she sprang out of bed. Home invasion. Burglars. Always a risk for empty properties, especially those on the Cape. And it was obvious from the noise they were making that they thought the cottage was empty. It was isolated, so they'd assumed that their presence would go undetected. They'd do what they wanted to do, take what they wanted to take and then leave. They hadn't factored in a witness.

She'd seen enough movies and read enough thrillers to know what happened to witnesses, and it was never good.

Fear swamped her. She forced her mind to scan the options.

Call the police, obviously.

She reached for her phone and then stopped. If she reported an intruder, they'd ask her what she was doing there, how she knew, and technically she was an intruder, too, so she couldn't do that. Also, if the intruders found her before the police arrived, it wouldn't end well.

She sat back on the bed, legs too shaky to support her, heart thundering in her chest, immobilized by indecision.

She should leave. Get out of here while she could. Then she would report it. She'd say she saw lights or heard voices. She could figure that part out later. But now she needed to get out before they decided to check the whole cottage for valuables and found her instead.

She imagined them dressed in black, with masks covering their faces. Did they have weapons?

Would her shaky legs allow her to escape? Maybe she should just hide under the bed. She thought about all the movies she'd seen where the first thing the bad guys did was look under the bed, so she dismissed that. No hiding. And no screaming, because there were no immediate neighbors so no one would hear her and, anyway, they'd be back to the thorny issue of what she was doing here in the first place.

No, as far as she could see there was only one option.

If she could make it to the second bedroom, she could drop from the balcony onto the sand dunes below and be gone before anyone was aware of her existence.

As silently as possible she pulled on her jeans and a T-shirt and stuffed everything into her backpack. She rolled up her sleeping bag and stuffed that inside, too.

Then she tiptoed down the narrow flight of stairs that spiraled up to the loft, and paused on the landing area that was open to the living room below. She flattened herself against the wall, terrified that one of them might pick that exact moment to glance up. It was just a few steps to the comparative safety of the bedroom, but Lily found she couldn't move. From here she could see down into the living room and her heart raced as she saw a figure move into view. The figure grabbed one of the sketches hanging on the wall, stared at it for a moment and then made an anguished sound and smashed it on the floor.

Lily jumped, identifying the source of the breaking glass. Not a window, but the paintings. And not a group of masked men, but one person. A woman. She yanked another painting from the wall and sent it the way of the others. Lily watched open-mouthed. Part of her wanted to stop the woman because this place was her responsibility and she was going to have to clear up the mess in the morning.

She was going to have to explain to the company (and to the owners, whoever they were) that she must have forgotten to set the alarm. Would that invalidate the insurance?

If she was right and the paintings the woman was smashing were valuable, then she was in even bigger trouble than she'd thought.

As far as she could tell, nothing else had been damaged so far. Why would someone want to break in just to smash up paintings? Why not steal them? None of it made sense. And then the woman turned slightly, and Lily slapped her hand over her mouth to stop her gasp from escaping because she recognized her.

It was Cecilia Lapthorne.

She'd met her once, when she'd visited the Lapthorne Estate with Hannah, and there was no mistaking her slight build and short, carefully styled silvery-white hair.

She watched as Cecilia reached up to remove the final painting from the wall. The one Lily had been admiring for months. She had to stop herself from crying out. *No. Not that one.* Lily felt an almost visceral attachment to the work. And if she was right and it was a genuine Cameron Lapthorne, why would Cecilia be smashing it?

But she didn't smash this one. Instead, she left it where it was and sank down onto the sofa. And then she started to cry. There was something about those heartrending sobs that tore at Lily. And now she faced a dilemma.

The urge to go to her and offer comfort was strong, but then she'd have to confess that she'd been staying here. She'd be arrested. And, anyway, Cecilia thought she was alone. The tearing sobs were raw and real, and Lily sensed that she'd only given in to this unrestrained display of emotion because she believed that there were no witnesses. Cameron Lapthorne had died a year ago. Cecilia and Cameron had been together for fifty years. Cecilia had lost Cameron.

Cecilia's heart was broken.

Lily knew she needed to get out of the cottage, and not only because she needed to save her own skin. She was trespassing, not just on Cecilia's property (if this was indeed Cecilia's property), but on Cecilia's emotions. She was witnessing something that wasn't supposed to be witnessed.

She needed to give Cecilia privacy, even though part of her was reluctant to leave someone who was in so much distress. But would revealing herself help? It wasn't as if Cecilia knew her. Her presence would bring awkwardness, not comfort.

Forcing herself to move, she took those few final steps to the second bedroom. Moving stealthily, she opened the door that led to the small balcony and dropped her shoes and her backpack onto the sand below. They landed with a quiet thud, which Cecilia was unlikely to hear above the sound of her own sobbing. Pushing the balcony door closed behind her, Lily eased herself over the wooden railing and let herself drop onto the sand dune below. It was farther than she'd estimated, and she caught her breath as she landed, but the sand was soft and she scrambled to her feet with no apparent injury. Grabbing her backpack and her shoes, she sprinted away from the cottage.

Using the torch on her phone, she'd managed to put two sand dunes between her and the cottage when she remembered her bike.

She stopped and glanced over her shoulder. If she went back for it now, she risked being caught. Better to go in the morning and pretend she'd just arrived to check on the place. That was her job after all. And judging from the scene she'd witnessed, she had a significant amount of cleaning ahead of her.

But that wasn't her real problem. Her real problem was

that she'd lost her home and her sanctuary. No more nights gazing at the ocean and the stars.

She'd never find accommodation this far into the season, at least nothing that fell inside her budget.

She closed her eyes, feeling defeat close over her.

She was going to have to call her parents and ask for help.

6

Kristen

"Me time? Who decides to disappear and have 'me time' in the middle of her own party?" Stupefied, Kristen read the note for the twentieth time and then dropped it back onto the bed where her mother had left it. Her head throbbed and her feet hurt.

Her plans for the evening were in shreds.

All she wanted right now was for Jeff to sweep her away to a little bistro near the coast, where they'd share a seafood platter and talk long into the night. He'd listen to her in that way only he listened, with his gaze fixed on her face so that he could focus on every word. She would spill out her feelings and he would catch them (unlike Theo, who usually let them fall on the floor where he trod on them on his way to the hospital) and she would feel warm, and heard, and understood and best of all no longer lonely.

But that wasn't possible. Jeff had left several hours earlier, and Kristen knew she was supposed to be grateful for that because she didn't need more complication, but she didn't feel grateful. She felt resentful and feeling resentful made her feel guilty because she knew she shouldn't be thinking about herself at a time like this.

After she'd intercepted him in the rose garden and told him what had happened, Jeff had behaved impeccably. He'd played the role of "guest" perfectly. Instead of being Jeff her almost lover, he'd turned back into Jeff the art editor, only a softer version of his usually acerbic self. He'd studied the paintings on display, asked intelligent questions (she'd always found a sharp mind more of an erotic draw than broad shoulders) and mingled with colleagues. Jeff had even laughed and chatted with Theo. At some point as the evening progressed Jeff had left without a word. Kristen didn't know what that meant, and she didn't have time to think about it now.

As dinner with Jeff wasn't an option, all she wanted to do was go to bed and close her eyes and pretend her life wasn't falling apart, but she didn't have that luxury because she had to support Theo, who was an emotional wreck, and figure out what was happening with her mother. First the party, and now this.

"Where has she gone? And why?"

Winston looked exhausted. He'd played his part talking to journalists and guests and he looked as if he'd be happy not to have another conversation for at least a fortnight. "There are no clues in the note?"

Did he really think she'd be wondering where their mother had gone if there were clues in the note? Kristen hid her irritation, because she knew she was only irritated because she was worried, and snapping at Winston wasn't going to help that.

"No clues."

"What do you think we should do, Kris?" He looked at her expectantly and she knew that whatever she suggested he'd go along with because that was what he always did.

"I don't know." She was used to being the one in control, but right now she wished someone else would take over. She was tired of responsibility. Tired of doing the right thing when everyone else just did what they wanted to do. Tired of keeping every ball in the air by herself. "If you have suggestions, I'm listening."

She sat down and removed her shoes, flexing first one foot and then the other. She'd walked miles today, striding between paintings and problems, managing and trouble-shooting and smiling until her face ached. All without the help of the most important guest.

Outside it was dark. The guests had left. The champagne had been drunk and the food eaten. Most of the clearing up had already taken place, although the crew would be back in the morning to pick up any remaining detritus.

Kristen lay back on her mother's bed. When she was discharged from the hospital as a child having almost died, she'd slept in this bed and Cecilia had slept next to her, watching her breathe. Every time she'd opened her eyes, her mother had been there. For the first two nights her father had slept there, too, and she remembered feeling happy and a little smug because she'd reunited a family that she'd been sure was broken.

Her memory of the accident was blurry. She remembered her mother telling her that they were divorcing. She remembered feeling as if her life had collapsed. She'd yelled at her mother and run out of the house. Her next memory was of waking up in the hospital and seeing her parents standing by her bed. Together. They'd talked to the doctors together. They'd watched her bleeping machines together. They held hands at the same time as holding her hand.

Cecilia had cried on Cameron's shoulder, and he'd hugged her and held her and cried a little himself.

Kristen had never seen her father cry, but he'd cried over her when she was in the hospital and that, together with the suffocating level of attention that followed her accident, made her feel loved and safe and part of a family that just might stay together.

She sat up, pushing those memories away.

Why was she thinking about that now? Possibly because unpredictable parental behavior unsettled her.

The door opened and Theo entered carrying a tray loaded with wine, beer and glasses.

Kristen glanced at his face, trying to gauge his mental state. How was he doing?

When he'd arrived at the party, she'd been terrified that he was going to have some sort of emotional breakdown and that she was going to have to try and find a way to support him while still running a major event and managing the absence of her mother. Theo had surprised her by appearing to be his normally controlled self.

Instead of coming straight from the hospital, he'd stopped off at home to shower and change. He'd arrived looking like the calm, steady man she'd married, and he'd brought Hannah with him.

Kristen had been relieved. On the phone he'd sounded broken and she'd been nervous about how she was going to deal with it. This version of Theo she understood. This version she could handle. Hopefully those unsettling few minutes of unleashed emotion during their phone call were in the past.

"Hannah is on her way up." He put the tray down on the table and dropped his jacket over the back of a chair. "Bring me up-to-date. What do we know?"

"Not much. This was a good idea, Theo." Winston poured wine into the glasses. "Genius."

"I thought we needed it."

Kristen watched him closely. "Her note simply says that she has gone away for a while and not to worry about her," she said. "There are no clues as to where she has gone or why."

"Did she take a taxi or drive herself?" Theo drank his glass of wine quickly and Kristen thought that maybe he wasn't doing that well after all. Maybe he was just doing well at disguising how bad he felt.

"I don't know."

He had been drinking steadily all afternoon and evening, and Kristen hadn't said anything or tried to intervene because she knew he was on edge and thinking about Michael and she sympathized. She was thinking about Michael, too (and Trisha), but she'd also had to think about all the guests, her speech, Jeff and also Todd who had apparently had champagne thrown in his face by Amelie, which might or might not be linked to the fact that her phone was telling her she now had twelve missed calls from Amelie's mother. (What was *wrong* with the woman?)

The way her life was right now, Kristen was ready to snatch the bottle out of Theo's hand and drink it herself without bothering with the glasses but if she did that who would unravel the various strands of their family mess?

Winston was looking to her to make decisions and it was becoming clear that despite his valiant attempts to disguise his personal crisis, Theo was incapable of thinking of anything except the loss of his friend. Todd might have had some insight because he was close to his grandmother, but no one had seen him since Amelie had tried to drown him.

"No one saw her leave as far as we know." And it didn't matter how many times Winston said they shouldn't worry. She was worried. And angry with her mother for adding yet another stress to her already stressful life. Why couldn't she just have said where she was going like a normal person? And why couldn't she have waited until after the party?

"Perhaps we should wait for her to get in touch. We know she's not in danger." Winston was practical. "She said she wants some time to herself. What's wrong with that?"

"What's wrong is that this was supposed to be her party. And Dad's exhibition. People were asking questions. There were a hundred people ready to sing her happy birthday and I had to pretend she had a headache. It was awkward."

Winston looked helpless. "You handled it well, Kris."

Kristen stood up and walked to the window. She didn't want praise. She wanted—what did she want?

Not this.

Her entire life was imploding. Her mother was supposed to be here, and she'd vanished without a word. Theo was supposed to be at the hospital, but instead he was here at the party, clearly counting the hours until they could leave and he could stop pretending everything was fine. Jeff had gone. Todd had disappeared. No one seemed to be doing what they were supposed to be doing.

Theo picked up the letter and read it carefully. "Where does a person go for 'me time'?"

"I don't know, which is why I'm worried." Kristen rubbed her forehead. She felt guilty that she had so little insight into the thought processes of her mother. If her mother had needed "me time" why hadn't she said so? Why leave a note? "We need to find her, obviously."

"Why obviously?"

"Because she must be having some kind of breakdown. Why else would she leave without telling us? She was behaving oddly all day."

Hannah walked into the room carrying a bottle of sparkling water and a fruit plate. "Is this the Lapthorne missing persons committee?" She was wearing a fitted navy dress and her hair was loose around her shoulders. She looked young and pretty and very tired. "My preliminary investigations confirm that wherever Nanna has gone, she's driven there."

Kristen stared at her. "How do you know?"

"Her car is gone. Detective Work 101."

"Where did you look?"

"By the stables. That's where she parks." Hannah put the fruit plate down and poured herself water. "What am I missing here? Nanna has gone AWOL. I don't see why it's a big deal."

"Today was her birthday party."

"Who hasn't wanted to run away from a party in their time?" Hannah helped herself to a grape. "Parties can be exhausting, all that small talk and smiling and saying things you don't mean to people you probably don't like. Having to share your cake is a big enough reason to cry."

Kristen didn't manage to raise a smile. "Have you seen your brother? He might know where she is."

"Haven't seen him." Hannah put the water down and

helped herself to wine instead. "He's probably trying to keep Amelie happy, which is a full-time job I can assure you. Doesn't leave a lot of time for anything else."

Kristen felt she should defend Amelie, but she couldn't bring herself to do it.

"Do you know why Amelie threw champagne over him?"

"Did she do that?" Hannah brightened. "Mmm. Interesting. Well, he can't say I didn't warn him."

"Hannah—"

"They're adults, Mom. Let them get on with it."

If only it were that easy. "You're still my children and I will always worry about you." Although she would rather not have worried about them today when her worry quota was already overflowing.

"Remind me never to have kids," Hannah muttered as she put her glass down. "We're fine, Mom."

Theo looped his arm around Hannah. "It's good to spend a bit of time with you. Everything going well at the hospital? I'm proud of you. I hope you know that."

Hannah shot him a look of alarm. "Are you okay, Dad?"

"Yes. Why?"

"Because you're—" Hannah shrugged "—I don't know. Acting a bit weird."

"What's weird about telling my daughter I'm proud of her?"

"Nothing, except when it's coming from you. You don't normally..." Hannah coughed awkwardly and Theo gave a tired smile.

"And I'm sorry for that. From now on, expect to hear it a lot more from me. It's important to say things in case you miss the chance."

"I...right." Hannah glanced at Kristen and then back at

her father. "As long as you don't embarrass me in public." She patted his hand and carefully pulled away from him.

Kristen sighed. They were so alike. Both single-minded and focused. They pushed themselves to their mental and physical limits, and sometimes beyond.

Ever since she was young, Hannah had put a ridiculous amount of pressure on herself. Kristen had been one of the few parents who spent her time trying to stop her child studying and encourage her to take a break. It was as if Hannah had taken it upon herself to fulfill her father's expectations for Todd, too. She was the golden child. Todd was the rebel, although he wasn't really a rebel of course. He'd just stood firm about doing what he wanted to do, and Kristen had quietly admired that about him.

And right at that moment, Todd strolled into the room. His hair was ruffled, his collar undone and there were several marks on his previously pristine white shirt.

Kristen stared at her son. "We've been looking for you. What happened?"

"I was dealing with a personal crisis."

"Is that—blood?"

"Yes." Todd rubbed at the mark on his shirt. "But only a relatively small quantity. And it's mine. Nothing to worry about. There's plenty left in my body. I don't need Dad's attentions yet."

"Todd!" Driven by a whole new concern, Kristen hurried toward him. "What happened?"

"I fell against your holly bush and the landing wasn't comfortable."

"You fell—" She frowned. "How?"

Hannah helped herself to another grape. "Amelie pushed him."

Kristen looked at her daughter. "How do you know that? You said you hadn't seen him."

"I didn't. But I'm guessing he didn't throw himself in a holly bush voluntarily. He's not a masochist."

"Are you serious?" Kristen turned back to Todd. "Did Amelie push you? First she tries to drown you in champagne and then she tries to lacerate you? Why?"

"It's pretty obvious," Hannah said. "That's what happens when you hook up with a—"

"Thank you." Todd gave his sister a sharp look. "When I want your opinion on my sex life, I'll ask for it."

"I can't think of anything that interests me less than your sex life. Do you want me to look at that wound for you? My training is more up-to-date than Dad's."

"I'd rather consult with Dr. Frankenstein."

"Stop it." Kristen felt her blood pressure rising. "I have no idea what is going on between you two, or between you and Amelie, Todd, but it's time we talked about it."

Todd scrubbed at the blood on his shirt with his finger. "I'm handling it."

Hannah rolled her eyes. "Have you looked in the mirror lately? Because from where I'm standing it doesn't look as if you're handling much. Is that the holly bush or her fingernails? You should maybe have a tetanus shot."

He threw her a warning look and Kristen felt almost as worried about their relationship as she was about Todd's relationship with his girlfriend. Why wasn't Hannah supporting him as she usually would? Something had obviously happened between them. Was it to do with Amelie? And she still didn't know what had happened between Hannah and Lily.

Her head throbbed. She couldn't think about that now.

If Todd said he was handling it, she had to believe he was handling it.

She almost said as much, and then remembered that at some point she was going to have to call Amelie's mother back, so she needed some facts.

"Is this disagreement of yours the reason I have so many missed calls from Amelie's mother on my phone?"

Todd winced. "It could be related."

Hannah rolled her eyes. "I can't believe her mother is getting involved. It's not as if Amelie is sixteen years old. Which one of them are you marrying?"

"I'm not marrying anyone." Todd ignored the wine and grabbed a beer. "I broke it off."

Hannah's eyes widened. "You've only been engaged for a week."

"Longest week of my life."

"Judging from the blood on your shirt and the champagne in your hair, I'm guessing this parting of ways wasn't mutual."

"Your guess would be correct."

Hannah patted her brother on his shoulder. "You're not all bad."

He shrugged. "Amelie would disagree."

Kristen watched him, unsure whether to be relieved or concerned. Relieved. Definitely relieved.

"Why is her mother calling me?"

"No doubt to inform you of my deficiencies as a human being." He removed the cap from the beer and drank. "Apologies if I've embarrassed you."

"I'm not embarrassed," she said. "But if you didn't want to get married, why did you propose?"

Todd put his beer down on the table. "It's a long story.

We can talk about it another time. Why is everyone gathered in here anyway? Where's Nanna?" He glanced around him for the first time.

"We were hoping you might know." Hannah handed him the note and he scanned it quickly.

"Why would I know?"

"Because you're the top grandchild." Hannah poured herself a glass of sparkling water. "You're the one who sets up her phone, fixes the Wi-Fi on her laptop and tops up the oil in her car. You call in for tea when you're passing."

Todd gave the note back to her. "You are welcome to do any, or all, of those things."

"I'm too busy working and living up to parental expectation."

What was that supposed to mean? Kristen glanced at Hannah and then at Theo, but he was staring out of the window with a distant look in his eyes.

Her heart ached for him. He'd watched his closest friend die. He hadn't been able to save him.

That would rip Theo apart. She was surprised he hadn't told the kids, but maybe the only way he could hold it together was by not talking about it.

When she'd had to appear in public after her father died, she'd done the same. She'd told everyone she was fine and changed the subject, while inside she'd been terrified that she might fall apart in the middle of a crowd.

Was that how her mother had felt today? Had she been afraid of breaking down in the middle of the crowd?

"Let's focus for two minutes. Does anyone have any idea where Mom—Nanna—might have gone?"

Hannah shrugged. "I assume you've tried calling her?"

"I tried three times," Winston said. "It goes to voice mail. I left messages."

"Maybe she doesn't know how to pick up her voice mail."

"She does," Todd said. "I showed her."

Kristen felt a surge of anxiety. "I didn't think she was herself earlier. Did something happen? Did she say anything to any of you? Anything at all that might give us a clue as to what she was thinking and where she is now? She didn't want to give a speech, but I immediately said I'd do it so it can't have been that."

Todd shrugged. "Maybe she just didn't want to go to the party."

"Yeah." Hannah nodded. "Maybe it was all too much seeing Gramps's paintings everywhere. I mean, it must hurt, right? All those reminders in one place. We know she doesn't have any in her bedroom and presumably it's because they make her sad. Maybe the whole party made her sad."

Kristen felt a twist of guilt. If she could put the clock back, she wouldn't have organized the party. She'd thought it was the right thing to do, but now she wasn't so sure.

"Maybe it was the mention of journalists," Winston said. "She doesn't like them. Never has. She finds their questions intrusive, although I don't know why. It's not as if she has secrets."

Maybe she did have secrets, Kristen thought. Maybe there was something they were all missing.

"I think we all need to chill." Todd picked up his sister's glass and poured water onto the stain on his shirt. "If she wanted us to find her, she would have told us where she was. Her note was clear. She didn't sound upset or desperate. I say leave her alone. Let her have her 'me time' and wait for her to get in touch."

Kristen was sorely tempted to follow his suggestion, if only because it would mean she had one less immediate problem to solve. Theo was looking washed out and she wasn't sure if it was the alcohol, grief or the sheer effort required to seem okay when he was falling apart, but she sensed she needed to get him away from here fast.

In terms of her priorities, she was probably looking at it.

"Maybe we should wait until tomorrow," Winston said. "If this is all about the party, then maybe she left so that no one would try and persuade her to attend. She could be back in the morning."

"Yes." Kristen had to admit that there was sense in Winston's suggestion. "What do you think, Theo?" She tried to draw him out of whatever dark place his mind was currently inhabiting. "Theo?"

He flinched as her voice finally penetrated. "I think life is short and unpredictable, and we should all make the most of the moment. You never know what's round the corner."

"Whoa, Dad," Hannah muttered. "I think Mom was just hoping for your take on the best way to handle the Nanna issue, not your thoughts on the meaning of life."

"It's the same thing," Theo said. "If Cecilia wants space, then we should respect her wishes and allow her that." He swayed. "It has been a long day. I think I might head home."

"Maybe we should sleep here tonight," Kristen said. "In case she comes home."

Todd raised an eyebrow. "You don't think it would freak her out to discover that her entire family has moved into her home in her absence? If she left to avoid us, then that might make her turn around and leave again."

Had her mother been avoiding her family? Had she been avoiding *her*?

"I can't stay," Hannah said. "I'm due back at the hospital in the morning and it's too far to drive from here. I need to get a cab."

"I have to go back to the city," Winston said. "I'll drive you." He gave Kristen a look of apology. "I can come back tomorrow if you need me to."

"I need to go back, too," Todd said. "I'm driving to Hyannis to give someone a quote for a new hand-built kitchen using sustainable wood."

Kristen stood there, feeling lost and then Theo crossed the room to her and put his hand on her shoulder.

"I'll stay here with you if that's what you'd prefer. I know you're worried." His voice was kind and his touch firm and reassuring.

She felt a lump form in her throat. "You want to go home and sleep in your own bed."

"I want to do what's right for you. I love you."

Kristen saw Hannah's startled look. She saw her glance at her brother.

Theo was undeterred. "We can sleep in your old room. Haven't done that in years."

The same room where she'd read her message from Jeff. "I don't know—"

"It will be fine, Kristen." He pulled her close. "Your mother will show up tomorrow, having spent a night at a spa hotel or something. She'll wonder what all the fuss was about. Everything is going to be fine, honey."

Honey.

Theo never called her honey, even when he'd had a drink.

Theo, who never paid attention to her, had decided to pay attention.

Why was life so confusing?

7

Cecilia

She woke up aching and cold, the arm of the sofa digging uncomfortably into her neck. For a moment she was confused about where she was, and then she saw her suitcase by the door where she'd left it and remembered that she was in the cottage.

It had been dark when she'd arrived, which she'd thought might lessen the emotional impact of being back here, but it hadn't worked that way. From the moment she'd opened the door, the memories and emotions had engulfed her like a storm. Images had appeared from the shadows; images she'd tried to force from her mind. She'd seen Cameron everywhere. It was as if he'd been waiting for her.

Why didn't you sell the place, Cameron?

It had taken willpower not to turn around and drive back to the house and the sanctuary of her bedroom, which she'd stripped of all the reminders.

Instead she'd flicked on all the lights and the images had melted away, but that hadn't changed the way she was feeling.

It was surprising she'd managed to sleep at all.

The events of the day before came back to her. The party she'd left without even showing her face. Kristen in the rose garden, gazing up at Jeff.

Jeff.

Head thumping, Cecilia sat up. She rubbed her fingers over her forehead, trying to ease the throbbing pain. There were no words to describe how much she hated that man. And she was also afraid of him. Afraid of what he might know. What he might do.

And now she was also worried about Kristen, who she suspected was a pawn in whatever plan Jeff had. She wanted to warn her daughter, but what would she say exactly? It wasn't a simple conversation.

And there was every chance that even if she did call, Kristen wouldn't want to hear what she had to say. Daughters rarely wanted advice from their mothers, and it wasn't as if she and Kristen were close. She wouldn't be able to introduce the topic during one of their intimate conversations, because they didn't have intimate conversations. They didn't confide in each other. When they talked, it was about practical things. Cameron's work. Exhibitions. Auctions. Hannah's achievements. Occasionally they'd talk about the changes Cecilia was making to the gardens.

They never talked about marriage or feelings or Theo. And that was probably her fault. She'd never talked about her relationship with Cameron, so why would Kristen talk about her relationship with Theo? Cecilia had always assumed that Kristen and Theo were fine.

Unless she'd wildly misinterpreted what she'd seen in the rose garden, that wasn't true.

Poor Kristen. And poor Theo.

She stood up and felt something scrunch under her feet. Glass.

She stared at the mess strewn across the living room floor, shocked and mortified.

Had she really done that? It was a good thing no one had been here to witness it.

Just one painting remained intact. *The Girl on the Shore*.

Cameron had promised to destroy it. Cameron had promised to sell the cottage.

He'd never been good at keeping his promises, so she probably shouldn't be surprised that the painting was still intact.

She gazed at it with mixed emotions. What would their lives have looked like if that painting hadn't existed? It had changed everything.

She probably should have smashed that one, too, in the circumstances, but she couldn't bring herself to do it. And maybe it wasn't necessary to go to those extremes.

Who would look for it here? No one knew about this cottage. Not even the children. They knew about the apartment in Manhattan, the beach house in The Hamptons (Cecilia had refused to return to Cape Cod after that one awful summer), and the house in Provence where the children had spent several summers playing among vineyards and olive groves and swimming in the pool while their parents had painted. They didn't know about this place.

She needed to think and plan, but first she needed to clear up the mess she'd made.

Unpack. Shower. Clean up.

She flung open the front door and took a breath of the fresh, salty air. Then she made her way across the room, careful to avoid the broken glass. She picked up her suitcase and headed upstairs. The wooden stairs creaked in the exact same place they'd always creaked. There were the same chips in the paintwork.

She paused by the door of the master bedroom and then turned away. She couldn't bring herself to walk into that room yet, so instead she opened the door to the second bedroom and put her suitcase on the chair. The room was light and bright, although the paintwork had slightly yellowed with age. The bedding was clean but old-fashioned, but the view from the doors that led to the small balcony was as spectacular as ever.

She stepped into the bathroom, prepared for spiders and mold but the place was fresh and clean. A faint floral scent hovered in the air. Whoever had been maintaining the place had done a good job, she thought as she stripped off her clothes.

She took a shower, which was always something of a challenge in Dune Cottage because the water pressure wasn't great, and then dressed in the first thing she found in her suitcase before heading back downstairs.

The mess seemed worse each time she looked at it.

What had possessed her to smash the paintings? Why hadn't she simply removed them from the walls and piled them neatly where she couldn't see them, as she'd done in her own bedroom at home?

Maybe it wasn't so surprising.

Opening that letter and discovering that Cameron had lied about selling the cottage had left a deep wound. The fact that he'd waited until after his death to confess had made things worse. She'd had nowhere to put all the intense emotion that had been swirling inside her.

She'd tackle the mess, she promised herself, but first she needed coffee and something to eat. And painkillers for her headache, which was getting worse not better.

She made herself a mug of strong black coffee and took it outdoors onto the deck.

The breeze fluffed her hair, and the warm sun and blue skies promised her a pretty day. Maybe she'd walk later. Anything to avoid spending time in the cottage. She'd underestimated how difficult it would feel to be here.

Sadness seeped into her. She used to love it here. The cottage had been her special place. *Their* place. Even when Cameron's work had started attracting attention, and selling for good money, and then unbelievable (was she allowed to say stupid?) money—even when they'd bought a huge house and had the children—this was the place that made them both happy. Occasionally Cameron's mother would babysit, and they'd come here for a weekend and paint, and talk, and enjoy being a couple again and not just parents. The pressure seemed to slough away from them the moment they crossed the Sagamore Bridge.

And then there had been an occasion when Cameron had come by himself. He'd needed the space and the peace and the opportunity to paint undisturbed. It had been Kristen's ninth birthday and Cecilia had been organizing a party for ten classmates, so she'd decided not to join him. As she'd iced cakes and hung balloons and had her head pierced by the high-pitched shrieks of thoroughly overexcited girls, she'd felt envious of Cameron. She loved the children, but she also missed the days before kids when she and Cameron had spent long, lazy weekends at the Cape painting side by side on the beach. Cameron's career had soared ahead of hers and she didn't resent that, but she did envy the fact that he was able to devote his life entirely to art, heading to his studio daily, leaving her to fit her own love of painting into the small scraps of time that weren't taken up by running his life and caring for the kids. On her less generous days she thought, *That could have been me.*

She'd watched enviously as Cameron had loaded up the car early on that Friday morning and headed to the Cape by himself. The moment he'd driven away she regretted not asking him to postpone for a day so they could go together. The day after Kristen's party she'd woken with a yearning to spend time with him. She'd contemplated bundling the children into the car and taking them to Dune Cottage and surprising Cameron, but they'd never taken the children there and Winston was going through a stage of hating car journeys, so she'd dismissed the idea. She and Cameron had agreed from the beginning that the cottage was to be their secret hideaway. A place where they could spend time alone. And that approach had worked. It meant that the moment Cecilia stepped inside the cottage she transformed from being an exhausted mother and overworked wife and turned back into an individual. It made the place seem more romantic. It gave it a special intimacy.

She was working on coming to terms with a missed weekend on the Cape when Cameron's mother had shown up unexpectedly from a trip photographing wildlife in the Galápagos and offered to babysit her grandchildren.

It was so rare for Cameron's mother to appear (her own parents had died in her first year of college) that Cecilia had grabbed the opportunity.

She'd often wondered what would have happened if Cameron's mother hadn't offered to stay that weekend.

She wouldn't have gone to the cottage. She wouldn't have decided to surprise him.

She hadn't even knocked on the door or called his name. Instead, she'd crept into the cottage with a smile on her face as she anticipated his surprise and joy at seeing her.

He'd been in the bedroom and when he saw her there he had indeed shown surprise, but no joy. Instead there was shock on her part, and guilt on his because he wasn't alone. The girl lying naked on the bed (Cameron and Cecilia's bed, on Cecilia's specially chosen bed linen) was smoking a joint even though smoking in the cottage was strictly forbidden.

Cecilia had rushed from the room, and Cameron had rushed after her, excuses spilling out of him as he'd pulled on his clothes. He'd decided to paint a series of nudes. The woman had agreed to model for him. He hadn't intended to sleep with her. He'd met her on the beach. She was *no one*. He'd been worried about his work and lonely without Cecilia. It meant nothing.

It had meant everything to Cecilia. From that moment the cottage was tainted. Cameron might as well have spray-painted the walls in garish red. Their special place was no longer their special place. It would never again be just his and hers. She would never again associate it with happy memories.

It had changed the cottage and it had changed their marriage.

Cecilia didn't know what words were exchanged between Cameron and the woman, but she'd left immediately.

Cecilia did the same. She told Cameron not to follow her because she didn't want him back in the house. She couldn't bear to share the same space with him. How could he do this to her after everything she had done for him and everything they'd been through together?

He'd checked into a hotel overlooking Boston Common and she'd told the children that their father was staying in the city for a while because of his work.

Cameron sent her flowers. He sent her jewelry. He sent her a painting.

When she didn't respond to any of it, he sent her a frantic note. She was his muse. She encouraged him. She was the only one who understood him. She was everything. He said *I can't do this without you.*

This time Cecilia wrote back. *You're going to have to.*

A month after Cameron moved out, Cecilia decided to make it final. She'd told the children their marriage was over. Kristen had been hysterical. She'd refused to accept it. She'd blamed Cecilia. When Cecilia tried to talk to her, she ran out of the house and that was that.

Cecilia and Cameron had sat by her bed in the hospital day and night. She'd clung to them. Needed them. Separation and divorce were forgotten. They were forced back together by their love and fear for their daughter.

And they'd stayed together, even after Kristen had recovered, but Cecilia had never returned to the cottage.

She'd known that whenever she walked into that bedroom, she'd picture that woman. It would be like ripping open a festering wound again and again. She'd told him to sell the place, and he'd agreed.

Learning to trust him again had been a difficult task but with time and a great deal of effort, she'd managed it. And if a small part of her had sometimes wondered if that had been his only affair, she forced herself to ignore it.

When she'd opened that envelope and discovered he'd lied about selling the cottage, she'd been devastated. What had he been using it for? Why keep it?

She'd put the letter and the key in a drawer and hadn't touched it again until yesterday, when the painting had been mentioned.

But now she was here, and it was like stepping back in time.

Finishing her coffee, she walked back into the cottage and went to the fridge. She reached inside for the cheese, intending to make herself a snack with the bread she'd bought the day before, and as she did so she noticed the jug of lemonade. Had that been there the night before? It must have been, but she'd been too upset and distracted to notice.

The lawyer had told her that Cameron had kept the cottage maintained and ready (Ready for whom? How often had he come here?), but surely that didn't include providing a jug of fresh lemonade?

It was mystifying. Maybe the housekeeping staff made it for themselves to keep themselves hydrated while working. Thinking about that made her wonder when the cleaning company came. The thought that they might witness the havoc she'd wrought galvanized her into action. She didn't want people to know. She didn't want people asking questions. She'd clear up and then she'd find a way to cancel the cleaning service while she was here. And she'd do what Cameron should have done. She'd sell the place.

Maybe this was what she needed to do to be able to move on.

Grabbing a broom, she swept all the broken glass into a pile, scooped it up and then disposed of it. She'd thought she'd done a good job, but then she spied a piece of glass that had skittered across the floor and almost reached the kitchen. She retrieved it, then discovered more under the coffee table and another piece stuck to the rug.

It was the large shard under the sofa that was her undoing. She reached for it, not seeing the piece that lay sharp and deadly beside it. It sliced across her wrist like a blade and she gasped and jerked her hand back, horrified to see the volume of blood welling from the wound.

Blood slid down her arm and dripped onto the floor. The sight of it made her dizzy.

Cecilia had never been good with blood. When the kids had fallen over, it had been Cameron who had cleaned them up while she'd sat with her head low, trying not to pass out.

"Damn." She covered her wrist with her other hand, putting pressure on it but her fingers were slippery with the blood. She wanted to close her eyes and let someone else clean it up, but that wasn't going to happen. She'd wanted to be on her own, and now she was on her own, which meant clearing up her own mess.

Did Cameron still keep a first aid kit here?

She was afraid that if she stood up and searched for it she'd faint, or bleed everywhere and leave the cottage looking like a crime scene. She should never have smashed the paintings, and she wouldn't have done so if she hadn't been so angry with Cameron.

Had he kept the cottage so he could have more affairs, knowing that this was the one place she would never come?

She gave a loud scream of frustration, taking advantage of the fact that she had no neighbors and no one could hear her. It felt good, so she did it again, louder this time. It was cathartic. Why had she never screamed aloud before? She probably should have done it decades ago. She should have shattered Cameron's eardrums as revenge for shattering her heart.

And then she realized that if no one could hear her she might bleed to death and no one would know until the cleaning company came again, whenever that was. She was going to die alone. Here. In this place she'd avoided. Her body would be found, and no one would know who she was, or what she had been doing in the cottage.

She imagined the shock it would create. The poor soul who opened the door and found her might be traumatized forever and that would never do.

Pull yourself together, Cecilia.

Cecilia felt the blood escape from the pressure of her fingers and slide down her arm, and she was about to try and stand up without releasing her grip on her wrist when a sound came from the doorway.

She glanced across and saw a young woman standing there. Her face was pink from the sun and her hair, a rich oak brown, fell tangled and messy past her shoulders as if she'd had a dip in the sea and hadn't taken the time to rinse her hair of salt water. Sand clung to her running shoes, and she was out of breath.

She looked vaguely familiar although Cecilia couldn't think why that would be. She hadn't been here in years and knew no one.

The girl dropped the backpack she'd been holding and rushed across to Cecilia. "What happened? No, you mustn't— why did you—oh, there's so much blood. Don't move. I'm going to help you." She rushed to the kitchen, pulled open a drawer and removed a first aid kit. Then she sprinted back to Cecilia and dropped to her knees next to her. "You need to elevate the limb. That's it. Hold it up for me—right there."

She unzipped the pack, and dressings and bandages spilled out. "I'll call an ambulance but first I need to stop the bleeding. Just breathe steadily. You're going to be fine."

Now that she was no longer alone, Cecilia knew she would indeed be fine.

"I don't want you to call an ambulance." She didn't want a fuss. But it would be good to stop the bleeding. Looking at it was starting to make her feel dizzy again. "I'm feeling light-headed. Could you stay for a few minutes?"

"I'm staying for as long as needed. I'm not leaving you like this." The girl was calm and steady. She found what she was looking for, opened the packaging and pressed a dressing hard against the wound. "You poor thing. You must have been feeling terrible."

The unexpected sympathy brought a lump to Cecilia's throat.

She had been feeling terrible, but how could this girl possibly know that?

"What made you come to the door?" She winced as the girl's fingers pressed hard. "I didn't know anyone was around."

"I'm the caretaker. I arrived early. I was on the beach when I heard you scream."

"Oh." Her scream must have been louder than she'd thought.

Also, this really was early.

The girl lifted the dressing a little and checked the wound. "Are you still feeling light-headed? Could you stand up? I want to check this wound properly and irrigate it. We need to make sure there's no glass in it."

Cecilia noticed that the girl's shirt was creased and there was a smudge of makeup under her eyes as if she hadn't removed it properly. And didn't cleaning staff usually wear a uniform?

"There's no glass in it. I cut myself on a large piece." But she scrambled to her feet with the girl's help and walked on shaking legs to the kitchen. She stood with her arm above the sink and her head turned away as the girl prodded and examined, then cleansed it.

"I don't think it needs stitches. I've pulled the edges together with paper stitches so that should do for now." The girl swiftly and skillfully dressed the wound and bound it tightly. Then she helped Cecilia wash the blood from her other arm. "I'm going to make you a hot drink and we'll sit for a while. Are you still feeling light-headed? I'm Lily, by the way."

Cecilia felt herself wobble. Being in this place had left her feeling emotionally vulnerable and Lily's kindness threatened to snip through the remaining threads of her self-control.

"I feel guilty for taking up your time. I'm sure you're very busy."

"I have plenty of time. I'll make you more coffee. You should sit down. You're probably in shock." She moved around the kitchen confidently and in no time Cecilia found herself seated on the sofa with a mug of coffee in her hand.

Cecilia put the coffee down on the table. She didn't know if it was lack of food, or the shock of the blood, or the shock of being in the cottage after all these years but she really did feel strange. "You're a good first aider. Do you have medical training?"

Lily froze. "Not exactly."

Not exactly?

There was obviously a story there, but Cecilia knew when someone didn't want to talk.

"Well, it was lucky for me that you were close by."

Lily relaxed again and while Cecilia was drinking her coffee, the girl cleaned up the mess on the floor.

She brushed, she wiped, she polished and in no time the cottage was restored to its former state of cleanliness.

Unfortunately, it didn't make Cecilia feel any better about the place.

What had possessed her to come here?

"Thank you." She watched as Lily disposed of broken glass. "You're a wonder. You've been looking after this place?"

"Yes. I work for a management company. I clean a number of properties, but this one is easily the best. The position is incredible. How are you feeling now? Dizzy?"

"A little. I'll just sit here for a while and I'll be fine. You have work to do, I'm sure."

"My next job is to clean a beach house about fifteen minutes from here. The family won't be checking out until ten, so there is no rush. And, anyway, I can't leave you," the girl said. "Knowing that you're this upset. Whatever happened, however hopeless things seem now, there is always a way through. Is there someone you can talk to?"

It seemed like an odd question, and then she realized that Lily thought Cecilia had done this intentionally. She thought she had tried to cut her wrists with the glass.

Cecilia had been upset, that was true. But although there had been a few occasions during their marriage when Cecilia had contemplated dispatching Cameron, at no point had she ever considered such a fate for herself.

"It was an accident. I was clearing up the glass."

The girl sat down next to her and took her hand. "The glass that came from the smashed paintings. You were upset."

How did she know that?

She would have seen that the paintings were no longer on the wall, but how would she have known Cecilia had been upset?

Questions started to form in her head. The lemonade in the fridge. The floral scent in the shower.

"When I screamed this morning, you were quick to reach me. Lucky for me you were on the beach so early."

"I'm an early riser."

Cecilia nudged a little harder. "You must live nearby."

Lily stood up quickly and carried her mug to the kitchen. "I probably should leave if you're sure you don't need me. I wouldn't have come if I'd known you were going to be here. The company didn't tell me anyone was staying, but you should find everything clean and in perfect working order."

"The company didn't tell you I was going to be here because I didn't tell them. And it's lucky for me that you did come early this morning, or I would have been in some trouble. Please don't rush off."

"I should probably get home."

"And where is home? Where are you staying?"

Lily sent Cecilia a desperate look.

That look told Cecilia that she didn't want to lie but was scared of telling the truth.

That look confirmed Cecilia's suspicions.

"This is where you've been staying, isn't it? This is your home." She saw the panic in Lily's eyes and wondered what someone like her was doing staying all alone in a property that didn't belong to her.

It was oddly reassuring to know that she wasn't the only one whose life was a complicated mess.

"Sit down, Lily. We need to have a talk."

8

Lily

And now she knew who owned Dune Cottage. The mystery was solved.

Why hadn't she guessed? That was pretty simple to answer. She'd been to the Lapthorne house, and it was the size of a museum with grounds as big as a park. They owned a beach house in The Hamptons. Another house in Manhattan. They had a place in France—or was it Italy? Every property could sleep a dozen people comfortably.

Dune Cottage wasn't a statement property, like the ones she cleaned on a daily basis. It wasn't a spacious beach house with glass walls and a swimming pool. It was normal (as much as any property in this part of the Cape could be described as "normal"—it was all about perspective). She'd assumed that at some point it had been a much-loved family retreat, but that the children had grown up and the cottage forgotten.

It hadn't crossed her mind that the reason there were paintings by Cameron Lapthorne on the wall was because the place belonged to him.

According to the company she worked for, no one ever stayed in the cottage. Lily *never* would have chosen to stay here had she known the owner might show up.

She felt sick. She was also cold after her night on the beach, and her eyes stung from lack of sleep. "Are you going to call the police?" She imagined calling her family from the police station. *Hi, Mom, my new life isn't going so well...*

Cecilia raised her eyebrows. "Why ever would I call the police?"

"I've been staying here." Saying it aloud made her wonder what on earth had made her do such a thing. Her parents had raised her to be honest and law-abiding. Her life had been all about studying hard and getting top grades. About aspiration and achievement. She'd been on a carefully curated path, running to keep up with people until she'd fallen hard. Until something inside her had snapped.

She was no longer a high achiever. She was someone who stayed in properties that didn't belong to them. She was someone who broke the law. "It was wrong of me."

"I'm sure you had your reasons," Cecilia said. "Did you pick the lock on the front door or break a window to gain access?"

"No. I used my key."

"Exactly. You had a key. All you really did was stay a little longer than was probably expected of you. You appear to have kept the cottage in immaculate condition. Until I came along." Cecilia patted her arm. "I feel guilty for making such a mess. And I'm grateful to you because if you hadn't been here, I might have bled to death. You have excellent first aid skills and you've been very kind to me. I don't intend to repay that kindness by calling the police. You were here last night when I arrived?"

There seemed no point in lying.

"I was sleeping in the attic room. The noise woke me."

"The noise? Oh, you mean the paintings. I didn't know there was anyone in the place. I wasn't paying attention. I was—I had other things on my mind." Cecilia's cheeks flushed pink and she shifted in her seat. "You saw that? You must have thought it very odd."

She looked so uncomfortable and embarrassed that Lily wanted to reassure her—*no, I didn't see a thing*—but how could she do that?

This was the most awkward conversation she'd had in a while. What was she supposed to say? *I thought you were batshit crazy.* "You seemed upset. I was worried." And she was still worried. Without the paintings the walls looked bare and unfinished. The cottage was as bruised and damaged as its owner. She hoped the owners of the company she worked for didn't pick today to do a random check or she'd be arrested for destruction of property.

"I was upset. And the fact that you saw that explains why you thought my unfortunate encounter with the glass was something other than an accident. But it *was* an accident." Cecilia paused. "What happened after you heard me? Were you here all night?"

"No. I left the cottage."

"How? I would have noticed if you'd used the front door."

"I jumped from the balcony of the second bedroom onto the dunes."

Cecilia winced. "Did you hurt yourself?"

"No. It wasn't that far, and the landing was soft."

"You didn't think to just call out and let me know you were there?"

"No. You thought you were alone. I was intruding on a moment that was obviously personal." Lily felt her cheeks warm. "Everyone has the right to privacy if that's what they need."

Cecilia's gaze didn't waver. "And is that why you've been staying here alone? Because you wanted privacy? Some people would find this place too isolated."

"The position is part of the reason I love it," Lily said. "Being here has helped me and I'll always be grateful for that. But obviously I'll leave right away, and I won't bother you again. It's good to see someone using it after so long. Are you sure you'll be okay? You're not going to—"

"Cut my wrists or smash more paintings?" Cecilia shook her head. "There is only one painting left anyway."

Lily transferred her gaze from Cecilia to the painting that still hung on the wall. Why hadn't Cecilia smashed that one? She was relieved that she hadn't.

That painting had kept her company on so many nights. She wished now that she'd taken a photograph of it so that she could look at it sometimes.

"I love that painting."

"*The Girl on the Shore*?"

"Is that what it's called? Makes sense. I can't imagine how it must feel to paint something like that." Or to own a painting like that. "Of all of them, this is the one I would have kept."

Cecilia stared at the painting. "Really?"

"Yes. I have been looking at it for months, trying to fig-ure out what it is about it that draws me in. I want to know what that woman is thinking. What she's doing. What happened just before she walked to the water's edge. It's wonderful. Special. I thought I knew almost all his paintings of the Cape, but I've never seen this one before. Was it one of his earlier ones?" She saw Cecilia transform from warm to wary.

She gave Lily a long look. "You're an art lover?"

"Yes. And I love Cameron Lapthorne's work. I'm surprised this painting isn't in a gallery somewhere, surrounded by alarms and security guards."

"Are you an artist yourself?"

"Oh—no." Lily was embarrassed. "I paint a lot—all the time in fact—but I wouldn't call myself an artist. I've never sold anything, unless you count a couple of sketches of seabirds that a tourist offered me money for. My first ever sale. It paid for a couple of ice creams."

"If you produce art then you're an artist," Cecilia said. "Calling yourself that isn't dependent on the value that someone else places on your work. Did you study art at college?"

"No. Biological sciences. I went to medical school, but I dropped out." She waited for the inevitable judgments, but Cecilia simply nodded.

"Because you really wanted to be an artist, not a doctor." She made it sound as if that was a perfectly natural discovery and Lily felt a rush of warmth and connection. Cecilia was the first person she'd ever told who hadn't thought she was making a bad decision.

"Yes, but being an artist isn't exactly a stable career path. So I'm here while I figure things out." Whenever she talked about wanting to be an artist she felt like a fake, but that was nothing new. She'd felt like an imposter for most of her life. "I wonder when this was painted?"

And, more importantly, she wanted to know why Cecilia had spared that one. Maybe it was simply too large to lift it from the wall.

Cecilia was silent for a long moment.

"It was painted fifty years ago."

"Really? Well, I'm glad you didn't smash that one, Mrs. Lapthorne."

Cecilia's expression changed. "You know who I am."

"I— Yes." Why was that a shock? Had Cecilia not said her name? Lily had introduced herself, but it hadn't occurred to Lily until now that Cecilia hadn't done the same.

"When you first walked in, I thought you looked familiar," Cecilia said. "We know each other?"

Lily wished she'd kept her mouth shut. Maybe Cecilia would change her mind now and call the police.

"We don't exactly know each other. We met once, but I don't expect you to remember. I'm a friend of Hannah's." Or maybe she wasn't. Maybe that friendship was now in the past.

"A friend of—" Cecilia stared at her for a moment. "Oh dear. Lily. You're Hannah's Lily. Her best friend. Growing up you two were inseparable."

Lily felt something stab her insides. She wasn't Hannah's Lily anymore.

"Is that a problem?"

"I'm not sure," Cecilia said. "Since we're being honest here, I'll tell you that I came here to have some space from everyone, including family. No one knows where I am. And I don't want them to know. That probably sounds strange to you."

"Not really." The confidence touched her. And as someone who had come here to escape her own family, Lily didn't think it sounded strange at all. You could love your family and still need distance from them. She felt a rush of sympathy for Cecilia. "Won't they guess where you are?"

"No one knows about this place," Cecilia said. "Cameron and I bought it a long time ago. Right at the beginning, before we had children."

The cottage had been a hideaway. Somewhere special. She'd sensed it the moment she'd stepped through the door the first time.

"No one knows? Not even Hannah and—" She almost said Todd, but stopped herself. She'd vowed that she was going to stop saying his name and thinking about him. "How about the rest of your family?"

"None of them know. We never brought the children here, or the grandchildren. It was our place." Cecilia paused. "I thought Cameron had sold it, years ago. That was what he told me. It was only recently that I discovered he hadn't. My lawyer knows. And now you."

And now her. The fact that she knew Cecilia's secret, and Cecilia knew hers bonded them in some way.

"This is the first time you've been back since he died?"

"Longer than that." Cecilia stared into the distance. "It has been many years."

Lily tried to imagine how it must feel to be back here after so much time. After so much had changed. Was that why she'd smashed the paintings? Had looking at them made her sad? "I'm sorry for your loss." It was hard to know what to say, but she felt she had to say something. "It must be difficult to be here without him when the place was special to you both."

"Yes." Cecilia spoke quietly. "It is difficult."

And Lily was intruding on her private grief.

"I should never have stayed here. I never planned to. I've been maintaining the place for months, coming here weekly to check on things—that's my job, or part of it. In April I lost my accommodation. I was going to find somewhere else, but this place is always empty and—"

"And it isn't easy finding accommodation on the Cape in the summer. I understand. You said that this place is always empty. That no one ever uses it." Cecilia looked at her. "Do you know when it was last used?"

Lily shook her head. She'd expected Cecilia to be angry with her and instead she was asking about the cottage.

"The management company I work for has been in business for decades. It's family run. This place has been on their books since the beginning, and there is no record of anyone ever staying here."

"Never?" Cecilia's hands were clasped tightly in her lap. "You're sure about that?"

"Yes. I asked them specifically because I thought it was strange. And I wouldn't have stayed here if I'd thought there was a chance someone might use it." It seemed important to try and explain. "It wasn't only about the money. This place was a comfort to me. I was having a difficult time and being here made me feel better. Calmer. Happier. It has been a sanctuary."

Cecilia looked distracted, as if she was going over something in her head.

"Never."

"Excuse me?"

"No one ever stayed here."

Lily wondered why that was so important to Cecilia. "Apart from me."

"Apart from you." Cecilia seemed to relax. She smiled

131

for the first time since Lily had walked into the house. "That's good."

Was it?

"You're not angry?"

"That you stayed here? No. It makes me feel better to know that the place has had a use and that you found it comforting." Cecilia looked around the cottage, her eyes lingering on the spaces where the paintings had hung, and then moving to the painting that remained. "Cameron and I felt the same way in those early days. It's the reason we bought it. It has barely changed. It's full of memories."

Did Cecilia think she'd violated those memories?

"I haven't changed anything. I used the upstairs room but not the sheets. I rolled my sleeping bag on top of the bed. And it's good for showers to be used regularly—I would have run them as part of my caretaking duties, so it didn't seem too awful to stand under it myself occasionally." There didn't seem any point in holding anything back. "And I used the studio. The light is fantastic." Lily hoped she wouldn't ask to see something she'd painted. That would be too awkward. "I see now how totally wrong it was to stay here. You were expecting privacy and that's what you need."

Cecilia stirred. "Who knows you're staying here?"

"No one. No one comes out this far, unless something needs fixing."

"Friends? Colleagues? Do they not wonder where you're living?"

"I haven't made close friends since I've been here." She'd needed space to lick her wounds and decide what she was going to do. She hadn't wanted questions. "I've been vague about where I'm staying. I didn't want anyone to know, for obvious reasons."

Cecilia touched the dressing on her wrist. "You're sure you haven't mentioned it to Hannah."

Lily felt misery wash over her. "We haven't spoken in months. We had a falling-out. She doesn't know where I am, and I don't think she'd care." It was something she never thought she'd hear herself say, because Hannah had been the best friend she'd ever had. And she'd discovered that you could be angry with someone, and still miss them. And she missed Hannah. She missed her laugh. She missed Hannah's confidence, some of which had seeped into Lily. Hannah had never wondered if she was good enough. Hannah never felt like a fraud or a fake. She'd never had a panic attack before an exam. Hannah knew exactly what she wanted, and attacked life with an energy that was exhausting for everyone around her. Until Lily had met Hannah, she hadn't known it was possible for a person to survive on so little sleep. Hannah had joked that she'd been born to be a doctor. She'd teased Lily for being hopeless in the morning, for being almost incoherent until she'd had her first cup of coffee. She'd teased Lily for being in love with Todd.

Cecilia was watching her closely. "Friendships can be complicated, particularly as we grow older and our paths diverge. I'm sorry to hear you had a falling-out. For what it's worth I'm sure Hannah does care. I hope the two of you manage to sort it out. Relationships can bring the greatest pain and the greatest happiness."

"Yes." Lily had never heard anyone articulate it quite so perfectly. She found herself warming to Cecilia, and not only because she hadn't displayed the usual reaction to the news that Lily had chosen to give up medicine. They'd only just met, and yet it felt as if she'd known Cecilia forever.

Cecilia sat up straighter. "I don't want people to know I'm

here, so for my own selfish reasons I'm pleased you're not in touch with my granddaughter. I'm going to ask you not to tell anyone."

"I won't. But won't your family worry about you?" Lily imagined the Lapthorne family all trying to track down Cecilia. She hoped none of them would turn up while she was here.

The idea that Todd might show up with Amelie made her cold with panic.

"I left them a note saying that I needed some time to myself. I plan to message them later to let them know I'm safe. I'm hoping they will respect my need for some alone time. But either way they don't know about this place, so there is no way they will come here."

Lily wondered why Cecilia felt the need to hide from her family. She wondered why she'd smashed the paintings. Why she was here on her own. "Yesterday was your party."

"You know about that?"

"My mother bumped into Kristen. She mentioned it. The party was the reason you left?"

"Let's just say it was the trigger. The final straw." Cecilia stood up. "It seems we both have secrets."

"Yes." Lily waited. "Is there anything you need me to do around the place before I go?"

Cecilia frowned. "Go? Where are you going?"

"I start work at ten, and I need to find somewhere to stay tonight."

"There's no need for that. You can stay here."

"Stay?" Lily stared at her. "But you're here. You came here for peace and quiet. For an escape."

Cecilia glanced at the cottage. "That's not why I came. For me the cottage comes with memories. It's hard to escape when you're surrounded by reminders of the thing you're trying to forget." She took a breath. "I plan on selling the place. I doubt I'll be here for more than a few days. In the meantime, I'm sure we can share the space quite comfortably. I will use the second bedroom. You are welcome to the master or the loft room."

Stay? Share the space?

Her head spun, her brain circling through different scenarios. She hadn't thought for a moment that Cecilia would let her stay.

Staying would mean sharing the cottage, when really what she wanted was to be alone.

But staying would also mean she wouldn't have to spend time trying to find somewhere else to live. More importantly, it would mean staying in Dune Cottage, a place she'd grown to love.

And even though Cecilia was technically a stranger, she didn't feel like a stranger.

"If I stay, then I'll pay you rent." She hoped Cecilia wasn't going to charge too much.

"If you'd do a little housekeeping while you're here, we will call that rent. Our provisions are rather sparse right now. I was trying to keep a low profile, and I was afraid someone might recognize me when I went shopping yesterday so I grabbed a few things in as short a time as possible. On your way home from work today perhaps you could pick up some food for us. Do you cook?"

"Yes." Although it had been a while since she'd bothered. Her appetite had disappeared, and it never seemed worth making anything elaborate for one. But presumably Cecilia Lapthorne would expect something more than a bowl of cereal.

"Housekeeping and cooking for a few days will more than cover rent," Cecilia said. "I've just realized that it must have been late when you sneaked out of the bedroom. Where did you sleep last night after you jumped from the balcony?"

"On the beach." Although she'd barely slept at all. She'd lain awake for the rest of the night wondering what she was going to do next. "And I know I'm not allowed to do that, but it was too late to find anywhere else and it was only one night."

"Oh, you poor thing. You must have been so cold and uncomfortable. And tired." Cecilia took Lily's hands in hers. "No more sleeping bags, and no more outdoor sleeping. Go and take a hot shower and warm yourself up. I'll make us breakfast."

Lily felt a lump form in her throat. She wasn't used to being offered comfort. And remembering the smashed paintings it seemed to her that it was Cecilia who needed the comfort.

"You probably shouldn't be using that hand," she said. "If you're sure you don't mind me staying here, then I'll take that shower and make breakfast after. Why don't you go and sit on the porch? The view is an antidote to most troubles."

She kept the shower short, even though she was tempted to stand under the meagre flow of water forever. She washed her hair, dried it with a towel and scooped it back in a ponytail.

It was bliss to be clean.

She emptied out her backpack, pulled on the tunic she wore for work and headed downstairs. Knowing that she was going to be able to stay at Dune Cottage, and this time with the permission of the owner, lifted her mood. She wasn't going to be homeless. She didn't have to make any decisions.

She didn't have to call her parents. For now, she could legitimately think of this place as home.

Cecilia had followed her suggestion and was sitting on one of the chairs on the porch, a tiny figure with close-cropped white hair and delicate features.

She looked alone and vulnerable.

Lily felt a flicker of kinship.

She wondered what secrets Cecilia was hiding. Why she'd never told her family about this place.

Whatever the reason, Lily was determined to offer whatever support she could. "Mrs. Lapthorne?"

"Oh—" She gave a start and turned. "Call me Cecilia, dear. How was your shower? Frustrating?"

Lily grinned. "Possibly the best shower I've ever had. Sleeping on the beach is nowhere near as romantic as it sounds. I'll make you breakfast. What would you like?"

"There's not a lot of choice. Milk. Eggs. Mushrooms. Some fruit. I just grabbed a few things as I was passing a store."

"I'll stock up on my way home later." Lily headed back to the kitchen. She found the eggs and whisked them, then added a blob of butter to the pan and let it sizzle. Her mother always added herbs from the garden, but Lily didn't have any. She made a mental note to pick some up when she went shopping later.

The idea that she no longer had to hide the fact that she was staying in the cottage cheered her. And even though it made her feel sad that Cecilia planned to sell it, it wasn't an immediate worry.

The sun shone through the window as she slid the omelet onto a plate and took it to Cecilia, who was sitting in a pool of sunshine.

Lily put the plate in front of her and topped up Cecilia's coffee mug.

"This looks delicious." Cecilia glanced up at her. "Where is yours?"

"I'm not that hungry."

"Neither am I, so we'll share this. You can't go to work with nothing inside you." Cecilia walked into the kitchen and returned holding an extra fork and a plate. She sliced the omelet and slid half onto a plate which she gave to Lily.

Cecilia sat down and picked up her fork. "Did you come here after you gave up medicine?"

"I stayed with my parents for a while." Lily hadn't talked about it with anyone else, but there was something about Cecilia's calm acceptance and lack of judgment that made it easy to be open and honest. "It was a mistake. I never should have gone down that track in the first place. I really wanted to study art in some form, but my parents were worried that it wouldn't lead to anything. That I wouldn't be able to get a job. So I chose a science route. Not that I'm blaming them. They were just being caring. Encouraging. Doing what they felt was best for me. It was my decision."

"Pressure, however well-meaning, is still pressure." Cecilia sliced a piece from her omelet and ate it. "As well as doing something that wasn't really what you wanted to do, you felt you had to live up to their expectations."

It was a relief to talk to someone who understood.

"They were proud of the fact I was training to be a doctor."

"I'm sure they're still proud."

"They're not." Lily put her fork down without eating anything. Nothing ruined her appetite faster than thinking about the situation with her parents. "They're disappointed and worried. They sacrificed everything to give me a shot at a great career and I blew it."

"Is that how you see it?"

"It's how it is."

Cecilia finished her omelet. "Why the Cape?"

"I've always loved it here. We came when I was a child, so it has happy memories. I feel less—" it was hard to explain "—less claustrophobic when I'm here."

Cecilia nodded. "And you got a job with a property management company."

"I didn't have many options. I have no qualifications and so far my choices in life haven't worked out so well."

Cecilia reached for her coffee. "I've often thought it was ridiculous to expect a person to make decisions about their future at such a young age. How does anyone really know?"

"Hannah knew. Hannah never has any doubts. I always envied that about her." And it had made her friend impossible to talk to because she just hadn't understood.

Cecilia nodded. "But she is in a minority. Some people know, but far more just land on something and hope it works out. And it sounds as if you *did* know, deep down. You were passionate about art. But you didn't choose art. You chose with your head and not your heart."

"Art was a dream. Not a reality."

"That's your parents speaking." Cecilia pushed her plate away. "There's nothing wrong with having a dream. It's good to know what you want. But you also need a plan. A dream without a plan will never be anything more than a fantasy. But if you ask yourself how you can turn that dream into reality—if you figure out what it is you need to do, and then make sure you do it, you'll be living the life you want to live instead of thinking about it. Of course the dream loses some of its shine once you're living it. One of life's cruelest ironies I've always felt. I wish you'd eat something."

Lily picked up her fork. Cecilia's words played in her head.

She didn't really have a plan. The last few months had been about surviving.

And no amount of planning was going to help her sell a painting. Maybe if she'd been to art college things would have been different.

"I wasted all those years of college and medical school." And money. She'd wasted money.

Cecilia put her cup down slowly. "Better to waste a few years than a whole life. And is anything really a waste? We learn as much from what goes wrong as we do from what goes right. You tried it. You discovered it wasn't for you. You will have learned something from it, I'm sure. If you hadn't spent those years at medical school perhaps you wouldn't have been able to bandage my arm so skillfully."

Better to waste a few years than a whole life.

The words settled inside her and soothed her anxiety. "That's a good way of looking at it. Helpful." And she couldn't help wishing, just for a moment, that it had been her parents who had said those words. But they wouldn't, because they did think that she was wasting her life.

"It's accurate, although you're maybe too young to see it. You see it as a mistake. I see it as life experience."

"Maybe it would be easier to see it that way if my parents hadn't sacrificed so much to send me to college and medical school. They wanted for me what they never had for themselves. I understand that." And the fact that she understood it made it harder.

Cecilia nodded. "You're an only child."

"Yes. How do you know?"

"Because if there is more than one child the burden of parental expectation is spread. But whatever your parents want or think, in the end the only life you can live is your own. And that goes for them as well as you."

"Sometimes it feels as if I am their life. I'm their focus. After I left medical school I went home for a while, but their anxiety made me anxious."

"And you couldn't figure out what you needed, because all you were hearing was what they needed. So you came to the Cape." Cecilia nodded. "Smart move."

"Was it?" Lily slumped in the chair. "I wanted to prove to them that they didn't need to worry, that I'm going to be fine, but the truth is I can barely afford to live on what I earn and I don't see that changing. I'm not qualified to do anything although it turns out I'm great at clearing up after other people. My father wants me to try and go back to medicine. If they'll have me."

Cecilia was listening closely. "They do seem persistent. I assume you're not contemplating returning to a life you knew was wrong for you?"

"No." The thought of it made her stomach knot with panic. "But I hate the fact that I'm causing my parents so much anxiety and disappointment."

Cecilia nodded and her smile was faint. "I remember when I came here—I would have been younger than you— my parents were horrified."

"You dropped out of college, too?"

"No. I graduated, but then instead of finding a job I came to the Cape to paint. In those days we didn't have so many instantly available forms of communication, although I swear I could feel their worry and disapproval floating in on the breeze every day."

"But you didn't change your mind."

"No. Because the choice was between disappointing them and disappointing myself. I thought the first would be easier to live with." She paused. "You can't live your life for your parents, no matter how much you love them. You have to make your own choices. And a person should surely have control over how they live their own life."

"You make it sound so reasonable." And suddenly she felt a little less guilty. A little lighter. This was her life. She had a right to make her own decisions. And if she made mistakes, then they were her mistakes.

"You've swapped their dream for yours, your old life with a new life," Cecilia said. "Now you need to make it work. Give yourself time. Experiment a little. Don't make any decisions in a hurry. For what it's worth, I think you've done the right thing, coming here."

She thought so, too. This place had been nothing but good for her.

Because of Cecilia, Lily felt better than she had in a long time.

"Thank you for letting me stay," she said. "It's generous of you."

She could stay in the cottage and there would be no more worrying that she might be found out. No more feeling uncomfortable that she was trespassing.

Finally, she could properly relax.

And as no one else in the Lapthorne family knew the cottage existed, there was no chance of them turning up. The probability of awkward encounters was zero.

9

Kristen

Kristen stood in her kitchen, staring at the potato salad. She hated funerals. The concentration of grief was oppressive and the finality of it disturbed her. She was an optimist. She liked to tell herself that everything would be all right in the end, but a funeral was proof that things weren't always all right in the end and that happy endings were randomly allocated and far from assured.

Today was Michael's funeral. He was dead, and no amount of positive thinking or manifesting was going to bring him back.

She kept trying to remember him in happier times. On their wedding day, mortified because he'd left the ring in the pocket of his other suit. Hannah's first birthday party. A Christmas they'd spent together where they'd been snowed in. But nothing deleted the image of Michael, broken, being dragged from a mangled wreck of a car. It was stuck in her head, a macabre video playing on a loop, and she hadn't even been there.

Theo had been there, and Theo seemed as broken as Michael. He'd held it together on the night of the party but had then seemed to unravel. He hadn't been to work since it happened, and Kristen had been too worried about him to leave his side. It had been over a week now and during the day all he did was wander aimlessly round the house and garden. Occasionally she'd woken in the night and found him staring at the ceiling.

She'd reached for his hand, trying to hold him back from the edge of the dark pit that was threatening to swallow him up.

She'd spent years wishing they could spend more time together and just when she'd given up and tried to find a cure for her loneliness elsewhere, she now had her husband with her day and night.

Except he wasn't really "with" her. He was somewhere else. He was lost.

Remembering how she'd felt when her father had died, Kristen had given him the support she would have liked. She'd held him when the sadness overwhelmed him, she'd made him hot drinks and hot meals and encouraged him to go for walks and stay healthy. She'd listened when he wanted to talk but hadn't pushed him when he preferred to stay silent.

Everything she did signaled the same thing. *I'm here for you*.

She tried to ignore the tiny part of her brain that kept reminding her that he hadn't been there for her when her father had died (there had been other occasions in their marriage when he hadn't been there for her, either, but the death of her father had been the hardest to handle), that he hadn't once asked her what *she'd* needed.

That was in the past, and it would stay in the past.

But it had been a difficult week, made more difficult by the fact that her mother seemed to have gone into hiding. Why she couldn't say where she was, Kristen had no idea. Why the secrecy?

She'd had several messages from her, reassuring Kristen that she was fine, and simply taking some time to deal with a few things. She'd told Kristen not to worry. That she needed space.

Given that the Lapthorne mansion offered more than enough space for ten people to live comfortably, Kristen had deduced that what her mother was really saying was that she needed space from Kristen. Her mother wouldn't tell her where she was staying. Her mother didn't want Kristen to find her. Whatever crisis had driven her to leave her own party, she didn't want to share it with her daughter.

And that stung.

What did it say about you as a person that your own mother went into hiding to avoid you? When the person who was supposed to love you unconditionally was so desperate for space from you that they wouldn't even tell you where they were?

The whole thing was hurtful and mystifying, and the hurt increased with each passing day.

Cecilia had assured Kristen that she was fine, but not once had she asked how Kristen was. She hadn't apologized for walking out of her own party, leaving Kristen to handle a hundred guests. She hadn't asked how it went, or how Kristen had explained her absence. She didn't know that Todd had broken up with Amelie. She didn't know that

Theo had come to the party. She didn't know Michael had been killed. She didn't know that today was his funeral.

A normal mother, if not actually present, might at least have sent a message.

Thinking of you today with love.

But her mother wouldn't be thinking about her, because she didn't know anything that was happening in Kristen's life. She didn't seem to care.

Her eyes stung and her mood sank so low that she felt a moment of alarm.

Kristen was no longer worried about her mother; she was worried about herself.

She felt disturbingly close to the edge. She'd always assumed that resilience was like a piece of elastic that stretched when you needed it to, but lately she'd tugged and nothing had happened, and she wondered if it was more like string, if there were limits. If it might in fact snap if enough pressure was applied.

Had she reached her limit?

She wanted to talk to someone about it, but there was no one. It was hard to maintain friendships when life was demanding and during the limited time she spent with friends they always skimmed over the deeper issues. She sensed that they were fine (apart from Trisha of course, who definitely wasn't fine). Or perhaps no one wanted to admit that their lives weren't perfect. Either way, it meant she had no one to turn to.

Her children loved her, she had no doubt about that, but she was their mother. It was her responsibility to care for them and protect them, whatever their ages, not the other way round. And she didn't want to worry them. Hannah and Todd had their own lives to lead. They didn't need to know she wasn't coping.

The last week had shown her just how alone she was.

Her father would have noticed. Her father would have been there for her.

She had never missed him more. The pain of it gnawed at her insides. If she was stressed or sad, he'd stop whatever he was doing and pay attention to her. He'd say things like, *How's my girl?* Sometimes he'd just hug her and tell her, *You're the best.*

She badly wanted to hear his voice now. She missed the enveloping comfort, and the certainty of his love that had felt like a safety net when life had sent her spinning through the air. Her father had always been there to catch her.

Now there were nights when she lay awake for hours and worried about how hard she could fall without that safety net. She wondered who, if anyone, might catch her.

A few days before, she'd felt so alone that she'd called Jeff, even though Theo was in the house. She'd thought that just hearing his voice might make her feel better. She'd wanted someone to ask how *she* was. She'd wanted to remind herself that there were people who cared.

But Jeff hadn't picked up the phone. She'd called four times, and there had been no answer.

She'd left a message asking him to call her back, but he hadn't done so, and she was shaken by how bad that made her feel.

Jeff had been a tonic over the past couple of months. He had listened, and cared, and given her what she'd needed. Jeff had given her hope that life could still be fun and exciting, and that she could be wanted and important to someone.

But now she was beginning to wonder if wanting something badly had somehow led her to create it in her mind. She wondered if she'd conjured up a depth of feeling that wasn't there.

What had it meant to him? She had no idea, and she couldn't ask him because he'd basically ghosted her.

She'd told herself that he was probably just busy, but so many days had passed that no longer seemed a reasonable explanation. Why hadn't she heard anything? Perhaps meeting Theo at the party had made him retreat. Or maybe he'd simply decided he was no longer interested in her.

But she would carry on because that was what she did. She had responsibilities. There were people who depended on her and she didn't want to let anyone down, even though she often felt that people let her down.

Theo appeared, wearing a suit. "We should leave. I don't want to be late. What are you doing?"

"I'm making food to take with us." Kristen scattered fresh herbs over the potato salad. Trisha was having a gathering at her house after the funeral, and she'd asked Kristen to bring a few dishes even though she wasn't sure anyone would feel like eating. Kristen certainly didn't feel like eating.

The funeral made her think of her father's funeral. Her chest felt tight. Emotion spilled over.

"I'm dreading this funeral." She looked at Theo, but he was staring into the mirror adjusting his tie. "Theo?" *Look at me! Can't you see I'm on the edge?*

He frowned and tightened the knot. "You'll be okay. You're the strongest person I know."

She stared at his back, wondering how he couldn't see. Wondering why he didn't know.

He was a doctor. He was supposed to be able to tell when someone was in distress.

And now she wished she'd said nothing. Better to have stayed silent and imagine that he just wasn't tuned in to her emotions, than to speak and have her feelings dismissed.

She didn't feel strong. She felt fragile. She'd used the last of her strength propping him up. Losing Michael had stirred up all the feelings of loss she'd been struggling to handle since her father's death. Why couldn't he see that?

"I wouldn't have made it through the last week without you." He turned and held her gaze. "Thank you."

She didn't know what to say, so she nodded. "I need to make a vinaigrette."

"Right." He checked the time. "Have you heard from your mother?"

"Not since her last message. She made it clear she wanted to be left alone, so that's what I'm doing."

She waited for Theo to ask how she felt about that. To ask if her feelings were hurt. But instead he reached for the oil and vinegar.

Kristen took the bottles from him and mixed a vinaigrette in a jar which she then slotted into the bag she'd packed for Trisha. "Can you grab the cheesecake from the fridge? Then we should leave."

Theo didn't move. "I'm dreading this funeral, too." For a moment he reminded her of a little boy, vulnerable and afraid. "I wish we didn't have to go."

She wished that, too. It was an unfortunate feature of being an adult, that you ended up doing lots of things you didn't want to do.

"We have to go." She heaved the bag from the counter. "This is Trish. We have to support her." Although she still didn't really know what support Trisha would need. Technically speaking, Trisha wasn't the widow. She hadn't even been sure Trisha would be at the funeral but when she'd eventually found the inner strength to call her friend, it turned out that not only was Trisha going to the funeral, she was also organizing it. *She asked me to do it, can you believe that?*

Candy, the original party animal, apparently didn't do funerals.

Theo removed the cheesecake from the fridge. "It's my fault."

"What is your fault?" Kristen took the cheesecake from him and added it to the bag.

"The fact that Michael is dead." He'd said the same thing multiple times since that night. It was the first thing he said to her when he woke up and the last thing he said before he went to sleep. *My fault.*

She felt a rush of compassion and gave the same answer she'd been giving him every day since it happened.

"Theo, it's not your fault. You weren't the one who didn't stop at a junction and drove into his car."

"But I was the one who was supposed to be able to save him. I keep thinking of all the people I have saved over the years, but I couldn't save my best friend."

"You're a surgeon, Theo, not God."

He showed no signs of having heard her. "Maybe Trisha won't want me at the funeral."

"You're his oldest friend. Michael loved you. Trisha loves you. She wants you at the funeral." She hoped he wasn't going to fall apart, and she hoped she wasn't going to fall apart thinking of her father. She'd distract herself by making shopping lists in her head. Or maybe she'd think of fruits in alphabetical order. That was one of the tricks she used when her thoughts were spiraling out of control. *Apple, banana, cantaloupe.*

"I'm grateful to have you." He crossed the room and hugged her, and she was so surprised that she didn't move.

"We'll get through it." She leaned against him, breathing in the scent of him, feeling his arms tighten. And for a moment she felt less alone. She felt as if those arms were shielding her, as if he was standing between her and the emptiness that threatened to suck her down. Maybe he didn't always say the right thing. Maybe he didn't always do the right thing. But in this moment, she felt as if he cared. That was a start.

"I love you, Kristen." He muttered the words into her hair, and she closed her eyes and wondered whether this terrible turn of events, this pointless waste of a precious life, might in the end result in something wonderful. If it brought her and Theo closer together, then something good would have come from it.

"I love you, too."

And that was the problem of course. She did still love him, even though she didn't always love the way her life was with him.

He stroked her hair. "I'm going to make the most of every moment we have together."

She leaned her head against his shoulder and felt a flicker of hope.

She'd thought that they were stuck, that their situation would never change. That *he* would never change. She'd thought Theo was Theo. But holding him now, feeling him leaning on her, she wondered whether she might have been wrong about that.

10

Cecilia

Cecilia sat in the shade as Lily brought food out onto the porch. Inviting Lily to stay had proved to be one of her better ideas. Lily changed the way the cottage felt. It was as if her energy and presence had somehow swept the memories into a dark corner, helped by the discovery that Cameron hadn't been using the place as a love nest.

They'd been here together for a little more than a week and every day Lily brought home something new for the cottage. On the first day it had been a pretty jug that she'd found in a thrift store. She filled it with fresh flowers from the market and placed it on the kitchen counter. The froth of white blooms in the cheerful blue jug brightened Cecilia's day every time she walked past it. Since then, Lily had brought home a fresh set of cushions and a soft throw in a shade of sea green.

"You won't let me pay rent, so this is my contribution,"

she'd said when Cecilia had expressed concern. "I'm trying to cheer the place up. Make it somewhere you're happy to be."

Cecilia was touched by the sentiment, particularly as she knew how stretched Lily's budget was.

"You're extremely creative."

"I love decorating," Lily had said. "And money was always tight growing up, so I learned to do it on a shoestring. I made a patchwork quilt for my bed out of scraps of fabric that the school was throwing away."

As well as her obvious talent for interior design, Lily was calm, kind and, it turned out, an excellent cook.

Tonight, she'd pan-fried salmon fillets and served them with a lemon and dill sauce and a simple salad of watercress. There was a basket of fresh bread and a dish of creamy butter sprinkled with sea salt.

"This food is too pretty to eat. It's a work of art." Cecilia decided it wouldn't have been out of place in a top restaurant.

Lily flushed at the compliment. "It's just salmon."

"Maybe, but salmon never looked so good. You have a good eye."

"For fish?"

Cecilia smiled. "For the way things look. Everything, from flowers to food. Is tonight the night you finally show me your paintings?"

"Definitely not. I'm enjoying our friendship and I don't want to ruin it."

Cecilia rarely ate bread, but the smell was too good to resist. She helped herself to a chunk and broke it in half. "Why would it ruin a friendship?"

"Because you will either lie and say you love my work,

or you'll say you hate it. Either way, it would make me feel awkward."

"Perhaps I'll say I love it because I do."

"If you hadn't spent your life with Cameron Lapthorne then maybe I'd have the courage to let you have a peep at one or two things I've been fiddling with, but it's a bit like asking Mozart to listen to my piano composition. Tough audience. There's more sauce if you'd like it." Lily pushed the small jug toward Cecilia. "I paint for myself really. It gives me pleasure."

Cecilia tasted the salmon. "It takes great courage to put creative work on public display. It feels very personal. This is delicious, by the way."

"People judge. If they don't think you're good enough, then it's crushing. I'm trying to protect myself. Probably cowardly, but also necessary."

She'd had no one to encourage her, Cecilia thought. And confidence could be as fragile as spun sugar.

"Would it help if I told you that Cameron suffered from terrible imposter syndrome at times?" It was something she'd never revealed to anyone before, but it felt right to share it now. She sensed it might help Lily to hear it, and she felt Cameron would have approved. He'd always supported young artists.

"What?" Lily put her fork down. "No. I don't believe you."

"It's true, although I'm sharing this in confidence, obviously. He suffered terribly, particularly at the beginning, when his career took off." There had been a reason for that, of course, but she wasn't going to share that with Lily. "The point I'm making, is that many people suffer from imposter syndrome. The thing that matters most is that you don't let it stop you doing things. Are you proud of your work?"

Lily spooned sauce onto her salmon. "I enjoy doing it. I sometimes like what I produce. Not always. I feel like less of an imposter when I'm painting than I did when I was a medical student, so I suppose that's something."

"Maybe after we've eaten you could show me just one of your paintings." Cecilia focused on her food. "Now tell me about your day."

Lily took a sip from her glass of iced water. "I spent most of it trying to scrub tomato sauce from white cabinets. If I hadn't seen it with my own eyes, I wouldn't have known a family of six could make so much mess. This bread is from the new French patisserie near the marina, by the way. They'd just pulled it from the oven when I was cycling past, and the smell was incredible. I couldn't resist."

"I can see why." Cecilia spread the bread with creamy butter. She noticed that Lily was eating more than she had been at the beginning of the week. "How does tomato end up on cabinets? That's a story I need to hear."

"According to the mother, who stayed just long enough to apologize for the mess, they were making homemade pizza." Lily picked up her fork. "Judging from the amount I scrubbed off the walls, not much of it made it onto the pizza. I suspect they ate wood-fired dough. It has put me off ever having kids. I'm thinking I might settle for a dog instead."

"Dogs can be as messy as kids. And they chew more."

"Okay, then, maybe I'll have a rabbit." Lily finished her salmon.

Cecilia laughed. "Your partner might not go for that."

"No partner." Lily put her fork down. "Just me."

"For now."

"Probably forever."

"You've been hurt?" She felt a flash of sympathy because she knew exactly how that felt.

Love could be sweet, but it could also sting.

"Yes, but it was nobody's fault but mine. No drama there. No one to blame." Lily nibbled some bread. "I fell in love with someone who didn't share my feelings. I basically messed up my choice of job, and my choice of man. I'm winning at life."

The flippant tone didn't fool Cecilia. You didn't have to be a psychologist to see that Lily had been through a tough time.

"You're here," she pointed out. "This was one of your choices. And that seems to be working out."

Lily sat back. "That's true. Now it's your turn to tell me about your day."

Her day?

She'd spent far too long thinking about the past, but she wasn't going to admit that when Lily was trying so hard to make the cottage more welcoming for Cecilia.

"My day was productive. I cleared the second bedroom and the attic."

"Oh, well done. Not the master?"

"No." Cecilia spooned more sauce onto her plate. "Not yet." And she felt like a coward for not doing it.

Lily leaned forward. "I could help with that if you'd like me to. When my grandpa died, I helped my gran clear out his things. She found it so upsetting. It might help to have someone do it with you."

"You're very kind." If there was one thing she dreaded more than going into that room, it would be having someone with her to witness her distress.

Lily was looking at her. "Or I could do it for you if you

156

prefer. I could pile the personal stuff into a box, and you could go through it separately on your own, when you feel up to it."

She'd never met anyone as intuitive as Lily.

"I don't know what's in that room, but I don't want to keep any of it. Not a single thing." She said it with far more emotion than she'd intended, perhaps because Lily had already been so open with her, and she braced herself for the inevitable questions.

But Lily simply nodded. "In that case, why not let me clear it out? And why don't I freshen the whole room while I'm at it? I could change the bedding. The cover in there is old-fashioned. Maybe a fresh coat of paint on the walls. We could give everything a modern, beachy feel."

"There isn't much point. I won't be sleeping in there. I'm happy in the second bedroom." On the other hand, why was she refusing? Lily was offering to do a job she'd been dreading. Why not let her help? "I suppose if you have time to clear it all out, then that would be good."

"Great. It can be a job for this weekend. That reminds me." Lily stood up. "I have something to show you. I couldn't believe my eyes when I saw it yesterday. This is why I needed you to lend me your car today. Thanks for that, by the way."

"You've bought something else? Lily, you must let me pay you."

"It didn't cost anything because it was damaged. I found it outside a house that was being renovated with a note saying to help myself. So I did as I was told and helped myself. Close your eyes."

Cecilia dutifully closed her eyes, wondering what Lily had brought home this time. She heard the sound of something scraping along the floor and then a loud clonk as Lily put something heavy down on the deck.

"Okay." She sounded breathless. "You can look."

Cecilia opened her eyes and saw an old, battered bookcase, complete with splinters and chipped paint.

Lily blew strands of hair out of her eyes and sent her a triumphant look. "Isn't it fantastic?"

"I—"

"I happened to notice that you have a lot of books stacked on the floor in the second bedroom. I thought they needed a home, and this should fit perfectly in the little nook by the window."

Cecilia wasn't sure what to say.

Lily waited expectantly. "You're thinking it's hideous."

"I'm thinking it looks—distressed."

Lily grinned. "Well, that makes three of us, doesn't it? We can all be distressed here together. But not for long. At least, not for this bookshelf. Ta-da—" Like a magician, she produced a tin of paint. "It's called Seafoam Green. Just a hint of the ocean. I bet the marketing people had fun with that. More appealing than calling it Lizard Green, I suppose. Anyway, it's going to look great."

Cecilia decided it was worth giving houseroom to the hideous bookcase just to see Lily looking so animated. "Does it have woodworm?"

"I don't think so, but by the time I've finished the only thing living in this will be your books."

How could she say no?

"If you think we should keep it, then we should do that. I suppose it would be a kindness to give it a home. It needs some love."

And so did Lily.

Cecilia felt a ripple of frustration. Did Lily's parents not see how creative she was? It shone through in everything, from the way she dressed to the food she prepared. It was almost as if they didn't know their own daughter.

But she probably shouldn't be judging. She was all too aware of her own deficiencies as a mother. Parenting was never straightforward. And it was easier to see both the big picture and the mistakes when the child in question wasn't your own.

She was increasingly intrigued by Lily. There was no doubt that she had an eye for shape and shade, and for design. Cecilia was interested to see her paintings but so far hadn't been able to persuade Lily to share her work.

"You don't believe me when I say it's going to be beautiful. Wait until I've finished with it. I can't believe what some people throw away." Lily put the tin of paint on the table and sat down again. "I was thinking that if being in the cottage is difficult for you, then maybe we could change it."

"Change it?"

"Why not? Instead of tweaking things, let's be bolder. For example the walls where you removed the paintings look—"

"Truly awful?"

Lily smiled. "I was going to say 'bare.' And while we're thinking about the living room, we should consider moving the sofa so that it faces the view. And how would you feel about me painting the walls?"

"Did you have a color in mind?" The idea of redecorating the cottage hadn't crossed her mind. There didn't seem to be much point. But now she thought about it, moving the sofa was a good idea. Why on earth hadn't they done so before?

"I was thinking bright red for one of the walls and luminous purple for the other two. Maybe add a gold stripe or two." Lily looked at her, deadpan, and then laughed. "Sorry. Couldn't resist. You should see your face."

"You're a wicked girl. And now tell me what color you really have in mind."

"I thought I'd dilute the seafoam so that it's more of a pale wash. You might fall in love with the place all over again."

Was that what this was about?

"That isn't going to happen." Cecilia kept her voice gentle. "I don't want you to go to so much trouble if that's your objective."

"It will be fun. And even if it doesn't change the way you feel about the place, it will probably make it easier to sell if everything is freshly painted."

"I suppose there is some truth in that." Cecilia stood up and cleared the plates. "Stay there. You've had a busy day. I'll make us coffee."

"I'll help." Lily followed her into the kitchen. "*The Girl on the Shore* intrigues me."

Cecilia stacked the dishwasher. "In what way?"

"It's different from his later paintings. It's more whimsical. Dreamy. His later works are bolder. I'm glad you left that one on the wall."

She was probably a fool for doing so. She still didn't know why Cameron hadn't destroyed it as they'd agreed.

But Lily wouldn't understand the significance of that particular painting, so the fact that she'd seen it didn't matter. Still, Cecilia wasn't keen to discuss it in any detail.

"The coffee is brewing so now would be a good time for you to show me your own paintings." She saw the flicker of uncertainty cross Lily's face. "I promise to say nothing. Nothing at all. I'll just look."

"But then I'll be stressed trying to work out what you're

160

thinking. You were married to Cameron Lapthorne. You were surrounded by artistic genius. That's pretty daunting for the rest of us normal mortals." Lily looked anxious and then straightened her shoulders. "But if you're sure that's what you want. Probably best for me to hear the truth now, then I can give up dreams of being an artist before I waste as much time on it as I did medical school. Otherwise by the time I figure out what I'm going to do, my ability to do it will be long gone."

Cecilia looked at her sweet, unlined face, the nose smattered with freckles, the dark hair that curled and tumbled. Today Lily was wearing a pair of denim shorts with a T-shirt in vibrant shades of turquoise and aqua that brought out the blue of her eyes.

"That T-shirt looks good on you. The design is unusual."

Lily glanced down. "This is one of my more successful tie-dye experiments. There were a few disasters along the way, although I managed to salvage a few and turn them into hair scrunchies."

Cecilia was fast learning that there were no limits to Lily's creativity. "I want to see your work. Show me."

She grabbed Lily's arm and urged her through the living room to the studio at the back of the cottage. It was the first time she'd been in there since returning and she braced herself to be slapped in the face by the full force of memories.

Lily stopped dead at the door. "I'm really not sure this is a good idea."

Cecilia wasn't sure it was a good idea, either, although for different reasons.

She stepped past Lily and was pleasantly surprised to see the room almost empty. There were no traces of Cameron here. The sun beamed down through the tall windows, throwing light across the old, scuffed floorboards. Tall cupboards lined one entire wall. She knew they would contain paintings, but also paints, pastels, charcoal, old rags—everything. She remembered painting here in the early days, before she'd become part of the Cameron Lapthorne machine. There was an easel tucked into one corner and an old chair, paint spattered and with a spoke missing.

"I'll show you the last one I did. The one I like." Lily opened one of the cupboards and pulled open a drawer. "I know I shouldn't have left it here, but I didn't want to fold it and put it in my backpack."

"I should hope not. Show me." She stood over Lily's shoulder and studied the painting on top. It was a watercolor of the Cape seashore, light and delicate, the colors soft and luminous.

Cecilia felt something stir inside her. A trickle of excitement. "Show me another."

"If you hate that one then there's probably no point in—"

"Let's lay them out on the table." Cecilia took the seashore landscape and placed it on the long table that ran along the length of the wall opposite. "I can't see it like this. We need a frame." She opened a different cupboard and stared at the frames. She and Cameron had kept a few for their own use. She pulled one out and dismissed it. Too small. She selected another, and then took a mount. "Let's try this. Just to see how it looks."

"It's a beautiful frame, but it's wasted on my—"

"Hush. I need to concentrate." Cecilia flipped over the frame, inserted the mount and positioned Lily's painting. "This is temporary, obviously."

"Obviously." Lily sounded faint.

Having secured the painting, Cecilia propped it against

162

the wall and took several paces back so that she could study it properly.

She felt a thrill of excitement. Tears stung her eyes. It had been so long since she truly felt anything that she'd started to wonder if she'd be numb forever, but she felt something now. Something powerful and energetic that she hadn't felt in a while.

She put her hand to her mouth.

"You're trying to find something polite to say," Lily muttered. "Sorry. I knew I shouldn't have shown you. I'm just an amateur. I splodge paint on paper. That's it." Lily reached for the painting, but Cecilia caught her arm.

"Leave it. Don't touch it." She found it hard to speak, but she knew she had to. "Lily, it's stunning."

"Yes, it's a great frame. It could make a stick man look good."

"Not the frame. The painting." Her mind was racing. Who should she talk to about this?

It was so long since she'd been here she was no longer part of the community. Did Seth's family still own the gallery on Main Street? Probably not. Seth would be in his seventies. He was probably enjoying retirement somewhere.

She had no connections locally, and that was her own fault. But she knew, without vanity, that she could show up at any gallery and that they would pay her attention. But she'd need more than one painting. "Show me everything you have."

"Honestly, I don't think—"

"Lily! Show me."

"You're very bossy all of a sudden." Grumbling, face pink, Lily lifted the rest of the paintings from the drawer. "A couple of these are pastels. I was experimenting. I won't

163

show you the oil. That was a disaster. If it had been fabric, it would have been turned into a scrunchie."

"Give me the oil, too. Give me everything. I want to see all your 'disasters.'" Cecilia spread them out, one by one. Her hands shook. "Who have you shown these to?"

"No one. Who would I show them to? Also, why?"

"And before that? Who saw your work?"

"Er—my mother. She always said, 'very nice, honey,' because that's what mothers are supposed to say. Admiring what your child produces is sort of in the parental job description, isn't it? I sketched a bit during lectures at college to relieve the boredom, but as I was supposed to be studying organic chemistry at the time the professor wasn't impressed."

"What about school? Your teachers didn't say anything?"

"Not really."

"Criminal." Cecilia scanned the paintings and selected three. "We're going to frame these three." She almost confessed that she was going to show them to someone, but she stopped herself. If she was wrong, if she'd lost her touch, then Lily never needed to know. "Have you visited the gallery on Main Street?"

"There are several galleries on Main Street. You have to be more specific."

"It used to be called Atlantic Art." She'd spent hours there, soaking in the atmosphere, feeling part of something.

"It's still there. I gaze at the windows all the time. They have wonderful paintings. And sculpture."

The way Lily was looking at her made her wonder if the whole of her past was showing in her face.

"Maybe I'll pay a visit." She thought about Seth. She'd thought about him a lot since his card had arrived. "I used to know people, although I doubt they're still there."

"You're reconnecting with the locals. That's nice, but I don't see what it has to do with my paintings."

"Nothing at all." She didn't want to make Lily nervous or raise her hopes, particularly if nothing came of it. Maybe Seth wouldn't be there. Maybe whoever owned the place now wouldn't agree with her assessment of Lily's work. "I'm glad you showed me these. They're good, Lily. Better than good." She saw a brief flicker of hope and excitement in Lily's eyes and then it was gone.

"You're just saying that because you're afraid that if you're honest I will bring back woodworm-infested bookshelves into your home."

She had so little faith in herself. So little belief. But maybe that was what happened when you'd been trapped in the wrong pen.

"You may not be a doctor, Lily, but you're definitely an artist. And don't accuse me of being kind. I'm never kind. You have real talent. Raw, but full of promise."

"You *are* kind. You're letting me stay here."

"And in return you are transforming the place and keeping me fed." Cecilia took the paintings one by one and stacked them carefully. "I think you're looking at *artist* in narrow terms. There are many different ways of satisfying that creative urge. For example, these days I mostly focus on my garden—" Cecilia frowned and turned her head. "Did you hear something? A car?"

"Didn't hear anything. No one comes out this far."

But someone had.

They heard the thump of a car door, the crunch of footsteps and the sound of a voice at the front door.

"Hello? Is anyone around?" The voice was deep and male, and Cecilia put down the last of the paintings. She immediately felt on edge and defensive. The last thing she wanted was visitors.

"I must have forgotten to close the front door."

"Nanna?"

This time Cecilia recognized the voice. "That's—it sounds like my grandson. It can't be, surely. It isn't possible. No one knows where I am. Todd?" She raised her voice. "Is that you?"

"Todd?" Lily's face lost some of its color and she flattened herself to the wall of the studio as if she was trying to disappear. "You said no one knew you even owned this place."

"They don't. I don't know how he could possibly have found me." She felt a rush of frustration. Had he brought someone with him?

She patted Lily on the arm and walked out into the living area.

She was ready to be annoyed with him but then he strolled through the door, loose-limbed and handsome, strands of hair falling over his forehead. He gave her that warm Todd smile and irritation melted away.

She found it impossible to be angry with him. "Todd, what are you doing here?"

"I was trying to solve the mystery of the disappearing grandmother. I don't suppose you've seen her, have you? She's about this tall—" he lifted his hand to a point just below the height of his shoulders "—and fierce. Has a tendency to vanish without warning."

"How did you find me?"

"I tried the FBI but they were busy, so I had to settle for exploiting technology. I tracked your phone." He studied her, the laughter in his eyes replaced by concern. "Last time I saw you, you were upset. Then you disappeared. I was worried."

"I told everyone I was fine."

"Which is why I left you alone until now. But worrying about you was starting to keep me awake and I need my beauty sleep. I thought I'd come and check on you myself."

"You—tracked my phone?"

"Yes. Not something I've ever done before, and I only did it this time because I was worried. And now I can see you're alive and well and looking—" he narrowed his eyes "—actually looking a lot better than you have in a while— I'll leave you alone if that's what you want."

How did anyone resist him? You could hardly be angry with someone for caring too much, could you?

"We were about to have coffee on the porch. Would you join us?"

"Coffee would work. A cold beer would work better. I don't suppose you happen to have one stowed in that fridge? This place is great. Did you book it online?" He glanced toward the kitchen and then back at her, his gaze sharpening. "Wait a minute. You said 'we.' You're not alone?"

His eyes drifted to a point past her shoulder, and she saw his expression change from shock to pleasure. "Lily?"

Cecilia felt a flicker of surprise.

"You two know each other? Well, of course you do, as Lily is Hannah's friend. I don't know why that didn't occur to me. She's staying with me."

And judging from the expression on Lily's face she wasn't too pleased to see Todd.

She masked her dismay swiftly, but not before Cecilia had glimpsed something close to panic in her eyes.

She remembered what Lily had said about loving some-one who didn't love her back.

Was it a leap to assume that person was Todd?

If so, she might not be the only one who wasn't entirely pleased to see him here.

11

Lily

"Todd." Lily forced herself to step forward. What choice did she have? The other option was escaping through a window and once was enough for one week. And, anyway, she didn't need Todd wondering why she would go to those lengths to avoid him.

She needed to play the part of little sister's best friend. Which was what she was.

"Hey, Lily." For a second his gaze locked on hers and then he covered the distance between them in two long strides and pulled her in for a hug.

She shouldn't have been surprised. This was Todd. Demonstrative, affectionate and all-around good guy. Yes, he had faults, but it was her misfortune that she loved his faults as much as the rest of him. He could be annoyingly stubborn, often took ages to reply to messages because he rarely checked his phone when he was working, and he tended to give people the benefit of the doubt (which was presumably how he'd ended up engaged to Amelie).

And even if she had managed to hate those things about him, it was hard not to love a guy who went to such lengths to check his grandmother was okay.

For a moment she was pressed up against him, and she felt the hard wall of his chest and the strength of his arms as he tugged her close.

She breathed in the scent of him and sank into the power of him and felt everything she'd locked down explode. The feelings she'd tried so hard to bury escaped in a joyous bound. Her knees weakened. Her heart flew. She was scarily close to hugging him so tightly he'd never be able to escape back to Amelie.

Amelie.

Pulling away from him, keeping it casual, was brutal.

"Hi there." Did she sound normal? She felt anything but normal. "It's been a while."

She'd spent Thanksgiving with Hannah and the family. Before she'd dropped out. Before she'd fallen out with Hannah.

"What are you doing here?" He frowned. "Hannah mentioned that you'd left medical school. What happened?"

"Enough of the inquisition, Todd." Cecilia gestured to the kitchen. "The one rule in this household is that no one is obliged to talk about anything they don't want to talk about. Make yourself useful and bring the coffee outside."

Lily felt a rush of gratitude and then realized that Todd was still looking at her closely.

"I'll fetch the coffee," she said quickly. "You must be tired after your drive. I'm sure you two want to catch up."

And she needed to steady herself.

She headed to the kitchen and took as much time as she felt would pass as reasonable. She poured coffee into mugs, tipped a few of the lemon cookies Cecilia had baked fresh that morning onto a plate and added a jug of milk. She knew exactly how Todd took his coffee—black and strong, even this late in the evening. Everything about him was studded into her brain.

Todd.

She couldn't believe he was here. She'd been so absorbed by what Cecilia was saying about her paintings she hadn't even heard the car.

And now her head was spinning. Todd dominated her thoughts, but underneath was a feeling of dizzying delight that Cecilia liked her work. What had she said? *You have real talent.* Did she mean that? She'd spent a long time studying each one and muttering things Lily didn't catch. And she'd made the paintings look so much better by framing them.

For a moment Lily imagined her work hanging on a wall and then she brought herself back down to earth. She'd think about that later. For now, she needed to focus on Todd.

She wished she was wearing something dressier than her tie-dye T-shirt and her oldest pair of shorts. Amelie always wore dresses. Flowing, feminine dresses that cost more than Lily was ever likely to earn in a year.

Holding firmly to the edges of the tray, she walked back outside to find Todd standing next to Cecilia admiring the view. His arm was looped around her shoulders.

"This place is incredible. How did you find it?"

Cecilia glanced up at him. "More importantly, how did you find me? You said you tracked my phone. How? Who else should I be expecting?"

"No one. I used my laptop. I showed you, remember?" His tone was patient. "I set it up so that if you ever lost your phone, we could find it again."

"Oh. Yes, I think I do remember now. I often lose my phone, so it sounded a useful thing to do," Cecilia said. "But I didn't know you were going to use it to find me."

"It's a good thing you and your phone were in the same place." He kissed his grandmother on the cheek. "I wanted to check you hadn't been kidnapped and held for ransom."

Lily put the tray down on the table and unloaded the mugs. Because Todd wasn't looking at her, she allowed herself to look at him. Just for a few seconds. It was like eating one square of chocolate when really you wanted to devour the whole bar.

Cecilia lifted an eyebrow. "Did you receive a ransom note?"

Todd smiled, apparently undeterred by her crisp tone. "No, but I decided that maybe they liked you and decided to keep you. Maybe you made them your lemon cookies and they decided never to let you go. Don't be angry. It was done with the best of intentions and I promise never to do it again, providing you promise never to disappear again."

"You're a smooth talker, Todd Buckingham, but your charm doesn't work on me." But her tone had softened. "And there I was thinking that no one would ever be able to find me. You're sure no one else is on the way here?"

"Positive." His attention was caught by the bookcase. "What's this? I love it."

"You do?" Cecilia followed his gaze. "You and Lily are clearly seeing something I'm not."

"Look at the wood. It's an excellent piece of craftsmanship." He dropped into a crouch and ran his hand lovingly over one of the shelves. "This is well-made. Someone took time over it."

"And then someone let it go to ruin."

"It can be restored."

"That's what Lily thought."

"Lily found it?" He glanced up at her, curious, one hand still on the bookshelf. "Where?"

She couldn't believe he was here, looking at her with those blue eyes while the breeze played with his hair.

"Someone threw it out."

"They must have had a touch of the sun, don't you think? What are your plans for it?"

"I'm going to put it in the second bedroom. But first I'm going to sand it down, paint it. Remove the bottom shelf because it's damaged."

"Shame to lose a shelf. I could fix that." He ran his finger across the shelf, pausing where the wood was split in an ugly gash. "It would be like new. Better than new, because why buy something new when you can have this?"

Cecilia sighed. "It's two against one, so I guess that ugly splintered thing is staying in my house."

"Your house?" Todd rose to his feet. "That brings me to my next question. What is this place? Is it a rental? It's stunning. How did you find it?" He tilted his head back and shaded his eyes, studying the pitched roof and the windows. "I might be in love."

Lily heard the excitement in his voice and felt a pang because his reaction to the place mirrored hers, and that reminded her just how well they'd always connected.

She saw Cecilia hesitate, weighing her response.

"It's not a rental," she said quietly. "It's mine."

He turned, his gaze sharp. "You *bought* this place?"

"No. Well, yes, I suppose so. Technically. But it's not a recent purchase. Your grandfather and I bought it fifty years ago."

"You—" Todd stared at her, digesting that. "Does Mom know?"

"No one knows. Except you. Now you know. Which will no doubt complicate things." Cecilia suddenly seemed tired. She sat back down on the porch and reached for one of the mugs. "You shouldn't have come here, Todd."

Lily saw that her hand wasn't quite steady and wondered if Todd saw it, too.

She thought that maybe he did, because he was silent for a moment and then he nodded.

"You kept it a secret. I don't know why, and you don't need to tell me why. I can keep secrets, Nanna." He spoke softly, and there was no doubting the sincerity in his words and his voice. "If you don't want people to know about this place, they won't hear it from me. And if you want me to leave, then I'll leave. I really did just want to check on you. I know it's been a difficult time."

Cecilia lifted the coffee mug to her lips and Lily thought she saw a sheen in her eyes.

"I don't want you to leave. But thank you for offering. You're a very special young man."

Todd gave a wry smile. "There are a few people right now who would disagree with you. And now I'm going to steal a lemon cookie and a mug of that coffee. Lily?"

She'd been lost in her own thoughts, some of them about the earlier conversation with Cecilia about her paintings, and some of them about Todd. And now she saw that he was holding a mug out toward her.

"Thanks." She took the mug but didn't sit, instead staring

out across the ocean, watching as the sun dipped toward the sea. It was the best time of day, in her opinion. Normally it soothed her, but not tonight. Tonight, nothing could calm the flutter in her stomach and the crazy dance of her heart. Even though she knew it was hopeless, that nothing would ever come of it, she couldn't seem to help feeling the way she felt whenever she was around him.

Fortunately, his attention was on his grandmother.

"How often did you come here, Nanna?"

"I haven't been here for many years. I thought your grandfather had sold it. He was supposed to have sold it."

"That would have been a crime. Do you have any idea what you have here?"

Lily turned her head and saw sadness in Cecilia's face.

Todd saw the place as Lily did, in terms of position and potential. Cecilia saw only the past. Memories. It seemed to Lily that the place was furnished with them, and she'd been trying hard to make some changes in the hope that it might alter the way Cecilia felt. But she knew her contribution was probably too small to count.

And Todd's arrival had reminded her that although she and Cecilia had created their own little world in this cottage, the real world was still out there. It hadn't gone away.

"I know what I have," Cecilia said. "That's why Cameron and I bought it in the first place. And I will be selling it."

Todd put his mug down and leaned forward. "Why would you sell somewhere so perfect?"

Because it hurts her to be here, Lily thought. But he couldn't know that.

She was the only one who had witnessed Cecilia's distress on the night she'd arrived at the cottage, and sometimes family were the last people you could be honest with.

Her own experience had taught her that.

Cecilia paused and for a moment Lily thought she might be about to tell Todd the truth, but then she shrugged.

"I'm selling it because I have no use for the place."

"Sell it to me," Todd said instantly. "I'm serious. I've been looking for somewhere. This fits my criteria."

Lily was hit by a sudden wave of nausea. If Cecilia sold it to Todd—and why wouldn't she?—then Amelie would live here. Amelie would wake up in the mornings and be greeted by that glorious view. Amelie would wake up and be greeted by Todd. They'd sit on the porch together. They'd walk on the beach together. They'd make their own footprints and gradually erase the prints of all the people who had come before. Including Lily's.

Suddenly the cottage, the one perfect thing in her life, seemed tainted. Amelie might as well have thrown paint over it.

She stood up so suddenly the coffee slopped out of her mug and onto the table. "Sorry. I'll get a cloth."

"Lily?" Cecilia half rose. "Are you all right, honey?"

"I'm fine. It's been a long day, that's all." And seeing Todd was a special kind of torture. It hadn't occurred to her that she'd see him here, of all places.

But it had woken her up to reality.

Yes, she loved this place, but she wasn't making a new life here. She was hiding from her old life. She was avoiding making decisions. If she wanted her parents to treat her like an adult, then she needed to prove that she was one.

The fleeting rush of elation that she'd felt when Cecilia had admired her paintings had vanished, replaced by the usual heavyweight doubt. The uncertainty. And the guilt. Always the guilt. She had no idea how to shake it off. It might have been easier to do so had there not been truth in her mother's words.

She was right. It wasn't realistic to believe she could support herself as an artist.

How many people who dreamed of being an "artist" ended up making money? You only had to look at the statistics to know it was a fantasy. Art would always be her hobby, but what she needed to do now was find a way to make enough money to live on. Something she wouldn't dread doing. Something that didn't make her wake every day with a knot in her stomach.

"You should go to bed." Cecilia was still looking at her with concern. "You're up so early every day."

Todd vanished into the kitchen and returned with the cloth. "How did you come to be staying here, Lily?"

"She's here because I invited her," Cecilia said. "And where are *you* planning on staying tonight? You said you were doing a job out here."

"In Provincetown, but it doesn't start until next week." He mopped the pool of coffee. "I was planning on checking into a hotel."

Cecilia shook her head. "You won't get a hotel room now. Everywhere will be booked solid."

"You're probably right. I've been working today. Didn't think it through. I don't suppose—" he gave her his lost puppy look "—given that I'm technically homeless, could I crash on the sofa for one night?"

"Those sad eyes don't work on me, Todd Buckingham. That look didn't work when you were three and wanted chocolate cake instead of lunch. And it doesn't work now. Neither does the pretense that you're incompetent and somehow 'forgot' to book."

He looked sheepish. "All right, I was hoping to spend some time with you. Satisfy myself you really are okay. If you'll let me stay tonight, then I'll find somewhere more long-term tomorrow."

Cecilia eyed his long, rangy body. "You haven't been able to fit on my sofa since you were ten years old."

"It will be fine. If it's inconvenient I can always sleep in my car or on the beach. It wouldn't be the first time."

Cecilia looked at Lily. "Do you mind if Todd stays?"

What was she supposed to say? Yes, she minded. Having Todd here erased the sense of peace that the cottage gave her. It wasn't that she didn't want him here. It was that she really did want him here, desperately. And wanting him and not showing it required an effort and energy she wasn't sure she had.

But she was going to have to find the energy.

She was touched that Cecilia had even asked for her opinion, but there was only one answer she could give.

"Of course I don't mind."

Cecilia studied her grandson. "You can stay, but you don't think your family will want to know where you are?"

"No," Todd said. "Mom and Dad have been preoccupied since Michael died, so they're not likely to ask. You're not top of mind. I think Mom has decided that, providing you're telling her you're okay, she's going to believe you and leave you alone."

"Michael died? When?" Cecilia pressed her hand to her chest, visibly shocked by the news.

Lily had no idea who Michael was, but he was clearly someone who had been important to the family.

"The day of the party," Todd said. "Car accident. You didn't know?"

"No. I must have left before it happened, and I haven't been looking at the news. That's dreadful. I had no idea." Cecilia took a breath. "How is your mother?"

"Sad, obviously. Busy trying to make Dad feel better. He hasn't been to work since."

Cecilia gave him a long look. "She and your father have been spending time together?"

Lily thought it was a strange question, but Todd didn't seem to think so.

"Yes. A rare occurrence in our house. I don't suppose it will last," Todd said. "You know Dad. He'll soon be back working his usual hours."

"I must contact her. I should have done it before." Cecilia looked agitated. "And what about Amelie? Won't she be wanting to join you?"

"Ah. Amelie." Todd sat down. "She won't be joining me, now or in the future. We broke up."

Cecilia's brows lifted. "After a week of being engaged?"

"Yes. Shortest engagement on record, I know." He pulled a face. "It's complicated."

Todd was no longer with Amelie?

Lily's heart soared upward and her mood with it. Why? She had a hundred questions. Who was the instigator? *Why had Todd fallen for her in the first place?* Did it make her a bad person that she felt euphoria and not pity for Amelie?

Todd was no longer engaged.

Todd was no longer marrying Amelie.

Cecilia squeezed his arm. "You can stay. And you don't need to wedge yourself into the sofa and give yourself a backache. You can take the master bedroom."

"The master?"

"The master, and no questions."

"All right. If you're sure." But his gaze lingered on her face and then shifted to Lily, as if he was hoping to find answers there.

Lily couldn't think of anything except the fact that he was no longer with Amelie.

"I'm going to bed," she said. "Early start tomorrow and I'm tired."

But being tired didn't help her sleep.

An hour passed. And then another hour. She turned over in the bed, then turned over again and checked the time on her phone. She counted how much time she had left to sleep before the alarm woke her. Not enough.

But still she didn't sleep. Her mind was too active. She was too hot. She plumped the pillow, turned it to the cool side and tried a different position. The breeze and the sound of the sea wafted through the skylights.

She lay there, wide-awake, thinking about Amelie and Todd, and then just about Todd. And herself. And why people had to fall in love with the wrong person.

She wanted to know what had happened. Or did she? What if Todd was brokenhearted and that was why he was here?

Irritated with herself, knowing that she was never going to sleep if she carried on lying there, she slid out of bed. She might as well get up, go outside and see if that helped.

Trying not to make a noise, she pulled on a pair of jeans and a T-shirt and headed downstairs.

She tiptoed across the room, opened the door and stepped onto the porch.

She stood for a moment, breathing in the night air and the scent of the ocean. Then she walked to the beach.

The sand was cool under her feet, and she walked almost

to the water's edge. The moon sent slivers of silver across the water. She stared out to sea and imagined the early explorers navigating the shoreline and the shifting sands. The seabed in this area was littered with shipwrecks.

She felt a little like that herself. She'd been forging ahead, trying to navigate the storms of life, and suddenly she'd hit a sandbank and sunk.

She sat down on the sand, arms hooked around her knees.

One thing she knew for certain was that she couldn't stay here for much longer. She'd swapped her old life for this new life, but it wasn't real. It couldn't be forever. She needed to do something to earn money.

"Lily?"

His voice came from behind her and she turned, dismayed.

She hadn't expected or wanted company.

"I'm sorry if I woke you." There was enough light from the moon to be able to see him.

"You didn't. I couldn't sleep. Too much going on in my head." He'd pulled on track pants, and his T-shirt was a pale faded blue, washed until it barely held together. "Are you okay?"

"I'm fine. Why wouldn't I be?"

He sat down next to her, close but not touching. "Maybe because you're sitting on a beach at two o'clock in the morning when I happen to know from my grandmother that your alarm goes off at five thirty."

The thought made her wince. "I like it out here. It's special."

"I'm not arguing with that." He paused. "I didn't expect to see you here. How long have you known my grandmother?"

She was too tired to field awkward questions. "I met her

once when I was with Hannah. It must have been around ten years ago."

"So how did you come to be staying here with her?"

"It's a long story. Some coincidence involved. And some good timing. I'm working for a local management company, caretaking properties. I was looking after Dune Cottage and then your grandmother arrived. I needed somewhere to live. She let me stay here."

He waited. "That's it? That's all you're going to tell me? Cut me some slack, Lily. I'm worried about my grandmother."

"And you think I'm exploiting her in some way?"

"What? No. Of course not. Why would you think—" He shook his head. "I'm in the dark here, that's all. A week ago, my grandmother did a runner from her own party. I'm guessing you know about that. Massive cake. A hundred people gathered together ready to wish her happy birthday. Champagne. The only thing missing was the birthday girl. And while it's true that there have been plenty of parties I could happily have run away from in my time, I don't think that's what this was. She was behaving strangely. It's not that long since she lost my grandfather. My mother was worried sick, but she's scared of things she can't control and she had a lot on her mind, what with Dad and everything, so I wasn't too worried at first. But a week—a week is a long time, so I thought I'd check for myself. The plan was to put my mind at rest, and then melt away quietly."

"But here you are."

"Can I help it if I was born with a curious mind?" He grinned. "Not only do I discover that my grandmother is living in a property she has apparently owned virtually forever and told no one about, but you're staying there with her. I have a few questions. More than a few."

Lily sat up straighter. "I can't answer those questions. If there are things you want to know about your grandmother, you need to ask her."

He sighed. "You didn't inherit a gossip gene, did you? I should have remembered that about you. All right, so you won't tell me about my grandmother—I'm impressed by your discretion and loyalty by the way—but you're allowed to tell me about yourself."

"What do you want to know?"

"I know you gave up medicine." His voice softened. "I know you're living here now. Fill in the gaps for me."

It wasn't something she wanted to think about, especially not now, at two in the morning, when she was trying to calm her mind.

"I'm here because I needed to get away. That's all you need to know."

He was silent for a moment. "You used to talk to me about everything. School. Art. Your parents."

"That was a long time ago." Before she'd dropped out.

"Not so long. And I'm the same person."

Maybe he was the same, but the circumstances had changed.

If there were things she might have said to him before, she wasn't going to say them now.

"I'm here because I like it here. I like the way the place makes me feel."

He nodded. "That's a good reason to stay somewhere. Also, it's far away from your old life. If you're going to run away, this is a good place to be. I get it."

"I never said I was running away." But she was. That was exactly what she was doing. "You think I'm a coward."

"No. If you are, then I'm a coward, too. Why do you think I'm here?"

She couldn't imagine him running from anything.

"I thought you came to check on your grandmother."

"That, too." He was silent for a moment. "I don't expect you to betray confidences, but how worried should I be about her? And don't say she's fine, because I know she's not fine."

Lily thought about the night Cecilia had arrived. The broken paintings. The sobs.

She'd witnessed a deeply personal moment that shouldn't have had witnesses and she had no intention of revealing the details.

She was about to shut him down again but then she saw the worry in his eyes and relented.

"I can't share the detail because I don't actually know it. I do know that she was upset when she arrived and that she seems a little better after a week here." She hesitated. "I do know that she needed to come to this place."

"She thought my grandfather had sold it. Which meant they had secrets." Todd stared out to sea. "After all those years together, they had secrets. Imagine discovering something like that after someone has died. You can't ever find out why they didn't tell you. You can't ever have closure."

"Maybe there are always things we keep from those closest to us."

"From parents, definitely. Friends, maybe. But in a marriage?" He shook his head. "If you can't trust the person you've chosen to spend your life with, how is that ever going to work? If they have secrets, how would you really know a person. And isn't really knowing someone the point of a relationship?"

"I don't know. I don't consider myself an expert on relationships." She'd had two, both woefully thin and unimportant. There had been very ordinary sex and a depressing lack of depth and intimacy. She hadn't cared enough to wonder why they hadn't worked. The truth was she'd only ever loved one man, and he was sitting next to her.

"I'm not an expert, either." He gave a faint smile. "Which is probably the reason I'm sitting here now without a fiancée."

Was he hurting?

She didn't want to think about Amelie, but she couldn't bear to think of Todd hurting.

"Do you want to talk about it?"

"Maybe. But not right now. Now I'm putting some space between myself and the rest of the world. And this is a good place to do that." He leaned back on his elbows, his legs stretched out on the sand. "I can't believe she owns this. Also, that she never told me. Think of all the vacations I could have taken. I love the water. Do you sail?"

She was still thinking about him running away. What exactly had happened with Amelie?

"Sail? I—no."

"You haven't lived. I'll take you out. You'll thank me. It's the perfect escape."

"You need to escape?"

He gazed out to sea. "Have you ever done something you knew was the wrong thing for you, but you did it anyway? Made a bad choice?"

She thought about medicine. "Yes."

"Right." He nodded. "That was me. I did something. Made a bad decision. But I fixed it. It would have been better not to have made it in the first place, but perfect would

185

be boring and my friends would hate me. But I needed to get away. Needed time to think. How about you?" He turned to look at her and her heart gave a little bump.

"I'm definitely not perfect."

He smiled. "I was asking if you'd fixed your bad choice?"

She'd fixed the bad choice, but she didn't feel good about it. She suspected that wouldn't happen until she had her parents' approval, and for that to happen she had to do something to make them proud.

"It's a work in progress." She wondered what his bad choice was. Was he talking about Amelie?

He leaned forward and brushed sand from his feet. "I've been thinking about you a lot."

"Me?" Suddenly she couldn't breathe. "You were thinking about me?"

"Yes." He watched as the waves flowed toward them and retreated. "When Hannah told me you'd left medicine. I almost called you."

"Why?"

"She was shocked by your decision, but I wasn't. You used to tell me how hard it was living up to your parents' expectations. How much pressure you felt. I wanted to call and tell you that I know how it feels to take a different path from the one your parents want you to take. I've been there. What you did was brave."

Brave? She felt like the least brave person on the planet.

She wondered if he knew that she and Hannah hadn't been in contact for a while.

"They don't understand why I'd walk away from such a secure path. It's hard for them."

"Harder for you to be on the wrong track. I never did understand why you chose medicine. Seemed to me it was like trying to put a sheep in an aquarium." He ran his hand over his face. "Is that a terrible analogy? Blame lack of sleep. My brain isn't working."

"I'm not sure if it's terrible." She couldn't help laughing. "Are you saying I'm a sheep? I need a haircut?"

"Nothing wrong with your hair. I was trying to put a more original take on fish out of water." He grinned. "From now on I'll leave fancy words to someone else and stick to what I'm good at. What I mean is, it seemed like a waste for you to be a doctor."

"My parents think it was a waste for me to give it up." She didn't quite manage to keep the wistfulness out of her voice.

"That's because most parents want the predictable, secure option for their child. You would have been wasted as a doctor. You were always so creative. Remember when you came over and decorated Hannah's bedroom? You must have been about sixteen. I don't know what you did. Mixed different shades of paint. Did something fancy. It looked good. Even my parents commented on it. And you did some sketches one summer by the pool."

"You remember that?"

"Yes. I have one of them on the wall in my apartment."

"You—" she couldn't believe it "—you have one of my drawings?"

"Yes. My grandfather was an artist, remember? I was raised to think of art both as something aesthetically appealing to hang on your wall, but also as an investment. And don't ask for it back. I like it, and I won't sell it even when you're famous."

"I'm never going to be famous. I don't want to be famous." What did she want? "I just want to wake up every morning and look forward to my day. Not dread every moment."

He nodded. "Looking forward to the day is good. Enjoying your work is good. Knowing you're doing what you're supposed to be doing. Feeling as if you're living the right life."

"It doesn't sound like much, but it's everything. And not many people have that, I know. Plenty of people do jobs just to earn a living. And that's fine. But to love what you do…" She sighed. "That's the goal really, isn't it?"

"Yes. And it's a goal worth striving for."

It wasn't a surprise that he understood. He always had. He was one of the few people who really knew her, perhaps even better than Hannah did. It was one of the reasons that his relationship with Amelie had hurt so much. She hadn't just lost the dream of something more happening between them, she'd lost a friend because friendship had never been possible while Amelie was in the mix.

She turned to look at him. "Do you really have a job to do here or was that an excuse?"

"I do. Mr. and Mrs. Elliot from Beacon Hill, Boston, have bought themselves a four-bed, three-bath property on the waterfront, and who have they decided is the perfect person to remodel their kitchen? Me. Custom-made, sustainable. It will last a lifetime. I wasn't supposed to start the job until August but when I saw where my grandmother was, I juggled my schedule. And I surprised her, I know."

"You might have surprised her, but she was pleased to see you. That's the happiest I've seen her all week."

"There are no paintings on the wall." He sucked in a breath. "That's it. I knew there was something about that living room that felt odd. Just hooks, as if they'd all been taken down. Except that one."

"Yes." She didn't tell him about the frames that had been

destroyed. She and Cecilia had stowed the paintings them-selves away in the cupboards in the studio. "*The Girl on the Shore*. I love it."

"The—what did you say?" He sat up suddenly. "What is the painting called?"

"*The Girl on the Shore*. Why?"

"The day of the party—" He rubbed his fingers across his forehead, trying to remember. "I heard them talking about it. Someone was asking about that painting. They said it didn't exist."

Lily was mystified. "Why would they say that?"

Todd shook his head. "I've no idea. I don't understand."

Lily was silent.

What she didn't understand was why Cecilia had smashed every painting but that one.

12

Kristen

He'd picked a restaurant that overlooked the harbor instead of one of their usual haunts, and she wondered if it was symbolic that he wanted to be somewhere that came with no memories.

She didn't care. She was relieved that Theo finally seemed to be more in control. More like his old self. She'd been scared. She'd started to worry that he'd never leave the house again.

And then yesterday she'd woken to the smell of pancakes and found him making her breakfast in the kitchen. It had been a turning point, and now here they were in a restaurant. His suggestion. His choice. He'd even booked it himself, instead of leaving her to do it.

She was out to dinner with Theo, and for the first time in as long as she could remember she didn't have to worry about him being called to the hospital. She didn't need to rush her food, or leave half of it on her plate, or finish the meal alone. She could relax and enjoy the atmosphere. And the atmosphere was special. They had a table right beside the water, which had taken some sweet-talking on his part. It had been fascinating to watch. She'd forgotten how charming Theo could be when he wasn't distracted by work.

This was the old Theo, the Theo she'd fallen in love with, albeit an older, sadder version.

So here they were, at the best table, gazing at each other over a flickering candle.

True, they were hardly in a celebratory mood, but at least they were together.

On a date.

She was pleased now that she'd dressed up and taken time over her hair and makeup. She'd worn a new dress that she loved, and tried not to remember that she'd bought it for Jeff.

She wasn't going to think about Jeff. She was with Theo.

The funeral had been stressful and sad, but Theo had held her hand tightly throughout and even though she hadn't been able to stop wishing that he'd offered that level of support during her father's funeral, she'd been glad to have it anyway. It had brought them closer.

She ignored the menu in front of her and glanced across the water, watching as the setting sun streaked the sky and the ocean.

There was something about being near the ocean that soothed her. She loved the smells, and the sounds. The clink of masts, the gentle lap of the water as it hit the dock.

She reached across the table and took his hand.

"This is perfect. Great choice."

"Michael told me about it."

"Oh." She'd been trying hard not to think about Michael.

191

Not because she didn't care, but because she cared very much and was trying to keep her emotions in check. It wasn't a crime, surely, to try and pull a little joy from dark days?

Theo put down the menu he'd been holding. "I feel guilty being here, enjoying myself."

Were they enjoying themselves? That was an overly optimistic assessment of the evening in her opinion. They were going through the motions, but that was what you did until finally, one day, you found you really were enjoying yourselves.

"Michael would want us to be here. Michael would want us to be making the most of our lives."

"That's true. You're right." He stared down at their interlocked fingers. "I know you're right. I feel—strange, Krissy."

He'd called her Krissy when they were first dating, and whenever they made love.

And now he was calling her Krissy again.

"In what way, strange?"

"As if this is some sort of bad dream. As if it can't be real. I can't believe I'm never going to see him again."

She felt a pang of sympathy. "I understand. I felt the same way after my dad died. I still do."

He lifted his gaze from their fingers to her face. "You do? I didn't know that."

You never asked. You didn't listen when I tried to tell you.

She pushed those thoughts down. Later, maybe, they'd talk about it. But not now. She didn't want to damage this new, fragile connection. "It isn't easy to learn to live without someone you love."

"I'm discovering that. I've been thinking of all the times I've had to deliver bad news to relatives, and wondering if I could have done better. Could have offered more support."

You could have offered more support to me.

Kristen pulled her hand away.

"I think we should order and talk about something else. You're making yourself feel worse."

"You're right." He gave a brief smile. "You're an incredible woman. You hold everything together, no matter how tough life gets. You were a rock during the funeral. I don't know how I would have made it through without you. I'm lucky to have you. We're lucky to have each other."

She used to feel that way, but lately she hadn't been so sure.

All she knew was that she was glad to be here now, with him, with no risk of him rushing off.

They ordered fish and shared a bottle of chilled white wine.

"My mother called this morning."

"She did?" He raised his glass in a silent toast. "What did she say?"

"That she'd been worrying about me. Us."

Theo put his glass down. "Your mother said that?"

"Yes. She'd heard about Michael. I don't know how. Maybe she read something. She wanted to check that you and I were okay. And she apologized for leaving the party without telling me."

"Did she realize how worried you were?"

"I don't think so. I don't think she was giving any thought to me or anyone else on that particular day. Something happened." She frowned. "She said there was something she urgently needed to do."

"She didn't tell you what?"

"No. She said she'd explain everything when she next saw me. And she apologized for being difficult and thanked me for working so hard on the party. She sounded—different."

And she still didn't understand it. Something seemed to have changed, but she couldn't identify what exactly.

Theo picked up his wineglass again. "The important thing is that you had a good conversation. We should drink to that."

Kristen didn't raise her glass. She was thinking about her mother. It had been a good conversation. It had lacked the tension that punctuated most of their exchanges. Her mother had seemed softer, more receptive. Vulnerable. She'd asked about Kristen. Seemed concerned about Kristen, to the point that Kristen had almost blurted out how awful she'd been feeling, how lonely she'd felt and what a mess her life was. The urge to confide had been all the more unsettling because she didn't have those sorts of conversations with her mother.

She'd held herself back and instead they'd talked about Michael, and also Theo.

"She asked a lot about you." Kristen finally picked up her glass. "She wanted to know how you were." And now she thought about it, her mother had asked a lot of questions about Theo. Whether he was working a lot. How Kristen was handling that.

It was as if she'd somehow guessed Kristen was having problems in her relationship, but how? Kristen had said nothing.

Theo was watching her. "Did she say where she was?"

"She is staying on the Cape."

"Why the Cape?"

"I have no idea." But something flickered in her brain. A long-ago memory. "When Winston and I were young, our parents used to sometimes disappear to the Cape for the weekend to paint. Granny used to come and look after us."

"Where did they stay?"

"I don't know. I was young. I didn't ask. And then I think they stopped going."

Theo took a sip of wine. "This thing she needed to do so urgently—is it to do with your father, do you think? A trip down memory lane?"

"I don't know. I assume she'll tell me if she wants me to know. But I was glad she called."

"Yes. It's important to stay in touch with family. Make the most of every day." Sadness crossed his face and she knew he was thinking about Michael, so she changed the subject quickly.

She told him about an art dealer in Paris who was flying in to discuss one of her father's works and the private collector who continued to contact her about a painting of her father's even though she had informed him on numerous occasions that particular work he wanted had been gifted to a grateful nation on her father's death, and was currently hanging in a major gallery being enjoyed by millions.

It occurred to her as she talked that even though her father was gone, he still occupied most of her life. What did that say about her? She needed to change something. She needed to shake things up. But in the meantime, this was all she had.

She was partway through a story about a postdoctoral student who had contacted her about a research project when she realized she'd lost her audience.

"Theo?"

He blinked, bemused, as if he'd forgotten she was there. "Sorry. You were saying something about Paris."

Paris had been right back at the beginning of the conversation.

Maybe she was boring him. Maybe after all these years they had nothing to say that was new or interesting.

She waited while her appetizer was placed in front of her.

They'd both ordered asparagus but now it was here she wasn't sure she was even hungry.

All around them couples were dining and she wondered how many of them were having a great time, and how many of them were dealing with huge things in their lives but trying to inject as much normal as possible. People were like icebergs. Only a fraction of who they were showed on the surface.

How did she and Theo look to other people? Did they look like two people who were struggling?

"You're finding it hard to concentrate."

"Yes." He ran his hand over his face. "There's something I need to say to you."

"Oh." Something about his expression made her uneasy. "What?"

"This probably isn't the best place to have this conversation, but I need to talk about it." Theo glanced at the diners closest to them and lowered his voice. "The affair was a mistake, Krissy. It should never have happened."

"What are you talking about?" Panic squeezed her chest. She hadn't had an affair, not technically. She and Jeff had flirted and spent time together and maybe, just maybe, it might have turned into something more, but it hadn't. How had Theo found out?

"He told me that he regretted it right from the start."

Jeff had *told* him that? Why would he do that? And when?

Her mouth was dry. "What do you mean? When did you talk to him?"

Theo toyed with his wineglass. "A few days before he died."

196

Jeff was dead? No.

And Kristen realized that Theo wasn't talking about Jeff.

"You're talking about Michael." She saw Theo look at her strangely.

"Who else?"

"I don't know." She was so flustered, she stumbled over the words. "I suppose I'm finding it hard to focus, with everything that has happened. And you're not really making sense."

He was thinking about Michael. He didn't know about Jeff.

The relief was enormous.

She ate some of her asparagus. "Tell me what Michael said. Was this when you played golf a few weeks ago?"

"We've talked about it a lot over the past couple of years. His marriage breakdown was a rough time for him."

Remembering how Trisha had struggled, she felt a flicker of frustration. It had been a rough time for *Michael*? "What about Trisha? She had no choice in it. He wrecked their lives. She was devastated."

"Michael was devastated, too." Theo spoke quietly. "He never would have left, but she wanted him out of the house. She made that choice."

Kristen remembered the conversation.

I can't bear to be near him. I can't bear him to touch me.

She felt outrage for Trisha. "Do you blame her?"

"No. I'm not making any judgments. Just telling you how it was. How Michael felt."

"Why didn't he tell Trisha how he felt?"

"He tried. She wouldn't listen. She couldn't get past that affair. And the thing that made it harder for him was that it wasn't even serious to begin with. Maybe if it had truly meant something, if he'd been in love…" Theo shrugged. "I don't know. But it was just a fling. I'm not defending him. Just telling you his side of the story. He said he didn't know why he did it. Life seemed to be rushing past him. Trisha was always busy. He felt lonely. That's probably difficult for you to understand."

Feeling lonely?

Her mouth was so dry she could hardly speak. "No," she croaked. "Not so difficult."

"But a bit sad don't you think?" Theo gave a tired smile. "He still loved Trisha."

She'd never heard Theo talk like this before.

"He didn't love Candy?"

"For a while he thought he did. She came into his life at a low point. She paid attention to him. Made him feel attractive and interesting. I'm not blaming her, obviously. He made the choice. He was responsible."

Jeff had been attentive. Jeff had made her feel attractive and interesting.

She was bathed in a sweat of horror.

She felt pathetically relieved that she hadn't gone ahead with the affair. Nothing had happened. She'd had a few lunches with a man who wasn't her husband. That was it.

She took a large gulp of wine. "If he regretted it, why did he marry Candy?"

"Trisha told him it was over. That she'd never forgive him. He was trying to build a new life." Theo ate his asparagus and then put down his knife and fork. "Did you know that he and Trisha were seeing each other again?"

"No. I didn't know that."

But it explained a great deal.

She thought of Trisha sobbing at the funeral, distraught.

She'd made a speech about Michael, saying nothing but good things and Kristen had wondered where all the anger and hurt had gone, and how Candy would feel hearing all that. It had been a while before she'd discovered that Candy wasn't there. When she'd said that she didn't "do" funerals, she hadn't just been talking about the organization.

"The week before he was killed, he and Trisha had agreed that they were going to get back together permanently. They were going to get married again. He'd bought her a ring. He showed it to me."

Their main course was delivered to the table and Kristen watched as he boned fish with surgical precision.

A ring?

She didn't know any of this. Why didn't she know? Why hadn't Trisha told her? Come to think of it, why hadn't Theo mentioned it?

"What about Candy?"

"That was over."

Kristen was struggling to keep up. "Michael told you all this?"

"Yes. We used to talk a lot. Lately he was happier than I'd seen him in ages. Since before breaking up with Trisha. He said it felt like a fresh start. As if they were on the edge of major change."

She was stunned to discover that Theo knew so much personal detail about Michael. That they'd obviously had many conversations and he hadn't once mentioned it to her.

She poked at her own fish, trying to work up an appetite.

Michael and Trisha had decided to get back together.

Michael had bought her a ring.

It explained why Trisha had been so upset at the funeral. She and Michael had been on the cusp of a fresh start.

Life had a sick sense of humor. It would show you your dream, then snatch it away before you had a chance to live it.

She put her fork down.

When you were young you thought life was something you could control, and it was only later that you discovered that life often had a plan of its own that didn't coincide with yours, and that control was an illusion.

It made her wonder what nasty surprises life might have in store for her.

She stared at her plate. She didn't have Theo's talents for boning fish. Maybe she was about to choke on a fish bone and that would be it. She'd die right here, in front of a bunch of strangers who would no doubt film her demise and post it on the internet.

She picked up her plate and passed it across the table. "Could you bone mine?"

His eyebrows lifted. "Whenever I offer, you point out you're an independent adult."

"I am an independent adult, but I happen to be incompetent when it comes to boning fish. Part of being independent is knowing when to ask for help."

To give him his due Theo didn't question her. He simply pushed his own plate to one side and boned her fish.

One potential calamity averted, Kristen thought as she watched him extract a perfect skeleton, all bones intact. Nine million others to avoid.

"Had he moved back into the family home?"

"Last month, but they'd been seeing each other regularly before that. He used to spend every Sunday with them."

Kristen thought back to the beginning, when Trisha had told her how hard those days were.

"What happened to change things?"

Theo shrugged. "Michael didn't know, but thought it was probably that they were both making an effort because of the kids. They were polite. He told me that it was the best day of his week. He looked forward to it. Turned out, so did she. They realized that despite everything, they were still in love. Michael said he'd never stopped loving Trisha. What he'd done was stop paying attention. When things niggled, he didn't do anything about it. They didn't talk."

She tried to imagine Theo having these conversations with Michael. Theo, who rarely talked about emotions. And she tried not to feel hurt that he'd been able to have these conversations with his friend, but not with her. She'd told herself that he just wasn't the sort to open up emotionally to anyone, but now it seemed that wasn't the case.

It felt personal.

With an effort, she buried that hurt along with the other hurts and focused on what he was telling her.

"You're saying the affair helped their marriage."

Theo pulled a face. "I don't think he saw it that way. He saw it as a stupid choice on his part. A wild moment of desperation and stupidity. He'd been feeling lonely and unsettled. Instead of talking to Trisha, he talked to Candy. And that was that."

Kristen's mouth dried. She'd been feeling lonely and unsettled.

"So Trisha forgave him."

"In the end. And I'm sure it was hard. The affair meant nothing to him, but it meant everything to her." He looked at her. "What would you have done if you were Trisha?"

Her heart rate went from a steady rhythm to a sprint.

"I don't know. Why are you asking? Are you having an affair?"

"Of course not. I just wondered what you would have done if you'd been Trisha." He shook his head. "It seems like such a waste. Those years apart. Those years they could have spent together. And now they never will."

What would she have done if she'd been Trisha?

She had no idea. And then she realized she wasn't Trisha in this scenario, she was Michael.

She'd been contemplating doing all the things Michael had done.

She'd started down that road.

She'd been willing to risk her marriage because she'd been lonely, and desperately sad after her father died, and unable to find any comfort at home. Theo had been too busy to be there for her (although it seemed he'd been there for Michael, which stung).

Like Michael, she might have found herself in a position where everything important to her collapsed because she hadn't done more to save it.

But she hadn't. *She hadn't.*

She didn't know why Jeff had ghosted her, but she was grateful that he had. And she was grateful to Michael because in a strange way he had saved her marriage. Because of what happened to him, Theo was spending more time with her. Because of Michael, she had Theo back again. She had a chance to fix things.

Theo finished his glass of wine. "Talking to Michael made me realize how much work consumes me. I'm not looking forward to going back next week."

She wasn't looking forward to him going back, either. Even though he'd been sad for much of the time, and so had she, it had been good to be together. They'd talked more than they ever had, and she cherished those conversations.

She felt closer to him than she had for a long time. Surely they could build on that?

But in the meantime, they had to return to real life. They both knew it. And Theo needed it, even if he didn't recognize it quite yet.

This time she was sure things would be different. Michael's death had shaken him and made him reassess his priorities. She was sure that from now on he would be there for his family as well as for his patients. Even over the past few days she'd seen small changes. He brought her breakfast in bed and asked how she was feeling. When she'd mentioned that she was worried about Hannah, he'd taken her seriously and instead of dismissing her anxieties he'd called his daughter and arranged to take her to lunch the following week (at which point Hannah had called her mother because she'd been worried that there was something wrong with her father because he was acting strangely). Every evening they prepared dinner together, something they'd done only a handful of times since they'd met.

And she knew it was time to reassess her own priorities. She knew now that she needed more in her life. She needed to be more than just part of the Cameron Lapthorne machine.

"You're a good doctor, Theo. A great surgeon. You've helped many people over the course of your career." It seemed important to remind him of that. "And you were a good friend to Michael. He was lucky to have you."

His loyalty to Michael touched her and gave her hope.

If he could be there for Michael, she could rely on him to be there for her, too. She wasn't expecting something that he was incapable of delivering.

They finished their meal and took a stroll along the waterfront.

He held her hand, his grip warm and firm as if he was determined to stay as close as possible to her, and when he pulled her toward him and kissed her, she felt a flare of warmth that she hadn't felt in a long time.

She kissed him back, sliding her hands into his hair, holding on to him and this moment.

She'd almost made the biggest mistake of her life, but fortunately she hadn't.

And it was over now. Done.

She'd never have contact with Jeff again.

Theo would never know, and everything would be fine.

13

Cecilia

She parked in a spot reserved only for staff of the gallery and lifted her precious parcel out of the car. Before she'd even closed the door a man appeared from the back of the gallery.

"This is private parking. I'm going to have to ask you to—" He broke off and stared. "Cecilia?"

"Hello, Seth. Good to see you, too." She took pleasure in watching his jaw drop.

"No, it can't be. Is it really you?"

"It's me. I don't have to ask if it's you. You haven't changed at all." She closed the car door and watched as the scowl turned into a smile.

"I wasn't expecting today to turn out differently from any other day, but that just goes to prove you can always be surprised. And you look fantastic."

When she'd packed for her impromptu trip she'd swept

clothes into her suitcase without much thought, but when she'd riffled through everything that morning in an attempt to find something suitable, she'd been surprised by the choice. In the end she'd teamed a linen dress in a pale powder blue with a lightweight jacket and a scarf she'd bought on a trip to Paris decades earlier. Because this meeting felt like the most important thing she'd done in a long time, she'd added a pair of dangly earrings and a touch of lipstick.

It was clear from his expression that her efforts hadn't been wasted.

"What have you got there?" He narrowed his eyes as he saw what she was carrying. "I hope you're going to tell me you've been painting and you're here to let me sell your work."

"I'm not going to tell you that."

"Pity. It always struck me as wrong that your husband got all the attention when you were the one with the talent. But I would say that, wouldn't I? You were the one that got away, and that was all my own fault. I didn't know a good thing when I had it. I've learned a thing or two since then." He smiled without a trace of bitterness and opened the door wider. "Come in. Show me what you've got and tell me everything that has happened in the last fifty years."

Had it been that long?

Yes, it probably had. Longer in fact. Once, they'd been close. The best of friends. And some friendships survived the years, of course, but some were just too complicated. Particularly those that had once been something more.

She'd loved two men in her life. One of those was Cameron, but before him it had been Seth.

She walked past him, her arm brushing against his, her

heart beating a little faster than usual. She felt self-conscious and a little awkward.

Seth seemed to have changed little, which didn't seem possible given the years that had passed. He was lean and wiry, his face tanned and lined from so many summers spent on the Cape, and his hair was mostly white now. But he was still handsome, and his smile was as wide and warm as when she'd first met him.

Holding the parcel in her arms, she scanned the walls of his gallery and felt the familiar feeling of being home. How she'd loved this place when she was young.

"It's bigger than it was when your father owned it."

"I bought the store next door. Knocked it through and increased the space. You approve?"

"It's great." She glanced around her, taking it all in. One painting immediately caught her eye. It was hung by itself, for maximum impact. She stepped toward the large canvas, where bright blues merged with pale gold. The title was simply *Seashore*.

Seth moved to stand next to her. "You're not the only one to admire it. Sold it yesterday. They're picking it up today. Local artist. She'll be pleased."

"You always did have a good eye."

"I just take what I like. At home I surround myself with things I find beautiful. I don't care if they're unconventional or unfashionable. If I like to look at it, it can go on my wall. How long have you been back here, Ceci?"

He was the only one who had ever called her Ceci. It had irritated Cameron, who had felt it was an inappropriate intimacy. She'd often wondered if that was why Seth had done it.

Cameron had always been unsettled around Seth because

Cecilia had been dating him before they'd met. They were part of a large group of artists who had moved in the same circles, caring about little except their art and the moment.

"I read that he died," Seth said. "I wanted to call, but it seemed wrong after so many years. I wasn't sure if hearing from me would make it feel worse or better."

"You sent a card. Thank you for that."

"I didn't know if you'd even see it."

"I saw it." And kept it. It had given her comfort.

"Are you heartbroken, Ceci?"

How should she answer that?

"At times, yes. And at times I'm lost. Confused. And angry." She couldn't believe she'd just said that aloud, but this was Seth—Seth, who she'd once been close to, so maybe it wasn't that surprising. And what she said was true. She was angry with Cameron for having lied to her again. Angry that he'd left it to his lawyer to tell her the truth about the cottage and the painting. One minute she wanted to sob, and the next she wanted to scream. He'd left her with so many unresolved feelings. But at least it didn't seem that he'd been using the cottage as a love nest as she'd first feared. That helped. "How I feel changes all the time, which is a little unsettling if I'm honest. I'm sorry. You don't need to hear this, I'm sure. When people ask how you are, what they really want to hear is *I'm doing fine, thank you.*"

"Not me. When I ask a question, I appreciate a frank answer." There was no sign that her confession had shocked him. "Grief is a slippery beast. One minute it steps to one side to let you pass and just when you think you're doing okay, it trips you up and you're flat on your face again."

That was it exactly.

She felt a pressure in her chest and a thickening in her

throat. She was afraid she might lose control right here in this cool, contemporary gallery in front of this man she hadn't seen in years.

"It was a complicated relationship." Appalled, she felt emotion rush over her like the tide.

She needed to leave. She'd come back another time when she was more in control.

And then she felt Seth's hand on her shoulder and his touch was both familiar and unfamiliar.

"Cameron was a complicated person. But isn't everyone?" His fingers rubbed gently at the tight knots in her shoulders and then he smiled at her, lightening the moment. "I should never have let you go, Ceci. One of life's big regrets."

She saw the gleam in his eyes and remembered that his sense of fun was one of the things that had attracted her to him in the first place.

He'd been her first real boyfriend. Her first everything. She'd been heartbroken when he'd ended their relationship.

Over the years she'd thought about him. When things had been bad with Cameron. In those low points, she'd occasionally wondered how her life might have looked if she and Seth had stayed together.

But what was the point of looking back and wondering? That was then, and this was now.

And she was determined to build a new life in the now, but she knew that to do that she had to acknowledge and accept everything that had gone before.

"I loved Cameron."

"I know." He let his hand drop and gave a soft laugh. "But I won't hold that against you. No one is perfect. Are you staying in the cottage?"

"Yes."

"It's been empty for so long I wondered if you were ever coming back."

"You've been there?"

"Had some heart problems ten years ago. Boring. I'm determined not to turn into one of those people who talk about ailments. But let's just say that I changed my habits, or some of them at least. Since then, I exercise. Long walks. Sometimes those walks take me over the dunes to the cottage. I may have peeped through the window occasionally, for old times' sake."

She wondered if he thought about that time, as she did. It didn't feel right to ask.

"I heard about Sonya." She knew through the grapevine that he'd lost his wife ten years earlier. She'd never met Sonya, and she was curious about the woman who had convinced commitment phobic Seth to settle down. "I'm sorry. I should have contacted you."

"Don't apologize. I understand. We lost touch. Took me a few weeks to pluck up the courage to send you that card after Cameron died. It felt a little—inappropriate after so long. I suppose I didn't really know what to say. I'm better with paint than words, but you already know that about me. I'm glad you're here now. And you haven't told me why. Judging from that parcel I'm guessing it's business, not pleasure."

"I hope it's a little of both." She'd forgotten how direct he was. It was refreshing.

He was different from Cameron in every way.

When Seth had ended their relationship she'd rebounded hard, turning to Cameron to heal the wound. She hadn't expected the relationship to last. She hadn't thought about the future, just the present. But then before she knew it, she and

Cameron were an item. A couple. Their relationship was intense, and their love of art equally intense. They'd spent their days wrapped up in each other, needing no one else. Gradually the group of friends had thinned out as people had moved on to different things.

Seth had moved away and that had been the end of it, or so she'd thought.

But now she knew that despite the years, the connection was still there. The friendship was there. She felt it, and she saw it in his eyes. She'd forgotten how it felt to be looked at as if she was something special, but that was the way he was looking at her now.

His gaze lingered on hers and then he gestured. "Show me what you've got."

The paintings. Of course. Her excuse for being here.

Now that the time had come, she felt a moment of doubt. What if she was wrong? What if Seth didn't see what she saw?

She stood up straighter.

If that was the case, then Lily would never have to know.

She put the paintings down on the long countertop that stretched half the length of the gallery. It was early, so the place was still closed, but she could see people milling in the streets outside, enjoying the sunshine, browsing in shops and galleries.

"The town is busier than it was when we were young."

"Everywhere is busier than when we were young. We have it all here now. A jazz festival, a film festival—you name it. It draws the crowds, although in winter the place is still mostly ours." He stepped next to her and slid on his glasses, silent as he studied the paintings she carefully spread out.

She held her breath and watched him. Waited.

After a moment he glanced at her.

"I can feel you looking at me. It's distracting."

"I'm trying to read your expression."

"I've been in this business for too long to let people read me. Even you." He turned back to the paintings. "You didn't paint these. I know your work."

"No, I didn't paint them." But she was surprised that he would remember her style so well, given how many years it had been since they'd seen each other.

She didn't tell him that she rarely painted now, that her garden was her outlet for creativity. Time for that later. For now, she wanted to focus on Lily.

He lifted one and propped it against the wall before standing back. "It's extraordinary, but you already know that, or you wouldn't have brought them here. Why me? You have contacts everywhere."

"Because your opinion matters to me. And you have flawless taste."

"You flatter me." He gave a faint smile. "Tell me about her. What's the story? Not art college."

"How do you know it's a 'her'?"

"Educated guesswork."

"The first thing to tell you is that she doesn't know I'm showing you these."

Seth's gaze was still on the paintings. "If they are all as good as this then she'll have to know soon enough. It would be a crime to store these in a dusty closet. What else?"

"She reminds me a little of myself at the same age."

He turned his head, and she could see that she had his attention.

"You mean oblivious to her own talent?"

Had she been oblivious? "I'd say unsure of her own talent."

"Now I'm really curious," he said. "Show me the rest."

They spent an hour, heads close, studying and observing, exchanging thoughts and the conversation energized her more than anything had over the past year.

Seth scribbled a few notes on a pad. "I'm old-school," he said when she remarked on it.

At some point Seth's assistant opened up the gallery and immediately people wandered in, drawn to the art and the sculptures, keen to take a small reminder of the Outer Cape home with them.

Seth greeted them politely but left his assistant to deal with sales and queries so that he could stay with Cecilia.

"When can I meet her? Your artist."

Cecilia felt a ripple of anxiety. She hadn't thought further than this moment. "I'll talk to her. See what she says." What would she say? Would Lily be upset that Cecilia had taken her paintings without her permission?

"I'll meet her anywhere that suits her." He gathered the paintings together. "And now tell me about you. What are you doing now?"

"I'm spending some time at the cottage."

"I meant right now."

"Oh—nothing." She felt herself flush. "I mean—I've done it. I came here."

"Good. Then have lunch with me."

"Lunch?" The invitation flustered her. It had been so many years since they'd seen each other. So many years since their lives had been intertwined.

"Why not? We can catch up properly. There's a new beach restaurant that serves the best lobster rolls. We can buy ourselves a picnic and eat it at the beach."

A beach picnic. As if they were teenagers and not two sensible adults in their seventies.

She felt as if she should say no, but why? Her life was her own, to be lived in the way she chose. There was no one she needed to consult. And when had she last had a picnic? When had she last done anything just for the simple joy of it? If she wanted to start exploring a new life, without Cameron, then this seemed like a good place to start.

"A picnic sounds fun. Can you spare the time? Leave this place?"

"I employ good staff." He nodded to his assistant and to a girl who was currently discussing a painting with a customer. "I'll be back later, Francine."

She was young. Cecilia judged her to be a little younger than Hannah and Lily.

"Francine is elegant. Incredible bone structure. Have you painted her?"

"No. These days I focus more on other people's work than my own. She's the daughter of an artist friend of mine. Her mother is French. They live in Paris part of the time, but they're over here for the summer and Francine is helping me out. She is the assistant of my assistant, which makes me feel important. Let me pack a bag and then we'll go. Does a picnic rug work for you or would you rather a chair?"

She laughed. "Forty years of yoga, Seth, some excellent health genes and a splash of good fortune. A rug is just fine."

They picked up fresh lobster rolls and artisan coffee and took them to the beach, finding a spot away from the crowds. Cecilia didn't mind the crowds. She'd always been a people watcher. Her mind wandered. "I painted this scene once. A couple on a rug reading, a child building a sandcastle, someone flying a kite."

"I remember it. A red ball in the foreground."

She turned to him, astonished. "You remember that?"

"I remember all of it. They were happy times."

They were happy times.

She felt the sun on her face and the sand under her feet and felt lighter than she had in years. As you traveled through life you picked up scars and damage and baggage, and the weight of it could be crushing. But here, she was transported back to those early days when life had been uncomplicated.

"I love it here."

"Me, too. I love it even more at five thirty in the morning when I have the place to myself." He spread the rug on the sand, and she slid off her shoes and settled down. For a moment she felt like her twenty-year-old self.

"That's the best time of day. The light. Salty air. The sound of the ocean."

They shared a look, a memory, and then he handed her a napkin.

"Here."

"Never saw you as the napkin type. Did Sonya finally domesticate you? Seth, who never intended to settle down? Seth, who didn't even want to plan what he was doing that evening, let alone for the next twenty years?" The gentle teasing came naturally, which surprised her because after so many years their relationship shouldn't feel this comfortable, surely?

"To an extent, she did." His smile was an acknowledgment of his past self. "People change, don't they? But I've been on my own for ten years. It's funny how doing your own laundry can motivate a guy. Also, you're wearing a pale blue dress and although my fashion expertise is limited, I'm guessing it isn't compatible with the contents of a lobster roll."

"It's not precious. Clothes are to be worn." She didn't say that she'd forgotten she even owned this dress. That she'd grabbed it when her mind was on Cameron and the Cape and secrets.

"It suits you. You look good, Ceci."

For a moment she was worried he might think she'd chosen her outfit especially for him, and then she realized that she had chosen it for him. And what was wrong with him knowing that?

"You and Sonya lived here the whole time?"

"We had a house in Brewster. A year after she died, I sold it and used the money to convert the space above the gallery into an apartment. Didn't see the point in rattling around in a house that was too big for me."

She empathized with the lost feeling that was so much a part of grief. "It's hard, I know."

"Yes. And moving was hard, but it turned out to be the right thing to do. In the house I always felt as if something was missing, which of course it was. *She* was. Moving to a new place has helped me feel—" he paused "—more 'me' I suppose. Less 'us.' It's not about replacing what went before, it's about adding to it. Creating something new. If that makes sense."

"It makes perfect sense." It was what she needed to do. Discover who she was without Cameron. "And you've done that."

He nodded. "Not that I'm suggesting it was easy. My girls have been wonderful. The grandchildren have helped. Try the roll," he said, handing it to her. "I can guarantee you won't have tasted anything better. You're still living in that enormous place outside Boston?"

"Yes. Ridiculous, I know." She spread the napkin across her lap.

"I don't think so. It's early days. Doesn't pay to make big decisions too quickly, or so everyone told me."

She'd made no decisions. Apart from removing Cameron's paintings from her bedroom, she'd basically frozen her life. But now it was time to change that.

She felt a new sense of purpose. She'd been trying to work out how to push Cameron into the background, but what she should have been doing was working out how to step into the foreground. This wasn't about him. It was about her.

She thought about the planner Todd had given her. At the time she'd thought she'd have no use for it, but now she wondered whether she might have been wrong about that.

She nibbled at the roll. It tasted just the way she remembered. Sweet and satisfying.

"This is good. While I'm savoring it, tell me everything about you."

"You go first, although I know some of it of course because you're pretty much a public figure. I bet you hated that."

The fact that he knew her that well, warmed her. "Tell me what you know, and I'll fill in the blanks."

"You had two children. Boy and a girl."

"Yes." She told him about Kristen and Winston, and about her grandchildren and he told her about his two girls, and their two girls.

"I'm surrounded by women."

She smiled. "And you love it."

"Yes. And they're good people. The girls helped me clear out the house and make a fresh start here, and they visit frequently. Helps that I live by the beach of course. The grandkids love that. They're still at the age where making sandcastles is fun. And now let's get to the real stuff. Why haven't you been back to the cottage before now?"

She could have skirted over the truth. She could have muttered something about being busy, about the time never being right, but this was Seth. Seth, who had once meant everything to her. Seth, who had known Cameron and who had known her in those early days.

And so she told him everything. She told him about the affair, about the almost divorce and the rocky times that had followed.

"Even good relationships go through rocky times, but an affair—" He broke off and muttered something under his breath. "I always knew you were too good for him. Did it happen more than once?"

"He told me that it didn't."

"And you believed him?"

"I don't know. I wanted to. We made it work for the children, and by the time the children left home we'd fallen into a rhythm. It's a funny thing. You think you know exactly what you'd do when faced with a certain situation, but when you find yourself in that situation it isn't always so clear."

"Who was she?"

"A girl who modeled for him. He said that it shouldn't have happened, but she was there—he was flattered by her attention. I believed that part. Cameron was insecure. He suffered from terrible imposter syndrome. Even when his work started to sell, when he became famous and sought-after—he never quite believed it. He needed constant reassurance that he was as good as people said he was. He didn't believe in himself." She almost said more, but she stopped herself. No matter how honest she could be with Seth, there were some confidences she wouldn't break. Some secrets that were best kept. "When he was in public, he was a different person. Confident. Once he was simply an artist alone with a canvas the insecurity would hit."

Seth finished his roll and wiped his fingers. "So that was his excuse for the affair. Insecurity." He looked at her steadily. "You deserved better."

"I thought so, too, which was why I asked him to leave." She told him about the accident. Those horrific nights in the hospital, and the aftermath. "Kristen always blamed me. Our relationship never really recovered, even when Cameron and I were truly back together. She was always Daddy's girl."

"Did she know about the affair?"

"No. She was too young, and as she grew up I could never bring myself to shatter the image she had of her father. They worked closely together. She worshipped him. And Cameron was an excellent father. Engaged and hands-on, even when his work was demanding. I could never fault him for that."

"And you didn't want to tarnish their view of him." He sighed. "You're a good person, Cecilia."

"Oh no, not at all. There were plenty of times when I wanted to tell her—I had a childish desire to see her affections transferred to me. But common sense held me back. Fortunately, because I don't think telling the truth would have been helpful for anyone."

"You don't think she suspected?"

"I don't think so."

"And how about now? You're not close?"

She thought about Kristen laughing with Jeff. Kristen and Theo. The fact that she hadn't known that Michael had been killed. "We see each other regularly. She's attentive. Dutiful I suppose. But we don't talk about anything deep. And that's my fault." She felt a stab of regret. She should have done better. She'd resolved to do better, which was why she'd finally called Kristen. And it had been a good conversation, even though Kristen had told her little about how she was feeling. It was obvious that she'd been surprised that her mother had called. Even more surprised that she was asking how she was. Cecilia had found a mention of Michael's accident on a local news site, so there had been no need to reveal that the information had come from Todd.

It was going to take a while to shift their relationship into a better place, but Cecilia was determined to try. She'd even thought about inviting her to the Cape for a few days, but in the end she hadn't. It would trigger too many questions that Cecilia wasn't ready to answer. And, anyway, it sounded as if Theo needed her.

Seth was watching her. "Why are you blaming yourself?"

"For the fact that Kristen and I aren't closer? I think for a while I resented her." Another thing she'd never said aloud before.

"For being a daddy's girl?"

"No. For being the reason I didn't divorce him. Believe me, I thought about it. Before the accident I was going to do it. But after the accident..." Remembering made her shudder. "It felt as if I would have been sacrificing her happiness for mine."

"So instead you sacrificed yours for her."

"It felt that way for a while. But in the end things settled down. I should probably be grateful to her for being the reason we stayed together. I don't regret it. Despite everything, we had a wonderful life together."

He was silent for a moment. "I often thought about you, and hoped you were happy."

She felt something shift inside her.

Lately, ever since the lawyer had presented her with the letter and the key to Dune Cottage, she'd been more focused on the bad than the good but talking to Seth had made her remember the good.

She and Cameron had shared a love of art of course, but their relationship had been based on so much more than that. They saw the world in a similar way, and they understood each other. It was Cameron who had insisted they buy Lapthorne Manor rather than a more convenient home in the city, because he'd known how much she would enjoy designing the gardens. In the end it had become a joint project, with Cameron using the results of her careful planting as inspiration for some of his work. She'd written a book on garden design, illustrated with her own photographs and some of Cameron's paintings. It was precisely because she'd loved him so much that the affair had been so devastating.

"We had many happy years. And a few unhappy ones. But isn't that life?"

"Yes, it is. And all you can do is enjoy the good parts and survive the bad," he said. "Why did you stop painting?"

"At first, because I was busy. Life was busy. And I discovered that I preferred to be creative in other ways. I have a beautiful garden. It brings me as much joy as anything I ever painted. I enjoy watching it change and evolve with the seasons."

He stared out to sea. "Sonya loved your book. She copied

a few ideas for our own garden, although it was nowhere near as grand of course."

"She did?"

"Yes. And when she was sick, the garden was the place where she found joy—" his voice was rough "—so I should probably thank you for that."

She felt a flash of sympathy, but the idea that she might have brought pleasure to someone else through her garden design pleased her. "Art doesn't only have to be the process of splashing paint on a canvas."

"That's true." He let go of her hand. "And Cameron went down the traditional route. I read the story of how his career took off—a local exhibition. He submitted one painting."

Cecilia felt her heart beat a little faster.

"That was all that was permitted. But he was lucky. The work caught the attention of a gallery director from Boston. The rest is history."

He gave her a long look. "Sounds almost too good to be true. The whole damned fairy tale."

"Like many things in life there was an element of luck involved. Cameron was aware of that. He caught a break, but he was careful not to waste it. He worked it hard."

"You mean that if he hadn't had a painting that he could submit—"

"He wouldn't have been considered. Exactly. He made the most of an opportunity." She wiped her fingers on the napkin.

"Tell me more about those early paintings. How did he choose just one? When we knew each other, Cameron was all over the place. Full of doubt. He used to destroy canvases all the time. Remember the painting he threw into the ocean?"

"I remember." She'd rescued it, but it had been too late.

It wasn't the first or last time he'd destroyed a painting he wasn't happy with.

"But he had a painting he was happy with, ready to go. That was lucky." Seth opened a bottle of sparkling water and poured some into a cup. "Where is that painting now?"

She took the cup from him. "I expect it was sold. I lose track. It seems so long ago now. Why did you give up painting?"

"My father had a stroke and needed help running the gallery. I stepped in to help and discovered I enjoyed it. I painted a little, but the truth is I preferred working with artists to being one myself. I don't get anywhere near the level of excitement gazing at my own canvas that I do gazing at someone else's." He poured water into his own cup. "So, if your marriage settled down again, why didn't you come back to the cottage when it was such a special place for you both?"

"I think precisely because it was a special place. It felt tainted. We were trying to move on, and I associated the cottage with her. With betrayal and lies. I wanted him to sell it. He promised me he had."

"Given that the cottage is still there and you're staying in it, I'm assuming he didn't. And in the spirit of honesty, I must confess that in my opinion selling something so special would have been a terrible thing."

"At the time the terrible thing was discovering that he hadn't. That he'd lied to me again. Rebuilding the trust after the affair wasn't easy. This felt like another betrayal."

"I can imagine." He drank the water. "When did you find out?"

"After he died." She thought back to the day the lawyer had given her the envelope. "He left me a note and a key."

Seth gave a low whistle. "He kept it? Why?"

"Obviously my first thought was that he was using it as some sort of love nest, but I've discovered since that the cottage has never been used. No one has stayed there."

"But he had it maintained."

"Yes. For all those years."

He put his cup down. "What do your family think?"

"They don't know. No one knows about my connection to the cottage, apart from the lawyer and now Lily, who was caretaking the place."

"Lily is your artist?"

"How did you guess that?"

"Your protective tone. Why didn't you tell your family?"

"They didn't know the cottage existed, and it would have been impossible to tell them about it without revealing parts of our relationship history that I didn't want to reveal. I thought I could come back without anyone knowing. But I didn't really think it through. It was naive of me to think I could hide it." She sighed. "Yesterday, my grandson showed up to check on me. He tracked my phone, which was a possibility that hadn't occurred to me."

"Why would he feel the need to check on you?"

"Because he was concerned. I disappeared from my own party, you see. Or rather, I didn't exactly disappear as much as leave. But I told no one where I was going."

"You wanted to come here on your own."

"Exactly. I knew that if I told them about this place, someone would insist on being with me and this was something I had to do by myself. I didn't know how I'd feel."

"And how did you feel?"

She thought about the smashed frames. The broken glass.

"Emotional. I was angry. I came here intending to do what Cameron should have done—sell the place."

"And now?"

"Now?" She took a sip of water and stared out to sea. "Now I don't know. I was angry, but when I discovered no one had used it, I felt better. I don't understand why he didn't tell me about it, but I do know he wasn't using it as a place to entertain women. Knowing that changed the way I felt. It helped. Talking to you has helped, too. You've made me remember things that perhaps I'd forgotten. Talking to you has given me some clarity."

She'd been determined to sell the cottage, but now she wasn't sure. She felt a tug of regret. They'd had happy times there. Was that why Cameron had been unable to sell it?

"You don't need to decide right away, surely? There's no hurry." He took her hand again and she felt a flush of warmth as she stared down at their locked fingers.

"It's been years, Seth."

"So? A friendship isn't measured by time, it's measured by depth of feeling. My feelings for you haven't changed." He tightened his grip on her hand. "Have dinner with me tonight."

"We've just had lunch."

"So? You'll be hungry again by dinnertime."

"That isn't what I meant."

"I know that wasn't what you meant. Now you're here, I don't want you to disappear again back to Boston. I want to spend time with you."

She gently removed her hand from his. She hadn't given much thought to how long she'd be staying. She was taking it day by day.

"I'm not disappearing yet, but if you're saying what I think you're saying, then it's—too soon, Seth."

He smiled. "I'm seventy-six, Ceci. There is no such thing as too soon, only too late. And I don't want to leave it too late. Neither do you. And it's not as if this is a new relationship. Two dates in one day are perfectly acceptable when two people have known each other for as long as we have." As always, he made her laugh.

"You always were impossible to argue with. And sure of yourself."

"About some things. Not about others. Dinner. Your place. I'll bring the wine. I'll bring the food, too, if that helps sway the odds in my favor."

She thought about Lily. Todd. The explanations. "You're forgetting I have houseguests." And she was still adjusting to that. She'd come to the cottage expecting to be alone and suddenly she was sharing the space with two people. But it was hard to feel sorry about that when they were both such delightful people.

He nodded. "In that case I'll cook. Come and see my apartment."

It was tempting. "Not tonight."

"Tomorrow, then."

She laughed. "Do you ever give up, Seth?"

"I did that once, and I've always regretted it. It's not going to happen again."

She felt something stir inside her and she wasn't sure if it was fear or excitement. Maybe a mixture of both. What did this mean? Where would it lead? He'd broken her heart once before.

She almost laughed at herself. She should be long past the stage of guarding her heart, surely?

"Not tomorrow, but soon." She immediately felt nervous. "What am I going to say to Lily and Todd?"

He laughed. "I think you're past the age of making excuses for being out late at night."

"Maybe."

But an explanation would be expected, she knew that.

And that could be awkward. Even more awkward would be explaining to Lily what she'd done with her paintings.

14

Lily

"You showed him my paintings? Without telling me?" Lily put her coffee mug down and stared at Cecilia. It was horrifying to think of her work being assessed by a stranger. Like stripping naked and walking into a crowded shopping mall. She wished now she hadn't shown them to Cecilia. It was so personal. Painting was her joy and her escape. She didn't want that ruined by someone trampling all over it and telling her she had no talent.

"I thought if I told you, you'd be anxious. Also, you would have tried to talk me out of it and then I would have found myself being in the difficult position of going against your wishes. Easier to beg for forgiveness. He wants to meet you." Cecilia took a jug from the cabinet and filled it with water. "He wants to see more. This is good, Lily. An opportunity. Try not to look as if you're being tortured."

"It's terrifying."

"It shouldn't be. He's very excited about your work."

A stranger was excited about her work. A stranger who owned a gallery.

Lily felt something inside her lift, but she was afraid to hope.

"But you know this guy. He's a friend, so he would say that. He's doing you a favor." She eyed the bunch of cheerful sunflowers that had arrived an hour before. They'd been accompanied by a note, which Cecilia had read with a quiet smile and then promptly slipped into the pocket of her linen dress.

Lily's brain was buzzing with questions but felt it would be intrusive to ask them.

Cecilia arranged the flowers in the jug, snipping stems and moving them around until she was satisfied. "I've known him for a long time, although we haven't seen each other for many years."

Lily noticed that Cecilia seemed different. Calmer. Softer. As if she'd just returned from a long walk in the country or a spa day. Was that Seth's influence? The flowers?

"And you reconnected. That's nice. That flower arrangement is perfect. You could put them on the table on the porch and paint them."

"That's exactly where I'm going to put them, but you're the one who is going to paint them." Cecilia carried the jug outside and placed it carefully in the center of the table.

The deck was bathed in sunlight, the ocean sparkling under a cloudless blue sky.

Todd was on his knees, fixing one of the planks on the porch. He looked up as they came out.

"Nice flowers. Who is your admirer, Lily?" He wiped his brow with his forearm and stood up.

"Not me. No admirers." Her love life was moribund, but she'd made her peace with that. At least she thought she had until he'd shown up. "These were sent to your grandmother."

And Cecilia was smiling in a way Lily hadn't seen her smile before. As if everything was right with the world.

Todd obviously noticed it, too.

"Nanna?" He poured himself a glass of lemonade from the jug on the table. "Tell us everything. The more detail the better as Lily and I are both going through a fallow phase on the romance front. We need some vicarious action."

Lily's heart thudded. She would have preferred some real action, but since the only man she was interested in wasn't interested in her she was going to have to settle for vicarious. And as for Todd, she'd assumed that someone whose relationship had just ended would be more upset, but he didn't seem upset. She kept wondering what that meant, but wondering had a nasty habit of leading to hope, so she tried to shut it down.

Instead, she thought about what Cecilia had just told her about her friend admiring her paintings. The fact that he wanted to see more was terrifying and exhilarating at the same time.

"Nothing to tell." Cecilia made a final adjustment to the flowers. "There. That's better."

"Nanna!"

"What? He's an old friend, that's all. No one you know."

Todd wasn't about to give up. "And he lives here?"

"He owns a gallery in town. Took it over from his father. It's been many years since I saw him. Lily's paintings gave me the excuse to make contact again. I probably shouldn't have needed an excuse, which just goes to prove that even

someone of my mature years can still feel insecure and unsure."

If she'd felt unsure, Lily thought, then that must mean
she cared.

"It's good that someone has finally recognized Lily's talent. That's great. Long overdue." Todd rested his hip on the
edge of the table. "And now tell us more about this guy. You
said it has been years since you saw him. How many years?"

Cecilia raised her eyebrows. "Is this an interrogation?"

"That depends on whether you're hiding something juicy."

Lily was only half listening. She was still absorbing the
news that Cecilia had shown her paintings to someone who
owned a gallery. And that Todd thought she had talent.

Cecilia paused. "I knew him before I met your grandfather."

"Knew?" Todd folded his arms and waited. "An old boyfriend? Nanna Lapthorne, you've never talked about that
time in your life. This is a story I need to hear."

"You might need to hear it, but you're not going to hear
it. How is my porch? Can you fix it?"

"Easily. But first you need to give me details. No censor-
ship allowed. What's his name?"

"His name," Cecilia said, "is Seth. Now, will you finish
the boards? Because if I trip and break a hip, I'll be blaming you."

"I'll have it finished by tonight," Todd said. "Tomorrow
I will start on the window frames."

"What's wrong with the window frames?"

"Some of them are rotten. Don't worry. I can fix it, but I
work faster if my head isn't full of questions. It affects my
concentration. Is Seth married?"

Lily couldn't help smiling. He was asking all the questions she would have wanted to ask if good manners hadn't held her back.

Cecilia sighed. "If I asked you these questions, you'd be telling me to mind my own business."

"Not true. I'll answer any question you ask. Try me."

"All right." Cecilia narrowed her eyes. "What happened with Amelie?"

"Ah. Amelie. I realized I made a mistake." Todd answered without hesitation. "I'm making that sound as if it was a sudden revelation. It wasn't. I knew it was a mistake from the beginning."

"If that's the case, why did you propose?"

Lily held her breath, waiting to hear the answer to that.

Todd levered himself away from the table and pulled out a chair. "If it's confession time, then I need to be sitting. And the answer is, I didn't."

"You didn't propose to her?"

"No. She proposed to me." His eyes had lost the laughter, and Lily saw for the first time that under the smile and his easy manner he looked tired. As if he hadn't been sleeping well.

Cecilia sat down, too. "She proposed to you? How very modern."

"Yes. And at this point I should add that I have no problem with it in principle. But she chose to do it in public. With no warning." He tapped his fingers on the table, a tense rhythmic drumming. "It was her birthday. Fifty of her friends, looking on, waiting. Primed. Phones at the ready to record the moment."

Fifty friends? Lily tried to imagine it. She didn't have fifty friends. How did one even stay in touch with fifty people? But that was Amelie. She collected people like trophies as if the number of contacts in her phone was somehow a measure of her worth.

"She'd told her friends what she was going to do?" Cecilia looked astounded. "Why?"

"It was a filmable moment. I'm lucky she didn't live stream it."

"And because there was an audience, you said yes. Because you're you, of course."

"I didn't want to humiliate her," Todd said. "It was the wrong decision. I realized that pretty quickly, but in that single second, with no warning that it was going to happen, I couldn't think clearly. I intended to put it right before we even left the place, but it snowballed. I couldn't get near her for her friends screaming and hugging her. The right moment just didn't present itself."

Cecilia ran her fingers across her forehead. "How did she propose? Did she expect you to go shopping for a ring?"

"She already had a ring. She had everything covered. It was her grandmother's. She had it sized and gave it to me to give to her."

"Goodness. That doesn't sound like my dream proposal." Cecilia sat up straighter. "What do you think, Lily?"

Lily blinked. "I haven't ever thought about it. I wouldn't want it to be public, I know that. A proposal should be something intimate, surely. Something between two people." Her cheeks were hot enough to fry an egg and she saw Todd's gaze linger on her face as if he was trying to figure something out.

She felt a stab of acute longing and something else. Something much more complicated, and at the same time she felt a thrill of relief.

Todd hadn't proposed to Amelie.

He hadn't asked her to marry him.

All those hashtags, #soulmate #manofmydreams #true-love, had been wishful thinking on Amelie's part.

"She proposed and provided you with a ring to give her. She's obviously a woman who knows what she wants and isn't afraid to go after it," Cecilia said.

Lily thought about the Amelie she knew. Top of the class in everything. Captain of every team. A winner. "It probably didn't occur to her that you wouldn't be feeling the same way." In her experience, Amelie focused on her own feelings, not the feelings of others. And what Amelie wanted, Amelie always got.

But not Todd.

She didn't have Todd.

"Or maybe," Cecilia said, "she knew you were too much of a gentleman to turn her down. She knew that in the end your ingrained kindness and decency would ensure that you went along with it."

Lily thought about that.

And then what? A miserable marriage and a divorce? You couldn't force love, could you?

"I was cowardly." Todd topped up his glass. "I should have said no right away. I should have said that it wasn't the time or the place, but I was taken by surprise. I didn't want to humiliate her. I ended up doing that anyway, and by the time I found the words and the guts to end what never should have begun, she'd already picked a date and found a venue for the wedding."

Knowing Amelie as she did, Lily could easily picture it.

She could just imagine how much pressure Amelie had put on him.

But in the end, he'd resisted.

"She'd found a venue after just a week?" Cecilia sounded astonished. "Not a woman to hang around."

"At last count my mother had twenty voice mails from her mother. Probably a good thing you steered clear of your party. She turned up and threw champagne over me."

Cecilia gave a faint smile. "I saw that."

"You did?"

"I was in the window, looking at the gardens."

"And you didn't come and rescue me?"

Cecilia's smile widened. "You've always been able to take care of yourself, Todd. And having your grandmother riding to your rescue probably wouldn't have enhanced your reputation. Also, I had no idea what was going on and I've made a point of never interfering in other people's relationships. Your Amelie seems like a young woman who likes to live out the big life moments in front of an audience."

"Not my Amelie. And as I'm a person who likes a laid-back lifestyle, I think you can see we weren't a match made in heaven."

Lily said nothing. All she could think was that Todd hadn't proposed to Amelie. Todd hadn't even wanted to marry Amelie.

And that didn't really change anything of course, but somehow it made her feel better.

"So now it's your turn, Nanna." Todd removed his sunglasses and leaned forward. "Seth."

"Seth." Cecilia breathed the name like a sigh. "He was my first boyfriend. I was here for the season, with two girlfriends. There were a bunch of artists living here and we all spent time together. We hung out on the beach—painted, swam, ate, drank, talked about everything."

"You met Seth before you met my grandfather?"

"Yes. We arrived in spring, and Cameron appeared on the scene late in the summer." Cecilia paused. "Life was delightfully uncomplicated. We came from all over, but Seth was local. His father owned a gallery. He was influential in the art world, but I didn't know that then. We didn't care about things like that. We didn't think about the future. We lived for the day. None of us thought ahead. It was self-indulgent, but at the time we didn't see it like that."

Lily could picture it easily. Long summer days and lazy summer nights. Milky dawn mornings and rose gold sunsets. A group of young people with no commitments and no responsibility.

She felt a twinge of envy. She'd never experienced that carefree lightness. From the moment she'd moved to the exclusive school her parents had chosen for her, she'd felt the weight of expectation. Occasionally she'd felt as if she was drowning, and that the weight of those expectations was going to pull her right to the bottom.

Todd lounged back in his chair, his attention on his grandmother. "You were together. You and Seth."

"We were together for that whole summer." Cecilia gazed out across the ocean and Lily wondered which part of that time she was remembering.

Todd was obviously wondering that, too. "What happened?"

"What happened?" Cecilia turned to look at him. "We got a little too serious a little too quickly. Seth didn't want that kind of relationship. He ended it. And Cameron and I became involved." She said it as if that short statement should have explained everything, but of course it didn't.

"He broke your heart."

There was a long silence. "Yes." Cecilia gave a sad smile. "And that's when I started spending time with Cameron."

"Whoa." Todd sat back in his chair. "So you and my grandfather—major rebound relationship."

"I suppose it was, yes. At least, at first. But then it deepened to something more. You're going to ask me what it was about him, and I'm going to struggle to find the words to describe it. He was handsome and charming of course, but it was so much more than that. He had a fire inside him that drew me. At the time I saw it as passion. It was only much later that I understood that the fire was insecurity. That part of the reason he strived was to prove to people that he was good enough."

Todd shook his head, as if he was trying to reconcile this version of his grandfather with the version he knew. "You fell in love."

"Yes. Deeply in love. I was willing to sacrifice anyone and anything so that we could be together. I imagined us living this life forever. I didn't imagine anything would ever change. I had unrealistic expectations of relationships I think." She turned pink. "I can't believe I just said that aloud to my grandson."

"I'm pleased you did. I want to understand," Todd said. "You don't have to sugarcoat things for me. I'm old enough to know that all relationships, even good ones, can be complicated."

"Still, he was your grandfather. And I did love him very much. I don't want you to think I didn't. Many relationships hit bad patches and of course there are some circumstances when it's probably best to walk away, but the danger of giving up is that you miss the good. And there was so much good. The truth is our years together were extraordinary. I was lucky to have him in my life. Talking to Seth reminded me of that. And I needed reminding." She paused. "And Cameron was lucky to have me. And he knew that."

Todd nodded. "Were he and Seth friends?"

"They knew each other, but friends? No." Cecilia shook her head. "That was partly because of me of course, but also because they were so different. Seth was everything Cameron aspired to be. Confident, sure of himself. He didn't have Cameron's burning need to prove himself to everyone."

"If Seth hadn't ended it, do you think you would have stayed together?"

Cecilia was silent for a long moment. "I don't think so. Not back then. We wanted different things. We were different people. The person I was then needed Cameron. I admired his ambition. I respected his desire to be the very best he could be."

Lily swatted an insect away from her arm. "And this is the first time you've seen Seth in ages?"

"Yes. After all this time it felt like something I needed to do. I have no idea why. Maybe I wouldn't have done it if I hadn't been trying to work out who I could show your paintings to."

"Was it difficult?"

"The idea of it was more difficult than the reality. I wasn't sure what his response would be, but he was just Seth. In some ways he hadn't changed at all." Cecilia gave a half laugh. "But of course we both have. None of us can stay the same person we were at twenty. Perhaps it's more accurate to say we're a different version of ourselves."

Lily was intrigued. "You were gone all day."

"We went for a picnic on the beach. It was delightful."

Todd frowned. "Should Lily and I be worried? He broke

your heart once before. Should we be asking him his intentions?"

Cecilia smiled. "You should not. I can handle this."

"In that case you should invite him over," Todd said. "Lily and I can occupy ourselves somewhere. We will take a long walk on the beach. Or we can go out for a meal and give you the run of the place."

Lily nodded. "Definitely. Or we could just hide in the closet. Not make a sound."

Todd grinned and Cecilia turned pink.

"I don't know what you're both thinking, but—"

"We're thinking that you deserve some fun and happiness, Nanna." Todd eyed the flowers. "Did he used to come to the cottage?"

"No. This was our place. Cameron and mine. In the early days of our relationship, we lived here. And it was a blissful, perfect time." Cecilia was distracted. "Then Cameron was discovered and our lives changed. Suddenly he was in demand. And as his career took off, I became pregnant. After the children arrived, we used this place as a weekend escape occasionally."

"But then you stopped coming here altogether." Todd frowned. "I suppose you were busy."

"We were busy, but that wasn't why I didn't come here." Cecilia paused. "The place ceased to be special."

There was a long silence.

Lily caught Todd's eye.

She sensed they were close to getting an answer to the question that had been nagging at her since before Cecilia had arrived at the cottage that night. Why had such a special place been empty for so long?

Cecilia put her hands on the table. "Cameron had an affair, you see." Her voice shook slightly and the look she gave them was uncertain, as if she wasn't quite sure that she was doing the right thing by telling them. "Here. In our special place. In the bed that had been ours alone. And after that it ceased to be special. I never came here again."

There was a tense silence.

"Nanna—" Todd reached across the table and took her hand.

"It was hard." Cecilia took a deep breath. "And I can't believe I just told you that. Your mother doesn't know, and you must never tell her."

"Why?"

"Because she simply adored her father. He could do no wrong in her eyes and I don't want to be the one to change that, particularly now when it's all in the past anyway. All she has is her memories. She has a right to keep those."

It seemed from Todd's expression that he didn't agree, but he nodded anyway. "Whatever you want, Nanna. I'll respect whatever you decide. Did my grandfather come back here?"

"I don't know. For many months our relationship hovered on the brink. I couldn't see past the betrayal. If I hadn't loved him so much it wouldn't have hurt so badly but I did love him, and the hurt was almost unbearable."

Love, Lily thought. *Who needs it?*

"But you stayed together."

"We did. And I don't regret that. But for me the affair changed something. Before that I'd loved him totally. Unreservedly. But the affair took something away that never came back. If you break a pot there will always be a fracture line, even if you manage to glue it together again. There will always be that area of weakness. And I'm not sorry we stayed together, and I don't regret the life we had—but it wasn't the life it might have been."

She glanced back at the cottage. "It was two losses. I lost him, and I lost this place that was very special to me. I remember wishing he'd had his affair in a faceless corporate hotel somewhere. Anywhere but here. He promised me he'd sold it but after he died I discovered he hadn't. Another lie. At first I assumed he'd been using it, but then you told me no one had stayed here—" she glanced at Lily "—and I realized that whatever his reason for keeping it, it wasn't that."

"Maybe he thought that one day you might come back."

"He knew I wouldn't. Any mention of the place made me think of her. The cottage is forever associated with betrayal for me. I don't want to feel that way, but I do."

Lily felt her heart ache. "Perhaps he didn't sell it, because he couldn't. Because the place meant as much to him as it did to you." She thought about it. "What if we were to get away from the past altogether? What if we could make it feel different? I mean *really* different, not just a few pots and a bookcase."

"Different how?"

"This was your place, the two of you. It reminds you of your relationship. But what if we make it *your* place. What if it's all about you?"

Cecilia's eyes shimmered. "You're kind, but a coat of paint isn't going to erase the past."

"I think Lily is intending to give the place much more than a coat of paint, Nanna." Todd was on his feet, fingers in his hair. "I think it's a brilliant idea. Let's do a walk-through."

"A walk-through?"

"See the place with fresh eyes. Decide what could be done."

"But—"

"If you don't like our ideas, you can say so. The position is spectacular, but the cottage is tired. It hasn't changed at all, has it? So let's change it." He walked back into the living room and Lily followed.

She was excited that he agreed with her idea, but unsure how to proceed.

She glanced over her shoulder, but Cecilia was still standing on the porch looking at the ocean.

"Maybe we're wrong to push her."

"We're not wrong. You saw what I saw. You saw how much she once loved this place." Todd was restless, his gaze skimming over the building.

Lily thought about the paintings. "We need to make it feel different. But how?" She was starting to think she'd been a bit ambitious suggesting it. Cecilia was right that a coat of paint wasn't going to be enough. "The walls look horribly bare. I suppose we could find more paintings. Different paintings."

"Not paintings." Todd tilted his head, measuring the distance to the ceiling. "Bookshelves."

"Bookshelves?"

"Floor to ceiling. It will transform the place." He walked the length of the room and back again, muttering to himself. He seemed to have forgotten she was there.

Lily cleared her throat and he turned.

"What?"

"Just reminding you I exist, that's all."

He gave a funny half smile. "I know you exist, Lily. I'm hardly likely to forget." His gaze lingered on hers for a moment and her heart started to beat a little harder and faster.

"You're staring."

"I was just wondering something."

She was wondering something, too. She was wondering whether she should just tell him how she felt. Get it out there, because the strain of holding it in, of watching herself all the time, checking she wasn't giving anything away, was exhausting. Her feelings for him seemed to be growing by the day and she wasn't sure how much longer she'd be able to keep her love for him a secret. Maybe she should just kiss him, right here, right now.

It wouldn't be the first time, although he'd never mentioned it since.

It had been the summer before, at a party full of people who were mostly drunk. Lily had danced for a while, then retreated to a corner to worry about an exam she had in two days.

She'd been about to leave the party when Todd had arrived with a couple of friends.

He'd leaned in to kiss her hello as he had a hundred times before, except that this time they were jostled by the crowd and then somehow, and she could never figure out exactly how it had happened, they were kissing. Not polite greeting kissing. But properly kissing. Mouths locked together, hearts pounding. And having started, she couldn't stop. Or maybe she could have done, but she hadn't wanted to. Why would she want to? The kiss was the best thing that had ever happened to her, the gentle touch of his fingers against her cheek the best thing she'd ever felt. And then one of his friends had dragged him away and she'd stood for a moment, dazed, wondering what had just happened.

He'd never mentioned it, and so neither had she.

But that didn't mean she'd forgotten.

She tugged herself back to the present and realized he was still staring.

"What?" *What, what, what*…she sounded like a parrot. "You said you were wondering something?"

"How are your sewing skills?"

"My—sewing skills?" Of all the things she'd hoped he might say, that hadn't made the list.

"Yes. This sofa is the focal point of the room. It needs to change."

Lily tried her hardest to concentrate on the sofa. "Right."

"Don't waste time covering it." Cecilia joined them in the room. "It has been here for decades. Those cushions bear the shape of everyone who has ever sat on them and it's beyond resurrection. If we're going to do this, then we're going to do it. We'll change the sofa."

Lily saw Todd wrestle with his natural aversion to throwing things out.

"It's lumpy and horrid," she said helpfully. "It's the most uncomfortable sofa I have ever sat on."

"That's true. It has more humps than a camel. Okay then—" He looked at the kitchen. "Those cabinets—"

"Todd Buckingham, you are not ripping out my kitchen." Cecilia folded her arms, ready to do battle but Todd shook his head.

"I'm not ripping anything out. Unlike the sofa, those cabinets are good quality. They're wood. I'm going to sand them down, and Lily is going to paint them."

She was? Lily was still dealing with the fact that Cecilia had called it "my" kitchen. Her use of the possessive pronoun had to be a good sign, surely?

"And when are you planning on doing all this work? You're installing a kitchen in Provincetown."

"They called this morning and put it on hold. Illness in the family. These things happen. Sometimes it's frustrating, and sometimes it's fortuitous. This time it's the second. I'm free for the next month. I'll fix up the cottage, if that's what you'd like. Can I take a look upstairs?"

When he set his mind to something he was a bit like a bulldozer, Lily thought.

"Lily has a job," Cecilia said as she followed him up the stairs. "She won't have the time to help you."

"She can help me after work." Todd walked into the second bedroom, where Cecilia was sleeping. "I see why you thought that bookshelf would look good in here, Lily. And if it's my room, I'm going to need bookshelves."

Cecilia followed him into the room. "The master is your room."

"By the time Lily and I have finished with it, you're going to be kicking me out and claiming it as your own," Todd predicted. "I've already decided what to do with the master. Do you want to take a look with me and hear my plans?"

"No. Just do what you feel is right." Cecilia left the room so hastily she knocked her arm on the doorframe.

She can't even bear to go in there, Lily thought. If there was a room they needed to completely transform, it was that one. She was determined to do just that.

Todd caught Lily's eye and then nodded. "Whatever we want. Great. I love it when a client gives me free rein."

"And on the subject of clients, if you're going to do this, then I insist on paying you," Cecilia said. "You can't work for nothing."

"If you let me stay here for a few weeks and feed me, that

will be payment. I fancy a few weeks by the sea. It will be relaxing. I can work the way I want to work and not have to deal with a fussy client on a daily basis." Todd walked past her and headed up to the attic room that was Lily's.

Lily and Cecilia followed.

"This is a nice room." He peered out of the skylight and then looked back at the twin beds, which were tucked under the sloping roof on either side of the room. "We could remove the bed on one side and replace it with a rollaway that tucks under the other one. Gives more flexibility. What do you think?"

"I'm not going to be sleeping here," Cecilia said. "I don't mind what you do."

"Good. Because once we agree on the changes in principle, you won't go into the rooms until they're done. It's going to be a surprise so that you get the full effect."

Cecilia seemed torn between amusement and exasperation. "And where am I supposed to stay while you're remodeling my kitchen and living room?"

Lily noticed that she was no longer talking about rushing back to Boston. Did Seth have something to do with that?

Todd was obviously wondering the same thing. "Maybe Seth has a spare room?" He dug the tape measure out of his pocket and winked at his grandmother, who shook her head.

"You're trouble, Todd Buckingham."

Lily didn't disagree with that assessment.

Todd had just announced that he would be hanging around for the summer.

She and Todd would be working on the cottage together. And in the meantime, Cecilia would be seeing more of Seth. Seth, who liked her paintings. Seth, who wanted to meet her and talk to her.

She wasn't sure which was the most challenging—the idea of meeting Seth, or the idea of hanging out with Todd without revealing how she felt.

15

Cecilia

She stood at the rear entrance to the gallery. In one hand she held a bottle of chilled white wine, and in the other a box of handmade Belgian chocolates.

She felt like a teenager on a first date and that feeling didn't leave her when Seth opened the door.

He was wearing a lightweight shirt the same shade of blue as his eyes, and a pair of chinos. "You're right on time."

"Was I supposed to be fashionably late?"

"No. We're definitely too old for those sorts of games."

"Good, because Lily and Todd have been hammering and filling my cottage with paint for the past few days. They're determined to give the place a new look. My head is pounding from the noise, and I needed to escape before I was fumigated. Also, I no longer have access to the coffeepot."

"My coffeepot is your coffeepot." He opened the door

wider. "I hope I'm going to be given a tour when it's finished."

"You will. Until then, I'm looking forward to a tour of your home." She'd walked past the gallery so many times in the past and never given any thought as to what was above it. "I'm intrigued." She handed him her gifts and he took them with a smile.

"Thank you. You didn't have to bring anything. Come in." He stood aside to let her pass and she climbed the staircase that led to the apartment upstairs.

At the top it took her a moment to catch her breath, and not just because of the stairs.

"Oh, Seth—"

"Spectacular, don't you think? It's one of the best locations around here and people are always surprised to see it because they don't know it's here." He put the wine and chocolates down on the side and joined her in front of the expanse of glass that overlooked the ocean and the harbor. "I'm close to beaches, great restaurants, and my commute to work is less than a minute. Doesn't get better than this."

"The position is good, you're right, but the space—" She looked up at the vaulted ceiling and then at the flood of light through the glass. "I can see why you fell in love with it."

"It didn't look anything like this when I first saw it. It was a wreck when I bought it. It had been sadly neglected. I wasn't in too great a state myself, so let's just say this apartment mirrored my own journey. I like to think we healed each other."

They were both trying to move on, she thought. Leave the past behind and keep moving.

Seth was farther down that path than she was, but looking at him now gave her hope. She'd been struggling to form a new life for herself without Cameron, but perhaps she needed to take inspiration from Seth and look beyond her current life. She'd been determined not to sell Lapthorne Manor, but now she was rethinking that. Yes, she loved her garden and had put countless hours into developing it into what it was today, but staying there kept her firmly stuck in her old life. She needed a change that was more than simply removing a few paintings from the walls.

She glanced around Seth's home. "Who did the work? Local contractor?"

"I did it myself. Took me more time than I care to admit, and I did call for help when the roof sprang a leak."

"You did it?" Astonished, she turned to look at him. "I'm impressed."

"Don't be. The process was messy and full of mistakes, but there was no one but me to worry or care and I got there in the end. It was good for me. It's hard to feel sorry for yourself when you're trying to figure out how to fix the mess you just made. This room was in fact three rooms when I moved in. But I'm not a lover of small spaces."

"That's because you're tall."

The three rooms had been turned into one long room, which had been cleverly designed to give a living space with a comfortable seating area, a dining area and an open-plan kitchen. There was an abundance of white, with large canvases on the wall adding an explosion of color.

Cecilia crossed the room to take a closer look. "These paintings are striking. They're yours, aren't they?"

He laughed. "How did you guess?"

"I didn't guess. I recognize your work. Bold use of color. Abstract shapes, although—" She narrowed her eyes. "Yachts on the ocean?"

"You always did have a good eye for things."

"It's perfect. I thought you said you didn't paint anymore?"

"I don't usually, but the building costs escalated. I didn't want to cut corners on the construction, so I cut corners on the art and did it myself. Come and see the bedrooms."

She followed him through a doorway into the master bedroom.

It had windows on two sides and a bathroom with a skylight.

There were two further bedrooms, one with bunk beds piled with soft toys.

"For my grandchildren." He picked up a stuffed bunny that had fallen onto the floor and added it to the pile. "They love staying, and I love having them. Life seems simple when you're with young children. They live their lives in the present. All they think about is the next game, the next meal."

She felt a twinge of nostalgia, remembering her grandchildren as toddlers. She'd been busy for a lot of the time. The support act to Cameron's star turn. She'd loved spending time with them, but it had always felt fleeting. She'd done better when they were older, particularly with Todd. She'd worried that Hannah had sucked up all the oxygen in her household and had made a point of spending time with Todd so that she could get to know him outside the confines of his family. She'd discovered a smart, loyal and creative individual who had inherited a dose of his grandfather's artistic talent. He'd loved to make things, and over one summer he'd made her a birdhouse and a box for her garden tools.

Theo and Kristen had wanted him to be a doctor, and Cecilia had felt exasperated that they couldn't see how wrong that would be for him. Fortunately Todd, although not as vocal as his sister, was stubborn. He'd been determined not to be pushed down a route he didn't want to take. Through it all, Cecilia had offered him support, encouragement and a nonjudgmental listening ear. She suspected it was one of the reasons they were close.

Seth put his hand on her shoulder. "I've made you sad."

"No." For the first time in ages, she didn't feel sad. "You just made me think, that's all. I've been thinking a lot lately. Too much, I suspect."

"That happens when you lose someone. You have to recalibrate, and sometimes that means looking back."

"Yes." That was what she was doing. Recalibrating.

"Come and see the real reason I bought this place." He took her hand and led her toward a door at the end of a light-filled corridor.

Holding his hand felt so natural that she didn't consider pulling away. It felt right, as if Seth was the last piece of a jigsaw puzzle she'd been trying to complete.

And it occurred to her that the very best part of coming back to this part of the Cape was meeting him again. She hadn't expected that, which just proved that life could always surprise you.

"I can already understand why you bought this place."

"There's more. I've saved the best until last."

Enjoying herself, she stepped through the door he'd opened and straight onto a wide, spacious deck.

The breeze cooled her skin and she walked to the edge of the terrace. She stared across the rooftops to the shoreline, her attention caught by the yachts clustered in the bay.

The breeze lifted a few strands of her hair, and she tasted salt and sea.

"It's paradise."

"I think so. It's not Dune Cottage but it has its own special charm." He still had his arm on her waist. "This is the best reading spot. The best spot to drink the first coffee of the day. The best place to linger with an evening drink. Sunrise and sunset. You see it all from here."

They stood for a moment in companionable silence and then he drew away.

"Do you remember our trip to Florence?"

She hadn't thought of it for years. "You're thinking of the roof terrace on top of the building where we stayed. The room we rented overheated so badly we spent most of our time outdoors." Her mind slid back in time. "Italian coffee. The orange tree growing in the corner."

"Sounds of the piano coming from the ballet school next door."

"I remember all of it." She watched as a boat headed out to sea, the bow cutting through the water. "That was a memorable week."

"I went back last year, and the year before, for much longer than a week."

She turned to look at him. "To Florence?"

"Summers here are busy, but in the winter months I like to travel. I've been spending time in Europe, mostly Italy."

"Alone?"

"Yes. It took time to get used to my own company, but after a while you realize how freeing it is to travel by yourself. You can do exactly as you please." He paused. "You must have traveled a great deal with Cameron."

"Yes, but it was always very busy. There was a tight

schedule. We were rarely just relaxing." She thought about Seth in Italy and felt a stab of envy. "Where do you stay when you travel?"

"I find an apartment. It suits me better than a hotel. I like to pretend I'm local."

"Are you going again this year?"

"Yes. I've booked a month in Rome and a month in Florence. Those winter months are so much quieter. It's a different place without the tourists. Same as here, I suppose." He glanced at the water, and then gestured to the corner sofa and the table. "Are you happy to eat outside?"

"I can't think of anything I'd like more." She was still thinking about Rome, and Florence and the fact that Seth would be there this winter. Maybe she should travel. She'd traveled with Cameron of course. The life they'd led had taken them all over the world, and she was grateful for all the experiences they'd enjoyed. But almost all their time had been scheduled, with her playing the supporting role. When Cameron had needed time to paint, he often went alone or closeted himself in his studio and Cecilia had transferred all her attention to her garden. She'd never traveled alone.

The idea was appealing. Why hadn't she thought of it before? She'd been adrift, not sure what to do with her life, not sure how to shape her life now that Cameron wasn't part of it.

But Seth had done it. He could have stayed in the house he'd lived in with his wife, and carried on the life he'd always lived, but without her. Instead, he'd made major changes. Lily had made major changes, too, even though doing so had been difficult.

Was she brave enough to do the same?

Seth was watching her, and she had a feeling he could read her thoughts.

"I'll fetch the wine," he said. "Wait there."

He was back moments later with a tray loaded with wine, glasses and small plates of food.

"I'm a competent cook, but I didn't want to waste time that could be spent with you, so I raided the deli. The one near the beach." He put the tray down on the table and sat next to her on the sofa.

"I've heard about it. Lily has picked up a few things from there."

"Ah. Lily." He poured wine into the glasses. "I'm glad you mentioned her, because I have some news on that front. Good news for your protégé."

She took the glass from him. "She isn't exactly my protégé. I've not been involved in any of her work."

"Your mysterious lodger, then." He handed her a glass of wine. "I showed a couple of her paintings to a friend of mine."

"A friend?"

"Like you, I still have connections in the art world."

She did, but it had been a long time since she'd leveraged any of those connections. "And?"

"He's interested. He thinks her work is fresh and original. He would like to see more. But so would I." He touched his glass to hers. "When are you going to introduce me? Are you going to invite me to the cottage?"

"I'm not sure." She could imagine the looks she'd receive from Lily and Todd. "It might have been less complicated if you hadn't sent that extravagant bunch of flowers."

"You love flowers."

"That's true. But now my grandson is asking questions

about the man sending me flowers. I think he might have got the wrong idea."

Seth leaned back against the sofa and stretched out his legs. "Is it the wrong idea, Ceci?"

The question flustered her. "I don't know."

"I don't know, either." His gaze was fixed on her face. "But I'd like to find out. How about you?"

How about her?

She took a sip of wine. "I only planned to be here for a short time. A few days at most, but I'm still here."

"Is it wrong of me to hope I'm at least part of the reason you're still here?"

"No. You are part of the reason." But not the whole reason. "I have decisions to make. I have to decide which parts of my life to let go, and which to keep."

He nodded. "Sometimes the only way to move forward is to let go of what went before. You're thinking about the cottage?"

"Actually, right now I'm thinking about Lapthorne Manor and whether I should sell it." She put her glass down on the table, her hand a little shaky. "Just saying it makes my head implode. It has been my home forever. I've poured so much time and energy into the garden it feels like part of me. It would feel like selling a precious work of art. And as for the house itself—I don't know. It contains a lifetime of possessions. I wouldn't know where to start."

"The same way you tackle any big project. You don't think about the task as a whole, just the bit you're focused on today. You start by deciding what you will not, under any circumstances, part with. Then you ask your children and grandchildren to do the same. After that—" he shrugged

"—you clear it piece by piece. It's a challenge of course, but it can also be cathartic. You take it day by day."

Take it day by day.

She thought about the words in Todd's note. She thought about the planner. And now she had an idea of how she might use it.

"Did you find it hard?"

"To sell the house? Yes and no." He thought about it. "The task of clearing the house was emotional, but the girls helped and it brought us closer together. The decision to move— that was harder. I felt guilty. It felt like a betrayal of Sonya, as if I was turning my back on the life we built together, even though I knew that wasn't what I was doing. I was also worried that I was making a mistake. I was afraid I might hand over the keys to the front door and immediately want to snatch them back. After she died, everyone told me not to make any big changes and I can understand why, but I think people have to do what feels right for them."

"So how did you decide that moving was right for you?" She was looking to him for answers even though she knew that in the end she would have to find those answers herself.

"I used a simple formula. I looked at my life and tried to analyze which parts made me happy and which parts didn't. I worked out that I was at my most unhappy when I was trying to live the life I'd lived with Sonya. Doing the things I'd done with her. Walking into rooms in the house that we'd inhabited together. I 'survived' those times, of course, but happy? No. But there were times when I *was* happy—or certainly content—so I sat down one evening and thought hard about it. When did I feel good? What made me excited about the future?"

"And that's how you ended up here."

"Yes. I always wanted to be closer to the water. Sonya hated sailing, so I started doing more of that. I'd always wanted to renovate a house, but Sonya hated mess and disruption and we were always too busy anyway. When I saw this place, I knew it offered a chance to do something I'd always wanted to do. How about the cottage? Will you sell that, too?"

She helped herself to cold cuts and salad.

"When I arrived, I was determined to do exactly that. But now I'm not sure. Talking to you has helped me remember the good times as well as the bad. And Lily and Todd are determined to make me fall in love with the place again. Maybe they're even succeeding."

"You're feeling the pressure."

"In some ways, yes. They're trying so hard. It would feel churlish to turn round and tell them I still don't want the place after everything they've done."

He sat back in his chair. "But they're doing this for you. Because they're trying to make you happy."

"That's true."

"So why not let them get on with it and decide to shelve the decision for a while. When it's finished, you'll know. I doubt they'd be doing it if they didn't want to. Are they enjoying themselves or does it seem like a chore?"

Cecilia thought about the laughter and the banter. She'd seen an entirely different side of Lily over the past few days. And a different side to her grandson.

"They are definitely enjoying themselves. And they make a good team." Maybe this was something they'd both needed. "Lily is painting the cottage at the moment, so her talents don't just extend to canvases."

He helped himself to an olive from the dish on the table. "Are you matchmaking?"

"No. I don't believe in interfering. Let's just say I'm allowing two people to occupy the same space and work on something together. The rest is up to them." But that didn't mean she couldn't hope. "Lily hasn't had the easiest time. And Todd was with someone else until recently. A mistake. Fortunately he realized that, which is a relief because even though I know it's not my business, I was worried. Do you worry about your grandchildren?"

"All the time, although they're nowhere near at the relationship stage. At the moment I worry about busy roads, and shopping malls, and stranger danger. I think I worry more about my grandchildren than I did about my own children."

"I know what you mean." She watched as a gull swooped past them. "Maybe that's experience. Or maybe it's age. We no longer believe we're invincible."

"All the more reason to make the most of every moment." He topped up her wineglass. "Let's enjoy this evening and not think about tomorrow. But I'm here for you, Ceci. If you want to talk things through. If you need someone to listen. I'm here for you."

She reached out and took his hand, her throat thickened. "Seth—"

He was the last thing she'd expected to happen to her.

She'd thought about him of course, but only in terms of making contact, looking up an old friend, expanding her life a little.

But the feeling they shared was more than friendship. She knew that and so did he. It was the reason she'd been careful to have no contact after she married Cameron. A simple friendship would have been easy to maintain, but her relationship with Seth had never been simple.

And now he was back in her life, and she had no idea what would happen next.

16

Lily

"She didn't come home last night." Lily poured coffee into two mugs. She'd taken some vacation days that were owing to her and negotiated a few extra days unpaid. She and Todd been working flat out on the cottage for the best part of a week, and it was finally starting to take shape. Her arms ached and her shoulders ached. Her clothes were flecked with paint. She'd never been so tired in her life, and never been happier. "Should we be worried? She didn't call or anything. This must be how mothers feel about their teenagers."

"Don't ask me. I'm incapable of conversing intelligently on any subject until I've had coffee, you know that." He suppressed a yawn. "Don't be fooled. My body may be upright, but my brain is still asleep. What time did we finish last night?"

She liked the way he looked first thing in the morning,

with sleepy eyes and rumpled hair. "It wasn't last night, it was this morning. My phone told me it was 3 a.m. I did suggest taking a break at midnight, but you insisted we carry on. Are you listening to me?" She put the mug in front of him and waved her hand in front of his face. "Wake up! And I thought *I* was bad in the morning."

He picked up the mug. "I'm awake, I think. Mostly. Three o'clock. That explains a lot." He was silent for a moment as he drank half the mug of coffee. Then he put it down. "Right. You asked me if we should be worried. The answer is no. My grandmother isn't a teenager. It's not as if we don't know where she is. Dinner turned into dinner and a sleepover. Natural progression, I'd say."

She topped up his mug without waiting for him to ask. "Do you think something is going on?"

"I hope so. Her life has been pretty sad since my grandfather died. She just rattles round that big old house and tends the garden. Did you see her face when those flowers arrived?"

"Not only the flowers. When she talked about Seth."

"Yes. She lit up."

Lily picked up her mug and walked from the kitchen to the living room. They'd thrown open doors and windows to help let out the paint smells and she could hear the shriek of gulls and the sounds of the sea.

"He's obviously special to her. And maybe it's a good thing that she's not here. We're making progress." She felt a rush of pride as she surveyed their work. "I can't believe you managed to source the wood so quickly."

"I leveraged contacts." He nudged one of the strips of wood with his foot. "This came from an order that was canceled, so one person's indecision is our new shelving unit."

She was seeing a new side of him. Todd the craftsman.

"It's looking great. It transforms the room. Bookshelves were a good idea." She sipped her coffee. "Do you think this will work? Do you think she will still want to sell the cottage when we've finished?"

"I don't know. I hope not. I'm not sure she knows what she has here."

"She knows. But you and I see a gorgeous beach house with unbeatable views and masses of charm. She sees memories. And not good ones."

"Yes. Damn." He nursed his coffee mug. "I can't believe my grandfather had an affair. Not sure how much I want to think about that. I just saw them as my grandparents. I thought of them in the context of my life. As family, not as people with their own problems, needs and emotions. I never really thought about what was happening in their lives. Is that selfish?"

"No. I think it's natural. Also, parents and grandparents don't usually share intimate pieces of their lives with their kids and grandkids, so it isn't always that easy to put it all together. Were you close to him?"

"Not particularly. I was always much closer to my grandmother. When we were young, Hannah was usually the focus of attention. She was smart and funny and loud and dominated every room she entered."

The description so perfectly encapsulated her friend that Lily smiled. "Sounds like Hannah."

"Yes. And I was fine with it." He finished his coffee. "She's my little sister and I love her, obviously. We've always been close—until recently—but she always brought the drama. And she was so competitive. If it looked as if I was going to win something, she'd storm off. Sometimes I let her win because it led to a quieter life. I think my grandmother knew that and always insisted that she and I spend time together, without Hannah. I have special memories of those occasions."

"What did you do?"

"Different things. Sometimes she'd take me on a trip, and sometimes we'd paint or do something creative. I remember I made her a birdhouse once. It was my first piece of carpentry. But mostly we'd just sit and talk. She was a great listener, and she always encouraged me to be me. She was interested in me. And I suppose that was good for my confidence. She taught me that it was okay to be nothing like my sister."

It hadn't occurred to her that Todd might ever have felt insecure, or unsure about himself.

Thinking of her own conversations with Cecilia, Lily felt a pressure in her throat. "She's wonderful."

"Yes. When my parents and I didn't see eye to eye on my future plans, she was the one I talked to." He put down his empty mug. "She was the main reason I didn't do what you did and take the wrong path. She gave me the courage to do what I knew was right for me."

She thought she knew him well, but every day she was discovering something new. She felt as if she was accessing a secret part of him.

"But your parents are proud of you."

"Now, I think they are. At the time they thought I was throwing away my life, although they didn't say as much. Those were turbulent times."

Her parents had actually said as much. She badly wanted to be in the place Todd was in now and skip the turbulence.

"So how did you win their support? What did you do to persuade them this was right?"

"I didn't do anything to persuade them. I lived the life I wanted to live, and eventually they came round to it. It took a while and was probably helped by the fact that I was earning a living, and happy doing it." He looked at her. "In the end, there was no decision to make. I knew I would rather live this life without their approval, than the life they wanted for me with their approval. I left it to them to figure out how to handle that. The problem was theirs."

The problem was theirs.

Lily stared at the walls she'd painted the day before. She'd spent hours and hours figuring out how to make things better, how to fix this problem, but Todd was right. It wasn't her problem. It was her parents' problem. They were the ones who needed to make the adjustment.

"You were lucky to have your grandmother in your corner." Lily thought about how kind Cecilia had been to her. "She never passes judgment."

"She's the best. But now I feel guilty because I never really thought about her relationship with my grandfather, or the details of their life together. And she never said anything. Never mentioned it. I don't like to think of her suffering, with no one to talk to."

"Even if you'd asked, she wouldn't have talked to you. She would have protected you. She even kept it from your mother."

Todd nodded. "And I won't say anything. I hate to think of her alone, that's all. I'd like to think she has someone to talk to."

Lily thought about the flowers. "I think she probably does."

"Seth? I hope so," he said. "Did she take a bag when she left yesterday?"

"Wine and chocolates. That's all she took. If you're asking me if she packed for an overnight stay, then my answer would be no."

He grinned. "So she'll be doing the walk of shame later today."

"I don't think you should feel shame for finding joy in your life," Lily said, "particularly when you reach your seventies."

"Neither do I. I was kidding. And presumably she feels the same way, or she would have packed a bag." He gathered up both mugs and carried them back to the kitchen. "Enough slacking. We have a full day ahead. I appreciate you donating your vacation days, by the way."

"I'm having fun." Not just because of the work, but also because of him. Spending time with him didn't just make her happy, it made her feel stronger. More sure of herself. It was inspiring to see him living the life he wanted to live. And maybe allowing herself to get closer to him was going to make things harder for herself in the long term, but she wasn't going to think about that now. She enjoyed being with him too much to deny herself his company. Everything about him fascinated her. "When is the new sofa arriving?"

"Tomorrow. I persuaded them to sell us the one we saw in store. Otherwise we would have been waiting for two months."

"This must be the fastest makeover ever." She tensed as he reached out a hand and stroked her hair. "What are you doing?"

His fingers combed gently through the tangled strands. "You have paint in your hair. It's a whole new look."

Her heart was pounding. "You have paint on your nose."

He trailed his finger across her cheek and smiled. "Does it suit me?"

She wouldn't have cared if he'd poured the entire can of paint over himself. She still would have wanted him more than any man she'd ever met and standing this close to him made it almost impossible to concentrate. There was something in his eyes that made her wonder if he knew how she felt.

She hoped not. "We should get back to work."

He didn't move, and for a single breathless minute she thought he was going to kiss her, the way he had that night of the party. Then he let his hand drop and stepped back.

"You're right. We should. This place isn't going to transform itself." His voice was roughened, and he turned his back on her and focused on the shelving unit.

She stared at his shoulders, feeling as if something special had just slipped through her fingers. "I can't bear the thought of her selling it."

"I know. If she's going to sell somewhere, I'd rather she sold that big old house she is currently living in." He picked up the drill. "It's like a shrine to my grandfather. Interestingly she took all his paintings off the wall in her bedroom."

"She did the same thing here." Lily watched as he drilled holes in the wood, his T-shirt pulling tight over the width of his shoulders. She loved watching him. His hands moved over the wood with confidence, as if he was working with a friend he knew well. "Can I make a suggestion?"

"Go ahead." He turned to look at her, and this time his smile was friendly and neutral.

The intimacy that had been there only moments earlier had vanished.

Or maybe it had never been there. Maybe it was wishful thinking on her part.

"The attic room. I was thinking that instead of a rollaway, you could build storage under the beds." She outlined her idea and he listened and made a few suggestions of his own. Then he grabbed a pencil and sketched a plan.

"It would work." He studied the drawing. "It's a great idea."

Lily grinned and returned to the wall she'd been painting.

They worked side by side for the next few hours, Lily painting and Todd working on the shelves.

She was concentrating so hard on doing the best job she could that it took a moment for her to realize that the hammering had stopped.

She glanced over her shoulder and saw that he was watching her.

"You're a hard worker, Lily."

She looked back at the wall she'd just finished. "This doesn't feel hard, and it doesn't feel like work."

He wiped the back of his hand across his forehead. "Maybe you are looking at a future career. Do you know how much people around here will pay for a talented decorator? You might want to think about it. It would be a way of boosting your income while you develop your art career."

"I don't have an art career." She daubed paint on a spot she'd missed. "I don't have a decorating career, either."

"If my grandmother's instincts are correct, you will have an art career. And you could have a decorating career, too," Todd said. "Once word gets around, your phone will be ringing nonstop. Recommendation goes a long way in this part of the world."

"Who would recommend me?"

"I would for a start. You enjoy it, don't you?"

"Decorating? Yes. It's satisfying." Just how satisfying had surprised her. It wasn't something she'd ever entertained doing before.

"More satisfying than medicine?"

"For me, yes." But her mind was on what he'd said a few moments before. About decorating giving her an income. Why hadn't she thought of that? Maybe this was a way to find artistic satisfaction, while still earning a living. And if she was earning a living doing something she enjoyed, surely her parents might feel proud of her?

He wiped his hands on his shorts. "Sit down. Time for a break."

"I can't let the paint dry on my brush."

"Fine. Clean your brush, and then take a break. Unlike the rest of your life, there is no pressure here. We will do what needs to be done. We don't have to kill ourselves to get it done in the shortest possible time. No one is going to die if we haven't finished the place by next week."

She wanted to feel that way. She would have given anything to feel that way.

"I wish I could be as relaxed as you, but no matter how hard I try I just can't."

He crossed the room and removed the paintbrush from her fingers. "Only you would see being relaxed as something you need to try hard at. If you want to relax, you start by easing up on yourself. By deciding that you don't always have to push yourself to your limits."

She wished he wasn't standing quite so close to her. "I've always been this way."

"Why? You were born a perfectionist?"

"I don't know. Maybe." She'd never really thought about

it. Just accepted it as being who she was. Her personality. "The consequences of not being the best version of myself have always scared me."

"Consequences?"

"Fail an exam and you've missed an opportunity. My parents worked hard to give me those opportunities, and I've always felt I had to make the most of them. Not just because I didn't want to disappoint them, but also because deep down I felt that it was how my life should be. Work hard and pass this exam, and that exam, and then your whole life will come together. Fail, and it's over." She hadn't realized how much of that pressure she still had stored inside her. She'd been afraid to ever let it out. Afraid of letting her guard down even for a moment, in case revealing her true self stopped her from being the person she was pretending to be. But she'd shared her feelings with Cecilia, and now she was sharing them with Todd. "I suppose I felt that if I didn't fulfill my potential, if I slipped, if I failed, I would have lost my chance to live my best life. I would have let not just my parents down, but myself."

Todd was still holding the brush, but his gaze was fixed on her face.

"That's a lot of pressure you're piling on yourself there, Lily."

"I know."

"And when you were doing all that, working that hard at something you didn't love, did it feel as if you were living your best life? Were you happy?"

"No." She didn't even have to think about it, and it occurred to her that these past few days had been the happiest she could remember, and not simply because she was with Todd.

Her work had transformed the cottage, and witnessing that transformation was more satisfying than she could have imagined. She was making a difference. Surroundings could affect the emotions, and she was determined that by the time she and Todd had finished, Cecilia's emotions would be positive ones.

She took the brush from him, quickly finished the section of wall that still needed to be painted and then stopped.

"There. Done. And no more talking about my boring problems. Are you hungry?" She walked to the kitchen, washed her hands and then opened the fridge. Scanning the contents for a moment, she pulled out some cold chicken and salad items.

"Starving. I could eat a camel. And you're never boring, Lily."

She felt her cheeks warm. "I've checked the fridge and we're fresh out of camel, but would a chicken salad work?"

"It would work. What can I do?"

"Grab some plates. Forks." She worked quickly, rinsing, chopping, throwing everything into one of the large bowls that Cecilia kept on display. She made a dressing, added chopped chicken to the salad and took it onto the porch.

"I ache all over. Even this dish feels heavy."

"I know what you mean. This looks great, thanks." He served her first and then himself and ate hungrily, diving into the salad and pausing only to break off a thick chunk of bread from the Italian loaf she'd put in the center of the table. "How is the master bedroom coming along? When are you going to let me see it?"

"When it's finished. I'm nearly there. Finished the walls and all the decorating, but I'm waiting for the new bedding to arrive." She pierced a piece of chicken. "I hope your grandmother will love it. It looks like a totally different room to me, but I don't suppose that means she will want to sleep in there."

"You're kind to my grandmother. Thank you."

"She is the one who has been kind to me. She let me stay here when she should have thrown me out. Without her I would have ended up back at home. And she listened to me." She put her fork down. "For the first time ever, I felt as if someone cared what I thought."

"Why didn't you call me?" His voice was gruff. "You should have called me. You always used to when things got tough."

She picked up her fork again and focused on her chicken. "That was before."

"Before what?"

Before Amelie. "Before I realized that no one could solve this but me." She finished her salad.

"I know how much pressure your parents put on you." He glanced at her. "I've known you for a long time, Lily, don't forget that. This salad is delicious, by the way. What's in the dressing?"

"Lemon. Olive oil. Herbs. It's just something I threw together. Help yourself. I've eaten all I want to eat for now." It was true they'd known each other for years, but over the past few days something felt different. New.

He served himself another portion. "You can't live your life trying to please your parents, Lily. But you already know that."

"Yes. But disappointing them is hard. It's the reason I needed distance. I was worried that if I stayed at home, they might have persuaded me to go back."

He looked troubled. "Why would they do that? You didn't tell them how you felt?"

"I tried, but they didn't get it. They didn't understand that I found it emotionally exhausting. And terrifying." It stressed her to think about it. "And also nauseating."

"The blood and guts?"

"No. The responsibility. The idea that someone's life might depend on me having the right knowledge—I didn't find it empowering or fulfilling. It gave me panic attacks. It was the pinnacle of pressure. All my life I've been worried about failing an exam, of not living up to people's expectations, but that was just an exam. If you fail, no one dies. But medicine…" she paused "…that was on a whole different level. In medical school if you get something wrong, do something or miss something, someone can die. And plenty of people are fine with that level of responsibility. They thrive on it. Hannah is one of them. But I'm not Hannah."

"Which is a relief." He finished his salad. "I love my sister but sometimes her intensity makes me want to lie down in a dark room. Did you tell her how you felt?"

"I tried once, but she dismissed it. She told me I'd be fine. That I was great with people, that kind of thing."

His mouth tightened. "In other words, she didn't listen."

"I think it's more that she couldn't understand the way I was feeling. She didn't know what to say. But in a way that contributed to my sense of isolation. There was literally no one I could talk to about it. No one who understood. No one was in my corner." She could feel herself becoming emotional. "Do you want more food?"

"No thanks. I couldn't eat another thing." He reached for her plate and stacked it on top of his. "Was that why the two of you had a falling-out? Because you wanted to give up medicine?"

"She told you that we fell out?"

"Yes. It came out during a delightful shouting match. She was the one shouting, by the way. She obviously didn't like Amelie, but wouldn't say why, just accused me of being stupid for not seeing who she really was, and then she yelled something about how you'd feel about it, which made no sense to me."

Lily stared at him. "When was this?"

"I don't know. Not long. A couple of months?"

After she'd left medicine. After she and Hannah had stopped communicating.

Hannah had still been thinking about her. Worrying about her.

Hannah had been upset with her brother because she'd known how Lily would feel about him dating Amelie.

She'd thought Hannah didn't care, but maybe she did.

Hannah hadn't called her, but her friend was stubborn and proud. And Lily hadn't called her, either. All it needed was for one of them to give a little. All it needed was for one of them to believe their friendship was worth fighting for. And she did believe that.

"We should get back to work." She stood up, but he caught her hand.

"Wait. I want to ask you something." He held her hand tightly. "Why did Hannah think you'd be upset that I was dating Amelie?"

She tugged at her hand. "You'll have to ask her."

"Lily," he spoke softly, "you've always talked to me about everything. And I've talked to you. We've always been good friends."

Which was exactly why she couldn't talk to him about this. But she sat back down because he wasn't giving her much choice. She wondered if he even knew he was still holding her hand.

He wanted an answer from her, so she formulated one.

"Hannah didn't want me to give up medicine. She loves it so much. She really is living her best life and she can't understand why others wouldn't feel the same way."

"So why was she ranting about Amelie?" He kept his gaze fixed on her face. "She said she couldn't believe I'd been stupid enough to be taken in by her. Apparently she knew things about her, but when I asked her about it she wouldn't tell me what they were. I already knew I'd made a mistake of course and maybe I would have talked to Hannah about it, but she wouldn't listen to anything I had to say. The irony was, Amelie and I weren't even serious. It was just casual, for me at least. Although it's obvious to me now that she felt differently." He let go of her hand. "You knew Amelie, didn't you?"

Lily's lips felt stiff. "Yes."

"Are you going to tell me why Hannah disliked her so much?"

"I—you'd have to ask Hannah."

"I'm asking you."

"Todd—"

"Okay, so I'm going to take a guess at it." He studied her for a moment. "The girl who bullied you at school—that was Amelie wasn't it?" When she didn't answer, he nodded. "It took me a while to figure it out. Too long. Damn, Lily—"

"I don't know why you'd—"

"Because I put together all the things Hannah threw at me and added in Amelie's reaction when your name came up."

Her heart started to race. "My name came up?"

"Yes. Before we were dating. She wasn't really part of my social circle, but occasionally we'd find ourselves in the same place at the same time. We were talking about friends. You're one of my friends. But when I mentioned your name, Amelie changed. She became upset—moody."

"I don't see why us being friends would upset her."

It was a moment before Todd answered. "I think," he said slowly, "it was because she was jealous. In fact, I'm wondering now if that's why she got involved with me in the first place."

"That doesn't make any sense."

"It does. And I think you know it does." He leaned forward and took her hand again. "She knew you were in love with me, didn't she, Lily?"

The world stopped.

"Todd—"

"You were in love with me, and Amelie knew that. That was why she was suddenly interested in me."

This was a nightmare. She didn't know which was worse. Todd knowing, or Amelie knowing.

Todd. Definitely Todd. It was one thing loving him, and him not knowing. A completely different thing, loving him and knowing he knew. It was mortifying. She didn't want him feeling sorry for her. Pitying her. Everything would be awkward now. These past few days, where they'd worked together so closely and had such fun, were in the past.

She stood up suddenly and Todd stood up, too.

She freed her hand and turned to walk away but he caught her by the shoulders and turned her to face him.

"Wait. I have a question, and it's really important to me

that you answer it honestly." He was still holding her. "Are you still in love with me, Lily?"

Oh God, he was going to sympathize. He was going to be kind and understanding. This was her nightmare. The moment she'd always dreaded, and it was as bad as she'd feared it would be.

It was terrifying to be this vulnerable.

She opened her mouth to deny it. And then she stopped.

She was tired of denying who she was, and what she felt. She'd been honest with her parents, and even though it hadn't been easy, she didn't regret doing it. She could be honest with Todd, too.

"Yes. But it doesn't matter." She couldn't look at him, so she fixed her gaze on the middle of his chest. "People fall in love with the wrong people all the time. It happens. It doesn't mean anything."

"It means something to me. It matters to me." He was standing close to her now, so close that she could hardly breathe.

"Why?"

"Because I'm in love with you. I'm crazy about you, and I need to know if you feel the same way." He slid his fingers under her chin and tilted her face so she was forced to look at him.

And she saw in that moment what she hadn't seen right away.

He was nervous, too. He was vulnerable. He was feeling all the things she was feeling.

He was in love with her.

It seemed like such an impossible dream that at first her brain rejected it.

"You dated Amelie."

"I know. Big mistake, and I've made a few in my life. I'm hoping we can get past that." And right then, when she'd given up hoping it would ever happen again, he kissed her. He cupped her face in his hands and kissed her and it felt even better than she remembered. He kissed her until every one of her senses were screaming, until the desire was so acute, so excruciatingly intense that she desperately needed him to do something to ease it. She needed him to do *something*. She gave a low moan, and he finally lifted his head. "Lily?"

Did he expect her to talk? Her brain wasn't capable of stringing together a coherent thought. The moment his mouth had claimed hers, her brain had fused.

She looked at him groggily, saw that familiar gleam in his eyes, and finally regained her powers of speech.

"Todd Buckingham, are you laughing at me?"

"No. Definitely not. I'm smiling." He kissed her again, but briefly this time. "You still haven't said the words, but I'm taking that as a yes."

"Yes?"

"You do love me."

She couldn't resist teasing him. "You're very sure of yourself."

"I'm not sure of myself at all. I've never been this scared in my life. You still haven't said the words, by the way."

She'd said them so many times in her head that it felt as if the whole world must know.

"I love you, Todd. I love you." She tried to say it again, just so there could be no mistake, but he was kissing her again and this time there was no sign of him stopping.

His mouth still on hers, he backed her into the cottage, his hands ripping at her shirt while her fingers fumbled with the button on his shorts. It crossed her mind briefly that perhaps they should close the door, but they were too busy undressing each other and kissing, and then he pulled her hard against him and she was no longer thinking of anything but his mouth and the urgent touch of his hands and how badly she wanted him.

They tumbled onto the rug, and he rolled so that he was the one on the floor and she was the one on top. And she was happy with that because it meant she could see all of him, touch all of him. She trailed her mouth across his jaw, over his neck and lower, distracted from her purpose only when he made a few intimate explorations of his own. His skilled touch seduced and teased until she was drunk on sensation, dizzy with longing, needing more. Needing everything. She reached down, closing her hand over him and she heard the sharp intake of his breath. He shifted position and lifted her and then they were moving in a perfect rhythm, and she felt nothing but heat and sensation and the feeling that they were made to be together.

Afterward they lay on the floor, trying to catch their breath.

She stared up at the ceiling, drowsy and sated, thinking of the wonder that was Todd. "Are you alive? This floor is hard. We should have made it to the sofa."

"Wouldn't have made any difference. That sofa is as uncomfortable as the floor." He pulled her closer. "I'm alive, although possibly injured. You? Any bruises?"

"I don't care."

"Next time we'll aim for a mattress. Apologies for being impatient."

"Don't apologize." She wanted to tell him how good it felt to be wanted that badly, but her mind was drowsy, and her eyes were closing, which was annoying because she knew there was something she'd wanted to ask him. And then she remembered. "Why did you think Amelie was only interested in you because of me?"

He stroked her back with his hand. "Because she never showed the slightest interest in me until you and I kissed at the school reunion."

She turned her head to look at him. "You remember that?"

He frowned and rolled onto his side, propping himself up on his elbow. "I remember. Why would you think otherwise?"

"Because you never mentioned it." She put her hand on his chest and then moved it to his jaw. She couldn't stop touching him.

"You didn't mention it, either. I thought you regretted it. People do all sorts of things at those reunions. They're a nightmare. I was being a gentleman, but that was because I didn't know how you felt." He leaned down and kissed her slowly. "That's never going to happen again." And to prove it he pulled her close and it was another hour before either of them spoke again.

"Todd?"

He pulled her closer. "What?"

"I think we left the front door open."

He laughed. "I thought you were going to say something profound."

"I don't know about profound, but if your grandmother does come home unannounced it could be embarrassing."

"That's true." He eased his arm out from under her and sat up with a wince. "I'm going to lock the door, and then I think we should move somewhere more comfortable."

He dealt with the door and was pulling her to her feet when they heard the muffled sound of his phone ringing.

They both stared at each other and then at the discarded clothing strewn across the floor.

"Where is it?" She reached for his shirt, rummaging through the clothes they'd abandoned on the floor and finally he found the phone in his shorts.

He answered it before it went to voice mail. "Hi, Nanna. Yes, we're here. No, nothing's wrong—a long time to answer the phone? We were up a ladder, that's all—"

She tilted her head and mouthed, *Up a ladder?*

He gave a helpless shrug and carried on talking to his grandmother. "Yes, we assumed that was the case—" He paused and listened and then nodded. "Good plan. The place stinks of paint. Reeks. And I have wood spread across the floor so if there's an alternative place for you to stay, that would be a good idea. Stay as long as you like."

Lily raised her eyebrows and he winked at her as he continued the conversation.

"No problem...we'll be working until we lose the light anyway. There's lots to do...don't worry about food, we'll figure it out. Lily? She's fine, I think." He allowed himself a slow scan of her naked body. "Yes, I'll take care of Lily. No problem."

He ended the call and tugged Lily against him.

She lost her balance and had to hold on to his shoulders to steady herself. "What are you doing?"

"Following my grandmother's instructions and taking care of you." He kissed her jaw and then her neck. "Do you have any idea how hard it was to string a sentence together with you standing there naked?"

"Yes. I witnessed it. You were stammering."

"And whose fault was that? You did it on purpose, didn't

you?" His fingers trailed down her spine. "I mean, you could have been generous and pulled clothes on."

"I didn't see the point." She rested her forehead against his chest. After wanting him for so long, loving him for so long, any moment apart seemed like a moment wasted. "I can't believe this is happening."

"Believe it. And the good news is that my grandmother is staying another night with Seth, so we have this place to ourselves."

She looked up at him, digesting what he'd just said. "She's staying another night? That has to be a good sign, don't you think? How did she sound?"

"I have no idea. You were naked."

"Did she sound happy? Excited?"

"As I said, you were naked."

"I hope she and Seth are—"

"Can we stop talking about my grandmother?" He silenced her with a kiss, and she wound her arms around his neck.

"So, what are we going to do with the rest of the day?"

"I have a few ideas we can test out. But first there's something I need to say to you." He smoothed her tangled hair back from her face. "Something you need to know."

"What?"

He cupped her cheek with his hand and held her gaze. "You said you had no one in your corner. And I want you to know that I'm in your corner, Lily. Always. No matter what happens, or what choices you make, you will always have me in your corner."

It was possibly the best thing anyone had ever said to her. "Thank you."

"Also, I love you." He kissed her gently. "I may have told you that already."

"I have a terrible memory." She stroked her fingers through his hair. "Maybe you should tell me again, just so I'm clear about it."

"I can do better than that." He scooped her up and carried her to the stairs. "I can show you."

17

Kristen

Kristen arrived at the restaurant five minutes late. Theo was coming straight from the hospital and although he'd assured her he'd be on time, she knew him well enough that she chose not to arrive early.

She'd hoped he might take the whole day off as it was their anniversary, but having taken an extended leave of absence he understandably felt he needed to pull his weight in the department.

Theo had missed many anniversaries in their years together, and she was determined that this one was going to be perfect. It seemed symbolic somehow, that it came after what she thought of in her mind as a "rough patch." He wouldn't see it that way, of course, because he didn't know how she'd been feeling, but that didn't matter, because things were improving between them.

Losing Michael had made Theo more vulnerable, more

open to talking to her about his feelings. She was sure that from there it was a very short step to talking about *her* feelings.

Even his work-life balance had improved. Since returning to work, he'd been restricting his hours and he'd been home when he'd promised to be home every night.

She smoothed her hair and stepped into the restaurant. It had become the most talked about place in Boston, and the chef had won multiple awards. It was the perfect place for a celebration.

In order to secure a table, she'd done something she rarely did, which was to use her maiden name when she booked.

"Ms. Lapthorne?"

She was greeted with warmth and shown immediately to a table. The atmosphere was muted and sophisticated. Candles flickered and silver gleamed. It was perfect in every way but one—

Her husband hadn't yet arrived.

She was not going to stress. Traffic was probably heavy. When he walked through that door she was not going to say anything that might spoil the evening ahead, or risk threatening the new closeness that had emerged since the tragedy with Michael.

"You're the first to arrive," the woman said as she settled Kristen at the table, facing the view. "Can I fetch you a drink while you wait for your guest?"

She ordered a bottle of champagne, sure that by the time it arrived, Theo would have arrived, too.

She checked her phone, but there were no messages.

Five minutes, she promised herself. She'd give him five minutes, and then she'd call.

In the end she gave him ten, and by then the champagne had arrived.

"Shall I open it?" The sommelier hovered and she shook her head.

"I'll wait, thank you."

Ten minutes turned into fifteen and by twenty she was starting to worry.

After thirty minutes she called him, but his phone went to voice mail.

Maybe he was in a cab and taking another call. A colleague asking for advice, perhaps.

She gave it another five minutes and then called again, and this time she left a message.

"Theo, it's me. Where are you? I'm worried."

What if he'd had an accident? It was impossible not to consider that option, given what had happened to Michael. Michael had been driving his car, going about his business, not imagining for a moment that it would turn out to be the last car journey he ever made.

She stared out of the window, hoping to see Theo sprinting toward her, full of apology.

But there was no Theo. Just an oversolicitous member of the front of house staff, keen to know her intentions.

Kristen had no problem eating in a restaurant alone if she'd planned for it, but she hadn't planned for this and she felt increasingly conspicuous. She was dressed for a celebration, but there was no celebration.

Unable to stand the sympathetic glances from her fellow diners any longer, she stood up and gave her apologies. Embarrassed, she gave them a massive tip for nothing but the privilege of having allowed her to sit at one of their tables for an hour.

Then she walked out of the restaurant and called Theo again.

"Theo, I'm on my way home. I'll see you there. Call me as soon as you can just to let me know you're okay."

Her mind went into overdrive on the cab drive home.

She wanted to believe that he'd been held up, but if that was the case why hadn't he messaged her? He knew she was waiting in the restaurant. He knew this was a special occasion.

No, Theo wouldn't do that to her, which left only one explanation and that was that he hadn't been able to use his phone for some reason.

Theo had mentioned to her that Michael's phone had kept ringing even after he was dead.

Remembering that sent her mind and her thoughts spiraling out of control. There was no point in telling herself that nothing would have happened because these things *did* happen, and Michael was evidence of that. Some people arrived home safely, but some didn't.

Back in her house, she dropped her purse onto the kitchen countertop and called the emergency department.

She was probably overreacting, and no doubt she'd regret it once the staff started teasing her, but she'd take it because it was the only way to put her mind at rest.

"I just want to check whether Theo Buckingham is there. I'm sure he isn't. I'm being—"

"Theo Buckingham? He's in surgery."

"In surgery?" Kristen's knees gave way, and she sat down hard on the nearest kitchen chair. She felt dizzy. "How bad is it?"

"I'm not at liberty to disclose personal information."

"I'm his wife."

"Oh—Mrs. Buckingham? It's Clara Oats here. Sorry, I

287

didn't recognize your voice. It's pretty bad. It will be a few hours before we know more."

A few hours?

She couldn't think. She was shaking. How could two tragedies happen so close together?

"Mrs. Buckingham? Are you still there? Can I give him a message for you?"

"A message?"

"I can pass something to one of the team if there's something particular you want to say."

She knew from talking to Theo that hearing was often the last thing to go when a person was unconscious. It was the reason relatives were encouraged to talk to their loved ones even when they were in a coma.

What would she want them to say to Theo?

"It's our anniversary. I was waiting for him at a restaurant." She was choked by panic and emotion. This must have been how Trisha had felt. "I'd ordered a bottle of champagne."

"I'm sorry. This is bad timing."

Bad timing? Her husband was in surgery and all this woman could say was that it was bad timing?

"I'm going to drive over now." She tried to pull herself together. These were Theo's colleagues. He'd want her to be composed. "I'll be there as quickly as I can, but if you could just tell him that I love him."

"I'll do that. Nothing like a bit of romance to lighten a serious situation. You have a nice evening, Mrs. Buckingham. And hopefully Theo will be home in time to share that bottle of champagne with you. It must be frustrating for you. The downside of being married to a brilliant surgeon like your husband."

How could he possibly be home in time to drink champagne?

Downside?

And then she realized that when the woman had said that Theo was in surgery, she hadn't meant that he was the patient. She'd meant that he was the surgeon. Theo wasn't the one being operated on, he was the one doing the operation, but her mind had been hurtling so fast down the dark track toward doom that she'd interpreted the conversation in the wrong way. The misunderstanding was her fault, but in her defense Theo hadn't contacted her or asked anyone else to contact her. And yes, she understood the life-and-death nature of some emergencies, but this wasn't just about him being late home, it wasn't even about him leaving her stranded in an expensive restaurant on her own *on their anniversary*, it was about him not once thinking that she might be worried after what had happened to Michael.

Surely he wouldn't have done that to her? There must be another explanation. "Theo wasn't on call this evening."

"I know. It should have been Alison Hollister, but her mother had a fall this afternoon, so Theo said he'd cover for her. You know what he's like. He's always there for everyone."

Everyone except his wife.

She ended the phone call, skewered by a thousand volts of anger. All the energy she'd put into being anxious, now fueled her fury.

Theo wasn't trapped in a tangled heap of metal. Theo was at work. He was operating. He'd covered for Alison so that she could go home and take care of her mother, and he'd left his wife sitting alone in a restaurant on their anniversary worrying that something had happened to him.

Her eyes stung with tears of anger and frustration.

She couldn't believe they were back here again. After everything that had happened over the past few weeks, everything he'd said about appreciating his family, appreciating *her*, he'd prioritized work again without even having the courtesy to let her know.

Enough. *Enough!*

Vision blurred, she stomped up the stairs and dragged her largest suitcase from a cupboard. That hollow feeling inside her was back. The loneliness. The feeling that no one cared about her enough to make her their priority. Was it too much to ask?

Maybe it was, in which case she needed to make sure that she was at least the priority in her own life.

An hour later the suitcase was by the front door, along with a smaller bag stuffed with valuables and all her personal items.

It was dark, and past midnight, but she didn't bother turning on the lights.

She sat down on the bottom stair and waited.

Another hour passed and then she heard the sound of a key in the lock and Theo stepped into the house.

He closed the door quietly, turned and tripped over her suitcase.

"What the—" He steadied himself and flicked on the light, blinking as he saw her sitting there. "Kristen? What are you doing?"

She stood up. Her knees were shaking. Her hands were shaking. Her whole world was shaking.

"I'm leaving you, Theo." They were words she never thought she'd say. "But I'm doing you the courtesy of saying goodbye first, because that's the adult thing to do after so many years of marriage." And also because there were things she badly needed to say, and she knew if she didn't say them they'd burn a hole inside her.

"What? Wait—" He dropped his keys onto the table and put his bag down. "You can't be serious."

"Do you see a smile anywhere on my face?"

"Is this because I missed dinner? It was an emergency, Kristen. What was I supposed to do? Tell a husband that I can't save his wife because I have to go home to my own?"

"No, I don't expect you to do that. I respect what you do. But I would like some respect in return. Do you have any idea how I felt tonight?"

"It was all frantic, Krissy." He hung up his coat. "I knew you'd be okay. I knew you'd understand."

"Well, I wasn't okay. And I don't understand. Would you have left me sitting in that restaurant all night?" She was raising her voice, but she couldn't help it. "I would like you to just once consider how I might be feeling. A call, Theo, that's all I needed. A message. It didn't even have to be you sending it."

"It just went from my mind—"

"You mean *I* went from your mind, and that's because I'm never in your mind. There is always something, or some-one, more important."

"You're overreacting. And on that subject, why did you call the department and ask them to tell me you love me? They all had a big laugh over it. Were you trying to em-barrass me?"

"Embarrass you?" The thought of everyone laughing was the final straw. "Do you have *any idea* how I felt when you didn't show up at the restaurant? The restaurant *you* chose, by the way, as somewhere special to celebrate our anniversary. The date *you* fixed. Because you really want to spend time with your family, don't you, Theo, you really want to spend time with me. After what happened to Michael, you're a changed man." She knew she should be having this conversation in a calm voice, but it was impossible. She was so very hurt. So very upset. "Except you're not a changed man. You're exactly the man you've always been. And even now, with me spelling it out to you, you're not even *trying* to understand how I'm feeling. It's all about you. I didn't call the hospital to embarrass you, I called them because I was scared that something had happened to you!"

He stared at her. "Of course nothing had happened to me. Why would you even think that?"

"Because bad things happen. They happened to Michael!"

His expression changed. "I didn't think about that. It didn't cross my mind that you'd worry. I'm sorry. Next time I'll get a message to you."

Next time.

"There won't be a next time. I'm done, Theo." She gestured to the suitcases. "I've never been a quitter, but this is me quitting."

"Kristen—" he said, running his hand over the back of his neck. "Look, I get that you're upset. I understand. But can we talk about this tomorrow? I've been operating for the past eight hours and I'm tired. I'm sorry I messed up our anniversary. I'll make it up to you, I promise."

"If you think we can talk about this tomorrow, then you don't understand. And even now, you're still making it about you." And suddenly she realized something, and she wondered why she hadn't seen it before. "It's a type of addiction, isn't it, Theo? Being needed? Being the hero? The guy who rides in on his charger and saves the day. Or at least, saves the patient."

"Because the patient needs me. I'm a surgeon. That is my job."

"I know. And I've always admired that. I've always supported you. Which is why it's taken me this long to see things clearly. The patient does need you, but you need them just as much. You need the applause. You need the limelight. Yes, you make a difference, and sometimes you save lives, but there are other surgeons. You're not the only one. And a life doesn't have to be full of big moments and drama for them to count. Small moments matter, too. Those moments no one else sees. But you don't get high on those moments, do you, Theo? You can't handle the ordinary or the mundane or those life moments where you're not the shining star."

"Kristen—"

"You're a saint to your patients and staff, and absent when your family need you. We are nothing more than your support crew, here to back you up so that you can live this life you've chosen. You have your priorities, and I'm not one of them. But I deserve more than that. I deserve better than to be left in a restaurant without even the courtesy of a phone call. You are always there for your patients and colleagues when they need you, but never there for me." She was furious with herself for being so emotional, but how could she not be? This was her marriage. Her life. "I'm leaving, and we can figure out details later."

"Wait—" He caught her arm. "You're leaving because I didn't message you to say I'd be late?"

"No, I'm leaving because I'm not important to you." Her voice was shaky. "Even in my lowest moments, when I truly needed you, you haven't been there for me."

He let go of her. "That's unfair and untrue."

"Really?" She hadn't intended to rake up the past, but how could she not? "You missed Todd's birth because you were with a patient who you judged to be a greater priority than I was. It didn't matter that I was frightened and alone, and that Todd's heart rate was dipping and scaring everyone. It didn't matter that they had to rush me to surgery. The welfare of your wife and child was secondary to the patient you were dealing with."

"I knew you were in good hands, but you're right. I should have been there for that." His face was paler than usual. "Fortunately you were both fine—"

"Physically yes, although no thanks to you. Emotionally? I wasn't fine, Theo. I was traumatized. The gap between the happy birthing experience I'd hoped for and the panicked emergency I ended up having, was huge. And I had no one to share it with. You abandoned me." Her voice was shaking, and she stopped talking for a moment and pressed her hand to her chest, forcing herself to breathe slowly. She had to finish this conversation. "I buried that trauma and I forgave you, because deep down you're a good man and I was proud of you. I tried to forget and carry on. And on all the occasions that followed across the years where you weren't there for me when I needed you, I did the same. I swallowed it and carried on. I made excuses for you. I forgave you. And then my father was rushed into hospital."

"I was with a patient who had fallen from a window—"

"I don't doubt it. And I'm sure you felt you were justified in not being by my side when my father was dying, but ask yourself this, Theo—were you really the only person who could have helped that patient? Was there really no other surgeon who could have stepped in and covered for you the

294

way you always step in and cover for colleagues? I'm sure there was, but you didn't ask them because you didn't want to be with me." And suddenly it came to her in an explosion of clarity. "You were afraid."

"Afraid?"

"Yes. Afraid of my emotions. Afraid of your own emotions. You're good in a crisis when it is someone else's crisis." She wondered why she hadn't seen it before. "You're brilliant at being detached, but when it comes to dealing with your own emotions you will do anything to avoid it. That's why you had to take time off after Michael. You couldn't handle it. And it's why you weren't there for me after my father died, because you couldn't handle my emotions, either."

"Kristen—"

"At the hospital when he died, I handled it on my own. I cried on my own. I've become used to handling things on my own. But the thing about doing things alone, Theo, is that eventually you realize that not only do you feel alone, but you *are* alone. And when my father died, I realized just how alone I really am." She felt drained. Exhausted. She needed this conversation to end, or she wouldn't have the energy to leave the house and she was determined to leave the house.

"I know you felt terrible when your father died," Theo muttered, "but I didn't know what to do."

"Acknowledging it would have been a start. Saying *I'm here for you*, or offering some gesture of support. The type of support I've been giving you since Michael died. But you didn't give me that. You weren't there for me. You're never there for me. And do you know what makes it worse? You *were* there for Michael. You supported him when he needed it, so I can't even tell myself you're not capable of it. You're perfectly capable of doing that for other people. Just not for your wife." She picked up her jacket. "I'm always handling things alone because you're not around, so let's make it official. Let's formalize this arrangement and stop pretending we're a team. It's all about expectation, Theo. I end up handling everything by myself anyway, so I might as well be by myself."

"You're very upset," he said, "but we can't fix things if you leave. I don't understand why you'd leave."

"I know you don't. And that's why I'm leaving. Because even now you're not hearing me. I don't believe things can be fixed." What did she have to do to make him understand? What did she have to say to make him pay attention? "Do you have any idea how lonely my life is? I almost had an affair, Theo. I met a man who cared about me, who was interested in me, and who listened to me, and it was such a novelty after years of being invisible that for a short while I was truly happy. I'd forgotten how it felt to be happy. And I didn't sleep with him, I wasn't unfaithful—physically at least—but that relationship showed me just what was missing from my life."

Theo was breathing rapidly. "You've been seeing someone? That's why you're leaving?"

"It was a fleeting friendship and it's over. That has nothing to do with us. I'm leaving because I want more than you're able to offer. I deserve more. You've chosen your life, and your priorities, and I have to accept that. But I have a right to choose *my* life, and my priorities. The life I live matters, too. I deserve not to feel lonely. I deserve to find happiness, or at least contentment, where I can. I deserve to be more than your support team."

Theo looked shell-shocked. "Where are you going?"

"I don't know." She hadn't even thought that far. "I think I'm just going to follow my mother's example and disappear for a while."

"On your own?"

"I'll be fine on my own." She picked up her bag and her suitcase. "I've had plenty of practice."

18

Cecilia

"What if I don't like what they've done?" Cecilia parked the car outside the cottage and glanced at Seth. "I'll end up keeping the place just to please my grandson."

"Stop worrying." He reached for her hand. "Let's just look round and take it a step at a time."

His steady, practical approach to everything was calming.

She glanced down at their hands. "These last few days have been—"

"I know." He tightened his hand on hers. "Unexpected."

"More than that. They've been a gift. I hadn't realized how lonely I'd been feeling until I spent time with you. I was stuck in a place in my life with no idea how to move forward."

"And now?"

She smiled. "I'm following your advice and taking it a step at a time."

Still, she felt ridiculously nervous as they walked around to the front door of the cottage. She was nervous about the transformation, but mostly she was nervous about the fact that she was bringing Seth here. She was making their relationship public, and she wasn't sure how that would be received by her family.

"Nanna!" Todd had clearly been watching for their arrival because he sprinted down the steps and scooped up her bags. "You've been shopping. That's good."

"You left me no choice. You told me to stay away while you finished the place, and I hadn't packed anything."

"You wouldn't have wanted to be breathing in paint fumes and tripping over planks of wood. You must be Seth." Todd gave Seth a warm smile and extended his hand. "Great to meet you. Come in and see the place. Lily is waiting to give you the tour."

He was so easy with everyone, Cecilia thought. So comfortable and accepting. Her heart sank a little as she contemplated Kristen's reaction to this latest development. She was unlikely to be so open to this new change in her mother's life.

Still, that wasn't today's problem.

Todd seemed relaxed and for now that was all that mattered. She was pleased now that he'd come to check on her. There was no doubt that her life improved when he was around.

Lily appeared next to Todd. She was wearing a pair of cutoff denim shorts that showed off her long legs, a tiny hot pink top, and her hair was caught up in a ponytail. But what really caught Cecilia's attention was the smile she exchanged with Todd. It was intimate and loving. Familiar.

She glanced at Seth, who winked at her and urged her up the steps to the door.

"You must be Lily, the artist." He shook her hand. "I'm Seth, and I'd like to talk to you once you've given us this tour."

Cecilia expected Lily to protest that she wasn't an artist but instead she seemed to grow a little taller.

"Yes, I am an artist," she said and glanced at Todd with a little smile, "although for the past few days I've been using my paintbrush on walls and woodwork."

"I'm looking forward to seeing the results," Seth said, and Cecilia agreed.

She could see how eager they were to show her what they'd done to the cottage, and she was determined to be a receptive audience.

"Lead on. Where are we starting?"

"In the living room, and we'll work our way upstairs." Todd opened the door and Cecilia took a breath.

She'd set her expectations low. Not because she didn't trust Todd and Lily to do a good job, but because she didn't trust her own emotional response. This place had once been an important part of her life with Cameron, and she didn't think that a coat of paint and a few clever finds in a thrift store would make much difference to how she felt about the place.

The moment she stepped inside she realized she'd underestimated Todd and Lily.

Nothing was where it had been before. Nothing was the same.

The old hard sofa that Cameron had complained about had been replaced with a new, modern version. She could tell without even trying it that the deep cushions would be comfortable, that it would embrace the person choosing to sit on it rather than rejecting them. It was upholstered in cream and scattered with cushions in shades of green and blue.

"The sofa cover is washable," Lily said, "before you think I lost my mind choosing cream."

"It's perfect. And so is the position." Now the sofa faced the windows so that anyone sitting there could enjoy the spectacular view.

The large rug was new, but the coffee table was the same, which pleased her because she was the one who had found that table. She wondered how they'd known what to keep and what to discreetly remove.

But the major change in the room was the walls. What had once been a gallery of Cameron's work until she'd destroyed it, was now floor-to-ceiling shelving that extended over the doorway that led to the kitchen. The shelves were white and displayed books and various objects that she'd collected over the years. A vase filled with shells, a piece of driftwood, a photo of her as a young woman that she couldn't remember seeing before.

"This is spectacular." She stepped closer and ran a finger along the shelves. "Todd? Did you build these?"

"I built them, Lily painted them."

Lily stepped forward. "We chose white because we thought it was more adaptable. You can add pops of color with vases and candles."

"It transforms the room. Don't you agree, Seth?" She turned to look at him and found him staring at the one painting that remained in the room.

The Girl on the Shore hung on the wall above the fireplace, the soft colors drawing the eye and bringing the whole room together. It was as if the cottage had been designed around this one painting.

She hadn't thought about Seth seeing it and suddenly she was anxious about what he might say.

"Let's take a look at the kitchen." She turned to walk through to the kitchen, but he caught her arm.

"Wait. That painting—"

"Let's talk about it later."

He seemed about to argue and then nodded slowly. "All right. If that's what you want."

"It is."

"You don't think it looks good there?" Lily glanced from them to the painting, suddenly doubtful. "I love it so much I thought it should stay right where it was. So did Todd. But maybe you don't want a Cameron Lapthorne displayed with such prominence."

"We can decide that later." Cecilia moved quickly into the kitchen. She admired the newly painted cabinets and the blind that Lily had fitted above the back door, but her mind was back in the living room with the painting.

She should have destroyed it along with the others. She should have consigned it to the past.

And now Seth was watching her, and she knew why. He had questions, and she wasn't sure how she was going to answer them.

She delayed the moment. "I can't wait to see upstairs."

She followed Todd and Lily right up to the top of the cottage.

Lily opened the door. "Todd has worked magic with storage space in here."

"Lily was the brains behind it," Todd said. "I just did as I was told."

The room butted into the eaves and Cecilia saw instantly that the room had been transformed.

Lily gestured to the window seat. "You can sit on it and read while looking at the view, it also doubles as a bedding storage area—" she lifted the lid, proudly displaying neatly folded spare bedding "—and it can be used as an extra bed if needed. Isn't he clever?" She beamed at Todd and Cecilia reflected that while some couples found it impossible to work together, that was clearly not true of Lily and Todd.

Her fondness for her granddaughter's friend was growing by the day.

"It's perfect. Charming."

The second bedroom was equally charming, with Lily's newly restored bookshelf taking pride of place under the window.

"We've saved the best for last." Lily looked visibly nervous as she stood in front of the closed door of the master bedroom. "Are you ready?"

She'd never be ready.

She'd been dreading this moment. Even though she'd forgotten many things over the decades, the image that had confronted her when she'd opened the door so many years ago had stayed with her.

But Lily was so hopeful and optimistic, and she'd tried so hard to make everything feel different for Cecilia that she pushed past her own reticence.

What did it matter? It was all so long ago. And she wasn't doing this for herself, she was doing it for Lily and for Todd. There was no limit to what you could do when you loved someone.

She stepped into the room expecting ghosts and memories and for a moment felt disorientated because this wasn't the room she remembered.

The colors and textures were inspired by the ocean and the natural world, but the design was fresh and contemporary. The pale blue paint scheme that she and Cameron had chosen had gone, and now the room had white shiplap walls, a seagrass rug and glass lamps that reflected the light.

"We tried hard to make it different—" Lily was watching her every reaction, her anxiety palpable "—we bought a new bed. And moved it."

"I can see that." Instead of being tucked under the window, the bed now faced the balcony. The old bed had a heavy oak frame and striped linens faded from too much washing.

The new bed had a simple white rattan headboard, and the bed itself had been dressed in fresh white linens and stacked with pillows in toning shades of washed green and blue. Draped across the bottom was a pale sea green throw, perfect for cooler evenings.

The doors to the balcony were open, flooding the room with sea air and light, and offering far-reaching views across the dunes and the ocean.

Cecilia felt an instant sense of calm, and also relief, as if she'd been set free.

There were no ghosts here. No bad memories. Nothing at all to remind her of the past. The room was so tranquil and welcoming she immediately wanted to move all her things from the second bedroom to this one.

"I can't believe it." She touched one of the walls, running her hand over the line of the wood. "You did this?"

"Just on the one wall," Todd said. "We thought it added texture and a slightly 'beachier' feel."

She never would have thought of doing that. She never

would have thought that a room could be transformed the way they'd transformed this one.

There were bookshelves on either side of the bed, and they doubled as nightstands complete with reading lights.

Cecilia nodded her approval. "Clever idea."

"We wanted to maximize use of space. The room isn't that big. Everything has to work twice as hard."

"You can enjoy the view while you're lying in bed," Lily said. "I never understood why the bed was facing the wall before."

Because in the beginning, she and Cameron hadn't cared which direction the bed was facing.

She smiled as she remembered. There *had* been good times. Many of them.

Todd was watching her. "Take a closer look at the walls, Nanna."

What had she missed? She'd thought the walls were plain white, and only now did she see the small seashells, hand-painted in a creamy pearlescent shade that caught the light. Each seashell was subtle and exquisitely beautiful.

"Todd! You did this?"

He laughed. "I'm flattered that you think I have those skills. Sadly, I don't. This is Lily's work."

Cecilia stepped closer and traced one lightly with her finger. "It's beautiful. Did you do this freehand or use a stencil?"

"She did it freehand," Todd said, and Cecilia heard the pride in his voice.

"Which is the reason some of the seashells are different sizes. And it's not all shells—" Lily pointed to a spot above the bed. "There is the occasional seahorse, too. And a dolphin or two. I did sneak a killer whale in near the bathroom. I've never done anything like this before. It was fun."

Seth took a closer look. "This is extraordinary. I'm going to hire you to redecorate the room my grandchildren use when they stay with me. Gemma is obsessed with starfish. Could you do a starfish?"

"She can do anything. You see?" Todd gave Lily a triumphant look. "I told her she'd be booked up for the rest of the year once word gets out." He put his arm round her, not bothering to hide his feelings.

Cecilia glanced from her grandson's face to Lily, who was all smiles and flushed happiness.

"I wouldn't complain about that. We've had the best time doing this."

"You've both worked so hard."

She had no idea what had happened between the two of them during the few nights she'd been staying at Seth's, but it was clear that it wasn't just her cottage that had undergone a change.

"What do you think?" Lily was nibbling the corner of her nails. "Does the place make you feel calm and happy?"

"I think you've done an incredible job." She walked to the balcony and gazed across the dunes to the ocean. She remembered spending hours on that beach with Cameron, and before that with her friends. And with Seth.

Seth.

She'd only been back in the cottage for a short time and yet everything had changed. She'd felt trapped, like a butterfly in a net, not knowing what to do next.

But now she knew. She knew how she was going to move her life into the next phase. And knowing had freed her.

"Nanna?" Todd stood next to her, waiting, and she reached out and hugged him.

"Thank you," she said. "Thank you to both you and Lily."

"It was our pleasure. Come out on the deck and have breakfast." Todd stepped back into the bedroom. "There's freshly squeezed orange juice and pastries. I was in the bakery the moment it opened this morning, and I may have overdone the quantity. I hope you're hungry."

Cecilia was about to agree that breakfast sounded like an excellent suggestion when her phone rang.

She checked the caller display and felt a flicker of surprise. She answered it immediately. "Kristen?"

"M-Mom?"

Cecilia heard something in her voice and felt anxiety tighten in her stomach. She gestured to the others to go downstairs without her and waited until they'd left the room. "What's wrong? Has something happened?" She closed the doors onto the balcony so that her voice wouldn't carry outside.

"I've left Theo."

Cecilia closed her eyes briefly. So she hadn't been catastrophizing. They really were having problems. Where did Jeff fit into this? Why hadn't she asked Kristen about it? She should have found a way to offer support. She hadn't helped, but she could help now. And underneath her maternal anxiety was a feeling of relief and satisfaction that Kristen had chosen to call her.

It felt like a second chance, and she was determined not to waste it.

"You're upset. Are you driving? You shouldn't be driving."

"I'm not driving right now. I stopped because I needed coffee."

"Where are you?"

"I don't know. Brewster, I think. I decided that if the Cape could heal you, maybe it could heal me, too. I slept in my car last night."

"In your car? Kristen!" Her anxiety deepened. "Why didn't you check into a hotel? Or call me sooner?"

"Because it was already two in the morning when I got into my car. I didn't have the energy and I didn't want people to see me like this. Can I come and see you now? I'd really like to talk. I know you're upset with me, and I'm sorry. I'm sorry I threw a party that you didn't really want." Kristen's voice thickened again. "It was selfish and thoughtless of me, and I feel terrible that you felt you had to run away."

"Oh, Kristen—" Emotion settled like a lead weight in her chest. "You weren't the reason I left, and you have nothing to apologize for. I'm the one who should be apologizing." She felt choked. "I'll explain everything when I see you. But you can't drive. It isn't safe. Stay right where you are. I'll come and get you."

"No, I'm okay to drive, honestly. I've had coffee and the fresh air is helping. Where are you?"

Cecilia gave her the address without hesitation. "We'll see you soon."

"We?"

Cecilia thought about all the things that had happened since the party. "It's complicated. I'll explain everything when you get here. Drive carefully."

She ended the call and headed down the stairs to the kitchen where Todd was stacking a tray with mugs and plates while deep in conversation with Seth.

They seemed to be getting on well, and she was about to throw another complication into the mix.

"How many pastries did you buy? Because we have an extra person joining us for breakfast." And only now did she realize how potentially awkward this was. Kristen was in the middle of a marital crisis and was coming to her for sanctuary and comfort.

Presumably Kristen hadn't yet told her children that she'd left Theo. Maybe she didn't intend to.

But Todd was standing right in front of her.

"Your mother is joining us," she said carefully, and Todd gave her a curious look.

"You told her about this place?"

"I gave her the address. I'll tell her the rest when she arrives. I've had enough of secrets." Her own, at least. Kristen's secrets weren't hers to tell. "Let's make another pot of coffee. Make it a large one."

"Is my father coming, too?"

Cecilia added napkins and cutlery to the tray. "I don't believe so."

She'd leave that explanation to Kristen.

In the end Kristen was so pleased to see her son she didn't seem too interested in his reason for being there.

"I was doing a job nearby," was all he said, and Kristen accepted that without question, and greeted Lily warmly.

"Does Hannah know you're here?"

"No." Lily exchanged glances with Todd. "But I'm going to tell her. I'm going to message her soon. I should have done it before now."

Cecilia braced herself. "And this is Seth, an old friend."

She held her breath as Seth shook hands with her daughter.

Kristen looked more than a little dazed. "You have quite

a little gathering." She looked uncertainly at her mother and Cecilia walked toward her and gave her a hug. Not a perfunctory polite hug between two relatives, but a tight, comforting hug.

She wondered if Kristen might push her away, but she didn't. Instead she hugged Cecilia back, almost clinging to her.

When had they last hugged like this? When had they ever hugged like this?

"It's good to see you." Kristen sniffed and stepped back. "Thank you for allowing me to come."

"I'm glad you're here." Cecilia had to keep her own emotions in check. She released her daughter and took a closer look at her face.

Kristen gave a crooked smile and tried to smooth her hair. "I'm sure I look terrible."

"No, but you do look tired." And she could feel the misery coming off her in waves. "I'm worried about you. Come and sit down. You're just in time for breakfast."

If Kristen was delighted to have left Theo, it didn't show. Her eyes were shadowed, and she looked exhausted.

"Is Dad joining you, Mom?" Todd picked up Kristen's suitcases.

"No. He has to work. I'm having a few days to myself."

And that was what parents did, Cecilia thought. They hid their pain from their children. Protected them. But maybe there came a point where it was better to share than to shut them out. A time when it was better to tell the truth.

Kristen forced a smile. "Is there somewhere I can freshen up?"

"Of course. Let me show you around before we eat." Cecilia gestured to the front door of the cottage but Kristen stopped and stared at the name, freshly painted by Lily on a piece of wood fashioned by Todd.

"Dune Cottage," she said slowly. "This is the place you used to come to with Dad. When Winston and I were little. You spent weekends here."

Cecilia was taken aback. "You know about this place?"

"Not specifics. You were always secretive about it, which made me all the more curious. Whenever I asked Dad where you'd been, he'd always say 'paradise.' He said that you stayed in a cottage that perched on the edge of the dunes, with nothing but sand between you and the ocean. He told me that each bedroom had a balcony." She glanced upward, to the balconies and the shingled roof. "I assumed it was somewhere you rented. You own it?"

Cecilia realized how much she had to share with her daughter. "I thought your father had sold it long ago. I only found out recently that he hadn't."

Cecilia gave her a summary of everything that had happened and Kristen shook her head, confused.

"Why would he pretend he'd sold it?"

"Because he knew I wanted him to sell it."

Kristen didn't ask for her reasons for that. "But he kept it."

"Yes. It was a shock to discover that." She expected Kristen to defend her father as she always did and was surprised when her daughter took her hand.

"I don't understand any of it, but it doesn't matter." Kristen squeezed her hand and let go. "So, you've been renovating?"

"That was Todd and Lily's idea. I found it hard being here. They thought that a makeover might get rid of the memories." The moment the words left her lips she knew she'd misspoken. "I'm sorry—I know you find it difficult that I—"

"No, don't apologize." Kristen touched Cecilia's arm. "Whatever you need to do is fine with me. I feel bad that I didn't know. That you felt you couldn't tell me. I should have talked to you more and been more understanding."

This was a humbler, softer version of Kristen. It was as if this seismic event in her marriage had shaken the foundations of who she was and made her question everything.

They stepped inside and Kristen glanced around her.

"This is a beautiful room. Those shelves. I recognize Todd's work." She scanned the space and then stopped, her gaze fixed on the painting. "*The Girl on the Shore*." She said it quietly, as if she was talking to herself. Then she moved toward it and examined it closely. "This is it. This is the painting everyone has been asking about."

Cecilia stood quietly. This moment had been inevitable of course. And now it was here, the sense of dread left her, and she felt only relief. She wouldn't be able to move on until the whole of the past was cleaned up and this was the last remaining piece.

"Yes. It's *The Girl on the Shore*."

Kristen turned to look at her, questions in her eyes. "The day of the party—you said you thought it had been destroyed long ago."

"I did think that. I thought your father had destroyed it. He was supposed to."

"But why would he? It's stunning." Kristen studied the painting. She appeared to have forgotten that she'd intended to freshen up. She'd forgotten that she was tired, and sad. She appeared to have forgotten about Theo. It was all about the painting. "The brushwork. The use of color and light. It's extraordinary." She pressed her hand to her chest as if she was having trouble breathing. "All these years, it was here?"

"Apparently so."

Kristen rubbed her hands over her arms and turned back to Cecilia.

"When you discovered it, why didn't you call me? Do you have any idea of the value? People have been asking."

"You mean Jeff," Cecilia said flatly. "Jeff has been asking."

Kristen's eyes widened and streaks of pink touched her cheeks. "What do you know about Jeff?"

"I know he has an extraordinary interest in this particular painting."

"Is that surprising? Its value must be huge."

"That isn't why he's interested. And no one outside this family is ever to know the painting is here, particularly not Jeff."

Kristen shook her head, trying to clear it. "You have so many of Dad's paintings that you display openly. What's different about this one? If it's from early in his career, then it has both interest and value. Why wouldn't you want to share that with the world?"

Cecilia stared at the painting. She didn't know where to start.

"I think I can answer that question." Seth spoke quietly. "The reason your mother doesn't want this painting out in the world is because it wasn't painted by your father. It isn't a Cameron Lapthorne."

Kristen glanced at him with a frown. "Of course it is. Granted, it isn't his usual style, but it's an early work." She pointed to the initials. "CL."

Cecilia felt Seth's arm settle around her shoulders.

"In this case CL isn't Cameron Lapthorne."

"But—"

"It's Cecilia Lapthorne," Seth said. "*The Girl on the Shore* wasn't painted by your father. It was painted by your mother."

19

Kristen

"We never intended to deceive anyone," Cecilia said. "We were young. There was a competition locally. One of the galleries invited local artists to display one work in a summer exhibition."

"This was the exhibition where Dad was discovered?" Kristen ignored the pastry that Todd had put in front of her. "Are you saying Dad submitted *The Girl on the Shore*? That doesn't make sense. He must have had paintings of his own. Why submit yours?"

She'd taken a shower and changed into a cool linen dress. She felt tired, but slightly more human than she had when she'd arrived. And she was too captivated by the story unfolding to think about her own feelings right now. The questions were stacking up in her head. She wanted to know why Lily was here. She wanted to know what was happening between her and Todd (she'd seen the way their fingers had brushed and the way they looked at each other), and she wanted to know more about Seth.

But first she needed to know more about this painting and the secrets her parents had been keeping.

How was it that the people closest to you were sometimes the ones it turned out you knew least about?

"He didn't submit it," her mother said. "I did. And there was a mix-up. The initials were CL. The gallery thought it was Cameron's. It was a big exhibition. They were dealing with a large number of paintings."

Kristen was struggling to absorb it. "But when they made the mistake, why didn't you correct them?"

"We didn't know about it. We dropped off the paintings and went back to doing what we were doing, which was mostly painting and doing up Dune Cottage, which had been sadly neglected. We went back to the gallery two weeks later for the opening night of the exhibition, and the award presentation and that was when they announced Cameron as the winner. When we realized which painting had won, we were completely thrown. We didn't know what to do, and there was no opportunity for reflection. There were photographers and people wanting to interview him and see more of his work—it was crazy. Impossible to describe." Cecilia shook her head. "Suddenly he was the focus of all this fuss and attention and we couldn't find the right time to tell them that it wasn't his painting. It would have created so much complication. You're probably thinking it would have been easy to just tell them they'd made a mistake, but at the time it didn't feel easy. We were trapped in the moment. I don't expect anyone to understand."

"I understand," Todd said. "Sometimes circumstances

force you to make an on-the-spot decision that you later regret. It happens."

Kristen glanced at her son. Was he talking about his engagement to Amelie? They'd get to that later. Right now, her focus was her mother.

"Exactly." Cecilia sent Todd a look of gratitude. "Anyway, the whole thing spiraled. An important gallery owner from Boston asked to see more of his paintings, so Cameron showed him his work. It took off from there."

Kristen thought about *The Girl on the Shore*. "But his work was so different from yours. They didn't question it?"

"Cameron was experimenting a great deal back then. Style and medium. There were oils, pastels, watercolors, charcoal—he painted and drew nonstop and at that stage the style that everyone would later recognize as his, hadn't fully developed."

It was an extraordinary story, and one that impacted on more than just her father.

"But it was your painting." Kristen was struggling to incorporate this new information into everything she'd always believed. She knew that her father had been discovered by an influential gallery owner—she didn't know that it was her mother's painting that had been the reason for that initial interest. Why hadn't he ever told her that? She'd thought they were close. She'd thought she knew him well. Evidently not. And she also hadn't really known her mother. "It could have been you. It *should* have been you. This is awful. I never knew. It must have been hard for you."

"It was difficult for both of us. Cameron was insecure about his work in those early days—imposter syndrome isn't uncommon among creative people. And the knowledge that it was my painting that had given him his big break nagged at him. He never felt good enough. Always felt he had to prove himself." Cecilia stared at the basket of pastries that Todd had placed on the table. "That insecurity never really left him, although eventually he learned to live alongside it."

"But he robbed you of an opportunity." Thinking of it made Kristen feel terrible. She'd had no idea. Her father had never once mentioned it, even though they'd talked all the time.

"He didn't rob me of anything," Cecilia said. "It was a mistake, and I could have corrected it, but I chose not to."

"But your career took a back seat to his."

"That was my choice." Cecilia twisted the ring on her finger. "I could have focused on my own work, but I preferred to focus on his. In those early days I still painted, but for my own pleasure. The truth is I would have hated the attention Cameron had to deal with, and also the pressure. I enjoyed being engaged with his career."

"Dad must have felt guilty though."

"He did. He needed constant validation. Constant confirmation that he was as good as people said he was. And he was aware of that." Cecilia paused. "He used that as the excuse for the affair he had."

Her father had an affair? Who was this man? Not the person she'd thought, clearly.

Kristen sat in silence while her mother told her all of it. The cottage. The woman who had been with her father. The subsequent pressure on their relationship.

And she felt guilty because she remembered how distraught she'd been when her parents had separated, and how difficult. She'd punished her mother when she hadn't deserved it.

Emotions sat like a hard stone in her chest. "Why didn't you tell me?"

"Because it wasn't your burden to carry. Parents don't always reveal every aspect of their relationship to their children."

Kristen thought about the fact she hadn't yet told Todd the truth about her reason for being here.

"But if I'd understood—"

"You were a child, Kristen. A child can't possibly understand the nuances of adult relationships. And it was easier not to tell people. Easier to recover from it, and we did recover. We had many good years after that. Many." Cecilia smiled. "A marriage can hit a rocky patch, but survive. It depends on whether what you have is strong enough to be saved. In the end, I wanted to save it. And so did your father. We never regretted that."

Something about her mother's tone and the look in her eyes made her wonder if the words were meant for Kristen.

Kristen thought about Theo. About their marriage. They'd definitely hit a rocky patch. Could their marriage be saved? Did she want that? Did Theo want that?

It all felt too much to deal with right now.

"What happened to *The Girl on the Shore* after that competition?"

"We refused to sell it to anyone. We wanted the mix-up to end right there, so we took it back to the cottage. We agreed that we would never mention it again and never again show the picture. Cameron already had more attention than he could handle, and everyone seemed to have forgotten about that particular painting. And for a while it was fine. No one ever asked about it, and moving forward, everything was Cameron's work. All *The Girl on the Shore* really did was open a door. After a while we barely ever thought about that painting. We certainly never imagined that anyone else would remember it."

"But Jeff knows about it. How?"

"I'm not sure, but Jeff's father was at that first exhibition. He was an art critic with an interest in emerging artists. He saw *The Girl on the Shore* and from then on took a close interest in Cameron's career. He saw that his subsequent work was different, and he had his suspicions. We had an answer for that of course. We said that Cameron had grown—matured. That his style had changed. And all that was true. But Jeff's father raised it from time to time. He was sure it was someone else's painting."

Kristen pushed her plate away. She no longer felt like eating.

"And he told Jeff. So when Jeff asked me about it, he was basically digging for dirt." She felt a sense of hurt and betrayal. She also felt foolish. She'd fallen for his charm. She'd believed that his interest in her was genuine. It hadn't occurred to her for a moment that he was using her. She thought about the attention he'd paid her. The interest he'd shown.

She'd mistaken interrogation for intimacy.

How far would he have gone? Would he have slept with her to get the answers he'd been seeking? Maybe. And she'd been so lonely, so desperate for human connection that she wouldn't ever have thought to question his motives.

"Jeff can't know for sure," Cecilia said. "And neither did his father. Whenever he asked, we said that the painting had been damaged years before and no longer existed. And because Jeff's father would never let the subject go, we agreed we would destroy it. Cameron assured me that he had. When you told me on the night of the party that someone was asking about it, I panicked."

"That was one of the reasons you left in such a hurry?"

"Yes. I'd recently found out that Cameron hadn't sold this place. I no longer trusted that he'd destroyed the painting. Given that Jeff was asking about it, I needed to find out for myself."

Kristen shook her head. "And he hadn't."

"No. And I don't understand why. That part is still a mystery, and always will be."

"I don't think it's a mystery," Todd said. "The painting is yours. He loved you and he loved the painting. Why else would he have kept it hanging here in pride of place? He didn't want to destroy it. He couldn't bring himself to do it. It meant something to him. To both of you."

"Todd's right," Kristen said. "Dad was sentimental. Think about his office—every surface is covered in family photos and bits and pieces that the two of you picked up on your travels. He would never have destroyed anything as beautiful and important as that painting. And I'm glad he didn't. It's precious, Mom, not just because it plays a part in your history but because it's a wonderful painting."

"There's one thing I don't understand." Todd leaned forward. "Why is this Jeff person so interested? Why does it even matter? It's not as if you sold it and passed it off as an original Cameron Lapthorne. No crime was committed."

"That's true," Cecilia said, "but if the story had come out it would have damaged your grandfather's reputation. His integrity. It still would."

Todd reached for the coffeepot and poured it into mugs. "But even if he saw the painting, which he won't, he has no way of proving Grandpa didn't paint it."

"Not for sure, no. I'm the only person who knows the truth. And now you do, too, of course." Cecilia felt a flicker of anxiety. "I should probably do what Cameron was supposed to do and destroy the painting. That would put an end to it."

"No!" Lily half rose to her feet. "You can't do that. And everything you say makes sense—that it never had any real impact on Cameron's career. That part of its history isn't important. It's done and in the past. But the painting is special."

"I agree. It would be criminal to destroy it." Kristen finally voiced her thoughts. She had so many questions she wanted to ask, but one stood out. "Why didn't you paint more yourself? You clearly had a future if you'd wanted one. Your work was the one they picked as the winner of that exhibition."

"Art isn't only about painting, as I suspect Lily has discovered over the past week." Cecilia smiled at Lily. "There are many ways of expressing yourself creatively. When we bought Lapthorne Manor, I started experimenting with the gardens and treated the land around the house as my canvas. I found it more thrilling than painting because it changed constantly. I designed those gardens from scratch, and I had as much satisfaction from planting the borders as I ever did painting a canvas. More, in fact because the garden was alive. Living art. I was able to watch it change with the seasons and the years."

"The gardens are spectacular." She hadn't ever thought of them as art. But they were, of course, she could see that now.

And she realized how much she had to learn about her mother. She'd made so many assumptions, and so many of them had been false. And perhaps the biggest assumption was that her mother didn't care about her.

Her mother cared deeply, which was one of the reasons

she'd kept so much of this from her. But Kristen wished she'd known. Maybe it would have been painful to hear the truth, but she would rather that than not having the full picture.

She glanced across the table at her son, and decided that she was going to be honest with him about the situation with Theo. And she was going to call Hannah. She was going to try and help them to understand but not today, because she needed to rest and make the most of this time with her mother.

She'd called her mother out of desperation, never expecting to be offered comfort or sanctuary and yet here she was being given both. Another example of life taking an unexpected direction.

Her marriage might be imploding, but there were other relationships that were important to her. Other relationships that she needed to nurture.

Her mother smiled at her across the table and Kristen smiled back.

The past was behind them, and it was up to them to mold the future. The potential for a good relationship was right there in front of them.

All they had to do was take it.

20

Lily

"We should have made this bed wider." Lily was conscious that Todd's elbow was jamming into the wall. It wasn't the best sleeping arrangement for him. His shoulders were too broad and his legs too long, but somehow he'd managed to fold himself around her. "We planned this room for grandchildren."

"I am a grandchild."

She laughed and buried her face in his chest to muffle the sound. "You're about six feet longer than the version we were thinking of when we designed it."

"If we snuggle close together it's positively roomy." Todd shifted and pulled her against him. "This could fast become my first choice of sleeping position."

"Me, too." She curved her arm around him and found that her head fitted perfectly against the muscle of his shoulder. "What a day."

"I know. I still haven't got my head around the fact Nanna painted *The Girl on the Shore*."

"I'm the same." But it all made sense now. The reason Cecilia had smashed all the paintings but that one. It hadn't been painted by Cameron. The final piece of the puzzle had fallen into place. "I'm so tired but I don't want to sleep. This is the happiest I can ever remember being and I don't want to waste a moment of it."

She still couldn't believe that she was with Todd. She couldn't stop smiling. She'd smiled so much over the past few days that the muscles in her face should have been tired.

He kissed the top of her head. "Sleep. I promise I can make you happy in the morning, too."

But she knew she wouldn't sleep. She fought her way through the wisps of tiredness that tried to wrap themselves around her brain.

"Have you ever wanted to hold on to a moment because it's perfect?"

"Not until I met you." He murmured the words against her mouth. "But we don't need to hold on to this moment, because we have a million more moments just like this one ahead of us."

"Cecilia was pleased with the cottage, wasn't she?"

"Yes. It was worth the muscle aches, and the blisters and the lack of sleep. Of course you were partly responsible for the lack of sleep."

She smiled against his lips. "I'm not going to apologize. Do you think she'll still sell it?"

He eased away just enough so that he could look at her. "I don't know. I think we wiped away those memories, but maybe this place just isn't the life she wants."

"You mean because she and Seth are—"

"Together. Yes. Maybe it's time she swapped her old life for a new one. That's what she has basically done this summer."

"Like me." Lily stroked her hand over his shoulder and down his arm and wondered if the day would ever come when she didn't want to touch him. "Do you think your mom is okay with her being with Seth?"

"I hope so. She should be." He caught her hand in his and kissed the tips of her fingers. "In the end it's no one's business except Nanna's. It's her life. People should be allowed to make their own choices, and the people around them have to learn to accept it whatever their personal views."

"On that subject, I have something to say."

"You have?" He stilled. "It sounds as if you're about to say something profound. Is this the sort of conversation where we should both be sitting upright so I can give you my interested and supportive look?"

"If you sit up you'll probably bang your head. I'm fine with the lying down version." No one had ever been as supportive of her as he was. He didn't encourage her to be the person he wanted her to be. He encouraged her to be herself.

"Then tell me." He stroked her hair away from her face. "Whatever it is, I'm right there with you, you know that. I'm in your corner."

It was having him in her corner that had made the difference.

"This last week has been the best of my life. I know I've already said that, but I'm saying it again because it's true. And it's not just because of you, although a lot of it is."

"Go on. My ego is loving this."

"I loved transforming this place. And I learned a lot. It isn't just about how a place looks, is it? It's about how it makes you feel. And every single room is different. It's like starting a new canvas." She expected him to tease her for her enthusiasm, but he didn't.

"You're good at it. And I could see how much you enjoyed it."

"It's the first time in my life I've felt comfortable with the work I've done. No anxiety. No pressure. Just a sense of satisfaction and the confidence that I can do it." It was a revelation that she could feel that way. All her life she'd felt as if she was a breath away from failing. She'd thought that the feeling of pressure, the anxiety that almost smothered her in the early hours of the morning, was part of who she was. She'd thought it was something she'd have to learn to live with, to manage, but now she understood that wasn't true. That feeling had gone. "Do you know how good it feels to do something that you love? Yes, you do, because you're doing something you love, too."

"I can see from your face how good that feels." He stroked her cheek with his fingers. "I always said you were meant to be an artist. And Seth seems to think that it might be possible for you to go down a more traditional route."

"Whatever Seth says, I still don't believe I'll make a living from my art. But that doesn't matter. What matters is that I can see now that this life, or some version of it, is possible for me."

"Time will show us whether Seth was right, and in the meantime I can tell you that you *will* make a living using your artistic skills to decorate people's houses. And on that subject, I have a proposition to make. Set up in business with me. You can split your time between art and house renovation."

She sat up because she couldn't concentrate when she was lying this close to him. "Are you serious?"

"Yes. I'm thinking of basing myself here, on the Cape, as we both love it. What do you think?"

"Are you inviting me to join you?"

"Yes. It's a big decision, I know. You probably need time to think about it."

She smiled. "I've thought about it. My answer is yes."

"Yes?"

"Absolutely yes."

"What about your parents?"

Her parents.

Her excitement dimmed just a little, but nowhere near as much as it would have done a few weeks earlier.

"I hope they'll accept that this is what I want to do. I love them, and I want them to be proud of me, but I realize now that I can't make that happen." She shifted so she could look at him properly. "Talking of parents, how are you feeling about your mother being here?"

"You mean without my father?" He sighed and eased away a little. "It was unexpected, that's for sure. But I'm trying to roll with it."

"Was it awkward me being here?" It occurred to her that he probably hadn't intended to go public so quickly.

"I suspect it's more awkward for her. She wasn't expecting me to be here. Extra awkward because it sounds as if my parents are splitting up. She probably didn't intend for me to know yet."

She felt a shaft of sympathy. "I'm sorry."

"Me, too. It feels destabilizing, which is insane, I know, because I'm an adult."

"Being an adult doesn't stop you feeling unsettled by it. Did you know they were having problems?"

"No, but that's probably because I wasn't looking." He stared up at the slope of the ceiling. "My dad was never around that much when I was growing up. He was always at the hospital. Mum was busy working for my grandfather. I suppose I always assumed that their life worked for them."

"Maybe they're just going through a bumpy patch. Maybe they'll figure it out."

"Maybe. Although she left in the middle of the night, so that's not a good sign, is it?" He pulled her closer. "I'd like them to figure out whatever has gone wrong, obviously, but I suppose in the end all I want is for them to be happy. If they can't be happy together, they're better off apart. And I need to get my head round that. The truth is I feel sorry for anyone who doesn't have what we have." He leaned down and kissed her and she thought again that happiness wasn't always easy to find, but when you did the important thing was to hang on to it.

"Me, too. I don't want our time here to end, but if Cecilia decides to sell then we won't be able to stay here."

"If we can't live here, we'll live somewhere else. Together. And it will be just as good." He kissed her gently. "What will your parents say? Will they disapprove?"

"They'll love you, Todd." And if they didn't, it would make no difference to her choices because she loved Todd and wouldn't give him up for anyone.

And suddenly she made a decision.

She needed to do this. Now. Before she changed her mind.

"What time is it?" She reached for her phone, which she'd left on the floor. "It's only eleven. That's not too late."

"Too late for what?" He raised himself on his elbow,

watching as she tugged on her clothes. "What are you doing?"

"I'm going to call my parents." She zipped her jeans and pulled on a sweatshirt. "I'm feeling sure of myself and confident and I need to make this call while I'm feeling this way."

"Isn't it a little late for a chat? They won't be asleep?"

"No. My parents are never in bed before midnight. And I'm not calling for a chat. I'm calling them to let them know my plans. After that, it's all up to them." She slid her feet into her flip-flops. "Wait there."

"I'll come with you for moral support."

She smiled and bent to kiss him. "I'm grateful to you for offering, but no. This is something I need to do by myself. I need to know I can. I need to be okay with it. And you've already given me moral support. That's the reason I know I can do this."

He stared into her eyes for a moment and then nodded. "All right. But as it's eleven, you don't mind if I watch from a distance to check you're okay. You never know what's out there. Giant lobsters. Sharks."

"I'm just going to the edge of the beach, that's all. Far enough so that I don't wake everyone up. I'll be out of reach of lobsters and sharks."

"Fine, but I'll wait for you on the porch anyway, just to be safe."

He dressed quickly and together they crept downstairs.

Leaving Todd on the porch, Lily walked almost to the water's edge, far from listening ears.

For the first time ever, she didn't feel nervous about the call she was about to make. She knew what she wanted, and she knew what she had to say.

She couldn't spend her life trying to be the person other

people wanted her to be. It was exhausting and it made her miserable. She needed to live the life that felt right for her.

She'd been trying to work out how to fix the problem with her parents, but talking to Todd had made her finally realize that it wasn't her problem to fix. It was theirs. They were the only ones who could change the way things were.

She pressed the button on her phone and waited until someone answered.

"Dad? It's me."

21

Cecilia

"Florence?" Kristen paused and anchored her hair against the breeze as she studied her mother. "You're going to spend the winter in Florence?"

Above them the sky was a perfect azure, shot through with tiny wispy clouds. The sea sparkled in the sunlight, the surface calm and still.

"And Rome. Seth does it every winter. He rents somewhere and lives like an Italian for a few months. It sounds perfect."

"Has he always done that?"

"Since his wife died. He told me that trying to live the life they'd lived together was too painful, like stumbling along being only half of yourself. So he built a new life. One that wasn't full of things he'd once done with Sonya. His journey inspired me. And it gave me some of the answers I'd been looking for in my own life. This past year I feel as if I've been frozen in time. I had no idea how to move on."

"I wish you'd told me." Kristen looked tired, and it was obvious from her face that she hadn't slept well. "But that was my fault. I didn't make it easy. I should have asked. I wish I had."

"And I wish I'd asked you about Theo." The words needed to be said, but life was too short for regrets and guilt, she knew that now. Regrets were useful only when they provided a springboard for change. "Both of us were struggling. Let's agree to forgive ourselves, and each other, and move on."

"Yes." Kristen looked startled by that suggestion and then relieved, as if that option hadn't occurred to her. "I'm still adjusting to the fact that my father wasn't the man I thought he was."

"He was." Cecilia slipped her arm into her daughter's, and they strolled along the beach. "He was all the things you thought he was. But he was also human. He made mistakes and bad choices, as we all do. I think loving a person means accepting all of them, even the parts you wouldn't choose."

"I think you're an impressive woman," Kristen said. "You always have been. It's just that I never really thought about it. It was just who you were. You get on with things, no matter how hard. You find a way through. You're an inspiration. Dad was lucky to have you, but he obviously knew that."

"Thank you." Of all the things Kristen had ever said to her, this touched her the most.

"Still, it's a lot to take in. But I will. Life doesn't stand still, does it? As you say, we have to move on." Kristen glanced over her shoulder to Dune Cottage. "What's next for you, Mom?"

"I'm following Seth's example and changing things." She paused, unsure how her daughter would react to her next piece of news. "I'm going to sell Lapthorne Manor, Kristen. It's too big for me, and it's part of my old life, not my new life. When I'm there I can't seem to envisage any life other than the one I lived with your father."

"But what about your beloved gardens?"

"The gardens have been my life's work, but I'm happy to hand them on to someone else to enjoy. It's time."

Kristen stopped walking. "Where will you live? Here on the Cape? At Dune Cottage?"

"I haven't decided. Not Dune Cottage, although I have some ideas as to what I might do with that. I'm probably going to stay with Seth until winter and help him out in the gallery. Like him, I enjoy supporting new artists. It would make an interesting project for me. And when the season is finished, I'll travel with him. After that—well I'll see how I feel." She was already excited about the possibilities. "Todd gave me a planner for my birthday, and I've already started to fill it with things I want to do. We're going to visit galleries and gardens, drink good red wine and strong espresso. I'm going to improve my Italian. And we're going to talk and enjoy each other's company." Cecilia hoped it hadn't been a mistake to tell her daughter so soon. "Are you upset that I intend to sell the family home?"

"No. I'm a little surprised, that's all." Kristen pulled on the sweater she'd looped around her shoulders. It was early morning, and they had the beach to themselves. "It's a lot to take in. This place. The truth about Dad. Meeting Seth. Todd and Lily. I feel as if my world has totally changed."

"Todd and Lily." Just thinking about them made her want to smile. "How do you feel about that development?"

"I'm happy for them," Kristen said. "I'm happy for Todd. I could never understand why he and Amelie were together, but lately I've lost confidence in my ability to be a good judge of other people's relationships."

She'd never seen her daughter so vulnerable and uncertain.

"I don't think anyone can ever really understand another person's relationships."

"Maybe not. I'm very fond of Lily. I always thought she was good for Hannah. Calmed her down and kept her grounded. And Lily and Todd have always been friendly. Whenever she came round to the house, I could hear them laughing together. She sometimes spent as much time talking to Todd as she did Hannah. I'd say they're perfect together. Although what do I know?" Kristen gave a tired smile. "I never would have thought I'd leave Theo. I've shocked myself."

"I'm sure you've shocked him, too. But that could be a good thing."

"What do you mean?"

"Sometimes, when you've been with someone for a long time, you stop checking in with them. You assume you know how they feel. You stop paying attention. I suspect Theo is guilty of that." She felt a flash of sympathy for Theo, but more for her daughter. She knew how it felt to be with a partner whose work dominated everything.

Kristen stared out across the ocean. "Part of me feels guilty for feeling this way because I knew who Theo was when I married him."

"You mean his commitment to his job?" She didn't know the details of course, but she wanted her daughter to know she could talk to her. "What changed, honey?"

"I think I changed." Kristen slipped off her flip-flops and curled her toes into the soft sand. "It isn't really about his working hours, although that contributes because it reduces the amount of time that he's physically present. It's more that he doesn't see me. Or hear me. Even when he's there physically, he isn't there emotionally." She stopped and picked up her flip-flops. "I suppose when the kids were young, and even when they were at college, I was always busy, too. I didn't question my life. But after we lost Dad—well, lately I've been feeling pretty lonely. Even when Theo is in the house I'm lonely because he just doesn't seem to be tuned in to how I'm feeling. He assumes I'm fine all the time. I suppose that's why I was so receptive to Jeff. He listened. He was interested in me." She pulled a face. "Except he wasn't, was he? And it hurts to admit that he wasn't interested in me at all. I'm such a fool."

"Trusting someone doesn't make you foolish." Cecilia felt something tug inside her. "Did you love him, honey? Are you brokenhearted?"

"The only thing that is broken is my pride." Kristen stared across the water. "I didn't love him, but I loved the way he made me feel. For a while I wasn't lonely. I suppose I used him as much as he used me. Maybe that's why I don't feel worse about it."

Cecilia couldn't help feeling relieved that Jeff didn't seem to have made a dent in her daughter's heart. "I know something about feeling lonely. I wish we'd had this talk a long time ago. I blame myself for that."

"Don't. I didn't find it easy to talk about it. I didn't even talk about it with Theo, not properly, until something exploded inside me." Kristen bent down and retrieved a shell from the sand. "After Dad died, I felt so lost. His death left a big gaping hole in my life. I didn't know what to do. I didn't know how to be without him. I felt horrible, and I wanted to fix that because that's what I do when there's a problem. I find a solution. But there wasn't a solution to this. I couldn't fix it, and no one understood how I felt. Theo couldn't see how broken I was. How lost. Small resentments that I would have shrugged off in other circumstances, turned into mountains. I couldn't see past them."

Cecilia felt a shaft of sympathy. "It has been a difficult time."

"Yes." Kristen was silent for a moment. "I'm pleased about you and Seth, Mom."

Cecilia turned to look at her daughter. "Are you?"

"Yes. It's so hard to find someone you trust and love in this world. You deserve happiness. I'm glad you've found it. And I like Seth."

Cecilia was surprised. The last thing she'd expected was a vote of approval from her daughter. "I was afraid you'd think it was too soon."

"Too soon to find happiness again? It could never be too soon for that."

Cecilia felt a rush of warmth. She hadn't realized how much Kristen's approval and support would mean to her.

"Thank you."

"For what? For accepting what you want? The life you choose? I should have done that sooner. I'm sorry, Mom. I'm sorry for all the times I blamed you for the problems between you and Dad. I feel terrible about it."

"Don't feel terrible. I could have talked to you about it. Not at the time, perhaps, but when you were older. I should have tried harder to bridge that gap."

"When you left the party so suddenly, I thought maybe I was the reason. That you wanted to get away from me."

"Kristen! No. I was in a terrible state that day. Panicking

about the painting, and the cottage. Confused about my life. It wasn't you, it was the party. The thought of standing up in front of all those people was just too much."

"And I should have seen that. I should have closed the door on everyone and talked to you about it instead of running around with my to-do list in my hand, ticking off jobs."

"I love you, Kristen." It seemed important to say the words. "I've been bad at communicating it, but I do love you."

"I love you, too." Kristen sounded wistful. "Are we too old for things to be different?"

"I'm about to embark on a new life with a man who is a grandfather, so no, I think I can say with confidence that it is never too late to build on a relationship. And maybe with age and experience we'll do better."

"I hope so. I intend to." She paused. "Are you going to tell Winston all this?"

"Definitely. No more secrets. I plan on calling him when we get back from our walk. I'm hoping he might visit on the weekend." Cecilia gave some thought to her daughter's situation. "What are your plans? Where are you going to live? Or are you going to ask Theo to leave?"

"I don't know. I didn't exactly plan any of this. I didn't give it any thought at all. Leaving was an impulse." They strolled closer to the water's edge. "But I don't regret it. I'm sad, but I have to accept that Theo and I need different things. He isn't able to give me what I want. And I don't think he's interested in trying. Maybe we've just grown apart. Or maybe I've changed, and he hasn't. I don't know, and I don't suppose it really matters now."

Cecilia noticed the tall male figure, hovering uncertainly at the edge of the dunes.

"I wouldn't be so sure about that." She touched her daughter's arm. "You have a visitor. He's here."

"Who is here?"

"Theo."

"Theo?" Kristen turned her head. Her eyes widened. "No, that's not possible."

"Why isn't it possible?"

"Because he's supposed to be working. And nothing comes between Theo and his work. Also I didn't tell him where I was going. How can he be here? Why would he be here?" Kristen looked panicked.

"I assume he's here because he wants to talk to you. And given that he's driven all the way here, and presumably abandoned work in order to do it, you should probably at least listen to what he has to say." And Cecilia hoped with all her heart that the man would say the right thing. "Keep an open mind, Kristen. If there is one thing I learned from all those years with your father, it's that a bump in the track doesn't have to derail the train. Whatever you decide is best for you, you have my support. But listen to him first. Take him down to the beach. Sea air and the view always makes things clearer somehow."

She had a feeling that it was going to take more than a breeze and a beach to fix the dents in her daughter's marriage, but it was a start.

22

Kristen

Kristen walked back across the sand to the cottage. She felt nervous and on edge.

She hadn't anticipated Theo turning up here. She didn't know how she felt about that. She wasn't ready. She hadn't thought through what she would say when she saw him next.

She had no idea what she wanted.

She'd been so angry the night she'd left, but the heat had cooled and left only sadness.

She wasn't capable of hiding her feelings. She was sad, and she knew the sadness showed. And maybe that was all right. The years they'd spent together would have been diminished if she hadn't felt sad. Overall, they'd been good years.

She lifted her hand and scraped her hair back from her face. Her usually carefully styled hair was windblown and tangled. She wasn't wearing a scrap of makeup. Her flip-flops were dangling from her fingers and her skirt flapped against her legs in the breeze. Maybe this was what it came down to. Them being their most basic selves, devoid of artifice.

"Theo." She kept her voice steady. "What are you doing here? You're supposed to be working."

"I found someone to cover for me."

Her mouth almost fell open. He'd asked someone to cover for him? She couldn't think of a time when he'd done that. "Why?"

"Because I needed to see you. To talk to you."

"How did you find me?"

"I tracked your phone. Don't be angry. It's the first and only time in our marriage that I've done such a thing and if you want me to leave right away then I will."

"Why didn't you just call and ask where I was?"

"I was afraid you wouldn't answer. I was afraid you wouldn't want to speak to me." He took a breath. "And I wouldn't have blamed you if that was the case."

He seemed nervous around her. Theo, the calmest most in control person she knew, was nervous to be talking to her. His hair was ruffled and a couple of buttons on his shirt were undone, as if he'd dressed in a hurry and hadn't bother glancing in a mirror.

"You could have come after you'd finished work."

"I was afraid that might be too late," he said. "Seeing you was my priority, and despite what you may think, you *are* my priority. Our marriage is my priority."

She couldn't quite believe he'd asked someone to cover for him. It made the hurt inside her feel a little less raw. "What did you want to say?"

He glanced at her and then at the beach. "Can we walk for a bit?"

"If that's what you want." She stood still and waited as he walked toward her and then she turned and retraced her steps. There was no sign of her mother, so presumably she was back inside the cottage.

They walked side by side in silence for a few minutes, the only people on this stretch of sand.

Finally, he stopped. "Those things you said to me the other night—"

She wasn't going to apologize, and she wasn't going to take any of it back. "I meant every word, Theo."

"I know. I've had time to think about it, and everything you said was true. I wasn't there when Todd was born, and I should have been. I was in the middle of a difficult surgery, and I made a bad choice. I thought I could finish the tricky part of the operation and still get to you in time. I was wrong. I regret it, but nowhere near as much as I regret not being there when your father was brought into hospital..." He waited a beat, choosing his words. "Despite what you think, it wasn't because you weren't my priority. It wasn't because I didn't care."

She waited, saying nothing and Theo turned to look at her.

"I never felt as if you really needed me, Kristen."

She frowned. "Theo—"

"Let me finish, because this isn't easy to explain." He rubbed his fingers across his forehead. "You're the most competent, capable person I know. You are perfectly in control of every aspect of your life. There is nothing you can't handle. Or so I thought. As I said, my default is to assume you don't need me."

She stared at him. He thought she didn't need him?

He carried on talking. "The people I deal with at work—

342

they need me. I do what I can to make a difference. And I can handle it because I cut out emotions. To be an effective surgeon I have to be able to block out the knowledge that the relatives are in the waiting room, relying on me to save their loved one. I have to block out feelings altogether."

"I know this, Theo. And I know you're a gifted surgeon." She couldn't stay silent on that. "I've always known that."

"What I'm saying is that I learned how to switch it off and that became second nature to me. What was harder," he said slowly, "was being able to switch it back on. I'd programmed to stay detached. When your father died, you were bereft. For the first time ever you seemed to need me, and I had no idea how to comfort you. I had no idea how to fix it for you. I have never felt so useless. The one time you desperately needed me, and I was failing. It wasn't that I didn't care, Kristen. It was never that I didn't care. I cared deeply, and that was the problem." He put his hands on her shoulders and turned her to face him. "You said that I seem to be able to handle everyone's emotions except yours, and that's true. But that isn't because you're not important to me. It's the opposite. I can handle other people's pain because I can detach myself emotionally. Even with Michael, when he was miserable about his marriage, I was able to maintain a degree of emotional detachment. That's second nature. But with you? I've never been able to detach, and when your father died— your lowest moment—I was left trying to deal with emotions I had no idea how to handle, both my own and yours."

She looked into his eyes and what she saw there made her heart turn over.

His hands tightened on her shoulders. "You are the person I love most in the whole world. The person I care most about. I love the kids, obviously, but it begins with you. My whole job is to help people, that's what I do, but after your father died—" he swallowed "—do you know how it feels to not be able to help the one person you want to help? I felt impotent watching you grieve. Helpless. I had no idea what to do or say to make it better. I had no idea how to comfort you. I had no idea how to fix things."

She didn't know what to say so she let him talk.

"Despite my job, I had no experience dealing with grief," he said. "I break bad news and then I'm out of there, leaving someone else to handle the fallout. It wasn't until we lost Michael that I had some understanding of how it felt to lose someone you love. It made me realize that no one can make the pain go away. You can't rush a grieving person to surgery and fix it. The best you can do is be there for them, as you were for me. I'd wake up in the night and you'd be there beside me holding my hand. And when I was sad, you'd rub my shoulders and bring me a cup of coffee. It wasn't what you said. It was just the fact that you were there, and you made sure that I knew you were there." He paused. "You taught me that support doesn't always mean fixing things. Sometimes it means just staying close to someone and supporting them through all the bad things that they're feeling. I wish I'd known that sooner."

She felt her own throat thicken.

"Theo—"

"I'm not good at that, so I focus on what I am good at. You said I need the applause and the limelight, but that isn't true. What I need is to feel that I'm making a difference. That my contribution matters. That's why I work more than I should. Because I feel I'm making a difference. But somehow, with you, I didn't feel I could help. I should have sat down and talked to you. I should have asked you what you needed, what I could do. You were so busy all the time, so full on, I assumed you were fine. And that's no excuse," he said quickly. "Those things you said to me were hard to listen to, but the hardest thing was hearing you say you'd forgotten how it felt to be happy. That for a short time another man had made you happy."

"I didn't have an affair, Theo."

"I believe you. It doesn't matter anyway. I'm not losing us and what we have over that. I don't care. I only care about the fact that being with me wasn't making you happy. Of everything you said, those were the words that hit hardest." His hands tightened on her shoulders. "I didn't go to bed that night. I sat on the bottom stair where you'd been sitting when I came home, and I thought back over our marriage. You said I'd chosen my life and my priorities, but Krissy you're my priority. Nothing is more important to me than your happiness. And if you'll give me another chance, I'll prove it to you. I can't ever make up for not being by your side in the hospital the night your father died, and not being there for you afterward in the way that you needed, but if you'll give me another chance I swear I will be there for you from this point on."

She heard the love and sincerity in his voice and knew that he meant what he was saying.

But that didn't mean she believed he could do it.

On the other hand, he'd delegated work to someone else and driven out here to talk to her, so that told her something.

"We can't change who we are, Theo."

"Change?" He paused. "No. You're right. We can't change. Not completely. This is who I am. But can I do better? Yes, definitely. Can I make you happy? I believe I can, Krissy, if you'll give me that chance."

She respected the fact that he wasn't promising to change into a different person. And she wouldn't have wanted him to change who he was. Just the way he acted on occasion.

And the fault wasn't all his, she could see that now.

"You're right that I do try and hold everything together. I'm not good at saying when I'm not coping." Why hadn't she talked to him properly, before they'd reached the point of explosion? "I need to tell you how I'm feeling, instead of expecting you to read my mind."

He gave a tentative smile. "Given how bad I am at reading your mind, that would be helpful."

"And I need to put more things into my life." She thought about her mother, stepping forward into a new life so bravely. It was never too late to change things. "I don't know what yet. I haven't thought that far. But I can see that I let my life with my father consume me. It's time to broaden my horizons."

"Maybe we can think that through together. Maybe it's time we both broadened our horizons. What do you think?"

Together.

He was asking her if they could have a second chance and she thought about Trisha, who would have done anything to have a second chance with Michael. And her mother, who had forgiven her father the affair and gone on to have a long and happy marriage.

"Let's try it," she said finally. "Take it day by day."

"I'm on probation?"

"Maybe. To keep you on your toes." She smiled. "We'll see how many times you leave me stranded in a restaurant over the next month, and then reassess."

He grabbed her and hugged her tightly, muttering words into her hair that she couldn't quite make out. And she hugged him back, because it felt good to be held by him without a gaping distance between them.

They stood like that for a moment, locked together, and then eventually she pulled away.

"We should go back to the cottage. You must be tired after your drive. I'll make you coffee."

"Coffee would be appreciated. What is this place, anyway?" He glanced over his shoulder to the cottage and she smiled.

"It's a long story. I'll tell you another time."

Because there would be another time, she already knew that. She'd try again, and he'd try again, because that was what people did when they loved each other and she did love Theo and she believed that he loved her, too.

For now, that was enough.

23

Lily

The gallery was crowded, the space filled with the clink of glasses and the hum of conversation.

"How does it feel to see your paintings hanging on the wall?" Todd appeared by her side and handed her a glass of champagne.

"It feels surreal," Lily said, "although there are so many paintings here, I don't suppose anyone will notice mine."

She glanced across the crowd, but the two people she wanted to attend weren't here. Every time the door to the gallery opened her heart pumped a little harder, but it was never them. It was foolish of her to expect it. Definitely foolish of her to risk spoiling this once-in-a-lifetime moment by hoping for something that was never going to happen.

"Not notice yours? Have you looked recently? There's a crowd around them, Lily. I'll show you." Todd took her hand, but she held back.

"No, that's too embarrassing. What if someone realizes I painted them?"

"That's the idea. You're supposed to mingle and talk about your work. People are interested." He propelled her across the gallery toward the section where her paintings were hung.

A young couple were gazing at her watercolor of the dunes at dawn.

"It would be perfect in the living room, above the fireplace," one of them said and the other nodded.

"I agree."

Lily froze. It felt both uncomfortable and exhilarating to hear strangers talking about her work.

"I love that painting, too." Todd tugged her forward. "And this is the artist, just in case you had any questions."

"Todd, no." She dug in her heels and sent the couple a look of mortified apology. "I'm sorry."

"You're the artist?" The man shook her hand. "It's good to meet you."

They talked for a while and Lily answered their questions, aware that a small crowd had gathered around her.

When she finally extracted herself, she glared at Todd.

"That was so awkward! Why did you do that?"

"Because I'm proud of you." He kissed her briefly. "Better get used to it."

"What if they'd hated my painting?"

"I could see they loved it, but if they *had* hated your painting I would have tipped my champagne over them and insisted that they leave immediately. But they didn't hate it. You're a success. And talking of success, I heard back from the couple in Truro earlier. I sent them the photos of your wall with the hand-painted seashells. They want to commission you to do the same in their master bedroom and are willing to pay handsomely."

She felt as if she was floating. "Really?"

"Yes, really. They wanted to know if you could do a flower bedroom for their young daughter, and I said of course you could because you're a genius."

She felt dazed. "A flower bedroom?"

"Daisies and sunflowers were mentioned. Let's put it this way, it's safe to resign your job anytime you like. In fact, you should because you're not going to have time to do it after next week. We're in business." He was about to kiss her again when he caught sight of someone over her shoulder. "Wow. Have you seen my grandmother? She looks so elegant."

Lily turned, and saw Cecilia talking to a group of people, one of whom was Seth.

She was wearing a cream dress that fell to her ankles, with a matching floaty jacket and silver jewelry.

She caught sight of them, excused herself and walked over to them. "What a triumph." She took Lily's hands. "Has Seth told you he's already sold both your paintings?"

"Both of them? No."

"He intended to. He was on his way over to you, but he keeps getting waylaid. I can't believe how many people that man knows. And as for you," she said, squeezing Lily's hands, "congratulations. And this is just the beginning."

"I don't know how to thank you."

"You're the one who did it. I can't wait to see what the future holds for you."

Lily hadn't known it was possible to feel this happy and excited and she held the feeling close because she knew that whatever good times lay ahead, there would also be bad and that you needed to celebrate life whenever you could. And yes, she wished her parents were here, but with Cecilia, Seth, Todd and now Kristen in her corner she felt loved and supported.

The gallery was filling up now as more people arrived, and Lily was pressed into a corner between a display of ceramic pots and a sculpture in bronze, when she heard someone say her name.

She turned and there was Hannah, looking nervous and unsure.

"Hannah? What are you doing here?" Joy flooded through her and then she reined it in. Hannah was probably here because of Cecilia, or Kristen.

"I came because I heard a great deal of buzz about a certain new artist."

"You did?"

"Yes, she's supposed to be a major talent." Hannah gave an uncertain smile. "You have a lot of supporters, Lily."

"People have been great. Your grandmother, Seth, Todd—" She broke off. How would Hannah feel about her relationship with Todd?

"You look different." Hannah scanned her swiftly. "Stunning. I'm used to seeing you in track pants and sweaters hunched over textbooks and a laptop, and you look transformed. That red jumpsuit with your dark hair—you look like an artist. Which is what you have always been of course, it's just that I didn't want to see it." She hesitated. "I don't know what to say, so I'm just going to say I'm sorry. I'm sorry I didn't listen. I'm sorry I wasn't a better friend to you when you were feeling so down. I have missed you so, so much—you have no idea. If you'll forgive me, I promise to do better. But maybe you can't ever forgive me—oh," she gasped as Lily grabbed her and hugged her.

"I've missed you, too. I should be the one apologizing to you." She breathed in Hannah's perfume and felt the strength of her hug. "I should have tried harder to explain how I was feeling."

"It was my fault. You were struggling and all I did was tell you you'd be fine. I can't believe I said that." Hannah sniffed. "I'm going to be a terrible doctor."

"You're going to be a brilliant doctor. You were made to be a doctor." Lily eased away. "But I wasn't."

"I know. Maybe I've always known that, but I got so used to following a path with you I didn't know how to walk it alone. I was afraid to walk it alone. I was being selfish. I didn't want you to give it up." Hannah gave her a watery smile. "What kind of friend am I?"

"A good one. The best."

"So can we start again?"

"We don't need to start again. We've been friends forever."

Hannah blew her nose. "From now on I will always be there for you, even when I don't understand why you're doing something. Even when you're not telling me everything. You can count on me."

"And you can count on me. And from now on I will be telling you everything."

"That's a relief, because I didn't want to have a sister-in-law who didn't speak to me."

Lily felt herself blush. "We haven't—he hasn't—"

"But he will. And you will." Hannah grinned. "And quite right, too. It should have happened long before now. But better late than never, and all that. And now we've got all the emotion out of the way and everything is right with the world again, where's the food?"

Lily couldn't resist teasing her. "I thought you came to see my paintings?"

"I've put in two all-nighters and I can't remember when I last ate. If I don't eat, I won't be able to properly appreciate your genius."

"There are canapés."

"Better than nothing. We'll grab a plate. We can pretend we're taking them round but secretly stand in a corner and eat the lot. Oh, hi, Todd." She kept her tone casual as Todd approached. "Just catching up on all the family gossip. I just saw Mom and Dad holding hands in the corner, and I'm not sure if that's a bit gross or a good thing, so you'd better enlighten me."

"It's definitely a good thing." Todd put his arm around Lily and grinned at his sister. "Good to know you're speaking to me again."

"Yes, well, you were making some questionable decisions but you seem to have sorted yourself out thank goodness—" Hannah glanced between him and Lily and shook her head. "You two can't keep your hands off each other, Mom and Dad are smiling at each other again, and Nanna has fallen in love. There must be something in the air. I'm wondering if I should move to the Cape. Maybe if I stayed here for a while my love life might improve."

"You'd hate it here," Todd said. "It's too quiet for you."

"Maybe. So what happens now? Are you staying in Nanna's mystery cottage?"

"For now. And on that topic, I need to steal Lily away because Nanna wanted to talk to us and there's a local reporter who wants a photo of Lily with her paintings."

Hannah rolled her eyes. "Yeah, yeah, leave me. Go and be important." But she smiled and gave Lily a push. "See you in a minute. I'm off to forage for something to eat."

"I'm not sure I want to talk to a reporter." Lily glanced back at her friend and laughed as she saw Hannah holding a tray of smoked salmon. "I love your sister."

"I know. And she loves you."

"I'm so pleased you invited her. And relieved she came."

True friendship could survive most things, she thought, and what she and Hannah shared was true friendship. She imagined a future full of big family gatherings, but also times when Hannah and she would meet, just the two of them, sharing all their thoughts as they had when they were children. Whenever she had a health emergency she'd call Hannah, and whenever Hannah moved to a new apartment she'd call Lily to help with the decorating. Each had found their niche.

And here she was in her niche. She even managed to smile for the journalist as he took her photograph next to the painting.

And then Cecilia drew them both to one side.

"I love what you've done with the cottage," she said, "and I hope what I'm going to say next won't offend you."

"You're not going to live in it," Todd said, and Lily felt a thud of disappointment. It felt like failure somehow. Despite everything, she hadn't managed to make Cecilia fall back in love with the place.

"The cottage was once important in my life, but those days are gone. It's part of my past, not my future. You can't go backward. Or if you can, I wouldn't want to." Cecilia was positively glowing. "Seth has asked me to move in with him, and I've said yes."

Todd nodded. "Good decision, Nanna. He's a good man. I'm happy for you."

Lily smiled because it was a good outcome for Cecilia. "I'm happy for you, too."

Cecilia glanced between them. "Aren't you going to ask me about the cottage?"

"I assume you're going to sell it," Todd said. "And we'll help, of course. Just let us know what you need us to do."

Lily admired how calm and accepting he was because she knew he would be every bit as sad to leave the cottage as she would. But he didn't let his disappointment show. He wasn't going to put that pressure on his grandmother.

"I'm not going to sell it. Seth pointed out that property is an excellent investment, so for now I'm going to keep it. I won't be able to relax and enjoy my winter travels in Italy if I know the place is empty, so if the two of you wouldn't mind living in it, then you'd be doing me a favor."

"Living in it?" Lily stared at her. "You're going to let us rent it?"

"Your payment will be looking after it for me. It will give you a chance to see how you like living this far out. If it works out, maybe we can talk about you owning it. But eventually you might want to move closer to town. For now, the place is yours if you want it. If you're able to help me out. It's asking a lot, I know."

If they wanted it?

Todd was grinning. "I think we can manage it. Lily?"

"Oh yes." She imagined living there with Todd, just the two of them. She'd paint, and they'd run their business and when they weren't working they'd cook delicious food in the pretty kitchen and walk on the seashore. "I don't know what to say, except thank you."

"I should be thanking you," Cecilia said. "You've worked so hard on the place. You deserve to enjoy what you've created. And now that's sorted, you need to talk to Seth, Lily. There is a couple here tonight who want to commission something from you."

She was about to answer when she felt Todd's hand on her arm.

"Lily—"

"What?" She followed his gaze and saw her parents standing in the doorway of the gallery, looking lost. She'd been so certain they wouldn't come that she thought she must be hallucinating. "I don't believe it."

For a moment she couldn't move, and then she saw Kristen walk quickly toward them, hands outstretched in welcome.

"Come on." Todd grabbed her hand. "Time to show them who you really are. Relax. My mother is great at making people feel welcome."

She was glad he was with her, because she felt oddly nervous going to talk to her parents. They'd said almost nothing when she'd called them and told them her plans, and she had no idea what they were going to say now.

"Lily!" Kristen smiled at her. "I was just telling your parents how proud they're going to be when they see your work. And both paintings sold already. She has a great career ahead of her, and I consider myself something of an expert."

Lily felt a rush of gratitude and hugged her parents awkwardly. "I'm so pleased you came."

"Lily." Her mother blinked, as if she was seeing her for the first time. "I barely recognized you. You look wonderful."

"You look wonderful, too."

Her mother was wearing what seemed to be a new dress and her father was wearing a jacket and tie. They both looked self-conscious.

The next half hour was a whirl as they greeted Todd and then Hannah, and went to see the section of the gallery where Lily's paintings hung.

She was more nervous showing her parents her work than she'd been when she'd shown Seth.

They both stared at the paintings and then at each other.

Her mother clutched her father's arm. "Look at that, Stan."

"I'm looking, Moira. I'm looking."

"Our girl."

"Yes."

"Someone has bought her painting." Her mother pressed her hand to her mouth. "A stranger. A stranger paid money."

Lily understood how alien it must be for them, because that wasn't the world she'd been raised in. It wasn't the world her parents knew. But it seemed that the extra endorsement from someone who didn't know her made all the difference.

"Big money," her father said. "I'm thinking those paintings of hers that we have around the house are going to be worth something."

"Stan!" Her mother turned to him, horrified. "I hope you're not suggesting we sell them?"

"Sell them? We're going to keep them. Probably a better investment than a savings account." Her father reached out and patted Lily awkwardly on the shoulder. "Good work, honey. I might not understand how your brain works, but I admire it."

She felt as if she'd won the lottery.

Still, she was keen to reassure them.

"I don't know if I'm going to make a success of this," she said, "but I do know I'm happy. And it's my responsibility to make it work in one way or another whether that's painting walls or painting canvases. You don't need to worry about me."

"We're not worried," her mother said. "Not anymore. We can see how happy you are. And Kristen showed us a photograph of the bedroom you decorated. Those seashells! Wherever did you get that idea?"

They looked at her as if they were seeing her for the first time.

"Let me show you round the rest of the exhibition," Lily said.

They walked with her, pausing in front of different paintings, her mother effusive and her father a little bemused by it all. They greeted Hannah warmly, and Lily introduced them properly to Todd, who charmed them so completely that Lily fell in love with him all over again.

"You seem so comfortable here, Lily," her mother said. "As if this is your world."

"It is my world. I fit here."

Her mother nodded. "We're proud of you, honey."

"Of my paintings?"

"Yes, we're proud of that. But mostly we're proud of you for standing up for what you wanted, and what you knew was right. When you called that night—" her mother swallowed "—well, I'm just sorry we didn't make that easier for you. We didn't understand. This wasn't a world we could picture. But now we can."

Lily thought about what she'd learned from Cecilia, about moving forward. "Thank you for coming tonight. It means everything to me." She gave her mother a quick hug and then stepped back as Kristen approached.

"Moira! There's someone you must meet—" She bustled Lily's mother away and Lily watched as her mother smiled, chatted and tentatively sipped at the glass of champagne she'd been handed.

"Hi there, girl in the red jumpsuit," Todd's voice came from behind her. "Are you the hot young artist everyone is talking about?"

She turned. "I think you must have the wrong person."

"I don't think so." He curled his fingers around her hand. "Let's get out of here. I need some air. I can only stand a crowd of this size for so long. Frankly I can't wait to get back to our cottage on the dunes."

Our cottage.

She checked on her mother and saw her laughing with Kristen. "I should check on my dad."

"He's with my dad. They're talking about boats."

"He doesn't know anything about boats."

"Neither does my dad. It almost makes the conversation worth listening to, but I want five minutes alone with you."

They left the crowds behind them, crossed the road and strolled to the waterfront.

"I can't believe your grandmother is letting us live in the cottage."

"I know. It's going to be great. And if winter gets a little long and cold out here, we can always head back to Boston for a break."

"I can't imagine ever needing a break from this place." She leaned her head against his shoulder, and he wrapped his arms around her as they watched the sun go down over the ocean.

"I love you." He pulled her closer. "I love you so much."

"I love you, too. Remember when we were working on the living room, and you asked me if it felt as if I was living my best life when I was studying for exams? You asked if I was happy."

"I remember."

"I'm happy now." She slid her arms around his neck. "With you."

The sea. The sand. The cottage. Her art. Todd, and the future that stretched ahead of them.

This was her best life.

* * * * *

Acknowledgments

I've been lucky in my writing career to have been supported by many brilliant and generous people, some of whom I've worked with for many years. I'd particularly like to thank Loriana Sacilotto, Margaret Marbury, Susan Swinwood, Lisa Milton and Manpreet Grewal and the hardworking publishing teams at Canary Street Press and HQ Stories.

I'm grateful to my editor, Flo Nicoll, who I have been lucky enough to work with for the past eleven years. This will be the thirtieth book we've worked on together and I'm constantly in awe of Flo's ability to see exactly what a book needs to make it better. Not only is she a brilliant editor, but she's a brilliant person and we have so many laughs together.

I wouldn't want to navigate the stormy seas of publishing without my wonderful agent, Susan Ginsburg. When she agreed to represent me eleven years ago, I knew I was a lucky author and I've continued to feel that way every day since. I'm grateful to her, and to Catherine Bradshaw and the whole team at Writers House.

My family are endlessly supportive, and fortunately nowhere near as complicated as the families I write about in my books!

I'm indebted to my readers. To those of you who read, and reread, my books, take time to message me, engage on social media and write reviews—thank you.

Turn the page for a **SNEAK PEEK** at
the uplifting new Christmas novel from

SARAH MORGAN

The Christmas Cottage

SARAH MORGAN
Read
yourself
happy

COMING OCTOBER 2024

1

It began as a casual conversation and Imogen wasn't quite sure at what point things had started to go so wrong. It wasn't her fault. At least, not *all* her fault. She'd wanted to be friendly, that was all. To form a bond with her colleagues. That wasn't exactly a crime, was it? It was almost a requirement of open-plan offices. They created an atmosphere of familiarity. Sitting side by side and across from the people you worked with encouraged confidences, and chat, and allowed for the gradual absorption of tiny granules of information that you didn't even realize you'd overheard. It was intimacy by osmosis.

"Hey, Imogen." Anya glanced at her across the desk. She was a makeup addict and spent at least half an hour of every day extolling the virtues of her latest find. Today her eyelids glittered like an ornament on a Christmas tree. "Did you see the email from the boss? She's planning a 'bring your dog to work day' the week before Christmas."

"I saw the email." Her day had gone downhill from there.

Bonding with her colleagues was important, but she liked to keep her work life and her home life separate. "Did you get the costings for those venues, Anya? I have to get that proposal to Rosalind to check before it goes to the client at lunchtime."

Pets, clothes, makeup, diets, travel, food, movies, books, bad dates and irritating clients. That covered the bulk of the conversation that bounced around the office.

"Just waiting on the last two. Isn't it a brilliant idea? Every dog wears a festive outfit and Rosalind will pick the winner. All for charity. It will be so much fun. I'm wondering whether I can persuade my little Cocoa to wear antlers. Generally he hates having his head touched, so maybe not. But we get to dress up, too. I bought a new sparkly highlighter on Saturday. Perfect for Christmas. There was a discount if you bought two, so I got one for you, too." She passed it across the desk and Imogen felt a lump in her throat.

"That's for me? Why?"

"Just because." Anya shrugged and grinned. "Call it a thank-you for helping me out of that sticky client situation last week. Also, you have great cheekbones and it will look good on you."

Imogen was touched. She remembered her first day at the company when Anya had presented her with a frosted cupcake and a pen that glowed in the dark. *You're going to be working late so you'll need this.*

It was hard to believe she'd almost been here for a year. She'd started her new job a few days before Christmas and had barely got started before the office had closed for the festive break.

"I love it. Thank you." She checked the time and felt a flash of panic. She didn't miss deadlines. Not ever. And this one was too close for comfort. She wanted to call and get the costings herself, but she was Anya's manager and was supposed to be helping her develop so she needed to stop doing things herself. The restraint almost killed her. It was so much easier and safer to do it herself. At least then she knew it would be done on time, with no mistakes. "Will you chase those venues urgently? Those are the last numbers I need to finish this."

"Sure, I'll do it now. I saw a lipstick that would look great on you, Imogen. Maybe we could go shopping together one lunchtime. Also if you're looking for doggy outfits, I saw a cute red Santa coat on the internet that would look great on a golden retriever. Or do you already have something in mind?" Anya was more interested in the idea of everyone bringing their dogs to work than she was in doing actual work. "You will be bringing Midas, won't you?"

Realizing there was no chance of getting those costings until she finished the dog conversation, Imogen glanced at the photograph on her desk.

Huge brown eyes gazed back at her, and her heart tightened.

Bring your dog to work day.

She touched the photo with the tips of her fingers. "I'm not sure if I'll be able to bring him." She definitely wouldn't be bringing him, but she still had to work out how best to present that fact to her colleagues without alienating them. And then she had a brain wave. "He's not been well. The vet has kept him for a few nights."

"What? No! Midas is ill? And you didn't tell us?" Anya put her pen down and looked at Janie. "Janie, did you know Midas was ill?"

Janie glanced at them, her ponytail swinging across her

back. She was a fitness fanatic and used the gym for an hour every morning when everyone else was still asleep. Occasionally she paced up and down the office just to get her step count up.

"Midas is ill?" Janie rejected a client phone call and focused on Imogen. "That's awful. What happened? Was it the dog walker's fault? Did she let him eat something he shouldn't have eaten?"

"No, nothing like that." Maybe illness hadn't been the best way to go. She should have played along and then found a reason for Midas to be absent on the day. *He stepped on something and he has to rest his paw.* "It's not important. Look, if you could get the last of those costings that would be great, because I need to finish this document and the deadline is—"

"Of course it's important! This is your dog we're talking about. What is more important than that? The client can wait."

"The client can't wait," Imogen said. "We're in a competitive business. There are new events companies springing up every day. It's important that we exceed expectations."

"We will. We'll do a great job on the event itself, we always do, particularly with you in charge. But this is just a proposal. No one is going to die if it's a few hours late. You can pause for two minutes, Imogen," Anya said. "You worked over the weekend supervising those events, and you didn't take a day off Monday. You work too hard."

Too hard? There was no such thing as too hard.

She loved her job. Her job was *everything*. And she was good at it. She was a natural multitasker and handled twice as many accounts as everyone else. She did whatever it took to win business and keep the client, and she did that through experience, attention to detail, creativity and sheer hard work. She was good at what she did. And that wasn't only her opinion. In her previous company she'd moved up to the lofty heights of management so quickly a jealous colleague had left an oxygen mask on her desk.

But now she had a team of six to manage, and occasionally she wished she could just do all the work herself rather than manage them while they did it. Anya, in particular, seemed to feel no particular sense of urgency about anything. She was generous and kind, but also maddeningly slow to complete tasks. She told everyone that work/life balance was essential to her, but Imogen rarely saw her focus on the work part of that equation.

It was like trying to run a race with six weights attached to her waist.

She felt a rush of gloom. She was going to have to speak to Anya. There was no avoiding it. She needed to have a "conversation" about commitment and goals. Managing Anya would take her away from doing actual client work, which meant she'd be working longer hours.

Work/life balance? There was no balance for Imogen, but she didn't mind. This was her choice.

"The deadline is lunchtime, Anya."

"Relax, Imogen. You're going to get white hair and wrinkles before your time. It will get done. It always does." Anya dismissed the deadline and Imogen felt her stress levels ratchet up another notch.

It did get done because she invariably ended up doing it herself. She really liked Anya, which made it even harder. "Anya—"

"I know. You're stressed. And I understand why."

"You do?" Hearing that came as a relief. Maybe Anya was more aware of work pressures than she'd thought.

"Of course. How can you be so calm when your lovely Midas is ill? I can't believe you've been keeping this to yourself. I'd be totally freaking out."

Midas?

"I—"

"What does the vet say? When will they let him out? You must be worried sick. It's okay to be honest. We're a team. We're here to support each other. You're allowed to be human, Imogen. We can cover for you if needed. We can do your work."

Imogen blinked. Anya didn't seem able to do her own work, let alone anyone else's but this probably wasn't the time to point that out.

"Well, I—"

"Anya's right," Janie said. "You don't have to hold it in. I mean, this is Midas. He's your baby." She reached across and picked up the photo Imogen kept on her desk. "Look at that face. Poor boy. I'm sure Rosalind would give you time off if you explained. She was amazing when Buster had that lump on his leg. I suppose because she's a dog lover herself. She gets it."

"That's why I love this place," Anya said. "Everyone is so human. The last place I worked no one talked about anything personal. It was like working with a bunch of robots. Nightmare."

A place where no one talked about anything personal? Imogen was starting to wonder if that might actually be preferable. She loved her colleagues, but she would have loved them even more if they'd had the same focus on work as she did.

But there was no denying that her colleagues were good people, even if most of the time they seemed to fit work round their personal life.

Janie looked close to tears as she held the photo of Midas and Imogen reached across and gently removed it from her fingers.

"I'd rather not talk about it." She placed the photograph back on her desk, next to the one of her family. In her last job they'd had a hot-desk system, and no one had been allowed to display a single personal item. RPQ Events was a very different place.

There were plants, and a fish tank, and people were encouraged to personalize their work stations. Anya's computer was framed by fairy lights and no one seemed to mind.

Glancing around her on her first day, Imogen had seen everything from fluffy mascots to family photos. She'd stared at her stark, empty desk and decided she needed to do something about it.

Come on, Imogen, show us your family, Janie had said cheerfully and Anya had nodded in agreement. *Do you have any pets? We're all animal lovers here. Even Danny, although he'll tell you he bought the rabbits for his daughters. Don't believe him for a moment.*

She'd never had a personal photo on her desk before, but here the absence of it drew attention so she'd done the same. She'd appreciated how welcoming they were and wanted to be part of the team so she'd carefully selected one photo of Midas, and one family photo taken at Christmas. Everyone was huddled together, laughing for the camera as they struggled not to lose their footing in the snow. Imogen loved that photo. Everyone looked so *happy*.

"We're here for you, Imogen." Janie reached across and

rubbed Imogen's shoulder in a show of solidarity. "You're so brave and strong. You've been coming in every day and working hard and none of us even guessed! It must be awful not having your furry friend there to greet you when you get home. I'm sure you miss him horribly. We had no idea you were going through this. You seem so *normal*. Honestly, you're amazing, although I'm sure it helps having such a close family."

Imogen started to panic. She found personal conversations like this really unsettling. Any moment now they'd be suggesting grief counseling. She needed to shut this down before it went any further.

"I do miss him, but he's in good hands and I'm sure he'll soon be home. If you could get those costs now, I'd be able to send this through to the client by lunchtime."

"Working on it now. What's wrong with him?"

"What's wrong with who?"

"Midas." Anya's eyes were wide with sympathy. "Nothing serious, I hope. I don't know how you can concentrate on work when he's ill."

"They're not sure what's wrong," Imogen said. "They're running tests."

This was the problem with working in an open-plan office. People wanted detail.

Much of her time was spent out and about with clients at their offices, visiting venues or supervising events, but eventually she had to return to her desk and that meant being cocooned with her colleagues. And it wasn't that she didn't like them because she did. She liked them a great deal, but there was a fine line between fitting in and being welded together. If someone wanted to talk, then she was always willing to listen but sometimes the level of information became *too much* (close physical proximity didn't seem to be the moderating influence it should have been).

Take Janie for example. Because Janie never bothered to leave her desk when taking a personal call, Imogen knew that she lived with her mother, had one sister who was married and that she was currently dating two different men so that she had backup in the event that one of them ghosted her (Janie's father had walked out when she was ten, leaving her with a perpetual mistrust of the opposite sex).

Then there was Peter. Peter was head of tech, and he sat to her left. He'd been with the company for six months, yet despite this relatively short acquaintance she knew he had an appointment with his doctor on Friday to talk about a part of his body Imogen tried never to picture in a colleague. She knew his girlfriend wanted them to move in together and she knew Pete had no intention of doing that because she'd heard him on the phone to his landlord renewing his rental for another year.

And there was Danny, another account manager, who spent a large part of the day arranging gym sessions and after-work drinks so that he could arrive home after his wife had put their four-year-old twins to bed. Yes, he had rabbits, but judging from the conversation he'd never picked them up or cleaned up after them. That was his wife's responsibility (and his wife seemed to have a great number of responsibilities).

Imogen filed all the things she heard into a compartment in her brain labeled *things I wish I didn't know* and tried to forget about them. The thing she found less easy to handle was the fact that they wanted to know about her, too.

She was a private person and given the choice she would have revealed nothing about her personal life, but she wanted to fit in. She wanted people to like her. So she did what everyone else did and put photos on her desk. She chatted. And the chat requirement was about to escalate because they were heading into the worst month of the year for team bonding activities.

December.

Imogen knew that the "bring your dog to work" day would just be the start of many Christmas celebrations. There would be the office Christmas lunch, the Secret Santa, the charity quiz night *(which one of the following is not one of Santa's reindeer?)*. The list was endless and, although her colleagues knew a few things about her, the one thing they didn't know was that she dreaded Christmas. Last year had been easy because she'd only joined a few days before, but this year promised to be more of a trial.

"At least you'll have time off with him over Christmas." Janie flashed her a smile. "Only thirty-six sleeps to go. We're spending Christmas with my sister this year. I can't wait. She has a bigger house and a bigger TV. How about you, Imogen? Please tell me you *are* taking time off. The office closed for a week last year but still you sent emails on Christmas Day. I mean, who does that?"

"I'd just joined the company. I was keen." That wasn't really the reason, but it worked well enough. "I didn't expect you to look at them. But with the office closed and clients enjoying the holidays it seemed like the perfect time to catch up. I wanted to be able to hit the ground running in January."

"But it was your holiday, too. Why weren't you just hanging out with your family?"

"I was. I'm the family champion at charades." Imogen moved the photo of Midas next to the one of her family. "Also we all help with the cooking, so there's plenty of time to chat then. But there were a few hours in the day when everyone was either watching a movie, or sleeping off too much food, so I opened my laptop." And she didn't want to think about it. She really didn't.

"You're obsessed," Anya said. "Don't take your laptop this year, then you won't be tempted. It was a bit startling to turn on my computer on January 2 and find fifty-six emails from you waiting in my inbox."

"I like to end the year with everything tidy," Imogen said. "I spent plenty of time with family, don't worry."

Janie sat back and shook her head. "I don't know how you do it all. You hardly ever come out with us after work because you're either babysitting your niece and nephew or you're visiting your grandmother. You have a dog. You do everything for everyone, and still handle an inhuman work-load. And you never take time off. How many holiday days are you carrying forward into next year?"

"Er—I don't know. Most of them I think."

"Exactly! Would you slow down? You make the rest of us feel inadequate."

"You're all great," Imogen said. "We're a great team."

"We are, but if you're not careful you're going to burn out. You've been working every weekend, so you deserve a good break. Your family home looks like a dreamy place to spend Christmas. That gorgeous house. All that countryside. Midas must love it. Are you excited?"

Christmas, Christmas, Christmas.

As far as her colleagues were concerned, it was never too soon to talk about Christmas. It made her want to scream.

This year the conversation had started in July (July! What was wrong with people?) when Anya had indulged in a

Christmas movie marathon over the weekend and proceeded to talk about it for several weeks after.

In October Janie had returned from a trip to the supermarket to buy a salad and pointed out that the shelves were already lined with Christmas decorations and Christmas chocolate. She'd placed her plastic looking salad on her desk, along with a garishly wrapped chocolate Santa.

"I normally avoid chocolate, but Christmas is the exception," she'd told them happily as she'd stripped the Santa of its red foil and bitten off the head. "How about you, Imogen?"

Imogen had focused on her computer screen and hoped they'd lose interest.

"I refuse to think about Christmas in October. It's too soon." It was okay to say that wasn't it? Plenty of people refused to think about Christmas in October.

A month later, when someone had asked her about plans for the office Christmas party, she'd said the same thing.

"I refuse to talk about Christmas in November. It's too soon."

But in a week's time it would be December and Imogen would have run out of viable excuses. Decorations glittered in shop windows. Christmas music boomed relentless cheer over loudspeakers.

She couldn't avoid the topic any longer.

She'd have this one conversation and hopefully that would be it for a while.

"I'll be going home, yes. It will be chaos as usual. You know how it is. Big noisy family gathering. Tree too big for the room. Log fire. Uncle George singing out of tune. I'll be spending most of my time trying to stop the nieces and nephews squeezing the presents and making sure my mother isn't burning the turkey." That was enough information to keep them happy, surely? "We really need that costing, Anya."

"I'm on it. Oh and I forgot to tell you that Dorothy Rutherford called for you earlier. You were on the phone to that tech guy from the lighting company."

Imogen felt her breathing quicken. "You forgot—Anya, this is important. Dorothy Rutherford is our biggest client. When she calls, I stop what I'm doing and take her call. If I'm on with another client, then I call her right back when I'm done."

"She was fine about it. She loves you. We all know you're the reason she gave us the business. She wanted to carry on working with you when you left your last place. You can do no wrong. Also, you're the only one of us who genuinely loves her alcohol-free wine."

"I don't mind it," Janie protested, "it's a refreshing drink. But it's not—you know—alcohol. It doesn't give me the buzz I need on a Friday night. I know those bubbles aren't going to give me the headache I need the morning after."

"Just Friday?" Anya grinned. "What about the other nights of the week?"

"Those, too. It's the first thing I do when I get home. My mum and I open a bottle and share it. That's why I go to the gym every morning. I'd have more willpower if I lived on my own. You're so lucky to be able to afford your own place, Imogen."

Imogen waited for a break in the conversation. "What did Dorothy want?"

"She wanted to fix a time for you to present your ideas to the rest of the team. Sounds as if she wants to go ahead with everything you suggested. She was impressed. She asked for a bespoke and original concept and you gave her one. The outdoor festival, complete with a stage and tents and the works. Like a rock concert. She thinks it's a perfect way to showcase their products to customers. And she loved the idea of the drone display. This will be a huge piece of business, Imogen. Congratulations. You turned a virtually impossible brief into reality. We should celebrate—" she grinned at Janie "fancy a glass of non-alcoholic wine?"

"No thanks. I'd rather have a double espresso. I'll say this though, I love their packaging. Those bottles are classy. They *look* like champagne."

"And their sales are rocketing so someone is loving it."

Anya rested her chin on her palm. "I wonder if it's because the marketing is so clever. She has tapped into the whole healthy living trend. Pictures of her estate in the Cotswolds with its vineyard, lots of cool people toasting each other with glasses of Spearcante. I look at the ads and I want to be there, even if there is no alcohol on offer. I wonder how she came up with that name?"

"I think spearca is from an Old English word meaning spark," Imogen said and they both stared at her.

"How do you know these things?"

"Dorothy is my client. It's my job to know as much about her as possible. She hasn't always been in business. Originally, she read English Literature at Oxford. And then she did Medieval studies, which included Old English and Old Norse. I think she also studied Anglo-Saxon prose and poetry. I guess etymology was part of that."

Anya frowned. "Isn't that insects?"

Janie rolled her eyes. "That's entomology."

"Oh, right."

"Etymology is the study of the origin of words," Imogen

said. "Anyway, she told me that's how she came up with the name."

Right now, she didn't care about the origins of the name. The only thing Imogen cared about was that Dorothy had been kept waiting. Dorothy wasn't only their biggest client, but she was Imogen's favorite client. She was smart, interesting and surprisingly easy to work with. She embraced Imogen's ideas and rarely reined her in. She was in her early sixties and several decades earlier had switched careers to run her family's vineyard in the Cotswolds. After a few years she'd decided to experiment extracting the alcohol from the wine. She'd been producing no-alcohol wine long before it had become something of a cultural movement, but lately the business had taken off.

Imogen had worked with her for several years and found her enthusiastic, encouraging and supportive. She never whined and complained, which was more than could be said for most of their clients.

"I'll call her now."

"No point. She said she'd be tied up for the next couple of hours and you could catch her this afternoon."

Imogen managed to hide her frustration. She tried never to miss a client call, and if she did miss it she called them right back.

But if Dorothy was in a meeting, then it would have to be later and she would have to try not to stress about it.

And in the meantime…

"Anya, if you could get those costings now it would mean I could send this proposal on time—" she had a sudden brain wave "—and then I'll be able to make the call about Midas."

"Of course! Anything for Midas."

"Great. Thanks." As she'd hoped, the mention of Midas

galvanized her colleague into action and ten minutes later Imogen had all the costings incorporated into the document.

Relieved, she sent it through to Rosalind for final approval and sat back in her chair.

Done. Finally. Maybe she should try using Midas as a motivator more often.

Not that she wanted to be a killjoy. She wanted her colleagues to like her. She wanted to be one of them, and if that required a little personal sacrifice on her part then fine.

Soon the Christmas tree would arrive in the foyer and she'd admire it along with everyone else. Mistletoe would be hung in strategic places, even though office romance was banned (and, as Janie had once pointed out after several glasses of wine that most definitely had retained all its alcohol content, the number of kissable people in their office was depressingly limited).

And there would be the "bring your dog to work" day.

Midas.

She sighed and glanced at the photo on her desk. The photographer had captured the exact moment his tail had been suspended in mid wag.

He really was a gorgeous dog.

It was just a pity he wasn't hers.

Also a pity that her Christmas wasn't going to be a big, noisy family affair.

She loved the family photo she'd placed on her desk, but they weren't her family.

There was no big house in the country. There would be no oversize tree or a log fire. Uncle George wouldn't be singing out of tune because she didn't have an uncle called George, or any other uncle. She wasn't going to have to stop her nieces and nephews squeezing the presents, because she didn't have nieces or nephews. There would be no games of charades, and no burnt turkey because her mother had never cooked a turkey in her life.

But right now that wasn't her biggest problem. Her biggest problem was "bring your dog to work" day.

Everyone was expecting to meet Midas, but there was no Midas.

Imogen didn't have a dog. Imogen didn't have a loving family.

Imogen had no one.

The personal life she'd created for herself was entirely fake.

Can you find new beginnings with old friends?

Joanna Whitman's high-profile marriage held more secrets than she cares to remember, so when her ex-husband dies, she doesn't know what to feel. But when she discovers that he's left behind a pregnant young woman, Joanna is forced to act. She knows exactly how brutal the spotlight on them both will be...unless she can find a way for them to disappear.

Ashley Blake is amazed when Joanna suggests they lie low at her beach house in her sleepy Californian hometown. Joanna should be hating her, not helping her. But alone and pregnant, Ashley needs all the support she can find.

Joanna's only goal for the summer is privacy. All Ashley wants is space to plan for her and her baby's future. But when an old flame reappears, and secrets spill out under the hot summer sun, this unlikely friendship is put to the test...

'A PERFECT SLICE OF JOYFUL SUMMER ESCAPISM'
Clare Pooley

Could this Christmas be the start of a whole new chapter?

A long-lasting friendship

Every year, Erica, Claudia, and Anna reunite for their book club holiday. They're bonded by years of friendship and a deep love of books, but there is still so much they keep from each other . . .

A perfect Christmas escape

At the cosy Maple Sugar Inn, Hattie specialises in making her guests' dreams come true, but this Christmas all she wants is to survive the festive season. Between running the inn and being a single mother, Hattie is close to breaking point.

The start of a brand-new story . . . ?

Over the course of an eventful week, Hattie sees that the friends are each carrying around unspoken truths, but nothing prepares her for how deeply her story will become entwined in theirs. Will this Christmas be the end of the book club's story or the start of a whole new chapter?

Keep in touch with
SARAH MORGAN

For all the latest book news, exclusive content and competitions, visit Sarah's website and sign up to her newsletter at

www.sarahmorgan.com

Sarah loves to connect with readers on social media. Find her on:

f @AuthorSarahMorgan

◎ sarahmorganwrites

🐦 @SarahMorgan_

PS. Want even more great reads, giveaways and book news? Follow @hqstories

Berlitz®

Salzburg

Front cover:

The Cathedral on Domplatz

Right: Mozart statue

TOP 10 ATTRACTIONS

Festung Hohensalzburg The fairy-tale castle dominates the city it was built to defend (*page 30*)

Old Town A baroque treasure trove, with sights including the stunning cathedral (*page 36*)

Residenzplatz The most impressive square in the Old Town (*page 41*)

Mozart's Birthplace The house in which he was born is now a museum (*page*

Hellbrunn Palace and Gardens See the grand scale of living of Salzburg's prince archbishops *(page 63)*

St Peter's Abbey The city's spiritual heart and the oldest active monastery in Austria *(page 37)*

Museum of Modern Art This showcase for contemporary art also offers a great view of the city *(page 50)*

Mirabell Palace and Gardens Built for the mistress of an archbishop, here you'll find opulence on a grand scale *(page 56)*

Königssee Take a boat trip across the still waters of this beautiful Bavarian lake not far from Salzburg *(page 71)*

Grossglockner High Alpine Road This twisting and turning route is one of the world's great scenic drives *(page 75)*

A PERFECT DAY

9.30am Coffee

Even if you enjoy a hotel breakfast, a second coffee or tea at the Café Bazar (page 111) is the Salzburg way to start a day. Many writers have found inspiration in this smart café beside the river.

10.30am Mozart

Follow the footsteps of Wolfgang Amadeus Mozart to the Makartplatz, where, at house No. 8, you can find the 18th-century apartment of the Mozart family. Then stroll through Mirabell Gardens, used as a backdrop in *The Sound of Music*.

12.15pm Museum of Modern Art

The Museum (closed Mon) is not to be missed by art lovers. Its restaurant m32 is the place for an extravagant lunch with a superb view from the terrace. Alternatively, descend to town in the Mönchsberg lift and stop at Humboldt Stubn (page 106) for a traditional midday meal.

11.30am A walk

Cross the Salzach at Müllnersteg bridge and head for the pretty Müllner Kirche next to the huge Augustine Brewery. Lovely wooded paths wind south along the top of Mönchsberg, and scenic walking trails lead you down to the Museum of Modern Art.

2.00pm Shopping

Getreidegasse (with Mozart's birthplace at No. 9), Judengasse and Goldgasse are shopping heaven. Meander through the lanes and you'll discover top brands in carefully renovated Gothic houses next to old shops selling Dirndl and other local costumes. Tiny Café Fürst (page 109) at Alter Markt is the place to buy the original *Mozartkugel*.

IN SALZBURG

5.15pm **Squares and lanes**

Savour the atmosphere of the cathedral and the surrounding squares. Stroll from Residenzplatz to Domplatz and then to Kapitelplatz to see the giant chessboard and golden sculpture, *Sphaera*. To the south is the cemetery of St Peter, with catacombs carved into the rock face. Walk up Festungsgasse (Festungsbahn in summer until 7pm) to Stieglkeller to enjoy a local beer and panoramic city view.

4.30pm **360°**

Step into the Salzburg of 1829 at the Panorama Museum, Residenzplatz 9. Telescopes reveal the detail in the 360° panorama painting of Salzburg and its surroundings. Then head for Mozartplatz and peep behind the ornate doors of house No. 4 into a pretty 18th-century yard with a garden.

9.00pm **High above**

Traditional Gasthäuser like Zum Wilden Mann or Zum fidelen Affen (New Town) are cosy places to enjoy chatty evenings amongst locals. To finish off a day with an exotic drink and breathtaking views, the rooftop terrace lounge of the Stein Hotel (page 111) is the place to be.

7.00pm **Keynotes for dinner**

The restaurant Triangel (page 107), on Max Reinhardt Platz, is a favourite spot of musicians and singers – and a fine place for dinner. Or savour authentic Austrian fare at Zipfer Bierhaus (page 107) nearby. The Mozart Dinner Concert at St Peter's Stiftskeller offers the perfect evening entertainment for Mozart fans.

CONTENTS

28

103

8

41

14

96

INTRODUCTION

First time visitors to Salzburg are often awed by the consistent dignity and style of the city's Baroque architecture. And rarely is a city so delicately worked into a dramatic natural setting. Rising above Salzburg's skyline and visible for kilometres around is the Festung Hohensalzburg, a fortress that sits atop the Mönchsberg mountain and watches over the city.

Below, the Altstadt (Old Town) is dominated by baroque towers and church spires, built by a succession of independent bishops from the 16th to the 18th centuries. This historic centre became a Unesco World Heritage Site in 1996, recognised as an important European ecclesiastical area.

Salzburg is most famous for being the birthplace of Wolfgang Amadeus Mozart and, of course, as the setting for *The Sound of Music*, but the city's wealth of culture extends beyond that. With Easter and Whitsun festivals, as well as Mozart Week in January and the internationally known Salzburg Festival in summer, this is one of the world's top festival cities, vying with Vienna as the cultural capital of Austria. Salzburg also hosts renowned Christmas markets in December, when the city is transformed into a winter wonderland, with ice sculptures, ice rinks, music, stalls and copious amounts of *Glühwein* (mulled wine).

Geography and Climate

Salzburg is in the west of central Austria and close to the Bavarian border of Germany, in the northern foothills of the Alps. The city lies between two craggy hills, the Mönchsberg and the Kapuzinerberg, and is divided in two by the Salzach River. This was the life-blood of Salzburg for many centuries,

View of Salzburg from the Hohensalzburg fortress

Salzburg and the Salzach River

used for transporting salt (*Salz*), gold and copper mined in the mountains, and bringing much wealth to the city during the Middle Ages. Only a few kilometres from the city centre lies the closest real mountain, the Untersberg (1,853m/6,078ft).

Salzburg is influenced by the alpine climate, and generally has cold, dry, snowy winters and warm summers with a considerable amount of rain. When it rains here, it really pours. The locals call it *Schnürlregen* – 'string rain'. Whatever the season, the weather can be turned on its head by the warm south wind known as the *Föhn* (*see page 65*).

Politics and Religion

Home to approximately 150,500 people, Salzburg is the capital of the province of the same name (pop. 520,000). It is one of Austria's youngest provinces, not incorporated into the country until 1816 (it was previously an independent ecclesiastical state). Austria is a federal state made up of nine provinces, each with its own local government. The Regional Assembly of Salzburg, elected every five years by proportional representation, consists of 36 members who have considerable influence over the politics and economics of the region.

While the role of the church in Salzburg is by no means what it was in the era of prince archbishops, the diocese continues to be one of the most important in the Roman Catholic Church, and the archbishop has direct access to the Pope. The Catholic Church remains a powerful local institution – of the city's 43 churches, 40 of them are Catholic – and owns a lot of land in and around the city, with the final say on where street music, open-air festivals and sporting events can take place. It also has the right to a claim a yearly tax from every citizen's salary to help with its upkeep (this tax also extends to other denominations too). Nevertheless, although more than two-thirds of the population counts themselves as Catholic, not many are regular churchgoers.

The Salzburg Card

A useful money-saver for the serious sightseer is the Salzburg Card, which allows free use of public transport, including the fortress funicular and sightseeing boat, as well as discounts for various cultural events, tours and excursions. It also serves as an admission ticket to the city's most important cultural sights, including Mozart's birthplace, the Hohensalzburg fortress, the Residenz Gallery, the Salzburg Museum, and the Museum of Modern Art. Sights outside the town include Hellbrunn Palace, the zoo and the cable-car trip at Untersberg.

Cards are valid for 24, 48 or 72 hours and cost May–Oct €25, €34 or €40, Nov–Apr €22, €30 or €35 – half price for children (6–15 yrs). You can buy the Salzburg Card from hotels, ticket offices and tourist information offices, or visit www.salzburg.info.

Being a Salzburger

Salzburgers have a reputation for being aloof, and intimacy is reserved for their own close social circles. They are conservative in nature, though the younger generation is breaking the mould, becoming more outgoing and embracing influences from other cultures, especially on the music and entertainment scene. But this does not reflect the whole picture, and citizens are in general very friendly towards tourists. If you're staying in Salzburg for more than a few days, expect to be recognised and greeted by people as you walk the streets. Salzburgers in the main love their city and are delighted when foreign visitors express appreciation of its appearance.

Laws are for obeying in Salzburg: litter is prohibited, jay-walking is not tolerated (if you transgress, expect a lecture or a look of disdain at the very least), crime is almost non-existent and the police operate a zero tolerance policy. This

Downtown Salzburg, near Getreidegasse

might sound heavy-handed, but walking home at night is usually safe, disturbances on the streets are very rare and pickpocketing occurs only in crowded bars.

Salzburgers enjoy a leisurely pace of life. They do a lot of walking – not of the brisk kind – and they frequent coffee houses, beer gardens and taverns, relaxing and watching the world go by. There is no sense of

Breakfasting on croissants in a coffee house

urgency here and certainly not the hectic pace that can be felt in other cities of a similar size. Salzburgers are passionate about their dogs, taking their faithful friends everywhere – into restaurants, the hairdressers, on the bus.

Salzburg is a university town with a good nightlife scene. The city is dotted with wine bars and taverns where you can enjoy fine Austrian wine and beer (the city has one of the country's best breweries in Stiegl's Brauwelt). The main areas for socialising by night are along Rudolfskai, Gstättengasse and Kaigasse, although there are many taverns scattered throughout the city. The Augustiner Brewery is also a must when visiting the city, with its fine beer halls and huge, tree-lined, summer beer garden.

No matter what time of year you visit Salzburg, there is always something happening, from the street-café way of life in the summer to the harvest festivals of the autumn, from the Christmas markets and winter skiing to *Fasching* and Easter festivals in the spring. The beauty of the city is enhanced with each season, making Salzburg a perfect year-round destination.

A BRIEF HISTORY

Salzburg's strategic location, near to one of the passes running from north to south through the Alps, brought the city power and prosperity through trade – especially of locally mined salt. But it also brought the city into conflict, as the valley was a major trading route from Italy to Germany.

Neolithic and Celtic Developments

The history of human activity in the Salzburg region can be traced back 6,000 years to the New Stone Age and a settlement on the Rainberg (behind the Mönchsberg). During the Bronze Age, around 1000BC, the Illyrians settled here, lured by the copper that was mined on the Mitterberg, near Bischofshofen. But in the centuries that followed, salt mining became the

Open-air Museum in Grossgmain, south of Salzburg

primary industry, with mines at Hallstatt and later on the Dürrnberg, near Hallein. By around 500BC, the Celts had invaded the region and begun to mine salt and to build fortified settlements scattered around the hills. The area became a trading centre and the river was used to transport the salt, a valuable commodity.

Roman Occupation

Around 15BC, the Romans marched into the area, conquered the Celtic kingdom of Noricum and built a road over the Alps to Vivium (today's Klagenfurt). Known as Juvavum, the town acquired the status of

Latin inscription

When the foundation for the statue of Mozart was about to be laid in 1841, a marble floor was uncovered bearing the Latin inscription: 'Here lies happiness. Let no evil enter.'

a Roman *municipium* in AD45 and became the seat of one of the largest administrations outside Rome. Its focal point, the Forum, was quite likely to have been situated where Residenzplatz is today. During the reconstruction following World War II, the remains of a huge Roman temple were discovered in the Kaigasse area where the Kasererbräu hotel now stands.

Around AD500, the Baiuvari (Bavarians) laid waste to the city, after the Roman army stationed here had been laid low by an epidemic. They drove out the residents and set Juvavum's wooden structures alight. The ensuing conflagration destroyed most of the settlement, and was the cue for the Romans to withdraw from the province of Noricum.

Church and State Combined

Around 696, Bishop Rupert of Worms arrived as a missionary in Bavaria, whose ruler Duke Theodor granted him an area of land, including the remains of Juvavum. Here, Rupert founded the Monastery of St Peter and the Nonnberg Convent. Both institutions remain today, St Peter's as the oldest continuously active monastery in the Roman Catholic Church and the convent as the oldest surviving religious community for women.

Salzburg became a bishopric in 739 and, in the years that followed, one of the most important areas outside the Vatican. Among the early bishops of note was Virgil, responsible for the town's first cathedral in the mid-8th century. In 798 Salzburg was elevated to the status of an archbishopric by Pope Leo, and Abbot Bishop Arno was promoted to archbishop and a prince of the Holy Roman Empire.

In 996, Emperor Otto III awarded Salzburg a town charter and the right to levy customs duties and mint its own coins. Less than a century later, during the power struggle between the Holy Roman Emperor and the Pope, Archbishop Gebhard of Salzburg weighed in on the side of Pope Gregory II. As protection against the imperial armies, he commissioned the fortresses of Hohensalzburg, Hohenwerfen and Friesach.

Growth and Destruction

Under the reign of Konrad I during the 12th century, the Hohensalzburg fortress was developed into a heavily fortified bastion. The high walls that he added can still be seen today.

But the fortress was not able to prevent the events of 1167, when Frederick Barbarossa's troops set fire to the city during a dispute with the Pope (Salzburg sided with the Church), destroying the cathedral. In the years that followed, Salzburg was rebuilt under the direction of Archbishop Konrad III. He also started construction of an immense new cathedral.

By the 13th century, the salt that was mined in Hallein was proving to be increasingly important for the region. The mines produced so much that Salzburg could drop the price considerably, giving the city a trading advantage over the competition from the neighbouring salt mines in Bad Reichenhall and

Berchtesgaden. This added to the strength of the Salzburg archbishops who, once they had procured a monopoly on salt trading, were able to raise the prices again.

Although the archbishops had been imperial princes since the 12th century, the areas they ruled were still considered to be part of the Duchy of Bavaria. In the early 14th century, in the machinations between the Bavarian and Austrian royal houses, Archbishop Friedrich III of Salzburg sided with the Austrian Friedrich I ('the Handsome'). Civil war raged for seven years until Louis IV of Bavaria won the decisive

The Hohensalzburg fortress

battle of Mühldorf in 1322. Although Salzburg had been on the losing side, the result of this internecine strife was that Bavaria was forced to concede its independence. In 1328, Salzburg became an autonomous state, separate from both Bavaria and Austria. However, the city's prosperity was soon to suffer another blow when the plague hit it in 1348, killing around 30 percent of the population.

During the late 14th and early 15th centuries, the traders of Salzburg grew in importance. It was during this period that many of the merchants' houses that survive today in the 'old' and 'new' towns were built. Archbishop Leonhard von Keutschach ruled Salzburg from 1495 to 1519, adding significantly to the size and impregnability of the fortress.

The Peasants' War

Keutschach's successor, Matthäus Lang von Wellenberg, exerted political influence far beyond the boundaries of Salzburg. He was a cardinal, a councillor of Emperor Maximilian I and a politician with wide influence. He was decisive in the election of the Medici Pope Clemens VII, and the Habsburg Karl V would never have become emperor without his intervention. But it was on home ground that he faced his sternest challenge.

Salzburg's peasants were restless, suffering from increased taxation and the demands made on them by the nobility and monasteries. Inspired by Martin Luther, they also

The Prince Archbishops

For more than 1,000 years, Salzburg and its surrounding territories were ruled by prince archbishops: men highly placed in the Holy Roman Empire and wielding great influence. They could depend on the power of the Church to back their causes, commendable or not. And they controlled just about everything: tax collection, land ownership, mining rights, the building of churches, monasteries and places of learning, the armies and, of course, the salvation of souls.

The Church and the state were not separate entities, and the prince archbishop, as the title implies, was at the head of both – usually a head of state first and a religious leader second. The prince archbishop of Salzburg was elected to the position; he was not appointed by the Pope or the Holy Roman Emperor, nor was his position a hereditary title. Indeed, these leaders were not allowed to marry – but that did not stop many of them taking mistresses and having numerous children. Normally, the youngest son of a noble family was nominated for the post.

The prince archbishops displayed varying degrees of benevolence. Many were patrons of the arts, as well as being responsible for the design and development of the city, including the iconic fortress.

came to resent the hardline Catholicism and apparent arrogance of their archbishop. In May 1525, they rebelled; the miners of Gastein joined in. The revolt spread beyond the borders of Salzburg, into adjacent Carinthia and Styria, both ruled by the Habsburg dynasty. On 4 June the rebels seized control of Salzburg, and briefly controlled the

Statue of Emperor Maximilian I

city as well as parts of Carinthia, Carniola and Upper Austria. Archbishop Matthäus negotiated an agreement with the rebel leaders, which adressed some of their demands. He promised them a council that would address their grievances, and the peasants broke off their siege of the Hohensalzberg fortress.

But in December 1525, Archbishop Matthäus felt secure enough to act more forcefully. He had a number of rebel leaders arrested and executed. The promised council met in January 1526, but was dissolved without achieving anything. The peasants resumed their revolt, joining forces with the Tyrolean revolutionary Michael Gaismair. But Matthäus, too, had allies, notably the Swabian League, and a force of 10,000 soldiers. There were a number of indecisive battles in May and June 1526, until the rebels were finally defeated at Radstadt.

Matthäus overcame the threat posed by the peasants with a combination of patience, determination, deceit and outside help. Though the Salzburg peasantry continued to lean towards the Lutheran Reformation, Archbishop Matthäus and his successors remained steadfast Catholics, developing a style of absolute rule directed against Salzburg's Protestant elements.

The City Takes Shape

Wolf Dietrich von Raitenau was elected in 1587. He was a man of great vision who began to oversee the architectural design of Salzburg as we know it today, bringing Italian Baroque style to the city. He tore down the 'undesirable' areas and in their place built wide, open squares and magnificent residences. Schloss Mirabell was built for his mistress, Salome Alt, who is said to have borne him between 12 and 15 children. His reign came to an end when he quarrelled over mining rights with the prince of Bavaria, whose army attacked Salzburg. Dietrich lost his allies and the support of the Church because of his affair with Salome Alt. Attempting to flee the city, he was captured and imprisoned in the Hohensalzburg fortress, the very building that was designed to protect him.

His nephew and successor was Markus Sittikus. Even though his reign as archbishop lasted only seven years from 1612 to 1619, Sittikus is credited with continuing the reconstruction of Salzburg that Dietrich had begun, and also instigating new projects such as the palace and gardens in Hellbrunn. He also laid the foundation stone for the cathedral that dominates Salzburg today.

Sittikus' successor, Paris Graf von Lodron, is acknowledged as Salzburg's greatest prince archbishop. He was elected in 1619 at the start of the Thirty Years' War, the religious battle between Catholics and Protestants. He managed to keep Salzburg out of the dispute, maintaining neutrality and

Fountain fun

Markus Sittikus is noted for installing the famous water fountains in Hellbrunn Palace. He used to enjoy inviting guests to dinner at the palace and dining outside at the stone table that survives today. He had little water fountains installed in each seat (except his own, of course) and at a given signal, they were turned on, to the discomfort of his guests and the amusement of their host.

preserving the dominance of the Catholic Church. This was a major achievement as the war left most of Central Europe devastated. During Graf Lodron's 34-year reign, Salzburg's population rose from 40,000 to 80,000. A great believer in education, he founded the university in 1623. He brought new wealth to the city by imposing tolls on traders using the nearby Pass Lueg, and he also expanded the mining and mineral trade of the region. His body was laid to rest beneath the dome of the cathedral.

Music mural in Archbishop Sittikus' Hellbrunn Palace

The End of the Prince Archbishops

The prince archbishops' dominance over the land of Salzburg ended at the beginning of the 19th century. In 1800, Napoleon defeated the Austrians at the Battle of Marengo and crossed the Alps at the head of a 40,000-strong army, while another French army crossed the Rhine, captured Munich and pushed on to take Linz in Austria. In the years that followed, as the European powers challenged Bonaparte on several fronts, Salzburg was bounced around between its larger neighbours.

From 1803 to 1805, Salzburg was an electorate of the Holy Roman Empire of German nations. The religious principality was secularised, and the political authority of the prince

Mozart in Salzburg

In 1737, Wolfgang's father Leopold Mozart arrived in Salzburg and en-
rolled at the university, though shortly afterwards due to his obsession
with music he was expelled because he neglected his studies. In 1743,
he was accepted into the court orchestra and in 1747 married a local
woman, Anna Maria Pertl. The couple had seven children, though only
two survived, Maria Anna, known as Nannerl, and Wolfgang Amadeus
(christened Joannes Chrysostomus Wolfgangus Theophilus), born in
1756. Leopold began to tutor Nannerl and this eventually became a
point of interest and entertainment for young Wolfgang. As Leopold
realised his children's talents, he began to spend more time with them,
teaching them music with strict discipline and guidance. Mozart excelled
at the clavier and was already composing little pieces before the age of
five. At six, Mozart accompanied his father on tour, astounding the audiences with his skills. Then, aged only eight, he went to London and performed in front of King George III, dedicating six sonatas to the queen
(for which he received 50 guineas). When Mozart played in Italy at the
age of 14, the Italians were so amazed by him that they announced the
ring on his finger to be a talisman. Obligingly, Mozart removed it and
proceeded to play even more beautifully than before.

The prince archbishop at this time was Sigismund von Schrattenbach,
who had a genuine interest in music. He funded the Mozart family's
trips and allowed them to use court titles. It is no wonder that, after all
the excitement of international adulation, young Mozart found his home
town 'dull and boring'. Sigismund died in 1771 and was succeeded by
Archbishop Colloredo, who had little interest in the arts and considered
musicians to be among the lowest ranking courtiers. He put an end to
the support of the Mozart family, halting their tours, and instead required that they stay in Salzburg and perform to the court. Mozart grew
restless and left Salzburg for good at the age of 25. He moved to Vienna
after a major row with the archbishop and his secretary.

archbishops finally came to an end. As part of the 1805 peace treaty of Pressburg, Salzburg was incorporated into Austria. The independent state was now a province of a large empire – but not for long. The Habsburgs declared war on France in 1809, but were defeated. This brought Salzburg under direct French administration for a year and a half. But

The most famous Salzburger

in 1810, the area as far as the Leuken valley (Kitzbühel) was ceded to Napoleon's ally Bavaria. Salzburg's university was suspended and in 1811 the regional assembly was dissolved.

Following Napoleon's disastrous Russian campaign, Bavaria shrewdly switched its allegiance, and the Salzburgers found themselves once again in opposition to France. By 1814, Napoleon was being attacked on all fronts, and by the end of the year, he had been deposed and banished to Elba. The Great Powers – Austria, Prussia, Russia and Britain – convened the Congress of Vienna, at which the map of Europe was redrawn. Among many other realignments of territories, the Tyrol and Salzburg were assigned to the Habsburg rulers, and in 1816 Salzburg formally became part of Austria.

For the next 100 years, the ruling family left Salzburg to its own destiny, with limited funding and sparse resources to develop the city. The Habsburgs had little interest in residing there and likewise little interest in investing in the city. This turned out to be the saviour of Salzburg's distinctive appearance. Instead of knocking down and reconstructing buildings and infrastructure, there was no other choice than to repair and maintain what today is a vital part of its culture and history.

Early 20th Century

At the beginning of World War I, 49,000 Salzburgers were conscripted into the Austrian army to fight alongside Germany; 6,000 of them were killed and many more taken prisoner. Salzburg itself saw no battles, but the population suffered great hardship because of the lack of supplies. In 1918, the so called 'rucksack war' broke out. Thousands of people, mostly women, set off for the outlying provinces in search of food for their families. Many were caught by the local authorities and charged with black marketeering. At the end of World War I, the Habsburg monarchy was abolished and Austria was declared a republic for the first time, with Salzburg as a *Bundesland*.

In 1920, the first Salzburg Festival opened on the steps of the cathedral with the performance of *Jedermann* (*Everyman*). The festival was founded by many individuals, but notably the theatre director Max Reinhardt, the composer Richard Strauss and Hugo von Hofmannsthal, one of Austria's most renowned poets and lyricists. Its primary aim was to bring great music to the people with little or no influence from commercial contributions. In theory, this aim has been maintained, although today ticket prices range from just affordable to outrageously expensive. The festival was at its height from 1920 to 1938, growing in international stature every year.

Festival founder

Max Reinhardt (1873–1943) was one of the co-founders of the Salzburg Festival. Born in Baden near Vienna in 1873, he was forced into exile in the US in 1938. He was also the founder of the Max Reinhardt Seminar at the University of Vienna, a drama college that runs four-year acting courses.

With the annexation of Austria by Germany in 1938 (*Anschluss*) things changed. Many of the musicians, singers and conductors, who had helped make the festival what it was, were Jewish or had Jewish relatives. They were not allowed to perform. Before taking over the running of the festival, the Nazi Party accused the Jews and clerics of misusing the festival idea. Max Reinhardt fled the country for England and then the US in 1938. Artur Toscanini, who had conducted many performances prior to the arrival of fascism, had left the country a year previously to conduct in the US.

Austrian theatre director, Max Reinhardt

The festival continued in a diminished form with many performances only being held for army personnel until 1944. In 1947, it was relaunched under the patronage of the US Army. The festival flourished once again and was transformed into today's world-famous international music event that takes place every late July and August.

World War II and Beyond

During World War II, Salzburg again escaped the worst of the horrors. For the first few years of the war, life continued much as it had before. It was only the large number of refugees from bombed cities in Germany that reminded the population that

Walking down Getreidegasse

they were at war. But from autumn 1944 to the spring of 1945, a number of American bombing raids took place, killing 547 people.

The Americans were trying to destroy supply lines by targeting the railway tracks, but bombs caused much damage to the old parts of the town, including the cathedral, which suffered a direct hit. In May 1945, American troops entered the city and the war was over for the Salzburgers.

After hostilities ceased, the US Army oversaw Salzburg's post-war reconstruction. In 1955, the occupying troops left Austria and a new republic was declared. There followed a huge amount of construction work; the Festival Halls were built and also many new high-rise buildings and housing estates, so that the city expanded considerably. The university and the cathedral were also rebuilt and, in 1967, a preservation order was placed on the Old Town.

Austria joined the EU in 1995 and the European Monetary Union in 1999. In 2002, the euro replaced the Austrian schilling as the official currency. With the open border between Germany and Austria, the number of tourists visiting Salzburg has increased dramatically. The airport has been enlarged a number of times to cope with the influx of mainly British charter flights. In 1997 the city was placed on the Unesco World Cultural Heritage Site listing, which has attracted yet more visitors. The Salzburg Art Project was started in 2002. Within a decade internationally renowned artists created exceptional sculptures on the main squares of town – including the *Homage to Mozart* by Markus Lüpertz.

Historical Landmarks

4000BC Stone Age settlement on Rainberg.

1000BC Illyrian settlement.

500BC The Celts invade the region and settle; salt mining begins.

15BC The Romans conquer the region; Juvavum (Salzburg) emerges.

470 St Severin founds a monastic settlement at Salzburg.

696 Bishop Rupert of Worms is given the city of Salzburg.

c.700 St Peter's Abbey and Nonnberg Convent are founded by Rupert.

739 Salzburg becomes a bishopric and later an archbishopric.

8th century First cathedral built by St Virgil.

1077 Archbishop Gebhard commissions Hohensalzburg fortress.

1167 Frederick Barbarossa burns the city to the ground.

1348–9 Salzburg is struck by plague; a third of the population dies.

16th century Peasants' War.

16th–17th century Archbishops Wolf Dietrich von Raitenau, Markus Sittikus and Paris Graf von Lodron give the city its modern-day appearance.

1623 University founded by Archbishop Paris Graf von Lodron.

1756 Wolfgang Amadeus Mozart born at Getreidegasse 9.

1781 Mozart moves to Vienna after arguing with the archbishop.

1800 French troops march into Salzburg.

1816 Salzburg becomes part of the Austro-Hungarian Empire.

1861 First elected parliament and provincial government in Salzburg.

1917 Salzburg Festival Hall Association founded.

1920 Salzburg becomes a province of the Democratic Republic of Austria. First Salzburg Festival takes place.

1938 German troops march into Austria.

1945 US troops enter the city.

1956–60 Building of the Large Festival Hall.

1962 Paris Lodron University Salzburg reopens.

1967 Easter Festival founded. Old Town preserved by law.

1997 Old Town of Salzburg becomes a World Cultural Heritage Site.

2006 250th anniversary of Mozart's birth celebrated.

2012 Salzburg celebrates the 725th anniversary of its town militia.

WHERE TO GO

A lthough in tourist terms, Salzburg is geared towards everything Mozart, the city also offers a multitude of fascinating historical sights. There are ample churches, graveyards, gardens and alleyways dating back to medieval times. Salzburg is divided into an Old Town and a New Town, on opposite sides of the Salzach, and this chapter has been divided into areas of interest on both sides of the river, followed by a number of excursions. Depending on how much time you have, a walking tour is recommended to fully appreciate all that Salzburg has to offer (see page 125). As the exact opening times for some of the sights vary from year to year, you might want to check with the Tourist Information Office on Mozartplatz on arrival.

For the sights such as the zoo, the Untersberg and Hellbrunn Palace, you can take a bus from the railway station or Hanuschplatz. Hallein and Werfen can be reached by train from the railway station. A bus will take you to the Salzkammergut lake district (see page 79), but the area is better appreciated if you hire a car. You can also visit the Grossglockner High Alpine Road and the Krimml Waterfalls by car or on an organised excursion.

THE MÖNCHSBERG AND ENVIRONS

The great Mönchsberg rock which towers over the Old Town provides Salzburg with a spectacular backdrop of white cliffs. Some of the earliest people in the area settled on this mountain as it provided a natural defence against predators and invaders from nearby territories. A walk across the Mönchsberg's ridge, strewn with old battlements, crumbling walls and

The gardens of Mirabell Palace

contemporary sculptures, provides today's visitors with panoramic and tree-framed views of Salzburg and is an excellent introduction to the city's main sights. Below the eastern ridge is the Old Town, with the palaces and squares of the Prince-Archbishops' quarter and the cathedral's green domes. Further to the northeast, across the Salzach River, is the New Town, built in the shadow of the Kapuzinerberg. The Mönchsberg's western ridge looks out across the suburbs to the distant Untersberg.

As well as the funicular train on Festungsgasse, there are many routes up the Mönchsberg if you don't mind quite a steep uphill walk. A lift on Gstättengasse allows easy access to the Museum of Modern Art (see page 50).

The Festung Hohensalzburg

On top of the Mönchsberg sits the magnificent fortress, the **Festung Hohensalzburg ❶** (daily Jan–Apr and Oct–Dec

Hohensalzburg fortress

9.30am–5pm, May–Sept 9am–7pm, Easter and weekends in Dec 9am–6pm, last entry 30 mins prior to closing; the Festungscard (fortress card) includes the funicular to the fortress, access to the external parts of the fortress as well as to the interior area with an audioguide tour, all the museums, a multivision show and, from May–Oct, access to the lower

In the grounds of the fortress

Romanesque chapel; tel: 8424 301; www.hohensalzburg.com).

The Hohensalzburg is the largest and best-preserved fortress in Europe, its dominating bastions, walls and towers making it the symbol of Salzburg. It has had a fascinating history under its many ruling archbishops. Construction began in 1077 under the reign of Archbishop Gebhard and it was enlarged and renovated up until the 17th century. Its late Gothic appearance is largely due to the building work of the 15th-century archbishop Leonhard von Keutschach (1495–1519), who was not only a religious leader but also, like many archbishops, a powerful temporal ruler. He thus needed constant protection from outside invasion and even revolts from within his own territories. During this period, the main building of the fortress was significantly enlarged. There is a marble memorial to von Keutschach on the wall of St George's Church, and he is also commemorated by numerous insignia and coats of arms that include his curious personal symbol, the turnip, which was staple food in Europe before the introduction of potatoes. Since von Keutschach's time, the lion that is the symbol of the fortress has held a turnip in its paws.

Hangman's House

If you take the fortress tour up to the Reck watchtower, you will be rewarded with a spectacular view of the city and beyond. The white house in the middle of the open green space to the southwest is known as the Hangman's House. It is said that such was the desire of the citizens not to live next to the city's hangman that he was obliged to live alone in this isolated location.

The Hohensalzburg was more than just a defensive fortress and residence in war-torn times. During periods when there was no direct military threat to the city, it was used as a barracks and a prison. Archbishop Wolf Dietrich von Raitenau was held prisoner there by his nephew and successor, Markus Sittikus, for five years until his death in 1617.

The rich and lavishly decorated interior of the fortress is a breathtaking display of intricate Gothic wood carvings and ornamental paintings. Two rooms not to be missed are the **Golden Chamber**, which features stunning detailed wood ornamentation and a majolica ceramic oven from the 1500s, and the **Golden Hall**, with its magnificent wood panelling and carving, and a fascinating ceiling supported by large twisted pillars.

One unique exhibit is the **Salzburger Stier** (Salzburg Bull), possibly the oldest working barrel organ in the world, built in 1502 and lovingly restored, which roars out melodies by Mozart and Haydn.

The fortress contains no less than three museums, which span a variety of topics and can only be seen after an officially conducted tour of the fortress. The **Rainer-Regiments-Museum** is full of military paraphernalia recalling the Imperial and Royal Regiment of Archduke Rainer; the modern **Fortress Museum** (www.salzburgmuseum. at) has medieval art, weapons, instruments of torture and a variety of everyday objects that illuminate the history of the fortress and its occupants. The **Marionettenmuseum** in the cellars of the fortress captures the spirit of the famous Salzburg Marionette Theatre with a display of historical puppets.

If you do not have time to enjoy the splendour of the interior, the courtyard offers some more historical sights, such as the old lime tree, said to be several hundred years old, and the fortress well, which dates from 1539. Even if you're not particularly interested in ancient fortresses, Hohensalzburg is worth a visit just for the views. From the Reck watchtower, you get a panoramic sweep of the Alps, and the Kuenburg bastion offers a fine view of Salzburg's domes and towers.

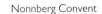

Nonnberg Convent

Nonnberg Convent

On the southeastern side of the Mönchsberg, to the east of the Hohensalzburg Fortress, is the **Nonnberg Benedictine Convent** ❷ (daily 7am–dusk; closed during Mass), which is the oldest convent north of the Alps.

Cemetery at St Peter's church

As with many buildings in Salzburg, fire destroyed the original and what we see today is a Gothic-style convent from the 1400s, though extensive renovations were done in 1895 and 1951. It is full of interesting artefacts, though visitors are only allowed into the church and St John's Chapel.

The convent was founded in *c.*712 by St Rupert, who promptly appointed his niece, St Erentrudis, as the first abbess. The founding patron of the Romanesque church, Henry II, built a basilica here in 1009, and the 12th-century frescoes are some of the most impressive wall paintings in Austria. The church was severely damaged by fire in 1423. In 1464, the abbess, Agatha von Haunsberg, began the reconstruction in a Gothic style, creating the unique crypt and the magnificent reticulate rib-vaulting. The tomb of St Erentrudis is located in the apse and most of the frescoes are from the 12th century. There is also a tombstone for Maria Salome, daughter of Archbishop Wolf Dietrich and his mistress, Salome Alt. In the nuns' choir there is a winged altar with a central shrine revealing the Madonna between the two patron saints, Rupert and Virgil.

St John's Chapel (near the entrance, ask for admittance at the porter's lodge, daily 9am–noon, 3–5pm) features a Gothic-winged altar from the late 1400s. The four figures on the south door pay homage to St Erentrudis, the Virgin Mary, St Rupert and Emperor Henry II.

The Sound of Music footnote: in 1927 the real-life Maria Kutschera and Baron von Trapp were married at Nonnberg Convent. Maria had been a student here in 1924.

Nonntal District – Kai Quarter

If you walk around the convent building and along the Nonnberggasse you will eventually come out at Brunnhausgasse. Follow this road to the right and you will get to the **Leopoldskron** district *(see page 61)*, while heading left you will shortly reach the quiet **Nonntaler Hauptstrasse**. Situated here is the Erhardplatz, which sits in front of the church of **St Erhard im Nonntal**. Built in 1685 by the architect Johann Caspar Zuccalli, it has a richly decorated interior of stucco and a high altar painting by Johann Michael Rottmayr from 1692.

Below the Nonnberg Convent to the north is **Kajetanerplatz**, whose notable feature is the **Kajetanerkirche St Maximilian ❸**. It was consecrated in 1700 and only properly finished after 1730, based on plans by Johann Zuccalli. The portrait of the Holy Family on the left side altar is by Johann Michael Rottmayr; all the other altar paintings and the ceiling fresco are the work of Paul Troger. The Holy Staircase (1712), to the left of the main body of the church, is based on the Scala Santa in Rome.

Leading off Kajetanerplatz is the quiet shopping street of **Kaigasse**, which is lined with shops, galleries and coffee houses. Most of these

Salzburg's signs

Salzburg is full of signs and insignias carved into walls and doorways. If you see 'C+M+B' and a year written in chalk above a door, this means that the carol singers dressed as the Three Wise Men have been to the house around 6 January and received a donation for charity.

buildings were once the homes of priests. On Chiemseegasse, off Kaigasse, is an even more elevated ecclesiastical residence, the **Chiemseehof ❹**. From the 14th century, this was the seat and residence of the bishops of Chiemsee in Bavaria, a filial diocese of Salzburg. The Chiemseehof is not open to visitors, as it now houses the province of Salzburg's regional parliament (Salzburger Landtag) and government (Salzburger Landesregierung).

THE OLD TOWN

The **Altstadt** (Old Town), is a combination of tall merchants' houses and narrow alleys, along with the baroque buildings and squares of the Prince-Archbishops' quarter. The area is compact and easily accessible on foot as most of it is a designated pedestrian zone.

Stiftskirche St Peter

St Peter's Abbey

Below the fortress, at the foot of the Mönchsberg, is the peaceful complex of **Stiftskirche St Peter (St Peter's Abbey) ⑤**, the oldest active monastery in Austria. Founded in *c.*696 by St Rupert, a Frankish missionary, St Peter's is recognised as the spiritual centre around which Salzburg grew. Having been destroyed by fire in 1127 and thereafter

Ornate gravestone in St Peter's cemetery

subjected to many alterations, the church shows traces of several architectural styles. Its Romanesque tower, for instance, is topped by a baroque cupola. Similarly, the interior is high Romanesque, but the altars are definitively in the rococo style. Most of the altar paintings are by Martin Johann Schmidt, and show his characteristic style with its contrasts of light and dark. There is also a plaque dedicated to Nannerl, Mozart's sister, and a memorial to the composer Johann Michael Haydn, the younger brother of the more famous Franz Joseph.

St Peter's bore witness to the music of 13-year-old Mozart in 1769: he wrote his *Dominicus Mass* (K66) for the first Mass officiated here by his childhood friend Kajetan Rupert Hagenauer, later the abbot of St Peter's. In 1783, Mozart's *Mass in C Minor* (K427) was first performed here under the direction of the composer, with his new wife Constanze singing the soprano part.

The church's **cemetery** is sprinkled with beautiful wrought-iron grave markers. This is the final resting place of many of Salzburg's aristocracy, and also of Nannerl Mozart, who died in October 1829. Bordering the cemetery are the famous **catacombs** (May–Sept Tue–Sun 10.30am–5pm, Oct–Apr Wed–Thur 10.30am–3.30pm, Fri–Sun 10.30am–4pm; charge). These were carved into the wall of the rock during early Christian times and emanate a spiritual eeriness.

On the right, next to the church, is Stiftskeller St Peter (daily 11.30am–midnight), a wine tavern since 803 and nowadays a traditional restaurant complex where you can enjoy the finest *Salzburger Nockerl* in town *(see page 97)* and the fantastic Mozart Dinner Concert *(see page 89)*.

Kapitelplatz

If you leave St Peter's by the cemetery exit, you will find yourself in **Kapitelplatz**, which is easily recognisable by the massive chessboard on the ground – right next to the stunning contemporary sculpture *Sphaera* (2007) by the German sculptor Stephan Balkenhol. The male figure on the golden shimmering sphere is the counterpart to the *Woman in the Rock* in court (west of St Peter's). Also on Kapitelplatz is **Neptune's Fountain**, built in 1732 by the sculptor Anton Pfaffinger on the site of one of the old horse ponds. During the summer months, Kapitelplatz is host to markets, sports events and many

Market stalls on Kapitelplatz

artists and musicians. On the far south side of the square, you will find the entrance to the Festungsgasse, which is the road up to the fortress and the **Stieglkeller** (daily 10am–midnight), a classic brewery pub offering good beer, food and a stunning panorama. The Festungsgasse also provides views of the city that you may recognise from *The Sound of Music*.

The Cathedral

Stepping through the northernmost arches of Kapitelplatz brings you onto the **Domplatz**, home to Salzburg's **cathedral**  (winter 6.30am–5pm, summer 6.30am–7pm). In the centre of the square is the statue of the Virgin Mary, a masterpiece of the Hagenauer brothers, created in 1766. Each year, the opening of the Salzburg Festival is celebrated here with a performance of *Jedermann (Everyman)*.

The cathedral, the most impressive baroque edifice north of the Alps, is the ecclesiastical centre of Salzburg. The original cathedral on

Salzburg's cathedral

this site was built by Bishop Virgil in 767. It was destroyed by fire in 1167, and ten years later a new cathedral was built on a grander scale, only to be destroyed once again by fire in 1598. The then archbishop, Wolf Dietrich, demolished the remains and dug up the graveyard in order to start rebuilding from scratch. But his plans were never realised as he was imprisoned by his nephew and successor, Markus Sittikus, who commissioned Santino Solari to rebuild the cathedral to a different design. The building escaped damage during the Thirty Years' War and was consecrated with much pomp and ceremony. Much later, it suffered a third calamity during a bombing raid in 1944, when the dome was destroyed. The cathedral was re-consecrated in 1959 after renovations. At the gates of the cathedral you can see the dates of the three consecrations: 774, 1628 and 1959. The towering white statues at the cathedral gates depict the patron saints Rupert and Virgil (outside) and the two apostles Peter and Paul (inside).

The cathedral's interior dates mostly from the 17th century. The only earlier survival is the 1321 font, supported by four even older 12th-century lions, where Mozart was baptised. One of the most impressive items in the cathedral is the massive and majestic organ, which is guarded by carved angels.

In the cathedral's magnificent baroque oratories is the **Cathedral Museum** (mid-May–Oct and late Nov–early Jan Mon–Sat 10am–5pm, Sun 11am–6pm; charge), which displays artefacts spanning its 1,300-year history, including medieval sculptures, baroque paintings and gold articles from the cathedral treasury. The oldest exhibit is St Rupert's 8th-century crozier. There are also natural history objects and curiosities including fossils, gems and carved ivory.

In the **crypt**, traces of the old Romanesque cathedral have been unearthed. The cathedral excavations (July–Aug daily 9am–5pm; charge), revealing ruins of the original foundations, are entered around the corner on Residenzplatz, left of the main entrance. Other artefacts from the excavations form part

Johann Michael Rottmayr

Johann Michael Rottmayr (1654–1730) was a renowned baroque artist, born in Laufen, Salzburg Province, whose style was influenced by the Venetian art of painting in the 16th century. His speciality was ceiling frescoes – he designed and executed most of those in the Salzburg Residenz and also in the Viennese Winter Riding School. He designed the altar in the Universitätskirche in Salzburg and the original painting *The Apotheosis of St Charles Borromeo* (the intercessor for people stricken with the plague), which can be seen in the Residenz Gallery.

of the Salzburg Museum's collection *(see page 42).*

Residenzplatz

Leaving Domplatz through the archways will bring you to **Residenzplatz**, the Old Town's largest square. It is used for seasonal markets and events, though one stunning constant is the **Residenz Fountain**, created by Tommaso di Garona between 1656 and 1661. The fountain is 15m (50ft) high and is said to be the largest and most beautiful baroque fountain outside Italy. If you are visiting in wintertime, though, you will find it covered up for protection against the elements.

The imposing Residenz Fountain

The **Residenz** ❼ (daily 10am–5pm, last entry 4.30pm; closed on certain special occasions and 3 weeks in August; charge) was the residence and seat of the prince archbishops. A bishop's residence had existed on this site since medieval times; the present building, an extensive complex enclosing three large courtyards, was built around the turn of the 17th century for Archbishop Wolf Dietrich von Raitenau.

The marble portal on Residenzplatz leads into the main courtyard. Take the staircase on the left up to the state rooms and apartments. Decorated in late baroque style, the rooms feature fine wall and ceiling paintings by Johann Rottmayr and Martino Altomonte. As a member of the Salzburg court music ensemble, the young Mozart would regularly perform before invited guests in the Rittersaal (Knights' Hall), which is still used as a concert venue today. On the third floor is the **Residenz Gallery** (Tue–Sun 10am–5pm), where European paintings from the 16th to the 19th century are displayed.

East of the fountain is the **Neue Residenz** (New Residence), built by Archbishop Wolf Dietrich as a 'guest wing'. In 1695, the famous **Glockenspiel** was added by Prince Archbishop Johann Ernst Graf Thun. Each day at 7am, 11am and 6pm, the 35 bells ring out across the city, with the tunes changing according to the season (guided tours Mar–Oct Thur 5.30pm, Fri 10.30am).

The Neue Residenz is home to the **Salzburg Museum ❽** (entrance on Mozartplatz, Tue–Sun 9am–5pm, Thur until 8pm, July–Aug and Dec Mon 9am–5pm; charge; www.salzburgmuseum.at). The collection features art and artefacts from all periods of Salzburg's history, ranging from prehistoric objects, such as a Celtic beaked pitcher and a Bronze-Age helmet, to a set of early 19th-century romantic paintings of the

A Controversial Statue

Right from the start, the statue of Mozart in Mozartplatz has been the cause of controversy. Intended to commemorate the 50th anniversary of Mozart's death, the statue was eventually unveiled a year late, at the 51st anniversary. As part of the unveiling ceremony, Mozart's son, a minor composer and musician, performed only a few of his father's works before moving on to play some of his own compositions. He was soon dismissed from the stage.

As for the statue itself, by all accounts it is not a very good likeness. And it includes a glaring anachronism. The composer is portrayed holding a pencil in hand, even though pencils were not invented until 20 or 30 years after his death. Mozart would have written with a quill pen.

city. Temporary exhibits will focus on local personalities, artists, photographers, writers, musicians and scientists. The **Panorama Museum** (entrance at Residenzplatz, daily 9am–5pm; www.salzburgmuseum.at) shows the fascinating 26m (85ft) -long panorama painting of Salzburg and its surroundings by J.M.Sattler, documenting life in Salzburg around 1829.

Mozartplatz

Next to Residenzplatz is **Mozartplatz**, a square dominated by a statue of Salzburg's favourite son. The disappointingly small bronze

Mozart statue in Mozartplatz

statue of Mozart was unveiled on 5 September 1842 as the composer's two sons looked on. His widow Constanze had died in March of that year, and at Mozartplatz No. 8 you will find a plaque dedicated to her memory. The statue, originally scheduled to be unveiled in 1841, had been delayed for a year because a Roman mosaic floor was discovered on the site during the preparations for its installation.

Alter Markt

There are two main exits leading off Mozartplatz. To the east is Kaigasse, the main street in the old Kai Quarter (see page 35). To the west is **Judengasse**, home to the Jews of Salzburg until they were expelled from the city in 1498. This

Mozart merchandise in
Alter Markt

cobbled pedestrian street
scores highly for charm and
unusual shops, including a
Christmas Shop, where you
can buy yuletide decorations
all year round, and a shop
selling beautifully deco-
rated eggs for use as Easter
decorations.

Judengasse ends as you
reach **Alter Markt ❾**,
another of Salzburg's busy
squares. Besides the impressive fountain that sur-
rounds a statue of St Florian, you will also find the chemist,
Hofapotheke, the oldest in Salzburg and still displaying its
medicinal preparations in old brown vials. Just opposite the
chemist, at No. 10A, is the smallest shop in Salzburg, formerly
a residence. If you are thirsty at this stage, have a coffee in
Café Tomaselli, which has been in the Alter Markt since 1705.
During both winter and summer, you will find markets and/
or mulled wine stands in Alter Markt.

Getreidegasse

Leading on from Judengasse, west of Alter Markt, is Salzburg's
most famous shopping street, **Getreidegasse ❿**. Whether
you like shopping or not, you should have at least one walk
down this busy pedestrian street. One of the first things you
will notice are the skilfully crafted wrought-iron guild signs
that hang above most of the shops and give the street its special
character. Also of interest are the numerous passageways and
courtyards leading off the Getreidegasse, notably the Schatz-
Haus-Passage which has an impressive relief of the Madonna
and child and enters onto Universitätsplatz. Looking up you

may notice that as the houses get taller, their windows get smaller, creating a strange optical effect. There are shops here selling traditional Dirndl (women's dresses) and *Loden* clothes (made of felt-like woollen cloth) and others offering authentic Austrian food.

The Getreidegasse is also part of the pilgrimage trail for Mozart fans: No. 9 is **Mozart's Birthplace** ⓫, the house where he was born on 27 January 1756 and lived with his family until 1773. The Mozarts' apartment on the third floor and the rooms on the second floor have been transformed by Robert Wilson into a museum with an extravagant twist (daily 9am–5.30pm, July–Aug 9am–8pm; last entry 30 mins prior to closing; charge; www.mozarteum.at). On display are manuscripts (facsimiles), documents and souvenirs, and portraits of the family members, including *Mozart at the Piano*, an unfinished 1789 oil painting by Wolfgang's brother-in-law, Joseph

The shopping street Getreidegasse

Lange. Also here are instruments that were played by the great musician: his concert piano and clavichord, his concert and child's violin, and a viola.

All of the passageways leading off Getreidegasse to the south reach Universitätsplatz (University Square), which is home to the academic district and the **Kollegienkirche** (Collegiate Church) ⓬ (daily 9am–6pm), one of Johann Bernhard Fischer von Erlach's finest achievements. The interior is immensely high and features an array of angels on stucco clouds surrounding the Madonna. Universitätsplatz is the site of the daily vegetable market, which can be rather expensive.

Festival District

Just east of here on Herbert-von-Karajan-Platz is the picturesque **Pferdeschwemme** (Horse Pond and Fountain), which incorporates a stunning mural of horses. The fountain was built in 1695 to serve as the washing area for the prince archbishops' horses that were kept in stables next door.

This adjacent site along Hofstallgasse has latterly been occupied by the famous **Festspielhäuser** ⓭ (Festival Halls, guided tours Jan–May and Oct–20 Dec 2pm, June and Sept 2pm and 3.30pm, July–Aug 9.30am, 2pm and 3.30pm; charge;

Horse Pond and Fountain

www.salzburgerfestspiele.
at). This is where, each year
in high summer, Salzburg
plays host to one of the
best-known music festivals
in the world, the Salzburger
Festspiele. The festival is
centred on the three main
venues here, though other
locations around the city
are also used. Based around
the old Riding School,
which was built in 1693 to

The Felsenreitschule theatre

train the archbishop's cavalry, the present Festival Halls still
preserve the original façade of the baroque horse stables.
Nowadays, the **Felsenreitschule** (riding school) is a theatre
with a retractable roof for open-air performances, hosting
high calibre operas and dramas. Next to the Felsenreitschule
is the **House for Mozart**. This, the former Small Festival
Hall, has been completely rebuilt with dramatically increased
capacity. Adjoining the Felsenreitschule on its other flank is
the 2,177-seat **Grosses Festspielhaus** (Large Festival Hall),
designed by the Austrian architect Clemens Holzmeister
(built 1956 to 1960) and inaugurated by the conductor
Herbert von Karajan. Guided tours – the only way to see the
Festival Halls – provide a fascinating insight into the world
of theatre.

The eastern end of Hofstallgasse opens into Max-
Reinhardt-Platz where the **Rupertinum** (Tue–Sun 10am–
6pm, Wed 10am–9pm; charge; www.museumdermoderne.
at) houses an important art collection of 20th-century
works with changing exhibitions. It is part of the Museum
der Moderne Salzburg, with the main exhibition high up on
Mönchsberg *(see page 50)*.

Altar in the Franciscan Church

East of the Rupertinum is Sigmund-Haffner-Gasse, where you will find the entrance to the **Franzisk-anerkirche** (Franciscan Church) ⑭ (daily 6.30am–7.30pm; closed during Mass), an elegant combination of baroque, Romanesque and Gothic styles. A church was originally built here in the 8th century, but the city fire of 1167 destroyed all but the nave. Rebuilding around this core soon commenced and the building was consecrated in 1223. More additions followed, and the church was finally completed in 1460 by Stephan Krumenauer. Originally a part of St Peter's Abbey, it was handed over to the Franciscans by Archbishop Wolf Dietrich. Definitely worth a look is the high altar by Johann Bernhard Fischer von Erlach and the Gothic statue of the Virgin Mary by Michael Pacher.

In the court Dietrichsruh just north of the church the sculpture *AWILDA* (2010), the 5m (16ft) -high head of a young woman, by the contemporary Catalan artist Jaume Plensa, contrasts with the baroque architecture of the university buildings.

Around Gstättengasse

At the northeastern side of the Mönchsberg *(see page 29)* is the **Gstättengasse** where old houses are snugly built into the rock of the hill. In 1669, a rockfall killed 220 people, which is why there are rock cleaners whose job it is to scale the vertical rocks after the snow has melted to chip away at any loose stones or potential hazards.

At the northern end of Gstättengasse is the site of another **Mozart statue**  – Markus Lüpertz' controversial sculpture, *Homage to Mozart*. It was erected in 2005 in anticipation of the 250th anniversary of Mozart's birth the following year and lends a modern touch to **Ursulinenplatz**. The former Ursuline Chapel is now called **St Mark's Church** (Markuskirche). After the original chapel was destroyed by the 1669 rockfall, it was rebuilt and completed in 1705 by the architect Johann Bernhard Fischer von Erlach, who had to accommodate his design to suit the complicated wedge shape of the site.

Around the corner at Museumsplatz is the **Haus der Natur** , Salzburg's modern Natural History Museum (daily 9am–5pm; charge; www.hausdernatur.at). As well as the usual stuffed specimens, it has an impressive collection of live reptiles and a 36-tank aquarium. Besides wildlife, there are also

African wildlife at the Natural History Museum

mineral and geology displays and the Space Research Hall, with a life-size diorama of man's first steps on the moon. The museum also stages exhibitions and has a lovely terrace café. Just past the southern end of Gstättengasse is the **Church of St Blasius**, one of the oldest Gothic hall churches in existence (1330–50). The former civic hospital adjacent houses the newly renovated **Spielzeugmuseum** ⑰ (Toy Museum; daily 9am–5pm; charge; www.salzburgmuseum.at). Displayed here are all kinds of old toys – such as dolls' houses, miniature trains and railways, optical illusions, musical instruments and paper theatres – giving a fascinating insight into the childhood pleasures of times past. The colourful interactive exhibition has very different play areas – be it with teddy bears or wooden tools to construct big cranes. This is fun for the whole family, starting with free felt slippers to feel at home right from the beginning.

Museum of Modern Art

A lift at Gstättengasse 13 allows access to the top of the Mönchsberg, where you will find the **Museum der Moderne** ⑱ (Museum of Modern Art; Tue–Sun 10am–6pm, Wed 10am–9pm; daily during festivals; charge; www.museumder moderne.at). Straight lines, shimmering glass and bright white stone create a stark minimalist edifice, which dominates the northwestern ridge of the Mönchsberg, 60m (200ft) above the shores of the Salzach. Built on the site of the old Café Winkler, which crowned the plateau for many decades, the building, designed by the Munich architects team Friedrich Hoff Zwink, opened in 2004. It respectfully incorporates the old tower into its new structure. The four levels, clad with bright white Untersberg marble, are designed to accommodate an ever-changing and diverse range of exhibitions, plus a permanent collection of works by Klimt, Kokoschka and other, lesser-known artists. The glass ceilings and the use of

The minimalist Museum of Modern Art

stairways as natural light shafts add to the viewing pleasure. If you are feeling peckish and have some cash to spare, then try out the m32 restaurant, which offers one of the best panoramic views of the city. The museum can also be reached by walking along the Mönchsberg from the fortress *(see page 30)*. Close to the museum you also find some contemporary sculptures including *Numbers in the Woods* by Mario Merz, forming part of the Salzburg Art Project 2002–2011. Since 2002 a different international artist has been invited annually to execute a work in a public space, so Salzburg has literally turned into an outdoor sculpture park.

Mülln

North of the Mönchsberg is the **Mülln** district of Salzburg. This neighbourhood is home to a celebrated brewery run by monks, **Augustinerbräu** ⑲ (Mon–Fri 3–11pm, Sat–Sun 2.30–11pm; www.augustinerbier.at). Visitors can enjoy the strong brown ale in a grand and delightfully traditional tavern, where the large beer garden is a place to meet locals and tourists during the summer months.

The brewery and tavern at the **Mülln Monastery** have been in existence since 1621, hence the unique taste of the beer, which is brewed using traditional, old-fashioned methods. The monastery, built on the northern slopes of the Mönchsberg between 1607 and 1614, was founded by monks of the Augustine order, who were called to Salzburg from Bavaria by Archbishop Wolf Dietrich. When the monks began to dwindle in number during the 19th century, the monastery was handed over to the Benedictines from Michaelbeuern.

The Salzach River divides the Old Town from the New

It is now the parish church of Mülln. The interior dates from 1738 and has magnificent examples of delicate Baroque detail.

THE NEW TOWN

Linzergasse

The Staatsbrücke (State Bridge) over the Salzach leads to the new side of town – though it's only new in comparison with its ancient counterpart across the river. Walking directly over the bridge you will reach **Linzergasse** ⑳ which brims with historical sights and stories. Many of the old houses were built during the 14th and 15th centuries, though a devastating fire in 1818 caused serious damage to the north side of the river. The Linzergasse was rebuilt and several of the old burgher houses were renovated and still line the street today. The house at No. 3 was the residence of the natural scientist Paracelsus (Theophratus Bombastus von Hohenheim), who lived here between 1540 and 1541. On the wall of the

St Sebastian's Church

Hotel Gablerbräu is a plaque dedicated to the operatic baritone Richard Mayr, born here in 1877.

St Sebastian's Church

Just opposite the Gablerbräu is the grand entrance to the climb up the Kapuzinerberg, the hill that dominates the skyline on the north side of town (see page 59). Slightly further up the Linzergasse is the entrance to the **Church of St Sebastian ㉗**. The original Gothic church was built between 1505 and 1512 by Archbishop Leonhard von Keutschach. Deteriorating over the years, it was torn down in 1750 and replaced with a baroque hall. The town fire of 1818 destroyed parts of the church, most regrettably the ceiling frescoes and high altar painting. The church was renovated again in 1820 (only the 1752 rococo doorway remains from the former church building), and more restoration work was completed in 1996.

Definitely worth a visit is the adjoining **cemetery** (summer 9am–7pm, winter 9am–4pm), which is surrounded by four arcades, and scattered with tombs, shrines and holy relics. Built by Archbishop Wolf Dietrich, the cemetery is dominated by the **Chapel of St Gabriel** in the centre, which contains his mausoleum. The chapel has a remarkable interior: the walls are clad with tiny coloured ceramic tiles, which contrast dramatically with the brilliant white stucco. The surrounding cemetery is the final resting place of many of Salzburg's best-known names, including Paracelsus, Mozart's widow Constanze and his father Leopold.

Makartplatz

A short walk northwest from the Staatsbrücke brings you to **Makartplatz**, dominated by the awesome Church of the Holy Trinity (Dreifaltigkeitskirche, 1694–1702). No. 8 Makartplatz is **Mozart's Residence** ㉒ (daily 9am–5.30pm, July–Aug until 8pm; last entry 30 mins prior to closing; may be closed in Mozart Week in Jan; charge; www.mozarteum.at), where the Mozart family lived from 1773 to 1780. The house does not offer much in terms of architectural beauty. It did, however,

The Stiftung Mozarteum

In 1880, the International Mozarteum Foundation was formed to 'perform and propagate Mozart's music'. Today, the Foundation runs two museums in the city. Its collections include the composer's original letters and sheet music and numerous performances of his work.

The Foundation is best known for its two long-running concert series. Mozart Week (*Mozartwoche*) is held in late January, with a 10-day presentation of the composer's works to mark his birthday on 27 January. Performances often include concerts by the Vienna Philharmonic Orchestra and concertos by star pianists. In summer, the Foundation's concert series forms a key part of the Salzburg Festival (see page 86).

For Mozart Week information and tickets, contact the Mozarteum Foundation's Ticket Office at Theatergasse 2 (tel: 873 154; www.mozarteum.at). For Salzburg Festival schedules and tickets, visit the festival website at www.salzburgerfestspiele.at.

Concert hall in the Mozarteum

offer exactly what Leopold Mozart wanted: more space than their former home on the Getreidegasse for the family to live and especially for Wolfgang to work. Indeed, Mozart produced many symphonies, concertos, arias, masses and other sacred music in this house. After he had flown the nest, his mother had died and his sister had married, only Leopold remained in the house.

After Leopold died in 1787, the house had many owners. It was only in 1989 that the International Mozarteum Foundation was able to purchase the building, which had been rebuilt as an office block after a bomb struck it in 1944. In 1994, the Foundation tore down the office building and began rebuilding according to the original plans of the house. Today it is a museum that displays exhibits from the Mozart family and old musical instruments.

Opposite Mozart's family house is the Landestheater (Regional Theatre) and, behind it, the Marionettentheater

(Puppet Theatre) and the Stiftung Mozarteum, making this area one of the artistic centres of the city. Built in 1892, the **Landestheater** is the centre of Salzburg's cultural programme, giving performances of all kinds throughout the year, including ballet and opera.

Performances in the **Marionettentheater** (Puppet Theatre) often include full operas enacted by the diminutive wooden characters on strings. The theatre's puppeteers have travelled the world performing their classic operas and plays.

The **Stiftung Mozarteum** ㉓ (Schwarzstrasse 26; www.mozarteum.at) is the headquarters of the foundation of the same name (*see page 54*), dedicated to the research and development of Mozart's music. The complex includes concert halls and recital rooms. This institution is not to be confused with the **Universität Mozarteum** (east of Mirabell Gardens), the world famous academy for music and drama (with a wide range of performances).

Mirabell Palace and Gardens

Next to the Landestheater is the entrance to the **Mirabell-Garten** (Mirabell Gardens) ㉔, comprising geometrically designed flowerbeds, fountains, an orangery, a rose garden and lawns adorned with sculptures based on classical mythology. In *The Sound of Music*, this was where Maria and the children danced around the statue of Pegasus singing *Do Re Mi*. The story of the Trapp family will be documented in a new Sound of Music museum (planned to open in 2013–14) in the building of the former Baroque Museum (this collection will move to the Salzburg Museum at Mozartplatz). On the west side of the parterre is an open-air theatre, with trimmed hedges marking the wings and entrances, and next to it an idyllic shady garden decorated with marble dwarfs (there is also a pleasant children's playground).

The **Mirabell Palace** was built in 1606 by Archbishop Wolf Dietrich, who wanted a residence outside the town walls for his mistress Salome Alt and their children (of whom 10 survived infancy). The archbishop named the palace Altenau. After his imprisonment in the fortress and his death, his nephew and successor Markus Sittikus renamed the palace Mirabell in an attempt to conceal the blasphemous memory of its original purpose. Between 1721 and 1727, the palace was remodelled by Archbishop Franz Anton von Harrach. The stunning marble staircase is the work of Johann Lukas von Hildebrandt, with acrobatic cherubs added by the sculptor Georg Raphael Donner in 1726. The richly adorned **marble hall**, where the Mozart family once performed, was at one time the dining room. Today it is used for concerts and is hugely popular as a wedding venue.

In the manicured grounds of Mirabell Palace

In 1818, the Mirabell was badly damaged in the great fire that ravaged the New Town. Fortunately the marble staircase and hall survived. The current neoclassical style of the

Salzburg and *The Sound of Music*

Film lovers will recognise Salzburg and its environs as the setting for *The Sound of Music*. Most people know that the film was based on fact.

The central character, Maria, was born in 1905. A strict upbringing developed an antipathy towards religion in her. After a chance meeting with a priest, she changed her views and joined the Nonnberg Convent. To aid her recovery from an illness, she was sent as governess to the home of Georg von Trapp, a widower with seven children. Love blossomed, Maria and the captain were married in 1927, and had three children of their own. The von Trapp children were a musical bunch before Maria arrived, but she developed their skills further. When the Austrian Bank closed and Georg was suddenly penniless, the children began to sing to audiences for money. The von Trapps fled Austria in 1938.

Today, fans of the movie come here to retrace the big-screen von Trapp family's footsteps. The song *Do Re Mi* was sung in the Mirabell Gardens around the fountain. St Peter's Cemetery was reconstructed in the studios and used for the scene where the von Trapp family hide between tombstones while trying to escape the Nazis. The façade of Frohnburg Castle became the front of the von Trapp villa, while Leopoldskron Castle was the rear. The children go boating on the lake there and the ballroom was modelled on one of the rooms inside. The opening scenes in the convent were filmed at Nonnberg Convent, the opening credit scenes around Lake Fuschl and the wedding at the church in Mondsee. The von Trapp family make their escape over the Untersberg, although in reality, this would not have been a wise move, as it would have taken them straight to Hitler's Eagle's Nest *(see page 70)*.

palace is thanks to Peter de Nobile, who was the court architect in Vienna and added the detailed work around the windows and the stuccowork.

Many well-known personalities have stayed at the palace, including Prince Otto of Bavaria, who later became the King of Greece, and the legendary Capuchin monk Joachim Haspinger, who died in the palace in

Mirabell Palace in the New Town

1858. Today, the palace is the office of the Mayor of Salzburg (*Bürgermeister*) and the administration. That is why only certain parts of the building are open to the public (staircase daily 8am–6pm; marble hall Mon, Wed and Thur 8am–4pm, Tue and Fri 1–4pm).

Kapuzinerberg

Opposite the Hotel Gablerbräu on the Linzergasse is the entrance to the path that leads to the top of **Kapuzinerberg**, Salzburg's highest point at 636m (2,087ft). The hill was inhabited during Neolithic times, and the two settlements above the monastery have been dated to 1000BC.

On the walk up you pass the six baroque **Stations of the Cross**, which were built between 1736 and 1744. Halfway up is the **Felix Gate**, dating from 1632, which offers the first panoramic view of the city. At this point there is another path called Imbergstiege, which takes you past St John's Chapel and meets up with another path at the *Kanzel* or pulpit, where you will be rewarded by the breathtaking views of the city. Not surprisingly, the forests

Stefan Zweig

An influential Austrian author, Stefan Zweig (1881–1942) lived in Salzburg between the two world wars. Much translated in the 1930s, Zweig's writings included short stories, novels, literary essays and biographies of Marie Antoinette and Maria Stuart notable for their use of psychoanalytical theories. Although of Jewish origin, he described himself as an 'accidental Jew'.

and quiet location of the Kapuzinerberg make it a haven for wildlife, including deer and badgers.

One cannot climb the Kapuzinerberg without visiting the **Kapuzinerkirche (Capuchin Monastery)** ㉕, which was originally a military tower and fortification system erected by nervous archbishops during the Middle Ages. It was Archbishop Wolf Dietrich who called the Capuchin monks to Salzburg in 1594 and transformed the fortification into a monastery and church. The monastery is surrounded by a wall, which runs from the Felix Gate and straddles the western, southern and eastern slopes. The towering cross and bastion of the monastery are dominant features of the landscape, though the monastery itself is very modest. The Gothic oak door of the inner portal is said to be a relic from the old Salzburg Cathedral. The interior of the monastery church is simple, befitting a life of devotion.

Kapuzinerberg 5 is the former residence of the writer Stefan Zweig, who chose the house for its tranquil location. Having lived in Salzburg since 1919, he fled Austria in 1934 following Hitler's rise to power. He first lived in England (in Bath and London) and then the US before moving to Brazil in 1941, where he and his wife both committed suicide because of their concern for the future of Europe. There is a memorial to Zweig next to the Capuchin Monastery.

SALZBURG'S ENVIRONS

Leopoldskron Lake and Palace

A short walk south from the Nonntal area of the Old Town takes you to the Leopoldskron district, which contains the lake and palace of the same name. The **Schloss Leopoldskron** (Leopoldskron Palace)  was built by Archbishop Firmian in 1736 in rococo style. The archbishops used the palace for centuries, but in the early 20th century, it was bought by Max Reinhardt, one of the founders of the Salzburg Festival. He had it totally renovated and the gardens laid out in their present form. Now the property of an American institute, it is used for conferences and seminars but unfortunately is not open to the public. However, you can see the palace from the lakeside path, which provides a lovely walk at any time of year. In the summer, the swans are wonderful to watch and in

Inside the spectacular glass dome at Hangar-7

winter, the Salzburgers love to use the lake for ice-skating and curling matches.

The lake and the house featured in the filming of *The Sound of Music*. The rear of the house was used as the von Trapp villa and the boating scene was filmed on the lake.

Hangar-7

If you are in the vicinity of the airport, it's worth paying a visit to **Hangar-7** ㉗ (Wilhelm-Spazier-Strasse 7A; daily 9am–10pm; free; www.hangar-7.com). Completed in 2003, it was built to house a collection of vintage aircraft. The hangar is a glass and steel dome in the shape of an aircraft wing and constitutes one of the highlights of modern architecture in Salzburg. Situated on the eastern apron of Salzburg's airport, there are two buildings. The first and largest is the hangar that is open to the public. Facing and mirroring it on a smaller scale is Hangar-8, the maintenance hangar.

The museum on the ground floor not only houses aircraft, but also Formula 1 racing cars from the Red Bull teams. During the summer months, many of the aircraft are at various air shows around Europe and may not all be on display. However, there are changing art exhibitions to view throughout the year. There is also a bar, a café and a top-class restaurant, Ikarus (see page 112).

Stiegl's Brauwelt

Not far from the airport and Hangar-7 is **Stiegl's Brauwelt** ㉘ (Stiegl's World of Brewing, Bräuhausstrasse 9; daily Sept–June 10am–5pm, July–Aug 10am–7pm, last entry 1 hr prior to closing; charge; www.stiegl.at). Stiegl, probably the favourite local brew in Salzburg, is served in many of the pubs and restaurants around town. The brewery has been here for over 500 years and is the oldest one that is privately owned in Austria.

Attached to the brewery is a museum housing the world's largest beer exhibition. There is a display of brewing techniques, machinery and unusual equipment through the ages. The tour reveals how the beer is produced and provides a chance to taste some samples.

Hellbrunn Palace

A short bus ride (route No. 25) from the railway station takes you south to **Hellbrunn Palace and Gardens**  (Schloss Hellbrunn; palace open end Mar, Apr and Oct 9am–4.30pm, May–June and Sept 9am–5.30pm, July–Aug 9am–6pm; charge; gardens open daily summer 6am–9pm, winter 6.30am–5pm; free; www.hellbrunn.at). The palace was built between 1613 and 1615 as a hunting lodge and summer residence for Markus Sittikus. Its architect, Santino Solari, was also the man responsible for the reconstruction of Salzburg Cathedral. The Hellbrunn Festival is held in the palace and gardens every August.

The 17th-century Hellbrunn Palace

Trick fountain at
Hellbrunn Palace

The palace itself is not very large, and the interior is no longer complete, but it's worth visiting to see the wonderful Italian murals in the banqueting hall and the adjoining music room in the octagonal pavilion. The palace's **trick fountains** also delight visitors. Markus Sittikus had these built to amuse himself and his guests (but particularly himself). The **Roman Theatre** has stone seats that spew out water without warning, so Sittikus' guests would be unexpectedly soaked (as visitors still are today). Funnily enough, this does not happen to the archbishop's chair at the top. There are also many charming grottoes featuring similar watery surprises based on mythological themes. If you are carrying expensive camera equipment, make sure you are ready to cover it up quickly. Hydraulics also drive a large **mechanical theatre**, with moving figures and an organ that runs on water power.

The park area surrounding the palace dates from 1730, although some of its sculptures are from the early 17th century and include a statue of Empress Elisabeth. The pavilion that was used in *The Sound of Music* was relocated here from its original place at Leopoldskron.

Also in the grounds, about a 20-minute walk from the palace, is the Stone Theatre, formed by a natural gorge, where the first opera in the German-speaking world was presented in 1617.

On Hellbrunn Mountain, still inside the park, stands the Monatsschlössl (Month Castle), so-called because it was allegedly built in only one month. It houses a **Folklore Museum** (Volkskunde Museum; daily Apr–Oct 10am–5.30pm; charge), which displays costumes, masks, religious artefacts and agricultural equipment from the lively history of Salzburg.

Also on the mountain is **Salzburg Zoo** (daily Nov–Mar 9am–4pm, Apr, May, Sept and Oct 9am–6pm, June–Aug until 7pm, last entry Apr–Oct 1 hr prior to closing; charge; www.salzburg-zoo.at). There has been a zoo on this site since 1421. Originally, it housed only alpine animals, but it has since been extended to include species from all over the world. Over 800 creatures can be seen here – many of them (no dangerous ones) allowed to roam freely around the grounds and beyond. There are often monkeys on the paths, storks in the nearby fields and vultures circling in the thermals above the Untersberg. In August, the zoo is open on Friday and Saturday evenings until 11pm (last entry 9.30pm) for 'Night Zoo' sessions, when

The *Föhn*

Situated so close to the Alps, Salzburg experiences a phenomenon called the *Föhn* for about 45 days of the year. A *Föhn* is created when air is forced up one side of a mountain range, causing it to expand and cool and lose its water vapour. When the dry air starts to move down the north side of the Alps, it warms as the pressure increases, creating strong, gusty, warm and dry winds. When a *Föhn* blows into Salzburg, it is enough to lay the whole city low. Headaches, asthma attacks and frayed nerves are common; the suicide rate, crime and traffic accidents increase. However, a *Föhn* day is generally a lovely day, bringing subtropical temperatures in summer and warm, pleasant days in winter.

Klessheim Palace

the nocturnal animals are the star performers.

Klessheim Palace

The main part of **Schloss Klessheim** (Klessheim Palace) about 1.5km (1 mile) west of the city centre (No. 18 bus), was built by Austria's greatest baroque architect, Johann Fischer von Erlach, for Archbishop Johann Ernst Graf Thun between 1700 and 1709. He used designs and ideas from Versailles palace and gardens and eventually completed the construction in 1732.

It was used by the archbishops until Salzburg came under the control of the Habsburgs. In the late 19th century, Emperor Franz Josef banished his homosexual younger brother, Archduke Ludwig Viktor, to Klessheim Palace after Ludwig had sparked a public scandal by making advances to an army officer in a swimming pool in Vienna. He died here in 1919.

Between 1938 and 1945, Hitler used the palace as his residence when he was in Salzburg. It was here that he met the Italian dictator Mussolini in 1940 and other heads of state from Hungary, Czechoslovakia and Romania. After the war, it became the headquarters of the occupying army. Then for a long time it was used by the provincial government to receive important state visitors such as Queen Elizabeth II.

Since 1993, it has housed the only year-round **casino** in Salzburg Province. You can enjoy the gardens and a few rooms of the palace free, but to enter the casino (open daily noon–3am) there is an admission fee which provides you with your first gaming chips. Minimum age for entry is 18 and you must provide some photo identification. As well as the No. 1 bus from the city centre, shuttle buses operated by the casino run from 4.30 pm from town to the casino (tel: 0662 2220 777) returning hourly from 5pm to any location in town.

SOUTH OF SALZBURG

Untersberg

The highest mountain in the vicinity of Salzburg is the **Untersberg** ③, to the southwest. It can be seen for kilometres around as it juts up from the flatlands and towers 1,853m (6,078ft) above sea level. The mountain is a limestone massif with deposits of salt and marble. The terrain is craggy and steep, making it a strenuous climb on foot. If you do not have a car, you can take bus No. 25 to the bottom station of the cable car in **Grödig** (daily July–Sept 8.30am–5.30pm, Mar–June and Oct 8.30am–5pm, Dec–Feb 9am–4pm). Alternatively,

View of the Untersberg from the Mönchsberg

there is a cycle path that takes you all the way there. On a clear day, the views from the top are incredible. You can see the whole of the Salzburg basin, into Bavaria, the Watzmann (the second highest mountain in Germany) and as far as the Lake District (Salzkammergut) to the east and the Hohe Tauern mountains in the south. There are a few easy walks from the top station of the cable car to the viewpoints. For those who do not want to venture too far, there is a panoramic view from the top station.

Tucked beneath the northwest slopes of the Untersberg is the village of **Grossgmain** ❸❷, which has an **Open-Air Museum** (Freilichtmuseum; Easter–Oct Tue–Sun 9am–6pm, July–Aug daily, last entry 5pm; charge). The museum is one

Legends of the Untersberg

According to legend, dwarfs, giants and wild virgins all live on the Untersberg. However, the mountain's main mythical character is Emperor Karl the Great, who is said to sleep within the mountain. Legend foretells a time when the ravens that circle the summit will stop and the Emperor's beard will have grown three times around a marble table. Then he will rise and fight the battle of good versus evil. The venue for this battle is quite specific: the pear tree in Wals. Once victorious, the Emperor will hang up his shield and an era of happiness and prosperity will follow. Other legends view the rising of the Emperor as Judgement Day, when the Antichrist will appear and do battle with angels.

Less portentously, historians debate the importance of the Untersberg during Celtic times, when Salzburg was geographically almost central in the Celtic empire. Given the pattern of early settlements found around Salzburg, it may be that the Untersberg was of great religious importance, and many of the mountain's legends have possible links with the political and religious propaganda of the early Middle Ages. Certainly few mountains in the Alps have generated such colourful mythology.

Countryside surrounding Berchtesgaden

of the top attractions in the area and has won numerous awards. It includes a collection of around 100 old farmhouses that have been transferred from different parts of Salzburg Province and reconstructed with meticulous care. They span the last five centuries, showing how building and farming methods have changed and developed.

There are also many old farm machines to be viewed, and on Sundays and public holidays craftsmen demonstrate the old trades, from woodwork to beekeeping, shoemaking to beer-brewing. The museum covers an area of 50 hectares (125 acres), so you will need a full day to see it all.

Berchtesgaden

Just 30km (18 miles) south of Salzburg, across the border in Germany, is **Berchtesgaden** ㉝. Set amid beautiful alpine scenery dominated by the impressive peaks of Germany's second-highest mountain, the Watzmann (2,713m/8,900ft), this delightful little town encapsulates all the attractions of the Bavarian Alps, including painted houses and wonderful views. But the area also has a dark side. The village of **Obersalzberg**, just above the town, was where in 1934 Hitler bought a chalet known as the Berghof (Mountain House), and had it decorated in the most pretentious style, with massive furniture and heavy fireplaces. It became his country retreat, where he entertained his cronies, Nazi Party functionaries and, in 1938, Neville Chamberlain, the British prime minister. A Gestapo headquarters was established nearby, and beneath it all was a network of underground bunkers. Most of these buildings, including the Berghof, were destroyed in an Allied air raid in 1945, and the remains were blown up by the West German government in 1953.

In the village, the fascinating **Dokumentation Obersalzberg** (Apr–Oct daily 9am–5pm, Nov–Mar Tue–Sun 10am–3pm, last entry 1 hr prior to closing; charge; www.obersalzberg.de) explains the bigger picture of the Third Reich.

You can still visit the **Kehlsteinhaus** or Eagle's Nest – the 'teahouse' built by Martin Bormann as Hitler's 50th birthday present from the Nazi Party (daily May–Oct; www.kehlstein haus.com). It sits precariously on the top of Kehlstein mountain at 1,834m (6,017ft). Parking for cars is in Obersalzberg, where you can catch a bus to the summit, up a mountain road that was built specifically to reach the Eagle's Nest, a remarkable feat of engineering. Once at the top, you board the original brass-lined lift for the 124m (406ft) ascent to the house itself. Part of it is now a restaurant and provides fantastic views.

Also located in the Berchtesgaden area are the ancient **Salt Mines** (Salzbergwerk; tours May–Oct 9am–5pm, Nov–Apr 11am–3pm; charge). Salt has been mined here since 1517, and still is today. Visitors are issued with old miners' clothing to take a tour of the mines, accompanied by a miner (you also get an audio guide), starting in a small wagon on railway tracks. The rest of the tour includes sliding down a miners' chute and taking a ferry across an underground salt lake. One feature not to be missed is the 'chapel', a grotto of oddly shaped salt formations illuminated to eerie effect.

Königssee

To the south of Berchtesgaden, and within the Alpen Nationalpark Berchtesgaden, lies **Königssee ㉞**, one of the most beautiful lakes in the region. The narrow fjord-like lake runs 9km (5.6 miles) north–south in the shadow of the Watzmann, its giant east face rising almost straight out of the water. There is a car park near the small village of Königssee, at the northern end of the 192m (630ft) deep 'fjord'. From here you can take a boat trip along the whole length of the lake. As only a small part of Königssee is visible from the village, the trip is highly recommended, to fully appreciate the stunning beauty of the scenery. The first stop (and final one in winter) is **St Bartholomä**,

A tranquil scene at Königssee with St Bartholomä

where there is a pretty baroque church with twin onion domes and a restaurant serving wonderfully fresh fish from the lake. The second is **Salet** at the lake's southern tip. There is a commentary on board in English about the lake's history, and the aims of the Alpine National Park Berchtesgaden and the Unesco Biosphere Reserve. To keep pollution levels down the tourist boats are electric and, apart from rescue boats and farmers' boats, they are the only powered craft allowed on the lake.

Hallein

About 15km (10 miles) south of Salzburg lies the busy little town of **Hallein ㉟**, the second largest town in Salzburg Province and the district capital of the Tennengau. You can reach it either by train or by car via the A10 Tauern motorway. Hallein has a delightful old town on the banks of the Salzach River. Most of the houses in the old town were built in the late Middle Ages, and many were renovated in the 1980s. Until the early 1990s, the town's Perner Island was an industrial site with a large salt processing plant, but it has now been turned into a cultural centre and every year stages a number of performances during the Salzburg Festival.

Dürrnberg Salt Mines

A large paper mill is the town's main employer, but in former years salt mining brought wealth to Hallein. Salt was discovered on the Dürrnberg by the Celts, and was mined there as recently as 1989. Now the mines are closed and have been turned into a museum. A tour of the **Dürrnberg Salt Mines** (Salzwelten; guided tours daily, Apr–Oct 9am–5pm,

Nov–Mar 10am–3pm; charge) demonstrates how salt was mined, explains the importance of salt and gives visitors the chance to go on an underground boat trip and to slide down an old miners' chute. Also included in the Salzwelten ticket is the **Celtic Village**, a reconstruction of a village showing how the Celts lived and worked.

Back in the town, the **Celtic Museum** (open daily 9am–5pm; charge; www. salzburgmuseum.at) houses a fascinating collection of archaeological finds from the area, including equipment used by the miners, as well as priceless burial offerings.

Franz Xaver Gruber's grave

The **Silent Night Museum** (open daily 3–5pm, Dec from 11am; charge; www.silentnightmuseum.org) is a celebration of the famous Christmas carol whose composer, Franz Xaver Gruber (1787–1863), is buried in Hallein in front of his house (museum). He was organist and choirmaster here since 1835, but composed the famous carol as early as 1818, when teaching at a primary school in the village of Arnsdorf.

Werfen

If you continue south from Hallein along the A10 for another 29km (18 miles), you reach **Werfen** ㊱, a small market town situated on what was an important trade route for salt. The town is strung along a wide road and is pleasant to walk through. The parish church, built between 1652 and 1657, contains a very impressive baroque altar and early baroque side altars.

Castle Hohenwerfen (Apr and Oct Tue–Sun 9.30am–4pm, May–Sept daily 9am–5pm, mid-July–mid-Aug daily 9am–6pm; charge) was built in 1077 to guard the trade route. Frequent additions up to the 16th century have given it a fairytale appearance. It was used as a prison for many centuries and among those locked up there was Archbishop Wolf Dietrich von Raitenau in 1611. According to folklore, the dungeons in these castles were sometimes filled to capacity with innocent people, including Protestant missionaries who had offended the archbishops of Salzburg in some way. It is said that these 'unwanted sorts' were locked up in darkness in solitary confinement for years and only set free after they had gone mad.

The castle has an interesting armoury and Austria's first **falconry museum**, and there are falconry displays several times

Hohenwerfen Castle

a day. The castle was used as a location for the 1968 film *Where Eagles Dare*.

Eisriesenwelt

The caves of **Eisriesenwelt** (World of the Ice Giants; guided tours daily May–Oct 9am–3.30pm, July–Aug until 4.30pm; charge includes cable car; www.eisriesen welt.at), northeast of Werfen, are the largest ice caves in

Rural encounter

Europe. They stretch for about 42km (26 miles), although only a fraction of that length is open to the public. Fantastic ice 'statues' and frozen waterfalls extend for about 1km (0.5 mile) from the entrance. The ice formations are created during the winter months when the water in the caves freezes, so the best time to see them is in the spring and early summer before the formations have started to melt again.

Drive or take a bus from Werfen's main square, to the car park by the visitor centre. Then it's a 20-minute walk to the cable car station. In order to enter the caves, you have to take one of the many guided tours that start at regular intervals. As the temperature inside is always around freezing point, wear warm clothing – and sensible shoes to negotiate the narrow slippery passages. The caves are not recommended for the elderly, infirm or young children. Although it's quite a strenuous excursion, it is certainly worth the effort.

The Grossglockner Road

One of the most spectacular scenic routes through the Alps is the **Grossglockner High Alpine Road** ③ (Grossglockner Hochalpenstrasse). The Grossglockner itself is Austria's highest mountain at 3,798m (12,460ft). It is situated in the Hohe Tauern range of mountains and in the national park of the same name, which straddles the provinces of Salzburg, East Tyrol and Carinthia.

The job of planning the road, running 48km (30 miles) between Bruck and Heiligenblut, was given to the engineer Franz Wallack in 1924. Construction started in 1930, taking five years. The road had to be rebuilt after World War II, having been seriously damaged by tank movements. Until the Felbertauern tunnel was built, this was the main road linking the provinces of Salzburg and Carinthia via the Alps. Since 1935, some 60 million people have made use of the road. It is popular with cyclists, motorcyclists – there are special facilities for parking motorbikes and equipment lockers along the route – car drivers and coach groups. On some sunny summer days, there can be thousands of people making the pilgrimage along this road.

The Grossglockner High Alpine Road

A toll road, it is officially open from the beginning of May until the end of October (daily May–mid-June 6am–8pm, mid-June–mid-Sept 5am–9.30pm, mid-Sept–Oct 6am–7.30pm, last entry 6.45pm), but sometimes summer snowfalls can close it for days at a time. Before you set off, it's worth checking with the Ferleiten Information Point (tel: 06546 650) whether the road is actually open or not. The ticket you buy at the toll-booth gives you access to the road's exhibitions and sights.

There are various **viewpoints** to stop at along the way. The Fuscher Törl, which lies at 2,428m (7,966ft) above sea level, has a memorial built by Clemens Holzmeister to commemorate those who died during the construction of the road. The highest point of the through road is the Hochtor at 2,503m (8,212ft). You will be quite likely to find snow up here even in August. But if you take the detour to the Franz-Josefs-Höhe, which is highly recommended, you can reach an even higher point called the Edelweissspitze, at 2,571m (8,435ft).

You have the best view of the Grossglockner from the Franz-Josefs-Höhe (2,369m/7,772ft), where there is a lift that takes you down to the Pasterze Glacier (note that the glacier is shrinking and so the bottom of the lift is now about 300m/yds away from the start of the glacier). This is where you are most likely to see marmots lying in the sun – or hear their whistles when alarmed. Access to walks and visitor centres are included in your ticket.

The road takes you through a variety of vegetation zones and is quite fascinating. There are also many activities to do with the family at places such as Fuscher Lake, at 2,262m (7,421ft), where there is an exhibition about the construction of the road. There is a geology path and, at Schöneck, a botanical path. Various restaurants are dotted along the route, but it is recommended to avoid lunchtimes at the Franz-Josefs-Höhe, as the restaurants there are very busy catering for the numerous coach parties.

Krimml Waterfalls in the Hohe Tauern National Park

Krimml Waterfalls

At the very western end of the Salzach Valley, just before the **Gerlos road** starts its steep ascent over the pass to the Tyrol, lie the **Krimml Waterfalls ③** (Krimmler Wasserfälle; daily mid-Apr–mid-Oct; charge; no charge in winter, but there is no guarantee that the path will be passable and safe). Like the Grossglockner, they are part of the Hohe Tauern National Park. With a drop of 380m (1,247ft), the Krimmler Wasserfälle are the highest waterfalls in Europe and make a magnificent spectacle as they plunge down the mountainside in three stages. The falls are at their most impressive in the spring and early summer when the melt-waters turn the stream into a torrent. The Krimmler Ache starts at the Krimmler Kees glacier before plummeting down the falls.

The path up to the falls is relatively steep, but not difficult, and there are benches and viewing platforms all along the route where you can rest your legs while admiring the rainbow colours in the spray of the falls.

The first waterfall is 140m (460ft) high and the most spectacular of the three. This one can be viewed from the bottom without any strenuous walking. The walk from the car park will take around 10 minutes. Walking from the bottom of the first falls to the second, which is 100m (330ft) high, will take half an hour. Then to the top falls (a 140m/460ft drop), it's another hour's climb. Allow plenty of time to get back before nightfall.

The falls have been popular with visitors for many years. The first rough steps to the top of the first falls were built in 1835. The existing path was completed in 1897, built by the local branch of the Alpine Club. For keen walkers there are several further trails that can be explored from the top of the falls.

In *WasserWunderWelt* (The Wonderful World of Water) at the bottom of the falls, information panels describe the flora and fauna in the area, as well as hydro-energy. There is also a multivision cinema.

THE SALZKAMMERGUT

The Salzkammergut (Salt Chamber Estate) refers to the wealth that salt brought to the region, but it is an area that today is more famous for its lakes and alpine scenery than for its salt industry, and is also known as the Lake District. The area extends from Fuschl near Salzburg to the Almtal in the east, with impressive peaks and more than 70 lakes. It is

On the shore of Fuschlsee

one of Austria's most popular tourist regions and often considered to be the jewel of the nation. The area has been popular with visitors since Emperor Franz Joseph spent his summers in Bad Ischl.

Fuschlsee

The first lake you come to heading east from Salzburg is **Fuschlsee** ❸. About 25km (15 miles) from the city, it can be reached by the A1 motorway or along the B1/B158 (the prettier route). The lake is 4km (2.5 miles) long and wonderfully warm in the summer. The steep, wooded slopes rising along its shore curve to its eastern shore where the village of Fuschl lies. This quiet little resort is popular with walkers in the summer and also offers watersports. If the countryside looks familiar, it may be that you recognise it from the opening titles of *The Sound of Music*, which was filmed here.

On the opposite shore, in its own extensive grounds, is Schloss Fuschl. This was originally a hunting lodge of the prince archbishops, then during World War II it was used as headquarters by Hitler's Foreign Minister Joachim von Ribbentrop. Since the late 1950s it has been a luxury hotel, with its own golf course, where Richard Nixon and Nikita Krushchev, among other notables, have been entertained.

Wolfgangsee

About 7km (4.5 miles) further southeast from Fuschl lies the quaint little village of St Gilgen. Stretched along the northern shore of **Wolfgangsee** ❹ (Wolfgang Lake), it is a popular destination for holidaymakers in summer and winter. The Wolfgangsee itself is 10km (6 miles) long and 2km (1.2 miles) wide. With water temperatures of around 26°C (78°F) in summer, it is popular for a variety of watersports.

St Gilgen is famed as the birthplace of Mozart's mother, Anna Pertl (1720–78). Although the composer himself never came here, there is now a **Mozart** multimedia show (June–Sept Tue–Sun 10am–noon and 3–6pm; charge) in the house where his mother was born. His sister Nannerl also lived in the house after her marriage, but she moved to Salzburg in 1801 when her husband died. The Mozart fountain and the parish church (1376) are also worth a visit.

For walkers and skiers, the Zwölferhorn lift takes you to the top of the **Zwölferhorn** mountain at 1,522m (4,993ft). In summer, the summit is a starting point for many alpine walks, while in winter, beginners and families ski here.

The village is also a good place from which to take a boat across the lake to **St Wolfgang**. The boats – some of which date from the 1880s – run a regular service from April to October. The journey is a wonderful way to appreciate the beauty of the countryside. Alternatively, you can drive the 18km (11 miles) along the whole of the southern shore of the lake and along most of

Picturesque facades in the village of St Gilgen

Sailing on the Wolfgangsee

the northern shore until you reach St Wolfgang.

This village is probably the most overtly touristy of all the locations on the Wolfgangsee, but when you see it hugging the shore and protected by the Schafberg towering 1,783m (5,850ft) above it, you will understand why. The village has a long history as a pilgrimage destination following its foundation in 976 by St Wolfgang, the bishop of Regensburg. According to legend, he built the village's first small church, which is allegedly a site of miracle cures. It is certainly one of the most beautiful churches in the region. Inside, it has a winged altar created by Michael Pacher in 1481 and three Baroque altars by Meinrad Guggenbichler from 1706.

The village is also famous for its White Horse Inn, a hotel with a wonderful lakeside terrace. It was the inspiration for Ralph Benatzky's operetta *Im Weissen Rössl am Wolfgangsee*, which was first performed in Berlin in 1930.

A trip up the **Schafberg** on the funicular railway (May–Oct) is not to be missed. On a clear day, you have the most breathtaking view of the Salzkammergut with its lakes and mountains spread below. The railway was built at the end of the 19th century and has been operational for over 100 years. For steam train enthusiasts, the old steam-fired train does occasional nostalgia trips. For timetable and fare information, see www.schafbergbahn.at.

Mondsee

The nearby lake of **Mondsee** ④ lies approximately 30km (19 miles) east of Salzburg and is easily reached on the A1 motorway. An alternative route is the Romantikstrasse from St Gilgen, taking you under the Schafberg and along the western shore of the Mondsee. The lake has a reputation for being the warmest in the Salzkammergut and it is popular for all kinds of watersports in summer. The market town of Mondsee is worth visiting to see its church, originally part of a large Benedictine monastery. It was founded in 748, although construction of the church began in 1470. Built in Gothic style, it has a 17th-century baroque interior. This was where the wedding scene in *The Sound of Music* was filmed.

The extensive Neolithic stilt settlements in the lake, which are well documented in the **Pfahlbaumuseum** (May–mid-June, Sept Tues–Sun 10am–5pm, mid-June–Aug until 6pm, Oct only Sat; Sun; charge; www.pfahlbauten.de) were given Unesco World Heritage status in 2011.

Mondsee lake

WHAT TO DO

Salzburg is a very agreeable city for sightseeing. Most of the major sights are within easy walking distance of the centre. You can stroll around the Old Town, wander into the cathedral and other churches, relax in the

large spacious squares, play outdoor chess, take a *Fiaker* (horse-drawn carriage ride) around the city or climb up the hill to see the fortress.

A pleasant way to relax in high summer is to sit on the grassy riverbank and watch the fast-flowing waters of the Salzach flow by, as well as the hustle and bustle of city life. If you want to get on the water, you can take a boat trip on the *Amadeus Salzburg*, which docks near the Makartsteg (pedestrian bridge). This takes you up the river as far as Hellbrunn and back again (www.salzburgschifffahrt.at).

CULTURE AND NIGHTLIFE

It is impossible to ignore Mozart in Salzburg. There is his birthplace, the house that he grew up in, Mozartplatz with its statue of Mozart, Mozartsteg (bridge), the Mozart Festival, *Mozartkugeln* (mini chocolate balls filled with marzipan) and the Wolfgang Amadeus Mozart Airport. But young Wolfgang is far from the only cultural feature of this city. The museums and galleries offer everything from Stone Age

Salzburg province is ideal for mountain bikers from novice to experienced

Production of *Measure for Measure* at the Salzburg Festival

relics and Roman remains to vintage aeroplanes and modern art.

Music and the performing arts are everywhere. All year round, operas and concerts are performed in the Festival Halls. The Landestheater (state theatre) and smaller theatres host musicals, ballets, operas and drama.

Festivals

The internationally famous **Salzburg Festival** (Salzburger Festspiele) is held every year from the last week in July to the end of August. Throughout the day you can hear opera singers practising through open windows, and every evening the Festival Halls and squares play host to magnificent operas and orchestral concerts. During the five-week period more than 180 events take place, including operas, concerts, plays and ballets, attracting the highest calibre of artists. If you are visiting Salzburg at this time and have not booked well in advance, there is very little accommodation to be had.

Many other festivals take place in Salzburg throughout the year. Among them is **Mozartwoche**, held each January (*see page 95*). The **Easter Festival**, every March or early April, sees the Berlin Philharmonic relocate to Salzburg for two weeks to perform various operatic and orchestral productions. The **Pfingstfestspiele** (Whitsun Festival), a four-day festival of baroque music, takes place in May over the Whitsun weekend.

Karneval (Carnival) is the ball season all over Austria, and in the Roman Catholic areas of Germany. The ball season begins properly with the New Year's Eve celebrations and continues right up to Shrove Tuesday (*Faschingsdienstag*), the last day before Lent (normally in February), when it culminates in a big celebration in which everybody dresses up in fancy dress and goes out to party. New Year's Eve and *Fasching* are the only two days of the year when the bars and taverns do not have to close.

All through the summer many individual streets hold festivals as well, with stalls and street theatre. In late August or early September, the **harvest festivals** begin, running until Austria's National Day on 26 October. Numerous events take

Winter Wonderland

From the beginning of December until 6 January (Epiphany), the city becomes a winter wonderland, taken over by Christmas market stalls, ice sculptures, food and *Glühwein* stands and carol singers. It is a great social occasion enjoyed by residents and tourists alike. The largest Christmas market is held on Residenzplatz and Domplatz, while Mozartplatz becomes an ice rink. There are other markets in Mirabell Platz, Sterngarten (near the Sternbräu restaurant just off Getreidegasse), the Fortress Courtyard (weekends only) and Hellbrunn Palace.

On 6 December, St Nikolaus Day, the saint delivers his bag of goodies (traditionally chocolate) to well-behaved children. However, on 5 December, the city is visited by the Krampus – a devil-like horned creature who rushes around punishing naughty children. In fact, there are usually several Krampuses at large; you will know they are near when you hear their bells or the screams of the children. Keep a safe distance: Krampuses have permission to hit people!

place in the city of Salzburg and all the towns and villages in the province. These include church thanksgiving services, brass band music (with sausages and beer), craft and farmers' markets, carved pumpkin displays, petting farms and other activities for children, and the taking down of the maypole that has been standing since the beginning of May. You will recognise the places holding harvest festivals by the large hay statues creatively constructed from bales and other paraphernalia. Take the opportunity to sample the local products, such as *Sturm* (fermented grape juice). Stiegl (the local brewery) normally brings out an autumn beer too.

Nightlife

Salzburg's varied nightlife offers bars, pubs, wine bars and taverns to suit all ages, tastes and budgets. Taverns like Zum Fidelen Affen and Gasthaus Zum wilden Mann are a must for

Enjoying home-brewed ale at the Augustiner Brewery

beer lovers who want to experience the Austrian brew at its finest. Food is normally served here as well. The main streets for bars are Rudolfskai, Gstättengasse, Kaigasse, Giselakai and Steingasse. Clublike bars, such as Republic and the Shamrock Irish Bar, have designated dance areas and live music.

For fans of Mozart, the **Mozart Dinner Concert** in St Peter's Stiftskeller (tel: 828 6950) is the perfect evening entertainment. Exquisite soloists and a small chamber orchestra perform pieces of *Don Giovanni*, *The Marriage of Figaro* and *The Magic Flute* between the three courses of a meal prepared according to traditional 18th-century recipes.

Between mid-May and October, you might consider the 'Sound of Salzburg Dinner Show', an entertainment-and-dining package all in English. The show takes place at the Sternbräu Dinner Theater, Getreidegasse 34 (tel: 826 617, www.thesound ofsalzburg.com), and begins with a video entitled *Maria von Trapp – the True Story*. The stage show includes melodies from *The Sound of Music*, a 'Trapp Family Folk Music Revival' and a tribute to Mozart, performed in period costumes.

SHOPPING

Salzburg has plenty of outlets for the dedicated shopper: modern shopping centres, specialist stores and antique shops, designer boutiques and high-street fashion, and several wonderful markets selling fresh produce, arts, crafts and souvenir trinkets. The shopping centres are just a short bus ride from the centre of town (Europark, route No. 1 or 6, and Alpenstrasse, No. 3, 5 or 8), but everything else is within walking distance.

The main shopping streets in the city centre are **Getreidegasse**, in the Old Town, and **Linzergasse** across the river in the New Town. Here you will find individual designer boutiques and chain stores alongside bakeries, jewellers and supermarkets. If you explore the many lanes that lead off Getreidegasse to Universitätsplatz, Judengasse, Kaigasse, Papagenoplatz and Steingasse, you will come across shops that deal in antiques, art, sculptures, perfumes, handmade soap, shoes, music and gifts. You can even buy Christmas tree decorations and Easter eggs all year round.

There's a fresh produce market, called **Grünmarkt**, Monday to Saturday on Universitätsplatz, where vegetables, fruit, meat, poultry, fish, seafood, pastries, cheeses, flowers, crafts and spices create a feast of colours and smells. The **Schrannenmarkt** is similar, held every Thursday 5am–1pm in front of St Andrew's Church on Mirabellplatz. In both of these markets are many snack stands selling traditional treats, which are worth trying. From the end of May until September there is a market called **Salzachgalerien** held every two to four weeks at weekends on the Old Town river bank of the Salzach. This is where local artists and craftspeople come to display and sell their work.

Shopping on Universitätsplatz

SPORTS

The city and the province of Salzburg offer a wide range of activities for all seasons. During the winter you have the option of downhill and cross-country skiing, snowboarding, ice skating and tobogganing. In summer you can choose from golf, hiking, horse riding, summer tobogganing, mountain biking and climbing, paragliding, watersports and canyoning or white-water rafting. Check with the tourist information office, the receptionist in your hotel or in youth hostels for up-to-date information on companies offering activity excursions.

Winter Sports

Salzburg's professional ice hockey team, the Red Bulls, have their home arena in the Volksgarten (Eisarena). The hockey season starts in late August and continues until March. If you are in Salzburg and the team is playing, you should get tickets as early as possible from the Ice Arena (tel: 630 752). It is advisable to dress warmly.

From the first snowfall, children make the field behind the fortress their winter playground. Makeshift toboggans compete with high-tech versions in sliding down the hill. Anyone is free to join in, and there is no entrance fee.

Salzburg is a well-located city for skiing and snowboarding, with some of the best slopes in the world within relatively easy reach. The province has hosted the Alpine Skiing World Championships, as well as ski jumping and snowboarding competitions. Whether you are an absolute beginner or an experienced skier, you will find a slope to suit your needs. Most of the major ski resorts are to the south of Salzburg, the nearest being just 20 minutes away and the best of them between 45 and 90 minutes from the city. The resorts offer a wide choice of accommodation, including slope-side alpine cabins, as well as numerous shops, restaurants, banks and a

Off-piste skiing

good nightlife. Off-piste skiing, cross-country, ice skating, tobogganing and night skiing are just some of the additional activities. Among the ski areas within comfortable travelling distance of Salzburg are Flachau, Obertauern, Badgastein, Zell Am See and Saalbach-Hinterglemm.

The best way to get to the resorts from Salzburg is by train, leaving early in the morning. The information desk at the railway station will be able to advise you about the best way to reach your destination. If you are staying in Salzburg during the winter season and would like to go skiing for just one or two days, a free ski shuttle bus leaves Mirabellplatz every morning at 8.30am to Flachau. There is also the Kitzbühler Alpen Shuttle from Mozartplatz (about €60 return), which allows you to spend 4.5 hours in this international skiing resort.

Watersports

Salzburg offers a choice of attractive outdoor swimming pools, which are well maintained and very clean. All have lifeguards on duty, as well as snack bars and restaurants. Some even have diving pools and crazy golf. The outdoor pools (*Freibad*) are at the following locations: Leopoldskron (bus No. 15), Volksgarten (bus No. 6 or 7) and Alpenstrasse (bus No. 3, 5 or

8). There is also an indoor swimming pool in the city centre at Paracelsus Bad & Kurhaus, Auerspergstrasse 2. If you would prefer to head out to the alpine lakes, with crystal-clear water and breathtaking views, the easiest thing to do is to catch a Post Bus from the railway station or from Mirabellplatz. All kinds of watersports are on offer at the lakes, including windsurfing, water skiing, sailing, kayaking and fishing.

The Alpentherme water park in Bad Hofgastein has everything from saunas and slides, to beautiful outdoor pools with a panoramic view of the Alps (Sun–Wed 9am–9pm, Thur–Sat 9am–10pm).

Cycling

Salzburg has been named Austria's most bike-friendly city. There are scenic cycle paths everywhere along the river, through Nonntal to Leopoldskron, Mülln and Anif (Hellbrunn). A few tips: stick to the cycle paths, know your hand signals, and be aware of other cyclists who tend to overtake at great speed. In Salzburg, it is not a legal obligation to wear a helmet, though it is much safer to do so. At night you must use front and rear lights. For pedestrians: do not walk on the cycle paths; when you hear a bell ringing, watch out, and move out of the way. If your hotel or hostel does not offer free bike loan, see page 116 for bike hire details.

Hiking in Zell Am See, a ski resort in winter

Hiking

Salzburg and its surrounding area offer all levels of hiking. A good city walk goes from Mülln, over the Mönchsberg, through town and finishes off on the Kapuzinerberg. For something out of town but not too demanding, try the Gaisberg (to the east) which has a road all the way to the top. You can walk parallel with it, which makes finding the way easy. The view from the top of Gaisberg is breathtaking. If you want to push yourself and get away from the city, the Untersberg is perfect. Really adventurous types will find plenty of trekking routes in the Salzkammergut. Make sure you have an idea of the weather and save your hikes for clear days. You should buy a hiking guide that details rest huts and routes along the trails.

SALZBURG FOR CHILDREN

The best attractions for children are Hellbrunn Palace with its water fountains and zoo, the Open Air Museum in Grossgmain, Salzburg's fabulous Toy Museum with creative play areas, and the Natural History Museum. The latter is interactive, so even though the descriptions are in German, children can still get involved. Ice skating takes place all year round in the Volksgarten and during the Christmas season on Mozartplatz. Children are thrilled by the Krampus runs in the first week of December. Summer brings swimming (pools supervised by lifeguards), cycling and street theatre. Outside the city, try the Alpentherme water park in Bad Hofgastein and the forest high ropes park, Untersberg Challenges, in Grödig.

Summer fun

Calendar of Events

For the most up-to-date information and comprehensive listing of events, contact the tourist information office *(see page 132)*. Also, keep an eye on posters and billboards around the city.

January New Year's Eve festivities continue through the night, with fireworks, live music and waltzing on Residenzplatz. Ball season is in full swing. *Mozartwoche* (Mozart Week) at the end of January sees 10 days of performances of Mozart's music to mark the composer's birthday on 27 January.

February Carnival season ends with *Faschingsdienstag* (Shrove Tuesday) when fancy dress and partying take over the city.

March–April The *Osterfestspiele* (Easter Festival) is celebrated with opera productions and orchestral performances over 10 days.

May The alternating *Biennale Salzburg* and *Aspekte Festival* are international forums of contemporary classical music. Baroque music is performed during the four-day *Salzburger Pfingstfestspiele* (Whitsun Festival).

June Midsummer festivals take place on the longest day of the year; beacons are lit on the highest peaks throughout Austria.

June–July The *SommerSzene* festival celebrates modern dance, with dancers and choreographers from all over the world.

July–August *Salzburger Festspiele* (Salzburg Festival) begins during the last week in July and continues until the end of August, commemorating the music of Mozart and other great composers. Attracts large crowds. Street theatre and markets.

September Harvest festivals take place throughout Salzburg province, with church services, craft and farmers' markets.

October–November Salzburg Culture Days *(Kulturtage)* is a four-week festival of opera and classical music, second only to the *Salzburger Festspiele*. The last few days of October see the beginning of two-week *Salzburger Jazz Herbst* (Salzburg Jazz Festival).

November The Christmas markets begin at the end of November.

December Christmas concerts take place throughout the illuminated city with its markets, mulled wine, carol singers and ice skating.

EATING OUT

Salzburg has a strong tradition of dining out. The oldest eatery in the city bears witness to this: the St Peter Stiftskeller was established as a tavern by the monks of St Peter's in 803. You will often see whole families gathered around a restaurant table, or large groups of friends out celebrating a special occasion. Meals are not hurried and it is not unusual for people to spend a whole evening in a restaurant relishing a hefty three-course meal, with beer and wine flowing freely.

Summer is the time for eating outdoors. Many restaurants have gardens or, at the very least, tables on the pavement. Remember, however, that Salzburg is near the Alps and that even in summer you might want a jumper or jacket.

Stopping for a lunch of bread, cheese and meat

WHAT TO EAT

Austrian cuisine is still more seasonal than in many other countries, especially regarding fruit, vegetables and herbs. Markets with fresh produce from the area play an essential part in the culture of home and especially restaurant cooking. Although the choice of fresh and packed products has widened immensely, you might not find the extreme array of convenience foods found in some supermarkets in the Anglo-Saxon world.

Salzburg has collected influences from all over Europe, especially the Austro-Hungarian Empire and, more recently, has been inspired by international cuisine. The Turks brought coffee and the coffee culture to Austria during the siege of Vienna in the 17th century; *Gulasch* and salamis come from the Hungarian part of the Austro-Hungarian Empire and some people even claim that the Schnitzel originated in Italy.

Meat

Traditionally, Austrian food has evolved around meat. Pork is the most popular item on the menu, closely followed by beef. Two of the classic meat dishes are *Schweinsbraten* (roast pork) and *Zwiebelrostbraten* (roast beef with gravy and onions). If you are a hungry carnivore and find it difficult to make up your mind, a *Grillteller* (mixed grill) is a good choice for sharing.

Vegetables

Vegetables are beginning to play a more important role as main dishes. As side dishes you will enjoy a lot of seasonal

Wienerschnitzel is veal or pork escalope fried in breadcrumbs

varieties. If you are here in the summer or autumn, the wild mushrooms (*Pilze*) are wonderful. In winter, pumpkins and root vegetables come into their own; *Schwarzwurzel* (black salsify) and *Kohlrabi* (a member of the cabbage family) are among the most popular. Finding good vegetarian food in Austria used to be a hopeless cause, but now nearly all restaurants offer a vegetarian alternative. There are also several vegetarian eateries *(see pages 107, 110, 112)*. Organically grown produce is very popular here and you will find several restaurants and shops offering *Bio* produce.

Seasonal Specialities

No matter what time of year you visit Salzburg, there is always some seasonal speciality on offer. In spring and early summer it's asparagus; in late summer it's *Eierschwammerl* (chanterelle mushrooms); in autumn it's game; in November it's goose; and at Christmas it is mulled wine and roast chestnuts. Austrians do not have a typical Christmas meal. Here it is traditional to eat fish on Christmas Eve, but steak or any other special treat are also options. Gingerbread and Christmas biscuits (*Kekse*) are the sweet specialities. On New Year's Eve, a fondue with either cheese or meat is a typical dish as it makes for a genial atmosphere around the table.

Bread and Cheese

If you are looking for a snack or a light lunch, the wonderful dark Austrian breads are perfect to enjoy with a plate of Austrian cheeses or *Speck* (a dry-smoked bacon). There are many different types of cheese, ranging from strong-flavoured hard mountain cheeses, to more gently flavoured soft cheese dips and spreads.

Desserts

During the hardships of World War II, people had to make do with the ingredients available to them. This has led to a love of desserts made from eggs, flour and milk. Many of the sweet dumplings, cakes and pancake-type dishes stem from these times. Although made from the simplest of ingredients, they can all be extremely delicious.

Coffee and Cakes

The city is awash with cafés of all styles, and anybody spending a few days here will see that they play an important role in the social life of Salzburg's citizens. Nobody is in a hurry. The coffee-house culture means that you can sit over one cup of coffee, reading the café's newspapers and magazines, for as long as you want. This is just as well, as the first glance at the menu

Marillenknödel are apricot dumplings

will reveal that coffee is not simply coffee. There are many types to choose from. All coffee served is made with espresso machines (the only time you might be served filter coffee is with breakfast in your hotel). The following list should help when choosing.

Verlängerter: A 'normal' cup of coffee made with one portion of espresso to two portions of water.

Espresso: One portion of espresso mixed with one of water.

Cappuccino: One part espresso to one of warm milk and one of whisked milk.

Latte macchiato: A double espresso in a large cup or glass topped with steamed milk and froth.

Melange: One portion of coffee, two measures of water and hot milk.

Einspänner: One portion of black coffee served in a tall glass with whipped cream (*Schlagobers*) and icing sugar on top.

Apfelstrudel

Fiaker: A single espresso served in a glass with a dash of rum.

You will also notice that you will be served a small glass of tap water with your coffee. This is a tradition that was brought in by the Turks. Their coffee was (and still is) famously 'sludgy', so it was normal to serve a glass of water with which to wash down the grounds. Nowadays this is no longer necessary, but the tradition has remained.

Of course, coffee is not the sole focus of these places – an amazing array of cakes and buns is on offer. Choosing a cake can be quite daunting when faced with so many different, delicious-looking cream cakes, fruit flans, biscuits and other sweet delights. The most famous are *Sachertorte* (a chocolate cake) and *Apfelstrudel* (apples and raisins wrapped in thin layers of pastry). But there are many others to tempt you. The *Cremeschnitte* is a cream slice; *Topfen* is cream curd used in many cakes that are often topped with seasonal fruits or berries; *Linzertorte* is a tart with jam and nuts. *Mandeln* (almonds) are also used in many biscuits and cakes; a particularly good one is *Bienenstich* (literally 'bee sting'), a cake base filled with whipped cream and almonds with honey on top. A wonderfully gooey biscuit is the *Florentiner* (nuts and candied fruit covered in chocolate).

WHAT TO DRINK

Salzburg is split between the beer and the wine lovers, and both are well catered for.

Beer

With three locally brewed beers on offer – Stiegl, Kaiser and Augustiner – all with long histories, you will almost certainly find a beer to your taste. You should try the *Weissbier* at least once. This is a cloudy beer as the yeast has not been entirely brewed out (though you can also get a clear variety). It comes in a light and dark form, with the dark version being somewhat sweet. *Zwickelbier* is another slightly cloudy beer, an unfiltered lager. *Bockbier* is available at certain times of year, usually Christmas and Easter, and is a stronger special brew which should be handled with care – perhaps start with just a *Pfiff* (0.2 litres) to test the effect. The beer-garden culture is alive in the summer, and sitting in one of the leafy gardens, enjoying a beer or two, is a wonderful way to spend an evening.

Salzburg's taverns or *Gasthäuser* are an excellent combination of beer-hall and restaurant. You will often find some of the best Austrian food served in these establishments at very reasonable prices. For the most part they are traditional old taverns that have retained their wooden interiors and are cool in summer and cosy in winter.

Wine

If you have never tried Austrian wines, then the wine bars and restaurants in Salzburg are a good place to start. Although this is not a wine-growing region, wines from Styria, Burgenland and Lower Austria are all worth trying. After the Austrian wine scandal in the 1980s, sales of

Austrian Fast Food

It is hard to miss the usual fast-food outlets in Austria, but the international brand names are popular mainly with youngsters and tourists. True Austrian fast food comes in the form of the *Würstlstand* (sausage stand). These are scattered all over the city and you can usually find at least one open at any time of night or day. Sausages are available in all shapes and sizes, including *Weisswurst* from Munich, *Frankfurters* (hot dogs), *Bosna* (served with mustard, ketchup and onions in a roll) and *Käsekrainer* (contains pieces of cheese).

Austrian wine plummeted. Many winegrowers had to lift their game, and now produce extremely high-quality wines in order to prove that most of the Austrian vineyards should be taken seriously. Both the red and white wines are very palatable and the most common are: *Grüner Veltliner*, a light, dry, crisp white wine; *Welschriesling*, a fresh, fruity white wine; *Zweigelt*, a full-bodied dry red; and *Blauer Burgunder* (Pinot Noir), a fruity, soft red. If you do not know what to choose, your barman or waiter will be happy to recommend a good bottle.

Steins of beer at the Augustiner Brewery

When in Austria in the late summer and early autumn, you should try *Sturm*. This is grape juice which is still fermenting and has about 4 percent alcohol and is very refreshing. The white variety tends to be drier than the red one.

Another Austrian speciality is *Schnaps*. This is a strong, clear spirit produced using a variety of different fruits. The most commonly available types are *Obstler*, made from apples and pears, *Marillenschnaps*, made from apricots, and *Vogelbeer*, made from rowan berries. Try one after dinner as a digestif. They are also commonly used as cure-alls in Austrian households.

TO HELP YOU ORDER...

Do you have a table for two/four?	**Haben Sie einen Tisch für zwei/vier Personen, bitte?**
Could we have the menu?	**Die Speisekarte, bitte?**
I/we would like...	**Ich hätte/Wir hätten gern ...**
Could we have the bill, please?	**Bezahlen, bitte.**

MENU READER

Auflauf	soufflé or a dish baked with cheese on top
Backhendl	chicken sautéed in egg and breadcrumbs
Bauernschmaus	meat with dumplings and sauerkraut
Blaukraut	red cabbage
Blunzn	black pudding
Bosna	spicy sausages in a roll with onions, curry powder, mustard and ketchup

Soak up the coffee-house culture when in Salzburg

Brot	bread
Buchteln/Wuchteln	yeast buns filled with jam
Debreziner	spicy Hungarian sausage
Eierschwammerl	chanterelle mushrooms
Fleischlaberl	meat rissoles
Frittatensuppe	clear soup with sliced pancakes
Gefüllte Paprika	stuffed peppers
Germknödel	big, fluffy yeast dumplings with poppy seeds (and custard)
Griessnockerlsuppe	semolina dumpling soup
Gugelhupf	Viennese sponge cake
Kaiserschmarrn	pancake served with raisins and apple sauce
Kartoffelsalat	potato salad
Kasspatzln	pasta with cheese and fried onions
Knödel	flour, potato or yeast dumpling
Krautsalat	shredded white cabbage salad with caraway seeds
Marillenknödel	apricot dumpling
Palatschinken	pancakes with various fillings
Ribisel	red or blackcurrants
Rostbraten	pot roast
Salzburger Nockerl	dessert with sponge cake, fruit and soft meringue
Schinkenfleckerl	baked noodles with ham
Schwammerlsuppe	mushroom soup
Schweinsbraten	roast pork
Semmel	bread roll
Senf	mustard
Tafelspitz	boiled beef
Topfenknödel	dumpling made with curd
Wienerschnitzel	veal or pork escalope fried in breadcrumbs
Zigeunerschnitzel	pork escalope in paprika sauce
Zwiebelrostbraten	beef steak with fried onions

PLACES TO EAT

We have used the following symbols to give an idea of the price for a three-course evening meal for one, excluding drinks and tips:

€€€ over 40 euros
€€ 18–40 euros
€ below 18 euros

OLD TOWN

RESTAURANTS

Da Pippo €€ *Alter Markt 2, tel: 843 861.* Superb Italian food with a buffet of cold starters and occasional live piano music while you eat. Located on the first floor overlooking Alter Markt; in the summer they have tables down in the square. Daily 11.30am–11pm.

Dubliner Irish Pub € *Kaigasse 8, tel: 0650 6110 967.* For anybody missing pub food, there is a wide choice of the usual fare from baked potatoes to fish and chips. Wash it all down with a pint of Guinness and, if the weather is good, there is outdoor seating too. Mon–Fri 4pm–1am, Sat–Sun from 3pm.

Goldener Hirsch €€€ *Getreidegasse 37, tel: 808 4889.* This famous restaurant in the very elegant hotel of the same name specialises in fine Austrian cuisine. Antique artwork and traditional decor create a relaxing atmosphere in the vaulted hall, where a farrier once used to work. Over the years it has won numerous accolades for its food and is the place to go for a special occasion. Daily noon–2pm, 6.30pm–9.30pm.

Humboldt Stubn €–€€ *Gstättengasse 4–6, tel: 843 171.* A traditional restaurant and bar with an international menu and many Austrian specialities. Humboldt offers some vegetarian alternatives and excellent lunch deals. In summer there is a large, shady terrace. Daily noon–1am.

Il Sole €€ *Gstättengasse 15, tel: 843 284.* Situated next to the entrance to the Mönchsberg lift, this Italian restaurant has friendly, efficient service and good pasta and pizzas (with vegetarian options) at very reasonable prices. Look out for the daily specials. Daily 11.30am–2.30pm, 5.30pm–midnight, closed Tue in spring and autumn.

Maredo €€ *Judengasse 5–7, tel: 843 894.* Fast and friendly service in this brightly lit steak restaurant, which is a perfect place to taste beef, pork or lamb Argentinian-style. The Maredo takes pride in the opulent salad buffet, which is a good choice for vegetarians, though not the only one. Daily 11.30am–11.30pm.

My Indigo € *(a number of outlets throughout the city, e.g. at Rudolfskai, near Staatsbrücke; opening times vary).* These small fast-food establishments are excellent if you want a quick snack during the day while sightseeing. They offer Thai and vegetarian cuisine and delicious sweets. Some locations have indoor seating.

Nagano €€ *Griesgasse 19, tel: 849 488.* Sushi restaurant in a small passage between Franz-Josef-Kai and Griesgasse. Wide choice, including meat dishes, all served in wooden boxes. Lunch deals. Daily 11.30am–3pm, 5–11pm.

Paul Stube €€ *Herrengasse 16, tel: 843 220.* Situated in one of the cobbled alleys below the fortress, this is an old, traditional restaurant serving Austrian food. It fills up quickly, so it might be wise to reserve a table in advance. Pretty garden in the summer, too. Mon–Sat 5pm–1am.

Triangel €€ *Wiener-Philharmoniker-Gasse 7, tel: 842 229.* A cosy, tavern-style restaurant close to the Festival Halls, popular with locals and visiting artists alike. Photographs of famous singers and conductors create an international ambience. Spacious outdoor seating in summer (200 places). Mon–Sat 11am–midnight.

Zipfer Bierhaus €€ *Universitätsplatz 19/Siegmund-Hafner-Gasse 12, tel: 840 745.* In a 14th-century building where Nannerl (Mozart's sister) lived for almost 30 years, this traditional tavern serves Austrian

food and beer in beer-hall style with a long line of hand pumps
for the beers. The decor of antlers is quaintly traditional. Not many
houses had their own well in the basement (still accessible) secur-
ing the water supply. Mon–Sat 10am–midnight; kitchen until 10pm.

Zirkelwirt €€ *Pfeifergasse 14, tel: 843 472.* An Austrian tavern
with an international twist in the corner of Papagenoplatz. Fabulous meals at affordable prices. Also a pleasant place just for a
coffee or beer. Mon–Thur 4pm–1am, Fri–Sun 5pm–1am.

Zum Fleischlaberl € *Kapitelgasse 11, tel: 842 138.* This small restaurant caters mainly for locals on their lunch breaks; breakfast is
also served. Homecooked food and the best cup of tea in town.
Mon–Fri 8am–5pm.

Zum Mohren €€ *Judengasse 9/Rudolfskai 20, tel: 840 680.* A
unique restaurant in Salzburg serving three wildly different cui-
sines: Austrian, Italian and Indian. Located near the river, with
the 13th-century town wall part of the building, it offers good
lunchtime deals and friendly service. Daily 11am–midnight.

Zum Wilden Mann €€ *Getreidegasse 20 (passage to Griesgasse), tel:
841 787.* Long wooden tables to share with the locals. The menu
is Austrian and the portions are huge in this Gasthaus dating back
to 1884. The Schnitzel are great fare to be enjoyed with local beer
and Austrian wines. Mon–Sat 10am–11pm.

CAFÉS

Afro Café *Bürgerspitalplatz 5, tel: 844 888.* In a very central location at the end of Griesgasse, Afro Café serves African specialities
from aromatic coffees and teas to mouth-watering snacks, breakfasts, salads, soups and tapas in a colourful, fresh interior inspired
by the African continent. Interesting wines from South Africa as
well as Austria. Mon–Sat 9am–midnight, Sun only during Salzburg Festival weeks.

Demel *Mozartplatz 2, tel: 840 358.* The famous Viennese Café
Demel took over this establishment, previously known as the

Café Glockenspiel. Located on the edge of one of the busiest squares in the city, the cosy café-cum-lounge makes a great place to sit and listen to the bells chiming in the Glockenspiel opposite. But be prepared to pay over the odds for your coffee here.

Fürst *Alter Markt/Brodgasse 13, tel: 843 759.* The place where the famous *Mozartkugel* was invented. A busy little café with great cakes, coffees and ice creams and a huge selection of newspapers and magazines to choose from while you relax between sightseeing expeditions. Daily May–Sept 8am–9pm, Oct–Apr 8am–8pm.

Niemetz *Herbert-von-Karajan-Platz 11, tel: 843 367.* With an enviable location next to the Festival Halls, this café is a favourite with concert-goers and is full of festival memorabilia. You can sit over coffee, cake and a newspaper for as long as you like. Mon–Sat 10am–6pm.

Tomaselli *Alter Markt 9, tel: 844 488-0.* Dating from the early 18th century, Tomaselli is the oldest café in Salzburg. It is worth a visit to see the traditionally dressed waitresses wheeling trolleys full of cakes, but it is not the cheapest or friendliest café in town. Daily 7am–9pm, during Salzburg Festival weeks until 10pm.

NEW TOWN

RESTAURANTS

Andreas Hofer € *Steingasse 65, tel: 872 769.* Located in one of the oldest lanes of town, through which farmers and salt merchants used to approach Salzburg with horse and cart. This old pub has the rustic ambience of times gone by. *Speck* (dry-smoked ham), *Knödel* (dumplings) and cheese are menu classics at 'Andi Hofer' – and provide a good basis for an evening of wine tasting. Mon–Sat and holidays 6pm–1am.

Bangkok €€ *Bayerhamerstrasse 33, tel: 873 688.* Excellent Thai food in a quiet little restaurant with attentive, friendly service and reasonable prices. Tue–Sun 11.30am–2.30pm and 5.30–11.30pm.

Die Weisse/Sudwerk €€ *Rupertgasse 10, tel: 872 246.* This restaurant incorporates a small brewery that makes its own Weissbier and serves excellent Austrian cuisine. Different rooms cater for different tastes and styles. The musical events are highly popular. Mon–Sat 10.30am–3am.

Köchelverzeichnis € *Steingasse 27, tel: 0664 5167 501.* Where medieval blacksmiths used to shoe horses next to the town gate, Andrea Hick established a welcoming wine bar with a small menu and a long list of fine Austrian wines, some from the family vineyard.

Shakespeare €€ *Hubert-Sattler-Gasse 3, tel: 879 106.* Easy-going, relaxed café and restaurant near Mirabell Palace serving Austrian and international food. Popular with students and the arty crowd. Daily 9am–2am.

Spicy-Spices € *Wolf-Dietrich-Strasse 1, tel: 870 712.* This little restaurant serves vegetarian food and also offers a take-away service. A pleasant casual place for lunch, if you are in the New Town and do not want to spend too long over your meal. Daily 11.30am–9.30pm.

Taj Mahal €€ *Bayerhamerstrasse 13 (corner of Lasserstrasse), tel: 882 010.* A popular Indian restaurant serving good curries in a relaxed atmosphere. British travellers should not expect the food to be as spicy as in some UK Indian restaurants, as Austrians prefer their curries to be on the mild side. Tue–Sun 11.30am–2pm, 5.30–11pm (closed for lunch Sat).

Zum fidelen Affen €–€€ *Priesterhausgasse 8, tel: 877 361.* Dark panelling, wooden tables and floors give this *Gastwirtschaft* a warm, welcoming atmosphere. Good food, friendly service and popular with locals. Mon–Sat 5pm–1am, warm meals until 10.30pm.

CAFÉS – BARS

Bellini's *Mirabellplatz 4, tel: 871 385.* An Italian café close to the Mirabell Gardens. Serves Italian coffee and snacks. Outdoor seating. Mon–Sat 8am–1am, Sun 10am–1am.

Café Bazar *Schwarzstrasse 3, tel: 874 278.* Slightly expensive, but with a lovely terrace overlooking the river. The art deco interior has been elegantly renovated. Sit and watch the world go by as all the famous literary figures in Salzburg did. Mon–Sat 7.30am–11pm, Sun 9am–6pm.

Café Classic *Makartplatz 8, tel: 882 700.* Located in Mozart's townhouse, this café is along the lines of a Viennese coffee house. Wonderful breakfasts, cakes and frothy coffee. Daily 8am–7.30pm.

Café Confiserie Sacher *Schwarzstrasse 5–7, tel: 8897 7254.* A sister of the famous Café Sacher in Vienna and 'inventor' of the chocolate cake of the same name. Treat yourself to a wonderful moist slice of this cake, or order a meal. In summer, there is a terrace on the river. Daily 7.30am–midnight.

Daimler's Bar & Late-Night Grill *Giselakai 17, tel: 873 967.* A lively popular bar overlooking the river. Serves delicious burgers, salads, sandwiches, fingerfood and steaks into the small hours. Tue–Wed 7.30pm–2am, Thur until 3am, Fri–Sat until 4am.

Fingerlos *Franz-Josef-Strasse 9, tel: 874 213.* Best ever coffee and cakes, all made on the premises. This is a popular place for breakfast too, if not the cheapest. The decor is modern and bright and in summer there are tables on the pavement. Tue–Sun 7.30am–7.30pm.

Steinterrasse *Giselakai 3–5, tel: 874 346-0.* Part of a trendy hotel, this is one of the most popular places in Salzburg and a great location for people-watching. The terrace affords a panoramic view of the city and in the evenings you can get what are considered to be the best cocktails in town. May–Sept Sun–Thur 3pm–midnight, Fri–Sat until 1am, Oct–Apr from 5pm.

BORDERS AND SUBURBS

RESTAURANTS

Augustiner Bräu Kloster Mülln € *Lindhofstrasse 7/Augustinergasse 4, tel: 431 246.* Genuine beer-hall atmosphere in a brewery founded by Augustinian monks on the northern slope of the Mönchsberg. Wonderful beer, beautiful garden and plenty of snacks to choose from. You can even bring your own picnic. Mon–Fri 3–11pm, Sat–Sun and holidays 2.30–11pm.

Bärenwirt €€ *Müllner Hauptstrasse 8, tel: 422 404.* A traditional restaurant serving Austrian cuisine, vegetarian and wholegrain food. There has been a restaurant on this site for over 350 years. Daily 11am–11pm, warm meals 11am–2pm, 6–9.30pm.

Esszimmer €€€ *Müllner Hauptstrasse 33, tel: 870 899.* Fine dining in a lovely location. This Michelin-rated restaurant has an excellent reputation (and correspondingly high prices). Its relaxed atmosphere makes it a popular place. Vegetarians are well catered for. There is a quiet garden in summer. Tue–Sat noon–2pm, 6.30pm–midnight (food served until 9.30pm and open Mon during Salzburg Festival weeks).

Hotel Friesacher €€ *Hellbrunner Strasse 17, Anif, tel: 06246 8977.* Friesacher has an excellent reputation as one of the best traditional restaurants serving Austrian food, wine and beer. Although slightly out of town in Anif, the hotel restaurant is worth making the journey here, particularly if you are visiting Hellbrunn.

Ikarus €€€ *Hangar-7, Wilhelm-Spazier-Strasse 7a, tel: 219 777.* This is a restaurant with a difference. Enjoy a first-class meal with a view of the collection of vintage aircraft and racing cars in Hangar-7, owned by Red Bull boss Dietrich Mateschitz. Top guest chefs from around the world spend a month at a time cooking up delights. Reservations essential. Daily noon–2pm, 7–10pm.

Krimpelstätter Augustiner Braugasthof €€ *Müllner Hauptstrasse 31, tel: 432 274.* Close to the Müllner church is this traditional tavern with a beer garden serving authentic Austrian dishes. *Schottnsuppe* (a cream soup with curd) and spinach dumplings are vegetarian delights. Very popular with the festival crowd. Tue–Sat 11am–midnight, Sun 11am–3pm.

Lemonchilli €€ *Nonntaler Hauptstrasse 24, tel: 842 558.* A Tex-Mex restaurant whose kitchen turns out spicy food, whilst the bar creates great cocktails – all amid a lively atmosphere. Popular with students. Garden in the summer. Reservations recommended. Mon–Fri 11am–1am, Sat–Sun and holidays from 4pm.

Magazin €€€ *Augustinergasse 13, tel: 841 584-0.* Mönchsberg is the dramatic backdrop to this 21st-century restaurant – its design as creative as the cuisine, though with a pleasant classic touch. Under the same roof you will find a shop with select kitchen utensils and wines. Mon–Sat noon–midnight.

Poseidon €€ *Neutorstrasse 34, tel: 842 918.* Probably Salzburg's best Greek restaurant. It is very popular and reservations are recommended. All your favourite Greek dishes served in warm and welcoming surroundings. There is a lovely garden in the summer. Daily 11.30am–3pm, 5.30pm–1am.

Riedenburg €€€ *Neutorstrasse 31, tel: 843 923.* This is considered by some to be the best restaurant in Salzburg. Chef de cuisine Martin Pichler serves wonderful food, beautifully presented, for which he has won international awards. Try the three-course lunch menu for less than €20. The wine list is also exquisite. Reservations recommended. Tue–Sat noon–2pm, 6pm–midnight, daily during Salzburg Festival weeks.

Wastlwirt €€ *Rochusgasse 15, Maxglan, tel: 820 100.* Located in a quiet corner, not far from the city centre, this traditional tavern is wonderfully cosy with lots of wood and a leafy, shady garden. Wed–Sun 11am–11pm.

CAFÉS

Café am Kai *Müllner Hauptstrasse 4, tel: 420 565.* With a terrace overlooking the river, this lovely pink café is a good place to take a break when walking along the river. Wed–Mon 9am–8pm.

Carpe Diem Lounge *Hangar-7, Wilhelm-Spazier-Strasse 7a, tel: 219 70.* An elegantly furnished café housed under the glass dome of Hangar-7. Enjoy your coffee while watching the goings-on in the museum through the glass wall. Daily 9am–6pm.

A–Z TRAVEL TIPS

A Summary of Practical Information

A

ACCOMMODATION (see also Camping, Youth Hostels and Recommended Hotels on page 136)

Salzburg has a wide selection of accommodation including the usual chain hotels such as Radisson, Sheraton, Mercure and Dorint, but also offers privately run hotels that tend to be friendlier and more characterful.

For most of the year it is not necessary to book accommodation in advance, but during peak times (July, August, December and Easter) advance reservations are essential. The Salzburg Tourist Office website, www.salzburg.info, offers an online booking service, in English as well as German. They also publish a booklet of accommodation every year, though this is not a complete listing of all the hotels and guesthouses in the city.

If you have not booked somewhere to stay before you arrive, the tourist information offices at the railway station and on Mozartplatz can assist with finding accommodation.

Pensionen are the equivalent of guesthouses or bed and breakfasts, and are less expensive than hotels.

a guesthouse	**eine Pension**
a single/double room	**ein Einzelzimmer/ Doppelzimmer**
with/without bath (shower)	**mit/ohne Bad (Dusche)**
What's the rate per night?	**Was kostet eine Übernachtung?**

AIRPORT (*Flughafen*)

Salzburg's airport, W. A. Mozart, www.salzburg-airport.com, is located on the western edge of the city. The airport is small, but offers all the usual facilities: restaurant, bar, banks, shops, cafés and a newsagent. There are regular buses (€2.10 for a single ticket) to the railway station (direct) and the city centre (change of bus). The journey to the station takes approximately 30 minutes. There is also a taxi rank directly outside the arrivals terminal. All car-hire offices are across the road in the multi-storey car park.

Arrivals are through Terminal I, but in winter the ski charter flights depart from Terminal II.

B

BICYCLE HIRE *(Fahrradverleih)*

Salzburg is considered Austria's most bike-friendly community. It has a superb network of cycle paths around the city and along the riverbanks. A number of hotels offer free bike loan. If yours does not, there are plenty of bike-hire shops (about €6 for 2 hours, €10 for 4 hours, €15 for a day). **Top Bike Salzburg** (tel: 0676-476 7259 and 062-724 656, www.topbike.at) has two offices – at Franz-Josef-Kai close to the Staatsbrücke and at the train station – and offers 20 percent discount with the Salzburg Card *(see page 11)*.

The Mozartradweg (Mozart Bike Trail) runs from the city through the Salzburg Lake District (Salzkammergut) on to Bavaria and its lakes, before ending at Berchtesgaden, near Hitler's former holiday retreat *(see page 70)*. The route stretches more than 410km (250 miles) and is primarily flat, with just a few hills along the way. It's ideal for families. Salzburg tourist offices will provide trail maps *(see page 132)*.

BUDGETING FOR YOUR TRIP

The currency in Austria is the euro. To give you a rough guide of how much things cost, the following is a list of average prices:
Drinks: Non-alcoholic drinks in bars and restaurants around €2.50–3.50, 0.5l beer €3, 0.125l wine €4 upwards.

Entertainment: cinema ticket around €8, entrance into a night-club or disco from around €5.

Hotels: a double room with breakfast will cost €160 and upwards per night in a five-star hotel, between €65 and €80 in a two-star.

Meals: a three-course evening meal in a mid-range restaurant will cost between €25 and €30 per head including a drink.

Museums: admission fees vary greatly; there are reductions for children and students. A Salzburg Card (*see page 11*) provides free admission to many museums.

Public transport: single tickets/day passes cost €2.10/5.00 if you buy them on the bus, €1.90/4.20 at the machines, €1.60/3.20 if you buy a block of 5 in advance. All fares included in the Salzburg Card.

Sightseeing: a *Fiaker* (horse-drawn carriage) trip for up to four people costs €40 for 20 minutes and €80 for a 50-minute tour. A boat trip on the *Amadeus Salzburg* costs €13–16 for adults and €7–10 for children. If you join a Salzburg city guide for a guided group tour, it costs around €10 per person.

Tickets: concerts €10–60; Salzburger Landestheater €6–32 for a play and €16–50 for an opera; Marionette Theatre €20–35 for adults, €14 for children. Salzburg Festival (www.salzburgerfestspiele.at): tickets vary greatly in price according to the performance.

C

CAMPING

There are three campsites in the vicinity of Salzburg: Nord Sam (tel: 660 494, www.camping-nord-sam.com) open mid-Apr–early Dec, Christmas–early Jan; Camping Panorama Stadtblick (tel: 450 652, www.panorama-camping.at, open end Mar–early Nov, early Dec and Christmas) and Camping Schloss Aigen (tel: 622 079, www.camping aigen.com, open May–Sept).

CAR HIRE (Autovermietung; see also Driving)

To explore Salzburg it is not necessary to have a car. It is easy to lose your bearings in the maze of one-way streets, and parking is expensive and very limited. However, should you need car hire for trips out of town, most of the major car hire companies have offices at the airport and will deliver cars to your hotel. Costs are around €70 for an economy class car for one day, €120 for a weekend.

For hiring a car, you need a driving licence, passport and one of the major credit cards. It is recommended to book third-party insurance, fully comprehensive insurance an option.

Arac-Europcar tel: 871 616, www.arac.at
Avis tel: 877 278, www.avis.at
Buchbinder tel: 8820 660, www. buchbinder-rent-a-car.at
Hertz tel: 876 674, www.hertz. at
Sixt tel: 0810-977 424, www.sixt.at

I'd like to rent a car	**Ich möchte bitte ein Auto mieten**
tomorrow	**für morgen**
for one day/week	**für einen Tag/für eine Woche**
Please include full insurance.	**Mit Vollkaskoversicherung, bitte.**

CLIMATE

Salzburg has a well-deserved reputation for being a rainy city and the watery weather even has a nickname: *Schnürlregen* (string-rain). It can rain for three seasons of the year, and in winter it snows instead. Salzburg can be quite cold in winter and stiflingly hot in summer. The best times of year for visiting the city in pleasant temperatures are spring and autumn. In spring the alpine flowers are in full bloom, and in autumn the colours of the forest are aglow. At these times the streets are not filled to bursting point with tourists. If you are looking for some romantic winter atmosphere, then December, when the Christmas Markets are in full swing, is also a good time, but much busier.

Below is a chart showing Salzburg's average temperatures and rainfall for the year:

	J	F	M	A	M	J	J	A	S	O	N	D
°C	1	4	11	16	20	24	25	24	21	15	8	2
°F	34	39	52	61	68	75	77	75	70	59	46	36
mm	54	49	41	52	73	110	134	108	81	67	53	46

CLOTHING

Whatever the time of year, it is always best to bring layers and something waterproof. It may be freezing cold outside in winter, but the buildings are all very well heated and insulated inside. There can be cold snaps in summer, so light jumpers or jackets will be useful.

Austrians dress casually for most occasions, but they do like to be smart when going to the theatre, opera, ballet or a ball. Evening dress is often worn to festival performances.

CRIME AND SAFETY

Salzburg is a very safe city. You do need to watch out for pickpockets in busy places (such as markets) and make sure you lock up your bicycle if you park it anywhere. Do not leave valuables in your car, and ensure that it is locked. In the event of theft or crime call 112 to get the nearest police station (*Polizeiwache*).

D

DISABLED TRAVELLERS

Salzburg Information has good website information (www.salzburg. info/en/service/salzburgfor/barrierfreevacation) and has published the free guide *Exploring Salzburg without Barriers*, listing sights, hotels and places of interest with their level of wheelchair access. It includes a map and plenty of useful information for wheelchair users. Most of the buses in the city are accessible with a wheelchair, although some of the older ones are not.

DRIVING (See also Car Hire)

If you are taking your car to Austria, you must have a valid driving licence, car registration papers, a national identity sticker for your car, a red warning triangle and a reflective high-visibility waistcoat in case of breakdown, and a first-aid kit. From 1 November to 15 April only cars with winter tyres are allowed to drive on roads with snow and ice (snow chains are recommended for the mountains).

For Austrian motorways you will require a toll sticker (*Vignette*) valid between 10 days and a year. They are sold at petrol stations, post offices and tobacconists.

Road conditions. The roads in Austria are very good on the whole. The north–south routes can get very busy at weekends in

driving licence	**Führerschein**
car registration papers	**Zulassungsschein**
Green Card	**Grüne Karte**
Where's the nearest car park, please?	**Wo ist der nächste Parkplatz, bitte?**
Can I park here?	**Darf ich hier parken?**
Are we on the right road for …?	**Sind wir auf der richtigen Strasse nach …?**
Check the oil/tyres/battery, please.	**Öl/Reifen/Batterie prüfen, bitte.**
I've had a breakdown.	**Ich habe eine Panne.**
There's been an accident.	**Es ist ein Unfall passiert.**

the summer, and in winter, when people are heading to and from the ski resorts. Information on road conditions and the traffic situation is available in English seven days a week 6am–8pm (tel: 0043-1 711 997).

Driving regulations. Austrians drive on the right. Here are some of the rules of the road that you might find useful:

• It is compulsory to wear seatbelts in front and rear seats.
• It is forbidden to use a hand-held mobile phone while driving.
• Children under the age of 12 are not permitted to sit in the front.
• It is forbidden to overtake on the right on the motorway.
• Headlights must be switched on at all times.
• The alcohol limit is 0.5 parts per thousand.

Speed limits. On motorways 130km/h (81mph) or 110km/h (68mph); on other roads 100km/h or 80km/h (50mph); in built-up areas 50km/h (31mph).

Parking can be difficult in Salzburg. It is not permitted to park in the bus lanes during the stated times. For the blue parking bays you will need to display a ticket (machines are located nearby).

Breakdowns. There is a 24-hour breakdown service for motorways and main roads. The two Austrian motoring clubs are ÖAMTC (tel: 120, www.oeamtc.at) and ARBÖ (tel: 123, www.arboe.at).

Fuel and oil. There are plenty of petrol stations around Salzburg. Not all are open 24 hours, but those on the motorway and at the major entrances to the city are. Petrol, diesel and LPG are available.

Road signs. Most road signs employed in Austria are international, but here are some written signs you might come across:

Anfang	(parking) start
Ausfahrt	exit
Aussicht	viewpoint

Bauarbeiten	road works
Einbahnstrasse	one way
Ende	(parking) end
Fahrbahnwechsel	change lanes
Fußgänger	pedestrians
Gefahr	danger
Geradeaus	straight on
Glatteis	icy roads
Halten verboten	no stopping
Licht einschalten	use headlights
Ortsende	town ends
Parken erlaubt	parking allowed
Rechts/links einbiegen	turn right/left
Rollsplitt	loose gravel
Sackgasse	no through road
Spital	hospital
Steinschlag	falling stones
Umleitung	detour
Vorfahrt	priority
Vorsicht	caution
Werktags von 7 bis 17 Uhr	weekdays 7am to 5pm
Zufahrt gestattet	entrance permitted

E

ELECTRICITY

Austrian plugs have two round pins, so an adapter is necessary if your device has a British or US plug. The voltage is 220 volts.

EMBASSIES AND CONSULATES *(Botschaft; Konsulat)*

Contact your consulate or embassy only for real emergencies, such as loss of a passport or all your money, a serious accident or trouble with the police. Citizens of most countries will have to contact their embassies in Vienna or a consulate in Munich. The consulate in Salzburg is:

UK: Alter Markt 4, 5020 Salzburg, tel: 848 133.

EMERGENCIES (See also Crime and Safety, and Police)

Normally, in the case of an emergency, your hotel receptionist will be happy to assist. If you do need to get hold of the emergency services yourself, the numbers are as follows:

Emergency (general): **112**

Police: **133**

Fire brigade: **122**

Ambulance, first aid: **144**

Emergency medical service: **141**

I need a doctor/ dentist/ambulance.	**Ich brauche einen Arzt/ Zahnarzt/Krankenwagen.**
Fire!	**Feuer!**
Help!	**Hilfe!**
hospital	**Spital**
police	**Polizei**

G

GAY AND LESBIAN TRAVELLERS

The gay and lesbian scene in Salzburg is not very evident, though there are good bars in the city that cater for gays and lesbians, including 2-Stein on Giselakai and Princess Bar in Priesterhaus-gasse. Mexxx is the latest party hot spot in Schallmoser Haupt-strasse 20. Outside Austrian cities such as Salzburg and Vienna, although it is unlikely people will be hostile, attitudes do tend to be more traditional.

GETTING THERE

By Air

Scheduled flights. There are regular flights year-round from several UK airports, and from Dublin, to Salzburg. Ryanair, www.ryanair.com, has daily flights to Salzburg from London Stansted, and Easyjet, www.easyjet.com, has weekly flights from London Gatwick during the ski season.

Charter flights. During the summer and winter seasons there are charter flights from a number of UK and Republic of Ireland airports. These are normally sold on a seat-only basis unless you are booking a package. Many UK tour operators offer Salzburg as a city break. Check with your travel agent for details.

Flying via Munich. The choice of scheduled flights to Munich is much greater than to Salzburg. Munich is about 1.5–2 hours away from Salzburg by train and 1.5 hours by car. If travelling by train, buy a Bayern Ticket from ticket machines at stations, which will give you all-day travel on regional trains within Bavaria and Salzburg province.

By Car

Salzburg is a long drive from the UK and you should allow two days' travelling time. Although the German motorways are pretty good, they can get very busy over the summer months. The quickest route is via Ostende, Cologne, Stuttgart and Munich.

Comfortable motor rails/car trains run between Hamburg and Vienna via Munich. Contact Austrian Federal Railways (ÖBB) for details (www.oebb.at) or Deutsche Bahn (www.bahn.de).

By Coach

Contact Eurolines (www.eurolines.co.uk) for coaches from the UK.

By Rail

There are regular train services from London St Pancras International to Salzburg via Paris and Munich. The journey takes about 16 hours. Sleepers and couchettes are available if booked in advance. Contact ÖBB (*see above*) for further information.

GUIDES AND TOURS *(Fremdenführer, Rundfahrten)*

There are two major bus tour companies in Salzburg that offer guided tours of the city in English both by coach and on foot, and also to places of interest nearby: Salzburg Sightseeing Tours (tel: 881 616, www.salzburg-sightseeingtours.at) and Panorama Tours (tel: 883 2110, www.panoramatours.com). Both have *The Sound of Music* tours, which visit all the film locations in and around the city.

The local tourist office at Mozartplatz also organises guided tours on foot with English-speaking guides.

Outside the Residenz you will find a row of horse-drawn carriages awaiting customers. These are known as *Fiakers* and will take you through the old town at a leisurely pace *(see page 41)*.

Boat trips on the Salzach aboard the *Amadeus Salzburg* are available between May and September. They leave at regular intervals from the Makartsteg (pedestrian bridge) in the Old Town and take you as far as Hellbrunn Castle and the zoo.

We'd like an English-speaking guide.	**Wir möchten einen englisch sprachigen Fremdenführer.**
I need an English interpreter.	**Ich brauche einen Dolmetscher für Englisch.**
How long will the ride take?	**Wie lange dauert die Fahrt?**
What does it cost?	**Was kostet es?**

H

HEALTH AND MEDICAL CARE *(Ärztliche Hilfe)*

The health service in Salzburg is excellent. There are numerous medical facilities, including the *Unfallkrankenhaus* (Accident Hospital) on Dr-Franz-Rehrl-Platz 5 (tel: 65 800) and the *Krank-*

enhaus und Konvent der Barmherzigen Brüder on Kajetanerplatz 1 (tel: 80 880). The *Unfallkrankenhaus* is renowned for treating injured skiers. Austria and the UK have a reciprocal agreement as far as hospital treatment is concerned. EU citizens should have the European Health Insurance Card (EHIC), available online at www.ehic.org.uk, which entitles them to reduced-cost, sometimes free, medical treatment. However, you should still take out travel insurance before departing as the EHIC does not cover every eventuality, such as needing repatriation.

If you are taking prescription drugs, bring enough with you to last the duration of your trip. The same drugs may not be available in Salzburg.

In order to buy any sort of medication, you will have to go to a chemist *(Apotheke)*. Should you require a chemist outside normal opening times, there is usually a duty roster posted on the door of all chemists, naming the nearest open chemist.

Where is there a chemist on duty, please?	**Wo ist die diensthabende Apotheke, bitte?**

L

LANGUAGE

German is spoken in Austria by 98 percent of Austrians, with Allemanic and Austro-Bavarian being the significant minority languages. However, as Salzburg relies heavily on tourism, many of the people here speak at least a little English. Even so, speaking a few words of German is always appreciated. A couple of phrases worth knowing are *Entschuldigen Sie bitte* (Excuse me, please) and *Sprechen Sie Englisch?* (Do you speak English?). The *Berlitz German Phrase Book & Dictionary* covers most situations you may come across in Austria.

LOST PROPERTY

The city lost property office is on the ground floor of the town hall in Mirabell Palace, open Mon–Thur 7.30am–4pm, Fri 7.30am–1pm, tel: 8072 3580 and 0900 600 200, fundamt@stadt-salzburg.at, www.fundamt.gv.at.

I've lost my passport/ wallet/handbag.	**Ich habe meinen Pass/ meine Brieftasche/ Handtasche verloren.**

M

MAPS

The tourist office and hotels have free street maps of Salzburg, which are detailed enough for walking around the centre. Bigger city maps are available from the tourist board and bookshops.

Maps of the bus routes can be picked up free in either the tourist information offices or from the railway station.

MEDIA

English-language newspapers are available at the airport, the railway station and some newsagents throughout the town. Most hotels also have a stock of the dailies. The English-language daily papers available in Salzburg are usually one day late. *Salzburger Nachrichten* (www.salzburg.com) is the leading regional daily. *Der Standard* (www.derstandard.at), *Die Presse* (www.diepresse.com) and *Kronen Zeitung* (www.krone.at) are the main national daily newspapers.

Most of the hotels in Salzburg have cable TV. If your hotel has satellite TV, you will probably have a greater choice of English-speaking channels. You can find English-language programmes on 104.6FM in Salzburg.

MONEY *(Geld)*

Currency. Austria's monetary unit is the euro. The euro is divided into 100 cents. Banknotes in denominations of 500, 100, 50, 20, 10 and 5 are in circulation. There are coins to the value of 1 and 2 euros, 50, 20, 5, 2 and 1 cents.

Changing money. You can exchange your money at any of the banks in the city. Hotels also offer money-exchange facilities, but their rates are not as good as those of the banks. All banks have ATM machines (cashpoints), most of them accept UK debit cards. Bureaux de change are also scattered throughout the city. These have the advantage of being open after the banks have closed. Travellers' cheques are widely accepted, but they do not give you as good an exchange rate as you would get in the banks.

I want to change some pounds/dollars.	**Ich möchte Pfund/Dollar wechseln.**
Do you accept travellers' cheques?	**Nehmen Sie Reiseschecks an?**
Do you have any change, please?	**Haben Sie Kleingeld, bitte?**
Where's the nearest cashpoint, please?	**Wo ist der nächste Geldautomat, bitte?**

Credit cards. The major credit and debit cards are widely accepted in Austria, but smaller shops, bars and restaurants still do not accept them.

O

OPENING TIMES

Shops. These can be divided into two categories when it comes to opening times. The first are the small shops in the shopping districts in town. These are mostly open from 9am until 6pm (some close for an hour or two at lunchtime) Mondays to Fridays and until 5pm on Saturdays. Supermarkets and shopping centres tend to be open from 9am until 7.30 or 8pm Mondays to Fridays and until 5pm on Saturdays. The only shops open on Sundays are those selling souvenirs.

Museums. These vary widely; for opening times check the individual entries in the Where to Go section.

Banks. Mon–Fri 8am–12.30pm and 2–4.30pm, Thur until 5.30pm.

Chemists. Mon–Fri 8am–noon and 2pm–6pm, Sat 8am–noon.

P

POLICE *(Polizei; see also Crime and Safety, and Emergencies)*

Police have blue uniforms with dark blue caps and carry guns. If you are fined for a traffic offence, you are likely to be asked to pay on the spot. Street parking in Salzburg is supervised by traffic wardens, who wear dark blue trousers and white shirts.

The main police station is at Landespolizeikommando Salzburg, Alpenstrasse 88–90, 5020, Salzburg; tel: 0662-6383; bpds.salzburg@polizei.gv.at.

In an emergency, contact the police on **112** or **133**.

Where is the nearest police station, please?	**Wo ist die nächste Polizeiwachstube, bitte?**

POST OFFICES *(Postamt)*

Salzburg's main post office is at Residenzplatz 9. Opening times are Mon–Fri 8am–noon and 2pm–5pm. The post office in the station is open Mon–Fri 7am–8.30pm, Sat 8am–2pm, Sun and holidays 1pm–6pm. If you just need stamps, you can also buy these from any tobacconist. Information on Austrian postal services can be found at: www.post.at. Salzburg's post boxes are yellow.

Express (special delivery)	**Express/Eilbote**
Airmail	**Luftpost**
Have you any mail for …?	**Haben Sie Post für…?**
A stamp for this letter/ postcard, please	**Eine Marke für diesen Brief/ diese Postkarte, bitte.**

PUBLIC HOLIDAYS *(Feiertag)*

On public holidays in Austria all offices and banks, most shops and some restaurants are closed. Note that on Good Friday, a holiday for Protestants only, shops etc remain open. On 24 December (Christmas Eve) all theatres and cinemas are closed, and most shops and restaurants close at midday.

1 January	*Neujahrstag*	New Year's Day
6 January	*Heilige Drei Könige*	Epiphany
1 May	*Tag der Arbeit*	Labour Day
15 August	*Maria Himmelfahrt*	Assumption
26 October	*Nationalfeiertag*	National Holiday
1 November	*Allerheiligen*	All Saints' Day
8 December	*Maria Empfängnis*	Immaculate Conception
25 December	*Weihnachten*	Christmas Day
26 December	*Stefanitag*	Boxing Day
Movable dates:	*Ostermontag*	Easter Monday
	Christi Himmelfahrt	Ascension Day
	Pfingstmontag	Whit Monday
	Fronleichnam	Corpus Christi

R

RELIGION

Most Austrians are Roman Catholics, but there are Protestant parishes everywhere and also Muslim communities. English-language Catholic services are held every 2nd and 4th Sunday of the month at the Sacellum on Herbert-von-Karajan-Platz at 5pm. Protestant services are held in the Christus Kirche, Schwarzstrasse 25, Saturday 6pm and Sunday 9.30am.

The synagogue is at Lasserstrasse 8.

T

TELEPHONES

Try to avoid using the phone in your hotel room: hotels can charge well over the odds. The net coverage for mobile phones is excellent, making roaming possible. If you are staying for a long time, it is cheaper to buy a local SIM card for your mobile.

The international dialling code for Austria is 43, the code for Salzburg 0662 (leave off the 0 if calling from abroad). To make an international call from Austria, dial 00 and then the country code (44 for the UK, 1 for the USA and Canada) and again omit the first zero from your area code.

TICKETS

There are a number of ticket agencies in the city and all charge booking fees. The most central and best known is Polzer Ticket Center, Residenzplatz 3 (tel: 8969, in Austria toll free 0800 846 500, www.polzer.at).

Salzburg Festival. Tickets for the Salzburg Festival go on sale in November and can be applied for online at www.salzburgerfestspiele.at until the first week in January. Remaining tickets go on sale from April onwards. Ticket office: Herbert-von-Karajan-Platz 11 (tel: 8045 500).

Mozart Festival. Tickets for the Mozart Festival in January can be booked with the Stiftung Mozarteum (tel: 889 400, www.mozarteum.at).

Other events. Tickets for the Marionette Theatre can be booked directly with the box office or online (tel: 872 406, www.marionetten.

at). The Mozart Dinner Concert can be booked with Salzburger Konzertgesellschaft at Getreidegasse 47 (tel: 828 695, www.salzburg-concerts.com), or at the box office before the start of a performance.

TIME ZONES

The time in Austria is Central European Time, which is one hour ahead of GMT. There is daylight saving time as in the UK with the clocks going forward one hour at the end of March and back one hour at the end of October. The time differences are as follows:

New York	London	**Salzburg**	Jo'burg	Sydney	Auckland
6am	11am	**noon**	noon	8pm	10pm

TIPPING

In bars, restaurants and cafés it is customary to tip around 10 percent, even though a service charge is normally included. For smaller amounts, it is good practice to round up the bill. Although service charges are included in hotel bills, porters and maids do expect a tip. Tour guides, taxi drivers and hairdressers also rely heavily on the tips they receive.

TOILETS

There are many public toilets around the city, especially in the centre. There is usually a 50-cent charge for toilets with an attendant. Signs in toilets are *Damen* (ladies) and *Herren* (gents).

TOURIST INFORMATION

The **Salzburg Tourism Office** has a website in English: www.salzburg.info/en. This includes a list of accommodation, plus all the sights to see, places to visit and events on offer in Salzburg. You can book accommodation online.

In Salzburg, the tourist information offices are at the railway station and on Mozartplatz. You can get help in finding accommodation, obtain maps, book day trips and guided tours, and buy tickets at the offices.

The website of the Austrian National Tourist Office (ANTO, www.austria.info/uk) also has a wealth of information about Salzburg. Contacts overseas:

Australia: tel: 02 9299 3621, info@antosyd.org.au.

Ireland: tel: 189 093 0118, holiday@austria.info.

UK: tel: 0845 101 1818, holiday@austria.info.

US: Austrian Tourist Office, P.O. Box 1142, New York, NY 10108-1142, travel@austria.info.

TRANSPORT

Buses. Salzburg has a very efficient public transport system. You will find maps of the bus and trolley bus routes at the railway station and at the bus information office on Mirabellplatz. It is possible to buy tickets from the driver as you board the bus and from the machines at some of the main bus stops, but it's cheaper to buy your tickets in advance. They are available from tobacconists (all marked with the Austria Tabak sign). You can buy blocks of five single tickets, 24-hour tickets or weekly tickets. Consider buying a Salzburg Card *(see page 11)*, which includes free bus travel for the card's duration.

Post buses. These serve the outlying districts. Timetables can again be found at the railway station. You need to pay the driver when boarding the bus.

Lokalbahn. This commuter-train route serves many destinations to the north of the city, including Oberndorf and Maria Plain. Information is available at the railway station.

Taxis. These cannot be hailed on the street, but taxi stands are scattered throughout the city. If you need to order a taxi, ask at your hotel reception or call 8111 for the taxi switchboard (www.taxi.at).

Taxis run on a meter; fares start at €3.50 during the day and €3.80 in the evening.

V

VISAS AND ENTRY REQUIREMENTS

A valid passport is required to enter Austria. If you are coming from an EU country, the US, Canada, Australia or New Zealand, you do not require a visa. See www.bmeia.gv.at/london for further information from the Austrian Embassy in London.

All goods brought into Austria from EU countries must be duty-paid. Visitors from non-EU countries can bring in the following duty-free items: 200 cigarettes or 50 cigars or 250g of tobacco; 2 litres of alcohol (of less than 22 percent), and 1 litre of alcohol (of over 22 percent).

Austria is a member of Schengen, the EU countries that have signed a treaty to end internal border checkpoints and controls. This means that if you are arriving from another Schengen state (e.g. Germany or Italy) there are no more border controls. Police do, however, carry out spot checks on some routes near the borders.

Currency restrictions. There are no restrictions on the amount of foreign currency that can be brought into Austria.

VAT reimbursement. Non-EU citizens are entitled to reclaim VAT paid on goods over a certain value (*Mehrwehrtsteuer*). On purchase you must obtain a form from the sales assistant, get this stamped either at the airport or at the border when leaving the country and send it back to the shop. They will then transfer the amount to your bank account.

I've nothing to declare.	**Ich habe nichts zu verzollen.**
It's for my personal use.	**Das ist für meinen persönlichen Gebrauch.**

WEBSITES

A great deal of information about Salzburg can be obtained from the internet. Some useful addresses are:

www.visit-salzburg.net Detailed information on sites, hotels and dining

www.stadt-salzburg.at Detailed website of the city's council with an excellent section on arts and culture

www.salzburg.gv.at/index.htm Facts , figures and information on culture, politics and tourism

www.weatheronline.co.uk/Austria/Salzburg.htm Reliable detailed weather data and long range forecasts

www.salzburg-alstadt.at Attractive site with news on restaurants, shops and events

www.salzburgfoundation.at Details on the unique Arts Project, started in 2002, which initiated the creation of fascinating sculptures in the city

www.viennaticketoffice.com/Salzburg_en.php Ideal website to get an overview of events with the possibility to book tickets

www.salzburg-sightseeingtours.at Hop on, hop off tours of the city by coach or open-top bus.

YOUTH HOSTELS

Salzburg has a good selection of cheap youth hostels. Probably the friendliest and most popular with backpackers is YoHo, Paracelsus Strasse 9; tel: 879 649, www.yoho.at. There is also the Jugend & Familiengästehaus (young persons' and family guesthouse) in Josef-Preis-Allee 18, tel: 05 7083, www.jufa.at. For more information on youth hostels in Salzburg, see the Austrian Youth Hostel Association website: www. oejhw.or.at.

Recommended Hotels

Thanks partly to the international reputation of its festivals, Salzburg has a fine selection of five-and four-star hotels. Three-star hotels tend to be less stylish – listed here are some of those that have their own charm and character. If you are on a tight budget, a *pension* (bed and breakfast) offers good value for money, and youth hostels provide basic, clean accommodation.

As Salzburg is not a huge city, even hotels slightly off the beaten track will be close enough to a bus route, and within easy reach of the city centre. Most listed below can help you organise tours and excursions around the city, while some are pick-up points on the tour routes.

You will be hard pushed to find a hotel that offers a large cooked breakfast, except the international ones. Elsewhere, breakfast is usually lighter, with bread, cereals, fruit, cold meats, cheese and yoghurt.

Prices are usually considerably higher in July and August, at Easter and for most of December. Some hotels take the opportunity to close during lulls between these peaks. Some smaller establishments, particularly *pensionen*, might not accept credit cards. Our price guide is for a double room in low season with breakfast:

€€€€€	over 220 euros
€€€€	160–220 euros
€€€	100–160 euros
€€	60–100 euros
€	below 60 euros

OLD TOWN

Altstadthotel Kasererbräu €€€ *Kaigasse 33, tel: 842 4450, www. kasererbraeu.at.* A charming, central hotel. The very different rooms have a homely feel about them. Some feature antique furniture, including solid, traditional wooden beds. Surprisingly, for a small central hotel, it features a luxurious wellness facility that includes a sauna and a Turkish bath. 45 rooms.

Altstadthotel Weisse Taube €€€ *Kaigasse 9, tel: 842 404, www. weissetaube.at.* Managed by the Wollner family, this traditional hotel is in the pedestrianised part of the Old Town, right next to Mozart-platz. It was built in 1365, on land belonging to St Peter's Abbey. Although the rooms are not particularly of any era or theme, they are friendly and comfortable. Breakfast room and bar, but no restaurant. 30 rooms.

arthotel Blaue Gans €€€–€€€€ *Getreidegasse 41–43, tel: 842 4910, www.blauegans.at.* The 'Blue Goose Art Hotel' calls itself a 'habitable work of art', and successfully fuses traditional and modern styles. The 37 rooms feature interesting works of art, crisp fabrics and warm lighting, all in a building that is nearly 700 years old.

Boutique Hotel am Dom €€€ *Goldgasse 17, tel: 842 765, www. hotelamdom.at.* Located in the heart of town, just minutes from the cathedral, this small hotel is a new icon of contemporary design in Salzburg. Each room is creatively designed and relates to a personality or event which shaped Salzburg's cultural image (Herbert von Karajan and Mozart).

Hotel Elefant Best Western €€€–€€€€ *Sigmund-Haffner-Gasse 4, tel: 843 397, www.elefant.at.* Over 700 years old, and located very centrally in the Old Town, in an alleyway off the shopping street Getreidegasse. There is a curious story that King Max of Bavaria had an elephant, which stopped to look in the window of the building, since when it has been known as Elefant. The rooms have a pleasant contemporary decor, and you can dine in the *Ratsherrnkeller*, formerly a 17th-century wine cellar. 31 rooms.

Hotel Goldene Ente €€€ *Goldgasse 10, tel: 845 622, www.ente.at.* A very central location in the Old Town, based on one of Salzburg's oldest (14th-century) inns. Rooms are decorated in the style of traditional country homes, with antiques and art on the walls. The restaurant is a favourite haunt of the locals, which means it has good traditional cooking. 15 double and 2 single rooms.

Hotel Goldener Hirsch €€€€–€€€€€ *Getreidegasse 37, tel: 80840, www.goldenerhirschsalzburg.at.* With 65 rooms and 4 suites, this hotel has the feeling of an elegant private home. All the rooms are unique, with their own colour schemes and themes reminiscent of a 15th-century inn, combining antique furniture and modern amenities. Guests have a choice between the gourmet restaurant of chef Gernot Hicka and the cosy traditional restaurant *s'Herzl*, both specialising in Austrian cuisine.

Schloss Mönchstein €€€€€ *Mönchsberg Park 26, tel: 848 5550, www.monchstein.at.* Situated on top of the Mönchsberg and surrounded by a park, the hotel, with its exquisite restaurants, is one of the most spectacular five-star establishments in Austria. The individualistic bedrooms and bathrooms are out of this world. Needless to say, the location offers some of the best views of the city. Only 24 rooms, so early booking is essential.

NEW TOWN

Altstadthotel Amadeus €€€ *Linzergasse 43–45, tel: 871 401, www.hotelamadeus.at.* Quaint and wholesome hotel in the centre of the New Town, set in a 15th-century building that has been extensively renovated in a blend of tasteful modern elements and traditional comfort, some have four-poster beds. The quietest rooms are at the rear, with views of the St Sebastian Cemetery. Breakfast is served in the spacious bistro-style café on the ground floor. 26 rooms.

Altstadthotel Wolf-Dietrich €€€ *Wolf-Dietrich-Strasse 7, tel: 871 275, www.salzburg-hotel.at.* A homely modern hotel in an old building in a quiet quarter, yet close to the New Town attractions. Ideal for families. Very attentive service. Bio breakfast (organically-sourced), complimentary afternoon tea and snacks. Lovely spa and indoor pool. Romantically themed rooms as well as family suites. 40 rooms.

Austrotel Salzburg am Mirabellplatz €€€ *Paris-Lodron-Strasse 1, tel: 881 6880, www.austrotel.at.* Conveniently located next to the Mirabell Gardens. The five-storey building was once the residence of Prince Archbishop Paris Lodron. There's an American-style lobby bar and a free coffee and juice bar (until 6pm). Breakfast served all day. Despite its history, the hotel has all the modern facilities you will need. 71 rooms and a spacious apartment.

Gasthof Auerhahn €€ *Bahnhofstrasse 15, tel: 451 052, www.auerhahn-salzburg.at*. A family-run establishment with tasteful rooms, all 15 of which are decorated in a different style. The excellent restaurant has won gourmet awards for several years. The shady garden offers al fresco dining in summer. Located north of the railway station.

Hotel & Villa Auersperg €€–€€€ *Auerspergstrasse 61, tel: 889 440, www.auersperg.at*. Family-run hotel in two buildings with historic charm and contemporary chic. Tasteful leather sofas and wooden panelling in the public rooms; bedrooms have a warm, elegant feel. The hotel also has a roof terrace, an idyllic peaceful garden and a small spa. Bio breakfasts with great choice. 55 rooms.

Hotel Bristol €€€€€ *Makartplatz 4, tel: 873 557, www.bristol-salzburg.at*. Built around 1890, the Bristol is located between the Mirabell Gardens and Mozart's house. The rooms feature luxurious antique furnishings and thick-pile carpets. Expect sumptuous beds, chandeliers, and rich fabrics. Fine dining in the Polo Lounge restaurant, or unwind in the cosy Sketch Bar & Lounge. Close to the Paracelsus Kurhaus (spa & pool), where special rates apply to hotel guests. 60 rooms.

Hotel Drei Kreuz €€ *Vogelweiderstrasse 9, tel: 872 790, www.hotel dreikreuz.at*. The name refers to the three crosses on the Kapuzinerberg. A modern, four-storey, family-run hotel featuring traditional rustic furniture and a lively bar. Breakfast room, but no restaurant. 24 rooms.

Hotel Hofwirt €€ *Schallmooser Hauptstrasse 1, tel: 872 1720, www. hofwirt.net*. A quiet, central hotel in a 100-year-old building at the top of the Linzergasse. The rooms (with noise-reducing windows) have a friendly, very modern feel. Airy breakfast room and stylish lobby bar. 60 rooms.

Hotel Mozart €€ *Franz-Josef-Strasse 27, tel: 872 274, www.hotel-mozart.at*. Six-storey family-run hotel, five minutes' walk from Linzergasse and the Mirabell Gardens. Rooms are spacious – some large enough to sleep four comfortably – and cosy in a traditional, homely way. Friendly service. Breakfast only, no restaurant. 33 rooms.

Sacher Salzburg €€€€€ *Schwarzstrasse 5–7, tel: 889 770, www. sacher.com.* Perhaps Salzburg's grandest hotel, founded in 1866 and the sister hotel to Sacher Vienna (famous for its *Sachertorte* chocolate cake). Located on the river with great views of the Old Town. The rooms range from standard to deluxe, though all are of five-star quality. The Sacher is large enough for a gym, sauna and steam bath, as well as a salon, a café and excellent restaurants serving both international cuisine and local specialities. If you look through the guest book, you will recognise many famous names. 113 rooms including suites.

Stadtkrug €€€ *Linzergasse 20, tel: 873 545, www.stadtkrug.at.* A popular base among performers at the Salzburg Festival, whose signed photographs adorn the walls. Rooms are sumptuously traditional with stone floors and ceiling beams. Good restaurant and roof garden with great views of the city. 35 rooms.

Star Inn Hotel Salzburg Gablerbräu €€€ *Richard-Mayer-Gasse 2, tel: 879 662, www.starinnhotels.com/de/salzburg-gablerbraeu.* This newly renovated complex of a brewery tavern with some parts dating from the early 15th century offer stylish family friendly accommodation and modern comfort just a stone's throw from the river at the foot of Kapuzinerberg. 77 rooms.

Stein Hotel €€€ *Giselakai 3–5, tel: 874 3460, www.hotelstein.at.* Directly on the river Salzach, the four-star hotel has been in operation since 1399. The décor is individual, some rooms with zebra themes, others with a subtle natural ambience. The grander rooms have marble bathrooms. At the top of the hotel is the famous Steinterrasse club/bar/lounge with commanding views over the old city – the place to be for an afternoon tea or evening drinks. 55 rooms and suites.

OUTSIDE THE CENTRE

Airport Hotel Salzburg €€€ *Dr-M-Laireiter-Strasse 9, tel: 850 020, www.airporthotel.at.* A modern hotel built in traditional Alpine style, with all the facilities of a four-star hotel, including a sauna, gym and indoor pool. Located right next to the airport (there are no flights at